Radiant Cool

Radiant Cool

A Novel Theory of Consciousness

Dan Lloyd

A Bradford Book
The MIT Press
Cambridge, Massachusetts
London, England

This book was set in Sabon and Meta by Graphic Composition, Inc. and was printed and bound in the United States of America.

With the exception of the author, the characters in this novel are fictions. Any resemblance to any person, living or dead, is coincidental.

Library of Congress Cataloging-in-Publication Data

Lloyd, Dan Edward, 1953–
    Radiant cool : a novel theory of consciousness / Dan Lloyd.
      p. cm.
    "A Bradford book."
    ISBN 0-262-12259-6 (alk. paper)
    1. Neurosciences—Fiction. 2. Consciousness—Fiction. 3. Philosophy—Fiction. I. Title.

PS3612.L56R36 2003
813'.6—dc22
                                                    2003059319

10 9 8 7 6 5 4 3 2 1

Lines 1–7 from "Howl" from *Collected Poems 1947–1980* by Allen Ginsberg. Copyright © 1955 by Allen Ginsberg. Reprinted by permission of HarperCollins Publishers, Inc.

"Thirteen Ways of Looking at a Blackbird" is excerpted from *The Collected Poems of Wallace Stevens* by Wallace Stevens, copyright 1954 by Wallace Stevens and renewed 1982 by Holly Stevens. Used by permission of Alfred A. Knopf, a division of Random House, Inc.

The passage in chapter 8 from "The Aleph" appears in *Collected Fictions,* by Jorge Luis Borges, translated by Andrew Hurley, copyright © 1998 by Maria Kodama; translation copyright © 1998 by Penguin Putnam Inc. Used by permission of Viking Penguin, a division of Penguin Group (USA) Inc.

Excerpts from the poetry of Emily Dickinson in chapter 9 are reprinted by permission of the publishers and Trustees of Amherst College from *The Poems of Emily Dickinson,* Thomas H. Johnson, ed., Cambridge, MA: The Belknap Press of Harvard University Press, Copyright © 1951, 1955, 1979 by the Presidents and Fellows of Harvard College.

For CG, RL, and ML, with love.

Contents

I saw the best minds of my generation destroyed by madness, starving
   hysterical naked,
dragging themselves through the negro streets at dawn looking for an
   angry fix,
angelheaded hipsters burning for the ancient heavenly connection to
   the starry dynamo in the machinery of night,
who poverty and tatters and hollow-eyed and high sat up smoking in
   the supernatural darkness of cold-water flats floating across the
   tops of cities contemplating jazz,
who bared their brains to Heaven under the El and saw
   Mohammedan angels staggering on tenement roofs illuminated,
who passed through universities with radiant cool eyes hallucinating
   Arkansas and Blake-light tragedy among the scholars of war,
who were expelled from the academies for crazy & publishing
   obscene odes on the windows of the skull. . . .
                              —Allen Ginsberg, "Howl"

I do not know which to prefer,
The beauty of inflections
Or the beauty of innuendoes,
The blackbird whistling
Or just after.
          —Wallace Stevens, "Thirteen Ways of Looking at a Blackbird"

Acknowledgments

Radiant Cool could not have been written without the knowledge, insight, support, and patience of many people. Cheryl Greenberg has carefully read the entire manuscript repeatedly from its earliest days. Her wise marginal comments shaped each draft, and insuperable problems of plot or character were frequent topics of breakfast conversation; she solved most of them before the coffee cooled. Super-editor Ed Henderson also inspired multiple waves of revision, and absorbed my endless tinkering with patience and humor. Katherine Almeida, Cindy Buck, and Yasuyo Iguchi freed the ultimate draft from errors and infelicities. Nely Keinänen, Kimmo Absetz, Sara Meirowitz, and Meghan Cole commented extensively on both the style and content of the penultimate draft. Earlier versions elicited useful comments from Nik Alksnis, Miller Brown, David Chalmers, Elizabeth Chua, Daniel Dennett, Lucy Ferriss, Anita Greenberg, Irwin Greenberg, Madelyn Kelly, Richard Lee, Alva Noë, Jon Opie, Michael Rutter, Rachel Skolnick, and Chris Westbury.

Vincent Clark generously shared fMRI data and expertise; I could not have learned the ways of fMRI without him. The fMRI Data Center enabled me to participate in virtual collaborations with the primary researchers whose data are archived at the Center, including Eliot Hazeltine, Alumit Ishai, Andreas Mechelli, Bradley Postle, and their many collaborators: Jeffrey Berger, Mark D'Esposito, Karl Friston, John Gabrieli, James

Haxby, Alex Martin, Russell Poldrack, Cathy Price, Alexander Taich, and Leslie Ungerleider. Jack van Horn and the Data Center staff have also provided essential support and encouragement. Along with fMRI, I also needed to develop skills in fiction, a genre I had forsaken in graduate school. Lucy Ferriss and her students in Advanced Fiction Writing were my guides; Lucy showed me many literary conjuring tricks that I am not at liberty to discuss.

Friends and colleagues from many places helped me think more clearly about the book and its ideas: Dina Anselmi, Cindy Buck, Jack Dougherty, Ben Dunn, Richard Goldberg, Irwin Greenberg, Sara Heinämaa, Ilmari Helin, Drew Hyland, Alumit Ishai, Eva Korsisaari, Richard Lee, Robin Lloyd, Bill Mace, Tom McHugh, Randy O'Reilly, Ilkka Pyysiäinen, Panu Raatikainen, Sarah Raskin, Antti Revonsuo, Mark Rollins, Anna Rotkirch, Judy Stiff, Ron Stiff, Maurice Wade, Katie Watts, Laura Werner, and Dan Zahavi. Four mentors have taught by their example that the imagination can be a way of knowing: Arthur Danto, Daniel Dennett, David Love, and David Young. One of them, Dan Dennett, has been an especially bright beacon in the philosophy of cognitive science, lighting my way with his percepts, precepts, and good cheer.

Many students at Trinity College participated in every stage of this project. Elizabeth Chua worked on fMRI interpretation. Jeff Harris and Greg Rubin assisted with data visualization. Students who have worked on data analysis for chapter 13 include Claudine Bitel, Ben Dunn, Julie Guilbert, David Herman, Nilsson Holguin, Hayley Ford, David Langner, Heather McAleer, Patricia Park-Li, Alison Rada, Tanya Suvarnasorn, Kate Weingartner, and Elizabeth Worthy. My Trinity seminars on phenomenology and cognitive neuroscience have been the scenes of many important conversations on the themes of this book. More recently, students in my courses at the University of Helsinki have shaped my thinking in the final stages of revision. The postgraduate seminar on Love and Literature has been a commune for exploring various entanglements of text and romance; our discussions inspired several new scenes in the novel. Participants included Hannele Koivula, Eva Korsisaari, Anu Kuusela, Virpi Lehtinen, Marjo Lemponen, Sanna Nyqvist, Floora Ruokonen, Leila Shotton, Katja Tuominen, and (our indispensable co-teacher and *taikuri*) Laura Werner.

The support of two communities has been essential. Trinity College has been an excellent context for interdisciplinary research in general, and the Philosophy Department and Neuroscience Program have both been consistently encouraging and supportive of my scholarly eccentricities. The Faculty Research Committee has provided me with something equally precious: time to work.

Late in the preparation of the book, I became a Visiting Fellow at the Helsinki Collegium for Advanced Studies. The support of the Collegium has been wonderful during the difficult final stages of writing and revision, and the community of Collegium scholars has been both welcoming and a continuous source of intellectual inspiration.

Books are born in solitude but mature in the company of others. The many colleagues and friends mentioned above suggest how lucky I've been (and how long the work has taken). All these collaborators have generously offered their ideas and teaching, and more too—their support and love. In the middle of it all, our sparkling girls Rianna and Morgan lightened every moment and every day. Throughout this adventure (and every adventure), I've been sustained by my steady flame, Cheryl.

My brother-in-law Michael Kelly was killed in the war in Iraq in April 2003. Mike was a loving husband and father. He was also an extraordinary writer with an eye for the telling detail and an ear for the most unlikely yet perfect phrase. His writings will let us keep his voice with us, a great gift. If any passage in this book sings, then let it be a tribute to him, and a reminder of his continued presence.

To all of you, *kiitos paljon,* many many thanks.

Prologue

In the first days of April of last year a young philosopher, Miranda Sharpe, was tempered in the furnace of extraordinary events. Beginning with a breach in her professional relationship with her graduate advisor, Sharpe found herself cast as the main actor in a drama that became both sinister and perilous. Thirty-six fateful hours derailed the life of at least one nationally prominent media figure, seriously strained U.S.-Russian diplomatic relations, and threw two institutions of higher education into a frenzy of self-examination—all in addition to the narrowly averted devastation of the Internet. At first, reports of these events were fragmentary and peripheral. A few articles appeared in the campus newspaper at Sharpe's university; on my own campus, the Sharpe saga ignited astonishment and dismay behind closed doors. With these disjoint sketches the matter might have ended, except for the appearance of a now-notorious exposé in *Lingua Franca* ("Through a Glass Sharpely: The Plot to Unweave the World Wide Web"). With that, the Miranda Sharpe story, notwithstanding all its gaps and distortions, took on a life of its own. By the summer of last year, Sharpe found herself, or at least her image, emerging as an icon representing, in various contexts, feminism transgressed, Generation Z redeemed, graduate study glamorized, the Internet made intimate. . . . It was only a matter of time before her face would promote animal rights or running shoes.

The *real* story, however, was slighted. This book tells its untold core. As a player in the pyrotechnic denouement of Sharpe's adventure, I was aware of the intellectual dimension of her sleuthing, and I felt that the world could use a full report of her discoveries. I first thought that Sharpe and I might collaborate, but when I approached her with this idea, she informed me that she was determined to write her own narrative, with the working title "The Thrill of Phenomenology." This story, in her own words, became the first part of this book. Her polyphonic narrative revealed, on one level, the depth of pain and terror she had experienced in April. But on another level, the real-life whodunit was interwoven with a re-alignment in the twenty-first-century view of the mind. This re-alignment occurred in Sharpe's thinking through the very encounters that embroiled her in a murderous drama. This, then, is the story that all the other stories have missed.

In early April, as Miranda Sharpe struggled to solve an apparently grave crime, she also discovered a new theory of human consciousness.

Scholarly books usually begin by announcing their conclusions, and follow with the support. But the process of *discovering* a new theory—of anything, but especially of consciousness—runs the other way. Like a detective solving a crime, discovery begins in the groping murk of half-thought doubts, and gestates in chance conversations, nagging metaphors, and backhand revelations. Halting soliloquy and endless side-trips hide its growth. Yet the discovering mind is easing itself into a new mold, foreshadowing the moment when the discoverer hews a roughcut keystone, and with its help the jumble of obstinate rock pulls itself into an unmistakable arch, still imperfect but intimating the vaults of a new science. From that climax all the switchbacks remap as the steady ascent of fate, a path that could not but lead to a new way of seeing. So it is with Sharpe's narrative as well.

And the new arch—should it turn out to bear the load of critique that will follow the publication of Sharpe's memoir—will span one of the great chasms of our world, the gulf between mind and brain. Our conscious mind is the great quaking stage of experience from first step to first kiss to last word. No place could seem less its home than that gelatinous organ known as the brain, a place of perfect darkness and bare chemical murmurs. For decades the drumbeat of philosophy, psychology, and neuroscience has insisted that mind is brain, and brain is mind. It *could* be so; it *must* be so. But *how* is it so? Not in snail brains or rat minds, nor in computer models nor other shadows of our selves, but in *us*. In you, in me. Sharpe's story culminates in a vivisection of consciousness. She offers us a rough sketch of the anatomy of the mind, the whole human show. As the police, the media, and public memory close the books on this very strange case, what should endure is a new way of thinking about thinking.

Some colleagues have suggested that credit for the new theory should be shared between Sharpe and myself. Although it is true that Sharpe found an important clue in a "virtual world" I had constructed to illustrate in three dimensions the high-dimensional space traversed by the thinking brain, I had never seen in my construct anything but a representation of the neurobiology of cognition. Sharpe recognized that the construct was also a theory of consciousness, and in a long conversation convinced me of the viability of her view. In recent months, as I've spackled the bullet holes in my living room wall, and repainted it to match the new rugs, I've often reflected on that dialogue in a diner, and I remain convinced that much of what is important and interesting in the theory is due to Sharpe alone. Nonetheless, I will plead guilty to having taken her insights and run with them. Accordingly, this volume has emerged as a different sort of collaboration. Its main text is Sharpe's tale, in which she not only makes clear what really happened during those freak snowstorms of last April, but fills in a rich memoir of her thinking as it moved so rapidly and so far. But in the second part, I have contributed some philosophical and scientific elaborations of Sharpe's theories, for those with an interest in the details. Miranda is also planning to contribute an epilogue, bringing the story up to date. [Editor's note: The epilogue, added in press, has been appended to "The Thrill of Phenomenology."] We hope that this combination offers something for readers of varying interests. By the way, the Web addresses Sharpe mentions late in her story remain operational as of this writing, and the reader is cordially invited to visit the sites and participate in the ongoing discussions there.

Dan Lloyd
Trinity College
Hartford, Connecticut

The Thrill of Phenomenology

1

He was a fool and a moron, but I never wanted to see him dead. All I wanted was a little slack between us, a space. That's why I was there, in that paper landfill he called his office, in the faint light of an icy dawn. The key he gave me long ago. I planned to slip in, take back what was mine, get out. He'd get the point. No talk needed. Just a little distance.

But, 6 AM or not, he's there. "Oh," I murmur, and as I see his current condition, "oh" again. The door clicks shut behind me. He's there, but not all there: slumping onto his keyboard, with both arms hugging the base of the monitor, like he wants to pull it off the desk. As if someone had blown his brains out, but without the spatter. I freeze into the jittery shadows, holding my breath. It is no dream. I'm about to speak his name, but pull back. Let sleeping senior professors lie, I always say.

I'm thinking I should get the hell out, but instead of moving I'm fixated on him, on the curve of his back. His sweatshirt hunches up at his neck. A tail of dark flannel sneaks out at the waist and drapes over the chair edge, weightless as a shadow. It could be the same shirt he wore last night. The image makes me shiver, reminds me why I'm there. This is not wrong. I remember to breathe, and step in toward the desk. Light folders and papers float on dim stacks, a million words submerged and smudged, silent in darkness. But one folder, lying next to him on the desk, shimmers red.

I already know what's scrawled along the tab: CONSCIOUSNESS. In it, *my* words. To own them again, I have to lean around him like a wife reading over his shoulder. A shiny black mug rests on one corner of the folder, empty except for a metal teaball. I ease the teacup aside like a dead rat, wipe my fingers on my jeans. Inches away, he smells like an old sneaker sprinkled with *Obsession*. I take the folder. My words.

As I straighten up, hugging my half-bodied dissertation, I have to see the scene again, repeating in the reflection of his dark monitor. At the bottom of the screen, his halo of Jerry Garcia gray. My face, round and startled and pale, hovering above like the double sunrise in *2001*. The gray glass washes out the difference between us, between his raggedness and the mathematical strands of my own dark hair, throwing my why-me face and his bald spot into a single deep well, a common dismal fate. I feel sick, uncanny, as if something has fallen out of a movie into my world. The room stills. Thought icicles. Absolute zero.

A second, one endless thick beat, falls. Colorless dark books loom around us, stacked from floor to ceiling. Way off, I consider gagging, and suddenly I'm filled with one thought: *Get out*. I take a step back, through the maze of lost time. And another, and then I'm in the hall, pulling the door shut behind me. Empty still. I am trembling, freezing all through.

I tremble all the way to the apartment, yawning compulsively, and do not stop even in the cocoon of my down comforter. The scene in the office drifts in fragments around me. What was he doing *there*? What was he *doing* there? Slowly it seems less and less like one of his mind games, like discussing Heidegger in total darkness or Sartre while sitting on your hands. Slowly it seems less like a nap. The smell is still with me, a bad mix of man smell and something else. Something like Christmas or old lace. Slowly it surfaces that I might well have seen my advisor—the Mr. Chips of consciousness, the jerk of my grad school life—that I might have seen him dead. Maybe still warm, maybe cold as ice, but all his fires out. I had stood there without seeing. Or hearing either—I can remember only streaks and shadows, and one red thing. I was so busy not stepping on overdue books, not losing it, that I throttled the main conclusion. *Maybe*.

And for two hours the strange shivering will not stop. It moves around like a cat caged in my ribs. *But maybe not*. Twice I jump up with the comforter pulled around me, the phone open in one hand, but I can't even think of my first line. I had been there at a strange hour, perhaps minutes after his crash. Why? I'd taken things from his office—secrets, truths, *evidence*. Why? And did I call anyone *then*? Why not? Every passing minute incriminates me. I didn't even check if he had been breathing. He got what he wanted after all, an accomplice in his moronic metaphysics, a me. Maybe already—it's 10 AM—he has been missed, or someone else has entered the office. *If he is missing at all.* At eleven, he will meet his first class. *Or maybe not.* I'm supposed to be there too. We will both be missing. Missing together. The moron.

Or, I can fake it. I fixate in my mirror, murmuring, *This morning did not happen.* I will simulate myself, Miranda Sharpe, on a typical Wednesday: ribbed sweater (black), denim jacket (same), jeans (of course), mascara but barely, impeccable high ponytail—the neo retro beatnik graduate student look. The plan: Be very, very normal. Go to class. In his decades of teaching he has never missed a class, he says. It's his jazz, his fix. Class will tell. If he appears, my job will be to sit with folded hands, study cuticles while he explains why appearance is reality. Then blend into the undergrads, flow toward the door and run away, run away.

And if he doesn't come? Then too, sit in class with folded hands, until Miranda Sharpe, TA, pulls the plug. As in plan A, run away, run away. Brave, brave Miranda. Rise and shine.

I drive to campus a second time that morning, parking again among the dirty snowpiles, winding across the quad to Ryle. The day droops badly, colder and grayer than at dawn. As the building looms, I zip my parka to my chin. A big fake Rodin Thinker broods at the main entrance. It had welcomed me two years ago, when being a philosopher meant a golden future of café ecstasies, casting off my body. I would become that thinker. A soul on speed. But then in one stroke, he—the mentor of thinkers—poisoned that dream with his infinite ego, and after a big night spent boiling poison into rage, I had come with the first light to reclaim philosophy for myself. *I will think outside of you.* But now, take three, all is lost. The weight bears down on the crouched figure, who cannot rise against it. My hopes and my defiance curdle. The Thinker is dead.

I take each step like I'm walking the plank, avoiding eye contact with the Thinker and the great wide world too. I heave up the stairs and through doors heavy as a tomb. Beyond, the corridors of gloom.

My normal first stop would be his office, to discuss the day's classes, or speculate about the secret lives of undergraduates. Instead, I imagine *discovering a body*. Will someone grab that shoulder—*his*—pull the body upright, feel for a pulse? Will the head roll, the eyes stare? Do dead men drool? Skip the office for today, I think. I climb the stairs to the second floor, a row of offices on one side of the hall, classrooms on the other. I'm still ten minutes early for class; the hall is empty, and no brighter than at dawn. His door, halfway down, glows. Full of brood, seething. As the screeching music rises, the Undead Philosopher will stagger blindly with his arms outstretched, clomp like a drunk into class, and lecture terrifyingly for fifty minutes. Only the Appointments and Promotions Committee can drive the wooden stake into its heart.

Miranda, get real. Hold on, honey.

I take a seat in the classroom, and cover my pounding heart by pretending to read, this time from *The Phenomenology of Internal Time-Consciousness*, the homework for today. The students float in like dust bunnies, settling in silent rows. I count them over my shoulder, as they stare at the cloudy blackboard, waiting for the movie to begin. Six so far, five still at large. I wait, the words rolling along:

> The foreground is nothing without the background; the appearing side is nothing without the non-appearing. It is the same with regard to the unity of time-consciousness—the duration reproduced is the foreground; the classifying intentions make us aware of a background, a temporal background.

The text fills my world with its fine dark words, the first solid point in this surreal day.

> We have the following analogies: for the spatial thing, the ordering into the surrounding space and the spatial world on the one side, and on the other, the spatial thing itself with its foreground and background.

Beautiful faraway Husserl with the long beard. Dear Edmund. Tell it like it is.

> For the temporal thing, we have the ordering into the temporal form and the temporal world on the one side, and on the other the tempo-

ral thing itself and its changing orientation with regard to the living now.

But I'm still here. So are they. I want to hose out the room. Scat. I turn again to words.

> The foreground is nothing without the background;
> *sitting in his chair, his swivel chair, collapsing onto his keyboard;*
> *stacks of books and planes of paper;*
>> the appearing side is nothing without the non-appearing.
> *His face, turned away from me;*
>> It is the same with regard to the unity of time-consciousness—
>> the duration reproduced is the foreground;
> *my day so far, endlessly looping*
>> the classifying intentions make us aware of a background,
> *and what a day*
>> a temporal background.
> *Where* is *he?*
>> And . . . this is continued in the constitution of the temporality of
>> the enduring thing itself
>> with its now, before, and after.
> What *is he, now?*
>> We have the following analogies:
>> for the spatial thing, the ordering into the surrounding space and
>> the spatial world on the one side,
>> and on the other, the spatial thing itself with its foreground and
>> background.
> *Across the hall, in his office, behind the door poster of Nietzsche, who*
> *is*
>> For the temporal thing . . . the ordering into the temporal form and
>> the temporal world on the one side,
>> and on the other the temporal thing itself and
>> its changing orientation with regard to the
>> living
> *also dead.*
>> now.

It was all already over before I even got there. He was a fool and a moron, but I had no wish to see him—at all. I didn't do anything. Did I?

Escape hangs in the future, infinitely distant, thanks to eleven temporally extended objects plowing through time like shooting stars. Everybody is in, and they will wait and wait. I walk to the front of the room. "It looks like, um, Professor Grue . . . Professor Grue isn't here. I guess this means no class." When did my mouth go dry? "So, bye." So *bye*. They look startled. They swivel their butts, looking at each other for confirmation that their good fortune is no dream. As an afterthought, I try to smile helpfully. It's always best to smile during a panic attack. Slowly they collect their books. But someone in the back row raises a hand.

"Yes?" I say. It's Elaine, the PG-13 image of sophomore enthusiasm.

"Could I ask you a question? You know, since you're the TA." Her gum snaps.

"Sure, Elaine, sure." She has Heidi cheeks and Bambi eyes; dresses like a hooker but carries it off as if she got the idea from her Barbie collection.

"Now that Professor Grue is gone, I have to tell you that I don't get any of this at all," she begins. The rest of the class stops. "Yeah," says one. They pause, and begin to condense again. We are shifting into help session mode, not my first choice with Dr. Death sliming across the hall. Maybe/maybe not. They all turn their eyes on me.

I suddenly have an overwhelming urge to tighten my ponytail, but instead I lean back on the table at the front of the room, holding on to the leading edge. Ms. Casual, in her fully locked and upright position.

"What don't you get?" I ask in my best probing TA style. But booming in my head, that word, "gone." Why has she said "gone"? Finally I begin to *think*. I really see them all for the first time, from Marie, at the left, her pencil poised at the top of a blank page, to Mickey along the window with his backwards baseball cap, rocking his little chairdesk to the brink of falling over. And I think, *murder*. Why not? I am looking at a room full of Motive and Opportunity and maybe even Means to Do It. What if Grue's metaphysical lechery settled on Elaine? Muddle her brains to meddle with her bra? From a tell-all office hour I know that she has a psycho jealous welder boyfriend back home, Stanley Kowalski to her Stella. Motive, check. Or Grue's famous harsh grades—add a few pre-meds with a chem lab, and bye bye prof. Even last night he had student goodies, some tea a student brought him from Russia, and a plate of brownies from someone else. Means, check. Now I'm thinking that a murderer in class would be a good thing, because the prime suspect wouldn't be me—the one with the key to his office and the shaky alibi. Opportunity, hell. Lock the door. No one leaves until the truth is outed!

"Well," Elaine continues. "How about superstition? Professor Grue keeps talking about that?" Snap snap.

"I think you mean 'superposition,'" I say.

"Whatever."

I'm about to explain it when a very round, very boy arm waves urgently. It's Gordon-the-nerd, founder of the campus fantasy club, the Guild of Doom or something. His amorous advance on me began perhaps ten minutes into the semester; it was dead in the water at eleven. "It's like in quantum physics. Two states can be superposed, like with Schroedinger's cat. The cat is dead and alive at the same time. Dr. Grue says that consciousness has superposition all the time." He nods at me with a conspiring grin. I imagine a puppy jumping up and down for a treat.

"No, Gordon, not exactly," I say. "Superposition means something else in the study of consciousness. It's not about physical properties. In this course, superposition refers to a pervasive property of our conscious experience. Does anyone remember it?" Does anyone know where Gordon was this morning, at say, 6 AM?

I squeeze the table edge. A fan thrums somewhere in the pipes and tubes above. To the blackboard, then. Layers of Spanish authors and algebra ghost through the smudges. I can't help trying to remember the word for chalk ghosts. *Pallindrome?* I draw a little random ouija thing: ⌒ My bean bag chair. Side view of a Wonderbra. My brain on philosophy. Zero, resting. I put down the chalk, dust my hands, thinking, if I ever do become a professor, I will have to stop wearing black.

I turn back toward my eleven phenomena. "What do you see?"

What do you see: Max Grue opening his apartment door, me with fuzzy scarf, to establish winter setting. Rumpled Max looked like he'd been sleeping in his clothes. He proffered a box, elaborately labeled in his own indescribable blockprint:

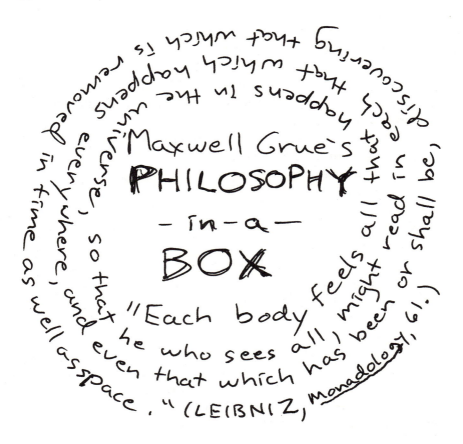

Maxwell Grue's
PHILOSOPHY
—in—a—
BOX

"Each body feels all, so that he who sees all might read in each that which is, might read in each that which happens in the universe, and even that which has been or shall be, discovering in time as well as space." (LEIBNIZ, *Monadology*, 61.)

"Oh. I guess you're doing the Monadology in Mod Phil. Cute."

He nodded and fumbled to open the box. His hands were shaking, oddly. He said, "A monad for Miranda." Inside, a dozen silver Christmas ornaments, each one a little mirrored world. A tiny bent Max and a tiny twisty Miranda reflected in each, beside infinite ranks of spheres in spheres, each with its mirrored scraps of both of us. I wasn't sure that Leibniz had plastic tree ornaments in mind when he pictured his ultimate atoms, the "windowless monads," each reflecting the universe from the beginning of time to the end.

"No thanks, I'm dieting," I said.

He took one out and handed it to me, took one for himself. He pulled on his coat, and led the way wordlessly along the hall to the lobby and into the night. Another fake adventure on the road to windowless enlightenment.

A beautiful snow was falling, the kind that sticks to even the skinniest branches and shimmers by the streetlights on the way down. He stopped beneath the first streetlight and turned to me. "What do you see?"

"What do you see?"

Gordon tries again to make the charts. Pointing to the board, he says, "It's chalk. Calcium sulfate rubbed on a surface of synthetic slate." He looks around at the women in the class, to see if any notice his existence.

"Thank you, Gordon." I wait. Snap. Pop. A hill, says Elaine at last. A kid's drawing to Marie. Sand. UFO. VW in a big bag. Cave. Drop of blood.

"Good," I say. "Not just chalk anymore. It's like this for *everything* we experience. Consciousness lives in a world heaped up with meanings. They are all *there* in my little drawing, and in every moment of awareness. A pig-pile of interpretations. That's superposition." I almost say, that's superposition, *man*. Just like Max.

I'm thinking something about the Bates Motel when a different voice joins. "Is that like an affordance?" This from Marie, the psych major. Maybelline makes a good profit by her, but she's the only woman in the class as tall as me, *and* she wears heels. I like that in a girl.

I ask for more explanation. She says, "Um, well, like we learned about it in my Perception class? And like I don't know, I'm probably getting it wrong, but like its when something lets you do something, like food lets you eat it, or rocks let you stand on them, but don't let you eat them. In his book about perception, Dr. Gibson says an affordance is what you can do around or with something?"

"Yes, that's a good connection." I pop back up on the table edge. I notice that I'm swinging my legs; I stop. "Max's point, I mean Professor Grue's, is that our conscious experience is not limited to just what we can see or hear. Many other possibilities are part of our awareness of things, non-sensory parts. We are aware of the affordances of things and situations and people. We *think* we live in a world of things. Maybe we do. But that's the tiniest edge of it. So Grue says, stop thinking. Stop *thing-ing*.

Then ask, What is really there?" At the moment, eleven new headaches, to judge from their faces, all pruny with thinking about not thinking. Elaine pops her bubble gum. Mickey by the window honks up a bit of last night, but, being a suave guy, doesn't spit.

"OK, here's another example." I point to the door. "Consider all the offices on this hall." Not to mention the little shop of horrors. "All these doors are closed. All of them are pretty much alike, right? You look at a door, and you think, a door is just a door. But some offices are empty and some are not. What difference does that make? Suppose your professor is in his office. His or her, I mean. Does that change anything about the way the door seems to you?"

"It might open?" ventures Marie.

"Exactly. A door that might open is a very different door from one that is likely to stay closed. At 6 or 7 AM, no one is in these offices, and the doors are just parts of the wall. You could pound on them, it wouldn't matter. But now, when your professor might be in, you respond to the door differently. Doors then and now are physically the same. They're visually the same. But they couldn't be more different. Even though the door looks just the same, your *experience* of the door changes. Remember the Sartre passage, from *The Transcendence of the Ego*, about streetcars-needing-to-be-caught. A streetcar-needing-to-be-caught gives us a different experience from one we don't need to catch. Max wanted you to get that." One beat— too late to correct my tense.

"Let's go back to the professor behind the door." Go go go. "Imagine him, now, in his office. Now suppose that he's not just sitting there like usual, but he's . . ." And here I pause deliberately, and look from face to face to see who has finished my sentence. Elaine's gum snaps. Marie frowns at me. Slowly eleven wandering streams of thought condense into a single confused anticipation, all focused on my face. It's like sitting in the sun without sunblock.

"He's what?" says a new voice. Alphonse, the quarterback of the WU Whales and president of the jock house, Delta Tau, stares sullenly from under the brim of his WU visor. He is as close to horizontal as you can get in a side-arm chair, but for all his lounging he still seems wound like a spring. Between his long legs and massive round shoulders he takes up half the room.

I fix him with narrow eyes, and in soft, deliberate tones I say, ". . . naked." Someone giggles, but Alphonse looks away suddenly. Then he jerks his head back toward me, snarls. "What I want to know," he says, "is why *the fuck* I should care."

They all freeze. Now we're getting somewhere. My cheeks feel hot. I'm on a mission now, and coiled. "Well, Alphie," I begin, and use the Smile again. "Let me ask you a question. Have you ever had an experience?"

He snorts. "What do you mean, experience?"

"Well, take right now. Are you aware of me? Can you hear my voice? Can you feel the body in your chair?" The questions work for me. Feet answer first, still hanging snug in their laces. Too snug. Clammy. And shoulders. I slouch with the guilty, or at least with the unseemly tall. I force myself to sit up straight, like a good girl in charm class.

The brim speaks again. "What do *you* think?"

"Oh, I know what *I* think! The question is about what *you* think." I like that move; learned it from Socrates. "What I want to know is, have you ever wondered what an experience *is?*"

"Everybody knows what an experience is." Good: still angry, but with just the slightest edge of doubt. "Experience is sensing things. I mean, you could look it up."

"Yeah, we could play the dictionary game here—sensing, perceiving, awareness, consciousness, feeling, thinking. Red herrings, every one. We can substitute these terms in and out, but you have to put the book aside and pay attention. Do some phenomenology. That's why we ask, 'What do you see?'"

What?

By streetlight I saw his eyes in deep shadow and crows' feet in high relief. His beaky nose and corkscrew beard. Snowflakes crashed into his afro, slushing to sparkling dew points. I was torn between fascination and wanting to punch him. He smiled and held his monad directly in front of his nose, in his palm like a glob of mercury. I thought, Bozo the Philosopher. "I meant, what do you see in here?" he said.

I held my globe before me. The streetlights reflected as a band of precise orange stars arching across the monad. Tiny luminous squares of lit windows gridded in behind the orange points. Max reflected in the shadows.

And me, nose leading cheekbones, a flow of hair looking very brown in the lurid light. Startled but also pleased. And snowflakes whirling down around the sphere from top to bottom, making the ornament and all that was in it seem to rise and rise.

"What do you see?" he repeated. It was a trick question, I decided. It was what I didn't see that mattered.

When in doubt, look at extremes—that would be Max's next move, and I make it mine too. "Tell me something radical that you experienced."

Mickey shares that he was really wasted Saturday night. Mm-hmm. "Well," says Marie, "I was there when my sister had her baby?"

And?

"Well, I'd seen the ultrasounds and stuff, and we had a name for him and his crib you know, but when his head came out it was amazing. Suddenly I could see a little ear and it was *his* ear and it wasn't just Matthew who was about to be born, or Matthew the baby someday, it was *him*. He got real just like that." She points over my shoulder at the board. "That's him. Crowning."

I'm about to ride the baby case when Alphonse interrupts, surly still: "I killed a guy."

That gets my attention. Elementary. Angry boy meets fuzzy hipster, a bad match. Now he'll jump up and say, "And I'm glad, glad I did it!" Case closed.

"It was in the playoffs, my senior year. Third and six. I was in the pocket, but their guard was coming in on me again, maybe the fourth time that game. I had to throw it away, and I was pissed. The asshole guard was charging, I dropped my shoulder and shoved hard right into his balls. Teach him about sacking me. The guy, he flips right over me and lands on his head. Then he just lays there. I go, 'Hey, no hard feelings.' But he didn't get up. In a minute the coaches are out there, and one of them rips off the guy's helmet and they start CPR, but he's already dead. Turns out he had some sort of congenital problem in his neck, a loose bone or something. He was just waiting to happen."

Alphonse still commands the room from his slouch, while everyone else shrinks from him without moving. "Hey, that's the game."

My move; I punt. "What was that like for you?"

"It wasn't *like* anything. All there was was him, lying there all limp for twenty minutes while everyone piled around him and the ambulance came. I kept staring at him because he kept moving."

How did he move? Around the room, the snapping, doodling, and fidgets all end. The play is Alphie's. Everyone locks on him. And checks out the shortest route to the door.

"When I looked away, he moved. If I looked at his foot, his eyes would blink, and if I looked at his face, I could see a toe move. Even when they covered him up, I could see him breathing. I had to go to the funeral, and even then I couldn't believe it." I think briefly of the stillness of my advisor, in the faint light.

"I'm surprised you continued to play."

"Hey, it wasn't *my* fault! If you've got a bad neck, you shouldn't play football."

There are events, I realize, that lie like a blanket across time. You just don't wake up from them. Alphonse playing possum, Alphonse the sullen. I would not have expected to see the world from his point of view, not ever, but it hasn't been a typical day. I'm staring at him, he's staring back. I'm startled by the shared intensity. But in what am I complicit? I feel a shadow, not the first of the day, and again I remember that I saw something of which I could not speak. Philosopher-in-a-box.

"So solve it," he demands. "Solve the mystery, teach."

"I would if I could." Nod pensively. "But that's just what this course is about, and that's why it's called The Mystery of Consciousness." Even a simple experience—point to blackboard again—is full of subjectivity. And how, I ask in a good soap opera voice, can you explain it? "That's really all I'm saying: *There is a mystery here.* You all know it, but you were born into it and live with it. Ordinary experience is full of the mystery—" which is what I should have said in chapter one of the famous soon-to-be-a-major-motion-picture Miranda Sharpe (auteur) dissertation, working title, "The Thrill of Phenomenology." Our story opens in a raging storm of footnotes, as the intrepid author attempts to say what phenomenology is. The *logos* of *phenomena*. *Logos*—words, order, argument—plus *phenomena*, what *seems* to be, appearances. The screen opens black, but then in extreme close-up a single match explodes and blazes. Pull back to reveal that the match is reflected in the pupil of an intense brown eye. Sandra Bullock? Julia Roberts?

Alphonse shakes his head with disdain.

"I can't solve it, but I can tell you about the search," I say. I tell them the starting point, scene 1, has to be descriptive phenomenology, the account of experience. That's why Max won't deal with psychology, with nonsense syllables and flashing lights. Too thin, too thin. Not when someone is sitting there, I mean, lying dead on the playing field. Not when you hold your baby in your hands. "Max wants us to understand and appreciate the richness and complexity of experience. He called it the structure of consciousness. Until consciousness is fully mapped, no theory of what it is made of can fly." Marie is taking notes furiously. Gordon nods, and Mickey is facing in my general direction. Not quite the mosh pit, but close enough.

"But the phenomenology is munchkinland." I tell them what we really need is a theory that tells us what Gordon told us about the chalk blob, that it's really just chalk on the board. Something that explains the phenomenology, the geology beneath the map of consciousness, the score for the symphony.

"Right," pops Gordon. "It's all neurons. That's all."

"Sure, Gordon. But what is it about neurons that makes them the medium of superposition? What is it about the neurons that makes seeing and smelling different? To say it's all neurons is *an* answer, and true too. But it's opaque. You have to take it on faith. What we need is a transparent theory. One that, once you get it, you see that anything built like *this* will have *this* particular conscious experience. It'll be about neurons, but once we get it, you'll be able to interpret the neurons *as* conscious states. And if you change the pattern of the neurons, the theory will tell you how consciousness will change. That was what Max wanted. He wanted to *read your mind*." Or mine, at least.

"What do you see?" I watched the snow arcing around my monad, and watched the real flakes stream by to vanish into the new whiteness that covered the sidewalk, street, and parked cars. The monad made everything straight bent. I listened to the hush of a billion flakes hitting a planet.

Max stared into his sphere, like a demon. I ignored him and thought about the question. What would Descartes say? In my twenty-nine-cent plastic ornament, there's a sort of fake mental representation of the world? Or Kant? The reality of snowflakes, forever out of reach except through the distorting mirror of perception. Or Max himself: He said snow is philosophy made physical. When the world is covered with snow, you realize that appearance and reality are different. That was his thing. What we see is not what's real. I let all those murmurs fade. Then my thoughts collected and condensed into words.

"I see two worlds."

"Ah!" burst Max. As if I'd said, "$E=mc^2$," just off the top of my head. "You're half right!"

Marie's face sinks into a scowl. Now she says, quietly, "You're talking like he was dead."

I know I'm over the top. I feel a blush rise along my neck and face. A secret rides you. "No, I was just referring back to previous lectures." I try a little laugh, but it sounds fake. "So while you're reading your Husserl for next time, think about the big questions: How is consciousness described? What is its phenomenological structure? And what sort of theory will explain that structure—transparently." Something else? I look up at the ceiling, wrestling with the feeling that I *already* knew. Superposition, layering—the orchestra saws and booms and every moment of this wicked day folds into a single frame. The music surges to a silent roar, collapses into a huge dissonance, and evaporates into ceiling tiles. Someone has stuck a pencil up there. I look back at the class. "Um, see you Friday." And again they seem startled, but this time it takes. They file out, leaving me alone with my own words ringing.

Now the room is very empty, just walls and chairs. I am dimly aware that I have done a little teaching. For a few seconds I was transparent, nothing but thought, the voiceover of the spheres. From now on the words would be mine alone, no matter where my advisor turned up. *Nobody creates Miranda Sharpe.* I erased the board, and the answer to one riddle came to me: *Palimpsest.* Now my consciousness squiggle was another smudge in the history of smudges, Wonderbra over algebra. How many layers down lay Maxwell Grue? The swish of the eraser sounded like a whisper, and I remembered a breathy voice in my ear.

"This is the secret of your life. Would you like to hear it?"

I touched the loops that circled through my earlobe, and ran my finger along the back edge of my ear. I did it to dispel the hot breath of my former advisor, and it worked. I noticed that just because a secret was secret didn't make it true. I noticed too that at the very bottom Max was clueless. He could rhapsodize about listening to Beethoven or smelling snow, but that big part about how consciousness is made, he knew nothing about that, and he knew he was empty, just like all his pals, Edmund Husserl and the other dead boys. Eleven students had signed on to the Grue Cruise, and now it was April second and Max *and* the big answers were absent. The breathy idea that had shocked me down to my toes, the mad ego of Max, was nothing. Hot, moist air. He really did miss class. And this morning— I shuddered at the David Lynch weirdness I had seen. Thought I saw. Alone in the room across the hall, I was not about to tango with Schroedinger's cat. Time to check out from the Roach Motel.

It would have been a good day to knot together some bed sheets and rappel down the outside of the building, but instead I pulled up a thoughtful expression and faced the door, and the Crypt that lay across the hall. I'll just slip on by, I thought, and wash my hair and burn my clothes later. Above all, avoid human contact. I fixed my eyes on the baseboard on the safer side of the hall, estimated the staircase to be about twenty seconds away. Waded into the ooze.

"Oh, Miss Sharpe," quavered a voice of biblical age and uncertain Britishness. I didn't need to turn around to know Professor Hemands, the logician who held half the department's reserve of awe and terror. The man could prove deductively through a five-minute quiz that you were a total moron. He looked up at me with his sad logician's eyes, pulling on his Fu Manchu beard and struggling to remember why he needed to talk to me. I noticed that the sleeve on his suitcoat was pulling away from the shoulder as its stitches decayed, like Frankenstein on a bad limb day. "Oh, um, yes. Um, Miss Sharpe. Would you have a key to Maxwell's office? He has my copy of *The Mind-Body Problem,* you see. I would be most grateful."

I might have said that I too had forgotten my keys, but my helpful hand beat my smarter brain to my bag. I held the keys. I blinked at him while my thoughts jammed, and slowly I turned to Max's door. "Sure," I said. I grabbed one hand with the other to steady myself, and there I was, opening *this door* a second time. My heart pounded. As the knob cleared the frame, I turned quickly toward Hemands. "Go ahead. Just pull it shut when you're done."

He thanked me, and I returned to my escape. The hall was surprisingly empty—lunch hour, I supposed, or a big funeral in another county. As I reached the stairwell, I turned back. I could see a triangle of gray light spreading from Max's open door, but there was no sound, no movement. I had to know. I slipped back toward the office, swallowing and trying to steady my breath. It was as if the hall was moving through me. Slowly the prospect of Max's office opened and resolved. I could see rows of books, the edge of his desk, and a man. Hemands. He stood there like a bookshelf, a worn copy of the Goldstein open in his hands. He read intently. "Oh, Miss Sharpe, pardon me," he said abruptly. "I had forgotten you were there." I was busy peering around him. Chair, desk, computer, with flying toasters crawling across the monitor. No Grue. No nobody. Just the solid and tangible psychic stain of him, the empty grid, the ghost. I had an urge to grab Hemands by the shoulders and pick him up, to see if he'd squashed Max. I stared at the logician and he stared at me, dismissing me as yet another of the inscrutable mysteries of human interaction.

"Where's Max?"

Hemands looked at me quizzically. "It appears that he is elsewhere."

2

I retraced my steps along the hall, unwinding the morning so it could start again. I'd spent four hours obsessing with a single image locked in time, Max immobile. *Maybe* he was growing cold on his keyboard. I knew it was unlikely—of course, she says *now*—but the mix of possibility, horror, and poetic payback made it real enough to take hold. I never really believed it, but I never really didn't believe it either. Now that Max had flown from the cuckoo's nest, my dread looked like bad comedy. It would be a day without a coroner's report after all. A regular day, the first day of the rest of my life spent avoiding him. It was possible that he did get the message of the missing folder, that he skipped class to make space for me. That would be nice, but not Max. Teaching is to him like blood is to vampires. Never mind. Skipping class would be his problem, not mine. I could get back to normal, thank you very much.

I walked down the stairs, plain, ordinary stairs, and went into the Department Office. Maybe I had mail.

"Hi, Maureen."

The department czarina looked up, cheerily cheery. "Oh, hi, Miranda." She wore half-glasses on a cord around her neck. With the smallest nose wiggle, she let them drop to her bosom. That was her sign of interest. We graduate students, crumbcatchers for any sign of care, love her for it. She said, "Did you get the bad news?"

Yes, but is he really dead? flashed to mind, leftovers of delusion. "News?"

Maureen nodded toward the office mailboxes. "Read the memo."

I pulled a pink photocopy from my box. The smudgy print looked like the death rattle of a tagsale typewriter.

```
April 2

TO: Whaleard University Computer Users

FROM: Harold Mulch, Director of Information Systems

RE: NETWORK SECURITY ALERT

At 2:20 AM this morning, the firewall protecting the
Frodo fileserver was breached by an unauthorized
remote user. Our staff immediately took Frodo off
line, and it will remain down until a full security
analysis has been completed. As a precaution, we have
also taken the following servers off line: Croft,
Britney, and Morpheus.

We have not yet determined whether this incident is
related to the "Chaos Bug" reported at other internet
sites. However, we strongly advise users toprotect
themselves from attack by observing these
precautions:

1. KEEP BOTH EMAIL AND WEB USAGE TO A MINIMUM.

2. WHENEVER POSSIBLE, DO NOT BROWSE WEBSITES IN
UNFAMILIAR DOMAINS. ESPECIALLY AVOID .EDU SITES.
In the temporary absence of campus-wide email
services , let me also appraise you of the current
extent of Chaos Bug incidents. Below please find an
updated list of universities and government agencies
reporting unexplained system failures. DIf you need
to contact individuals at these institutions, we
recommend that you use telephone, fax, or snailmail.
```

```
Oberlin College
Dartmouth College
Tufts
University of California ( Saan Diego, Santa Cruz)
 U niversity of Texas (San Antonio)
·Trinity College
MIT
   Yale
NIH/NSF
```

```
Every effort is being made to restore campus
network computing services, whileprotecting our
community from sabotage. We will keep you informed
as the current incident resolves.
PS.We apologize for the unprofessional appearance
of
```

```
this memo. With the LAN and our networked printer/
copiers down, we had to resurrect a mimeograph
machine, and deliver updates by hand to each
department.
```

I read it through, still with the sneaking idea that it would mention Grue, the bug's first human victim. He had looked rather breached himself, not too long ago. *Really quite sincerely dead?* The image was not letting go even still. I had an urge to go to the office again, to make sure that Max had not slipped in to pick up where he left off.

Maureen said, "I heard that over at Trinity an entire computer lab was wiped out. They wouldn't even turn on. And then they fixed themselves."

"Wow. That's close." They fixed themselves, he fixed himself.

"It's Wow all right. I hope you're being careful. I worry about you kids with your dissertations."

"You know me—I live for backup. The Queen of CD-ROM." He could be anywhere. He was in his office at the wrong time, and not in class at the right.

"Good for you." She planted her glasses back on her nose, and turned again to her computer. Our conversation for the day was now officially history.

"Oh, Maureen," I said, way casual. She looked up, but the glasses stuck. "Has Max called in today? He missed his class."

She frowned. "The faculty in this department. . . ." Caught herself—not in front of the children. With a sigh, she said, "No, he didn't call here. Maybe he forgot what time it was."

Not Max, I thought. He cared too much to minimize the Max hour. "He's usually pretty dedicated."

We both nodded. Maureen picked up the phone and started dialing. "Let's just get to the bottom of this," she said. She tapped a pencil eraser on the papers on her desk. "Well, he isn't home." She pushed a button on the bottom of the phone. "He's not in his office either." Then she pulled a card from her drawer. "Let's try his cell phone. I can always get him that way." She dialed that number too, and let it ring for a full minute. "Well," she concluded. "I guess he's buried in a snowdrift."

"Do you think he's had an accident?" I said.

She smiled consolingly. "Oh, I'm sure he'll turn up."

"Yeah." In a spring thaw. "Thanks." I bagged the memo like it mattered and left the office.

I exited through the side door into the slot canyon between Ryle and Trollope, passing under the flying bridge between the two buildings and into the patchwork Oz of car lots. Tan and white snow ridges, mouse alps, rose between the rows all the way out to the soccer fields. A loader at the far end revved and slammed its bucket into the slush.

Then I crossed beneath a large sign saying, "G: Faculty/admin. Student cars will be towed." The traffic lane was mostly clear, but the parking places were still outlined by a crust of mushy snow. Some of the cars were clean, others wore a sagging rug of white. I picked my way among oily puddles, watching the iridescent colors bristle in the wind. Between my crunchy bootsteps I could hear dripping.

Soon I found his badly beige Land Rover with the PHENOM plates, parked in the usual lot—he called it his G spot. A hat of snow made the car look even geekier than usual. The windshield was covered, and the side windows too. I circled it, mushing through unbroken white. No strings on you, Maxy. I thought there were traces of footprints leading away from the driver's door, but they had been almost completely covered in snow. I crouched down. Under the car were little patches of ice, like frosting. He had arrived with the storm, about eleven last night, not too long after our walk and all the rest, the spilling of secrets, the words that would make better silences. He arrived, he stayed.

The snow had slipped down on one side window, leaving a patch of wet black glass. I could peer in without disturbing the evidence. The inside of the car looked like a dim museum display of automotive life in the olden days. A brown wool coat was heaped on the passenger side, next to a scattering of 8-track tapes. It was the coat he'd worn last night, and the only coat I'd ever seen him wear in cold weather. One sleeve hung down to the floor mat, and the whole arrangement looked to me like a man in a great hurry, so rushed that he threw his coat in the car getting in, and forgot to take it with him getting out. Around eleven last night that forgetfulness would be an impressive mental achievement. By then the storm was in full fury, driving wet flakes hard into everything and everybody.

A dump of slush let go from under a car nearby. I looked again through the window, thinking that there must be something else. I had the same feeling I had in his office, the second time. His shadow lingered there, and now here too. The rest of him was a growing mystery. A cold, wet man on the run. Running to his office, not exactly sanctuary and rather skimpy in creature comforts. Running to get there, but staying for at least six or seven hours. To do what? Philosophy is the most portable profession. Max could just as well have stayed home. Or gone home. He did something else.

I left the lot and walked across the quad with my hands jammed all the way into my fuzzy pockets, so that my jacket pulled tight over my shoulders. The wind had died. It felt like the inside of a refrigerator.

I thought again of the scene at dawn. Was Max asleep? I remembered watching Seth, my former boyfriend with the Leo DiCaprio face and Peter Lorre ethics, snoring one night when I was up late with a bad case of Philosophy of Language. That was normal boy sleep. Max draped on his computer was more like wax. I shivered at the image, a memory strangely eroding toward a grainy black and white. When this ice age ends, I wondered, will they find some corduroy wrapped around the skinny skeleton of old Max Grue? A shinbone in bellbottoms? Looking back, it would have been ever so much nicer to see him rise from his keyboard, blink, yawn, and stretch both arms. Oh what a beautiful morning.

Then he would have done what comes naturally, teach. But that didn't happen either. Do I go to the police? If they looked into every case of odd behavior on this campus, they'd have to call out the National Guard.

I was halfway across the quad, walking to nowhere. I stopped and turned back toward Ryle and its chilly statue—from here the Fake Thinker just looked like a cold naked guy. The tree branches had all dumped their loads, and reached slick and black for the knotty wet sky. The snow everywhere already sagged, limp as wet socks, white fading to gray and brown. Crisscrossing this scene were the endless walkers, the undergrads with their cell phones and fleece, the grad students in their parkas from the Salvation Army. Walking, walking, with the heaviness of stale snow on their shoulders and in their gait. The trudgers trudged because the alternative was to fall face first into the muck, heave two bubbly gasps, and drown to *death*.

It would have been a good moment to have friends, but I must have left all mine on the bus. That included Seth, protohubby and artist-in-residence-in-our-apartment, a steady arrangement except for the matter of the spare girl. After Seth, I had relied on Max before he dabbled in the metaphysics of me. Fools all: I guess that would include Miranda Sharpe. I shivered suddenly, like I was shaking off icicles, and hugged myself to keep from crumbling. Max was somewhere. When I opened that office door, I let him out of the bottle. I had to know, for sure, that he was not only somewhere but *somewhere else*.

Talking to myself did not seem like the appropriate next step, but the idea reminded me of the Counseling Center, and my and Max's only mutual acquaintance: Dr. Clare Lucid, shrink to the stars and occasionally to pathetic graduate students. We hear she is a whiz of a wiz. I knew the way. Back when Seth was lost in his need for boyspace, the Doctor and I had thrashed over the eternal question, What do Men want? Actually, Lucid kept asking, What do you want? It was I, the poor fool with a comical look on her face, who thought it was about pleasing Seth. What does Seth want? It was obvious enough to his bimbo.

Grue and Lucid went way back too, and had a regular morning tea-for-two. Maybe she knew something.

"Sit anywhere you like," said Doc Lucid as I entered her cubby. Anywhere was the one chair in front of her desk, since every other surface was covered with high-end computer equipment and a Medusa of cables, gleaming in halogen light. I sat, feeling better already. "How are you doing, Miranda?" she asked. Max always said that I should wear purple, just like my prose, but on this campus the purple franchise was sewn up by Clare Lucid, a montage of Faye Dunaway and Anne Bancroft. Permanently in her prime. Today she wore a purple silk scarf with a pale blue suit, just right for lunch with the chancellor or her agent. She pushed back into her leather highback and knitted her fingers across her almost flat belly. Perfect clear nail polish, not self-applied. I tried to remember what she had worn for our sessions about Seth's loose fly problems last spring, and I couldn't shake the thought that it was exactly the same thing. And here I am, with boy troubles again.

"I hope you don't mind me dropping in like this."

"Not at all. I was lucky to have a cancellation."

"Yeah, me too," I say. "I wasn't sure where to turn."

"You weren't sure where to turn."

"Yes. I don't quite know where to begin."

"Is it because you don't quite know where to begin that you came to see me?"

I can tell this is going to get very deep. But surely the host of "Ask Dr. Clare" and author of *Deleting Prozac* and *Rebooting Your Soul* has something to say on the missing Max?

I'm about to speak when a cell phone tweedles. "Miranda. I know this is an extreme imposition, but would you mind if I took this?"

"No no, of course not."

She flips the phone to her ear: "Yes? . . . Next Tuesday? You aren't really saying that to me, are you? . . . No, *you* don't understand. I have a deadline for *Wired*. No computer, no column, no magazine. . . . Yes and I have a list too, but I turn to my urgent cases first. . . . No, second is not good en——. . . . oh. Be quick about it. If I'm down at the studio, my secretary will let you in." Snap; I imagine at the other end they got the message: bitch on speed.

She looks me over, a fashion check and reminder of our conversation so far. "I'm sorry, Miranda. My hard drive crashed." She points an accusing finger at one of the black boxes. "It's a disaster! But the monitors in the Infant ICU at the University Hospital hung for a minute this morning.

While the tech people take care of *that, I* lose a day! The computer people on this campus have a passive-aggressive sector a mile wide."

Now that computing is the ecstasy of the masses, I suppose she is right about her disaster. We graduate students have a saying, HMDYL—How Much Did You Lose? I say, "I hope you backed everything up."

"I hear that more than 'Have a nice day.' Yes, I have backups. But with computers so evolved, there is no excuse for even a minute wasted." She sighs, settles some boilerplate sympathy on me. "I forgot what sort of machine you use."

"It's just a G7 laptop, a low-end gigahertz machine. Go to grad school special, guaranteed not to be obsolete before midterms."

She frowns. "And your slow computer, is this the problem you wanted to talk about?"

"No. It's something else." Like: Why did I think you could help me?

"Oh. Well, before we turn to that, I'd like to suggest that sometime you look at what you are trying to accomplish by hobbling your computing power like that."

I'm definitely remembering why I had ended the Seth sessions, but before I can point out that my hobbled machine can download the entire multimedia *Encyclopedia of Philosophy* in three seconds, she says, "So. Let's talk about Seth."

"Actually, it's not about Seth. I'm over him."

"Oh?" Her precise black eyebrows rise, as it dawns on her that she might need to frame a thought about me. Then the phone beeps again.

I smile and nod encouragingly. She picks it up and swivels her chair away from me. "Clare Lucid. . . . Good. . . ." She turns back to me: "Miranda, would you mind waiting in the hall for just a minute?" I comply sweetly. And lean with complete casualness on the seven-foot cubby wall—halfway to the pipes strapped to the ceiling—and listen. "As I told you," she says, "he was supposed to come at nine. I tried his office, and home, and at ten too. . . . Where, in the G lot? A Land Rover, right? Plowed in? . . . I see." She pauses. I look down at my boots, still wet around the toes. Would I have long before the bloodhounds got here? "I have someone with me now. No no, that's all right. Please do call as soon as you find him. I really mean that, it's very important. . . . And could you keep it strictly between us? . . . Yes, discreet. Thank you."

She leads me in again. "Miranda, you're in the Philosophy Department, I believe." I nod. "They seem like such an interactive group. I'd love to be a fly on the wall over there, just to download some collegiality." I wait to see where this is going. "Just give me a feel for a typical day in Ryle. Were you there this morning?"

"Yes, I was just over there." Who had called?

"Ah. Were they all there? Having their morning tea?"

"Uh, no. It was pretty quiet." And why does she need it to be discreet?

"What, no professors at all?"

"Just one. Only one of them drinks tea anyway." And only one of them drives a Land Rover.

"Yes. So, whom did you see?" Why is she being so ulterior?

"Professors?" I'm waiting for the Doctor to swing her desk light into my face. This could only be about Max. We have ways of making you talk. "Uh, Professor Hemands. But that's it."

"I see. Well, what was it you wanted to see me about?"

I smile at her very nicely and helpfully while I rearrange everything. Someone is tracking Max, and I don't want the trail to point to me. I don't want to be the woman who knew too much. That honor seems to be hers, and something she knows is making her very worried. How will I get Dr. Discreet to talk? I vamp. "It's just that, that, my life is so meaningless."

She frowns, although I don't think she means me to notice, and sits back in her chair. "Where did this feeling of anomie begin?"

"I don't know." What *would* a typical neurotic say? That shouldn't be too hard. "I was walking on the quad, by the Fake Thinker, and the world just stalled on me."

"Fake Thinker. An interesting phrase. Why 'fake'?"

"Um, because the original is in Paris?"

"So says your conscious mind. But inside you are subroutines that are putting out propaganda to your conscious awareness, thoughts like the one you just uttered."

"Propaganda?"

"Yes. The real thoughts are all unconscious. The crowning achievement of the last century is the discovery of the unconscious, and nothing in cognitive science has yet threatened this profound truth." If you say so.

"OK, so what am I really thinking?"

"Miranda, what do *you* think about that?"

"You mean, do I think I'm really thinking that the Fake Thinker is a fake thinker—not really thinking?"

"Perhaps. And does that remind you of anything else?"

"Well, *I* think a lot."

"Exactly. The worry that your thoughts are not legitimate is typical in graduate students. But of course this would be a painful text to send to the monitor screen of consciousness. So your unconscious mind sends something else instead, a feeling that attaches to the world, and that distracts you from the painful truth about yourself."

"Wow," I say. Next caller.

"It works, doesn't it? The mind, Miranda, is a text. The text is stored in memory, accessed and updated all the time, even in our dreams. Freud knew this, but he was ahead of his time. He would have loved the computer. Now your life will change and you'll be happier."

Instead of thinking about that, I'm thinking about Max Grue instead, old, cold, wet Max. That old need to know. I say, "Doctor, you're amazing." Time to tango.

"Thank you." She smiles. I beam back with my kiss-ass good girl adoring smile.

"But," I say with my best perky worry, "you seem terribly upset about something."

She startles, stares at me like an eyeliner commercial, and then sags as much as a second facelift will allow. "Is it so obvious?" She draws a slow breath. "It's a personal matter."

One thing grad school is good for is cultivating the appearance of knowledge. But then, what else is professionalism? "I know," I say, nodding sympathetically.

She looks at me warily.

"He had a class at eleven, but he didn't show."

"Ah," she says. Zoom in. She blinks, the corners of her mouth pulled down still further, and as she looks at me her eyes narrow a little. I watch the gears of temptation turning. "And how do you know that?" Hello, Nosferatu.

"I'm his TA, you know."

"No, I didn't know. How strange. He didn't call? Email?"

"Nothing. Our department's off email. The Chaos Bug scare."

We are staring at each other, circling. I look down and pretend to pick some lint off my knee. Then Miranda the genius detective manages a convincing fake yawn, politely hidden in one hand.

It works. The Doc needs the spotlight full on her. "The voicemail he left *me* last night was very different. A breakthrough, he said. A new theory of consciousness. Do you know anything about that?"

"He's been talking all semester about the solution. Smoke and mirrored shades, I think."

"I suppose it would seem so to a graduate student. I would not underestimate him, Miranda. He is a very capable man." Ah, *man.* Do I detect some love among the subroutines?

I offer another teaser. "His idea was to find a transparent theory of consciousness, a Rosetta Stone—you'd put in phenomenology at one end and get spiking neurons at the other."

"Yes yes, he told me that too," she says. "Did he say anything about an aleph?"

"A what?"

"Aleph. It's from a short story, by Borges. The aleph is a place where the entire universe comes together, like a lens of space and time. Last night he said, 'I have seen the aleph of consciousness.' Those were his exact words. He said something about it being a blurry image, but a whole one. I take him to mean that he was reading some sort of a rough draft. He was tremendously excited."

If she does know him, she should know that he is always tremendously excited. Max Grue shouting his tales, laughing and waving his arms—that was part of his charm. Or maybe she does know him, and he really is where the wild things are. Hurricane Max. With a little spinal tingle I ask, "What do you suppose he saw?"

"Well," says Clare Lucid, back on home ground. "The rough draft notion is clearly an allusion to Dennett's *Consciousness Explained,* and his multiple drafts theory. Consciousness is not a single thing, all funneled through a magical place somewhere in the brain. But then, that idea is implicit in Freud. When I read Dennett I wondered what all the fuss was about. The mind is a text. That's obvious, isn't it? Freud's *Project for a Scientific Psychology* was his 'consciousness explained,' and 'unconsciousness explained' as well. The mystery is, why would Max get all worked up over old news?"

"Maybe he meant something else."

"But what else could he mean? Freud and Dennett have to be right. Our minds are full of codes—sentences floating around in mental soup, forming and unforming. Some are ongoing updates of the perceived world, some are expressions of infantile needs, and some are the ego overwriting its own datastructures. Only a bit of that is conscious. It's obvious, really."

"But how could a sentence be conscious?" How a neuron? How an anything?

"Miranda, they aren't literal sentences in English or Java."

"But. . . ." I'm vamping again. Everything is running backward. Max has been minimized. Miranda too. This shrink shrinks. She talks like she's the only game in town. "But when I look at something . . ." I look at something, so I don't have to look at her. The something is lines, tubes, cords, cables. ". . . at your computers here, I experience a lot more than a mental label attaching to the object."

"Of course. Every label leads to many different associations. It's a hypertext."

"Yes . . ." I say tentatively. "Sometimes I feel that way, I guess."

"You feel? Oh, Miranda, overwrite that bit of Enlightenment folly. Your feelings are only symptoms of the code. The mind works mainly in the dark, and we waste our time if we think a little introspection is going to show us anything useful. It can give us symptoms only, side effects of the real work, the processing out of sight."

"You mean, it's biological?"

She dismisses the idea with a wave of one hand. "Cells, silicon, that's mere implementation. Beneath even the operating system. No, I mean that your virtual machines, the cathedrals of the soul, are operating out of sight. It takes a master programmer, an artist—like Freud—to delete the subroutines that'll kill you. But here in the twenty-first century, the rage is drugs. Prozac and Pleasac. Pissing in the machine! That'll fix it! Hah!" She is blushing. I can't tell if it is from catching herself ranting or the heat of the rant itself.

"You think Max saw that?"

"I suppose he must have."

And if he did, why didn't he tell me? It would have made a nice appetizer for his interdimensional dementia. His big bolt must have struck after I left. So why wasn't he sharing his new thrillo vision with the class? Even a sick Max wouldn't resist the whole mad scientist genius 4-wheel-drive philosopher scene, and me there too. But then I realize that I'm completely forgetting the main thing, that I really had seen him, and very much left the scene of the whatever. How convenient to forget *that*, as the Doc would say. And what else would she say? I ask, "And then what happened?"

"That *is* the mystery, isn't it?"

3

Aleph. Max's white whale and holy grail, the intersection of all space and all time. The answer to all your FAQs. Here's one: Why did Lucid have someone look for his car? Why did she care so much? One thing Clare Lucid did not need was a new theory of consciousness. Her ideas were as fixed as her makeup, saving her the trouble of picking up when Max called. But somehow she needed Max. Or maybe, like me, she needed to know what was up with him. I had my reasons. Something happened, but maybe the something was nothing. He'd progressed from erratic behavior to erratic being, and until I could pull out the real story I felt like I was being stalked. Maybe Lucid had a Grue problem too. Maybe he didn't compute.

I walked as far as the bench in front of the Fake Thinker, but then I had to sit and do some thinking of my own. The Thinker had almost the right pose. Instead of chin on knuckles, I hunched down on the bench and clasped my fingers around one knee, massaging the kneecap. Stared with absent intensity at a trickle of gleaming meltwater crossing the asphalt in front of me, leaking from the dirty mash of snow heaped along the walk. It looked as far away as spring itself, and I wanted to melt along with it.

Aleph. I imagined a sheet of cigarette paper big enough to roll an elephant, big as a seminar. Start in the top left corner with "I am born"—I,

Miranda M. Sharpe the first—the one and only—and print carefully all the way in tiny letters to the other end, line by line until I hit the *now* right in the very center of my map, and then on into the future toward the grail-shaped beacon or death or whatever Sartre felt with his last breath. The end. Then fold the sheet in half, and half again, and again and again until you get the point. The aleph.

I imagined slipping my tissue paper aleph into the back pocket of my jeans, making not even the slightest lump. I thought of lettering my life onto the petals of a rose. Or I could just make it all simple and write a book—let them fold it up in a factory. But no matter how fine the paper or how little the print, shelf space is space. No coming together there. And time, I thought, can't be squeezed either. The past is gone, the future is not yet. Only the present instant exists, falling forever forward.

I sat up straight on the bench, and put my hands in my pockets. I was beginning to get cold, but didn't want to leave my bronze buddy. Two heads are better than one.

The intersection of space and time. Max said he saw it. He didn't read it, hear about it, or figure it out. Reflexively, I dug in my pocket for my monad, but of course there was nothing but a wadded-up Kleenex. I pulled it out anyway. It was the color of old snow, just like the landscape. Just the sort of thing Seth would turn into an art project, like his plan to fossilize a Chia Pet or collect all my cigarette butts for a year. The used tissue and I had a history, and I supposed it was in some sort of relationship to every object in the universe. How nice for it. But that was nothing special, nothing cool for consciousness. The shiny globe idea didn't help either. The universe inside the plastic monad wasn't really in it at all. Inside it was dark, and the spreading bright world was just an illusion.

From the other pocket I took out a pack of cigarettes and a lighter. I thought again of Doc Lucid. She had told me that my thinking was fake and I had been comforted, sort of. But could she really know that about me, even sort of? Motive, Means, and Opportunity. My eleven students this morning, each one passed the MMO test. Suppose Alphonse is on his way home from some rave at DT, 4 AM. Alphonse sees Max's light on. Alphonse remembers that Max is about to nail him for plagiarism and sleeping with the Dean's wife, wiping out his hopes for an NFL career. So, he confronts Max, threatens him. Max holds firm, reaches for the phone to call Campus Insecurity. Alphonse has done what needs doing before, on his way to a touchdown. He even learned a little about the forces required to break a neck cleanly. In a panic, the perpetrator leaves the scene. But later, maybe at seven, he works out phase two, how to dispose of the body. Then, for plausibility—or maybe an alibi—he shows at class and makes sure he leaves a pleasant impression with everybody. A quarterback might be able to do all that, and a smart quarterback named Alphonse really might. With a few phone calls I could confirm my suspicions about the motive, but for a charmer like Alphie plain orneriness and bad timing might have been sufficient. So, I told a plausible tale, just like Doc Lucid's tale of the fake thinker, me.

I lit up, put the paraphernalia back in my pocket. Thin clouds of smoke and warm breath unwound from me and fled past the Thinker.

In a movie, this Sherlocking is half the fun. *Things are not as they seem.* Here in the world, a piece of string or a crumpled shirt is just something in the way, but when the soundtrack runs they are *clues*, and a shlumpy guy with BO and bad driving habits is not just a pain in the ass, he's a *suspect*. In the movies everything has a second meaning. If it shows at all, it is part of a hidden order, ready to be all snugged up before The End. How we love the hidden order. How we love things that stand for other things, the moronic chaos of reality transfigured and transfixed as part of a grand screenplay where nothing is out of place. Cut to Sig Freud, smoking a cigar. Our personal microcosms, the mental landfill. With Sherlock Freud at the glass, our frets and hiccups are clues, and the Moriarty within is scheming always, once we know how to spot his droppings. That mess I call me gets shaped into a good read. We all like good reads and good flicks, and a dash of Happily Ever After. Doc Lucid might be right, and Alphonse might be a murderer too. Both work for a good read. But if I'm not ready to believe the one, why should I believe the other?

I took a drag and my gaze rose from the clutter of slush to a thin, untouched bank of white, a wavy meringue of drifted snow beyond the sidewalk. I exhaled slowly. The smoke turned inside out and thinned to a white streak. Pallindrome for the snow. Make that palimpsest, I thought. I tapped my thumbnail on the cigarette filter, and flicked the ash.

This—I ran my senses over the whole scene—this can't be a crust of text hiding the real flick. It can't be text at all. Nothing makes a text conscious all by itself, no matter how hyper. Before me spread snow, smoke, sound—no fonts nowhere.

I smushed the cigarette into the grit at my feet and threw it out, thinking, as always, vile habit. A black smudge remained amid the gray. The smudge—vile, dirty, guilty, Miranda's, burnt, gray, gritty, ashy, dusty, dead, there—one smudge is all of that at once.

Doc Lucid's strings of code might fit a computer, but they don't fit me. Compared to Lucid's little rationalization, I'm too much, I'm over the top, I'm all at once, I'm here. And whatever it was that Max saw, it just couldn't be as bitty as that.

I shivered. The afternoon had not topped forty degrees yet. In a second shiver I remembered again that I was still in the middle of someone else's weird flick, and I didn't like it. I looked up at Ryle, a random grid of lit and darkened windows, glooming in this day-for-night afternoon. One of them, somewhere along the third floor, was Max's office. A light was on in the fourth office down, and nowhere else. And then that light went out too. Just like philosophers, to sit in the dark. I looked for the dead plant in Max's window, the one he said he kept to remind him that cities were better than nature. There it was, and the lopsided blinds too, in the fourth window down. With a different sort of shiver I realized that the light had just been on in that very window.

As I climbed the Ryle stairs once again, I imagined asking Doctor Clare why I kept coming back. But I knew why. If the phantom of the third-floor office was Max, I just had to know. Then the mystery might subside, and the sharp sinister shadows might brighten. This would be nice. Take two, day for night.

By the time I got to the hallway it was once again empty and silent. Even the lights were off, leaving only a few gray bands shining through open classroom doors. I knocked lightly on Max's door. Again. I found I could believe that he was crouched in there, and then I could snuff that thought and just as firmly believe that the office was empty. Ambiguity, possibility, dread. I could not shake the idea that this office could settle me, resolve the queasy feeling that breathed in and out of my day. With that old rumbling of fate, I slipped my key in once again, and for the third time returned to the scene. Roll soundtrack.

The office was empty again, and gloomed out. It looked just the same, a scatter of file folders across the desk and floor, with the biggest pile right in the middle of the desk, facing the window. No place even for your elbows. The dark computer was ringed with yellow stickies fringing the monitor, like autumn leaves. I turned on the lights, and frowned. The computer—it had been on earlier. I approached, and pulled over the chair. No, not *this* chair. I'll just stand, thank you very much.

I turned around and leaned back on the desk, arms folded. The fluorescents flattened all the faded paperbacks into bound compost, but they made something on the floor shine. At first I took it to be a hole through to some bright underworld, then a puddle, and then a CD, gleaming in a plastic sleeve. Someone must have slipped it under the door, and now someone picked it up and looked it over. (Me.) Completely unlabeled, this mystery disk. I tapped it gently on my palm, looking for a convenient rationalization for what I was about to do. A CD-ROM, slipped under the door: It couldn't be personal. I leaned over the computer, and hit a key. But the computer had its own scruples, and played dead. Nothing. Off. I pressed the power key, and just about squeaked when the big fake elevator music chord announced a happy desktop about to rise and shine. The box whirred a bit, the screen flickered to life, the little Mac icon popped up midscreen, but where its happy little face should have been, was only

?

Same to you, I thought. This was a dead computer, the nightmare of every grad student. Even someone else's computer lobotomy panics a person, and you reach for your diskette. (Mine was safe in my bag.) I laid the CD in the middle of the big pile. Getting ready for some secret agency, I slipped my bag off my shoulder and set it down under the desk, next to Max's open briefcase. I took off my coat and hung it on the empty coathook, then sat down and nudged the briefcase with one toe. The flourescents hummed. The satchel was empty except for an appointment book. Touching it seemed only a little bit worse than touching his computer. I set the datebook on top of the nearest desk pile, opening it as tenderly as a first edition. Max had clipped all his past days together, leaving the future open to my eyes. Here was his day. Nine AM, "CL"—the Doc, just as she said. Nothing else until noon, then "Scan. MRI facility, Med School." Below that, in red ink, a phone number. How convenient for the amateur detective. I thought it best not to call from there, so I copied it into my own datebook: 1–717–986–9209. Then I noticed that I was looking at Tuesday. I turned over the page and found Max's eternal return, with CL at nine again. Nothing until two, when he had written "Fescue." I looked at my watch: 2:05. One reason why Gordon Fescue might not show is that he knows that the man was out. But then there was a knock knocking at the chamber door. I shut his book and shoved it back into the briefcase. No exit for me: Whoever was knocking knew from the lights that someone was here. A peephole in the door would have been nice, but I opened it anyway. You know how it is with curiosity.

4

"Hello, Gordon."

He immediately blushed, part of what I loved about him. He looked around me for Max. "I was supposed to meet Dr. Grue to talk some more about my project."

"Of course. Do come in."

Gordon Fescue lived with the unfortunate conjunction of a round body and a flat face, each tending to be wider at the bottom than at the top. To use his own way of speaking, he seemed to be something of a distortion in the space-time continuum. I suppose he looked like a very young Mel Gibson—if you happened to be sitting in the very front row beneath a very large screen. In real life, he could be Santa in training, and he kept you interested because he seemed always to be about to topple backwards. When he was not beheading orcs, he majored in artificial intelligence.

"You look, uh, very very nice today." It was true. I was the very image of Gordonic desirability—female and not unconscious.

I thanked him, and cleared a chair of its ratty manilla folders. Then I eased myself toward Max's chair, thought better of it, and leaned casually against the desk. Looking down on him helped. He had a little boy's face, even a few leftover freckles, and except for the chronic circles under the eyes from self-administration of gallons of Mountain Dew, he seemed just made to have his hair mussed. I invited him to tell me about his project.

He swung an overstuffed backpack onto his lap and began to unzip it. He stopped and looked up at me. "Really? Can I really tell you all about it?"

I assured him that he could. Whatever. My profound compassion unleashed the boy; he blushed again and I was sure his downcast eyes were teary. "All semester I've tried to get it right, but Dr. Grue keeps making me do it over. I have a 3.9 average. This course is going to kill me." He finished unzipping the pack, and pulled a loose pile of paper from his backpack. The edges curled and folded, and I guessed that the strata of Gordon's thought included a few coffee rings, at least one smashed M&M, a flattened bug, and a foldout from last year's *Playboy.* No wonder Max liked him.

Gordon spread both pudgy baby hands on the top page. Incanting to himself, trying to levitate. Maybe just hesitating. Somehow I didn't think telling him the mind was fragments of text would help. But my hours were unbillable and in this Grue sprout I might find something. I invited him to tell me the whole pathetic story. Just between us. Grue for two.

The project was to program a computer to be conscious. Of course. Max would not have opened his very crowded schedule to anything less, and he probably judged Fescue to be smart enough to back. Gordon was certainly the type to read C+++ code late at night, for the suspense. He began, he told me, by bringing Grue his software outlines, the basic flowcharts for intelligent computers à la Fescue. He handed the top sheet to me. It was a maze of boxes and labels with arrows to and fro. Items like "Speech Input Buffer," "Long Term Memory," "Working Memory," "Motor Preparation," and many others. In the thicket, with many arrows in and out, was a black box labeled "Conscious Awareness." With total disregard of the crisp layout and impressive technicalities, Max had scribbled all over it. On the consciousness box, he had written WHY WOULD THIS BE CONSCIOUS? On many of the other links and boxes he'd written WHY NOT THIS?

"Every time he sent it back to me it was the same thing." Gordon dealt me one after another, variations on the flowchart theme, all thoroughly Maxxed. Why why why why. I was used to it, and I told him. Usually Max kept the moral buried in the experience. If you call that teaching. I asked Gordon where all this got him.

"It got me fired from my part-time consulting for blackbox.com, is where, OK? You see? I went 24/7 for Professor Grue."

I pressed him, and found he had taken another message too. Just hooking up the arrows could never make a you. The boxes in the flowchart couldn't know where they got their data from; rah rah labels like "Short Term Memory" make no difference to functionally illiterate datastructures. For them, it could be long-term hallucination or stolen credit card numbers. Garbage in garbage out. Fescue got that at least out of his all-nighters.

"So OK. So OK. I figured that Professor Grue wanted me to look inside. He wanted me to make it all real complex."

We were busy nodding at each other, OK OK, when the phone rang. And Max spoke from beyond the crypt, or at least from his own answering machine:

Hello, you are experiencing the voice of Maxwell Grue in the Department of Philosophy at Whaleard University.

It would be polite to the startled students lurking in your office to turn down the volume on that thing. The Grue eruption flooded the office and I felt myself cower. Buffeted Gordon tilted back in his chair.

It's the twenty-first century. I will be in and out of the office this decade. Please leave me a message and I'll return your call promptly, especially if you take the long view.

After the beep, a female voice played in real time: "Professor Grue, this is Monica Chua over at the Brain Scanning Facility, calling at about 2:15 on Wednesday. I just wanted to let you know that I happened to be in your building, so I dropped off your raw scan from yesterday and the other file. We post-processed last week's scan together with your speech output, using the software you sent us. You'll find the post-processed file on the disk along with the scan from yesterday. Hope it meets your needs. Dr. Clerk and I wanted to say thank you again for volunteering last week for the study on covert speech. It looks like you're the only faculty member willing to spend two hours talking to himself in a scanner, so we expect your data to be very helpful to supplement the student volunteers. Anyway, I slipped it under your door. Thanks again."

Door? What door? Fortunately, Gordon was more concerned with his own brain than Max's. Aren't we all. He handed me another sheet.

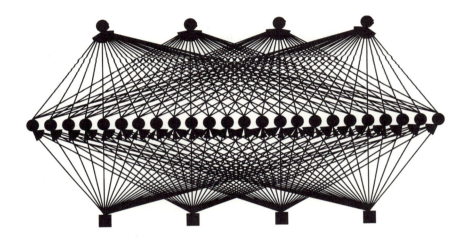

I asked, "Isn't that a neural network?"

Gordon brightened considerably. I studied the page intently just in case he was looking for meaningful eye contact, but if he was, the urge was swamped in neuroenthusiasm. "Yes!" he exclaimed, pointing out each of the three layers from the bottom up: the inputs, hidden middle layer, and outputs. His baby was a simulated brain, with most of the action in the middle. Each dit was a "neuron," and the forest of lines "synapses."

It was prettier than his earlier efforts, but I was skeptical that Max let it fly. "So why hasn't he questioned all your nodes?" I asked. I didn't mean it to seem lewd.

"Individual neurons don't matter. It's the *pattern*." For emphasis, he spread his arms like he was holding a very large balloon. Clearly a big moment. "It's like you were talking about in class, OK? To get all that super, superposition into a state of consciousness you've got to make it simultaneous and distributed all across the brain. This is it, parallel processing."

Brainwise, his drawing looked like flameout to me. You wired this yourself, I said. Gordon explained that it was simulated on his computer. What looked like lines was a "connection matrix." No two connections were the same, and so complex inputs could bring on complex outputs. Lots of each. To make it interesting or at least not insane, you could train the network by giving examples of the inputs and outputs you wanted to mate. A "learning algorithm" enabled the net to correct itself, finding just the right connection settings to get the job done. Sure beat tweaking thousands of connections. Gordon, still motivated by the ever-receding A, made many baby brains in his incubator. He fluttered them into my lap, one after the other. One recognized handwriting. One finished your sentences for you. One made your past tenses into present. Picked your face out of a crowd. Sorted fruit. Selected a good Merlot. Train it, and it could do, and will. I felt like I was taking a rocket tour of forty years of cognitive science.

I noticed that we were still only a few inches into his pile. "You've been working hard," I said, and saying it awoke a little mommyness in me. His shoulders sank like he'd just had a full backrub. His was clearly a story that wanted to be told. "I'm still confused, though," I said. "These nets of yours are full of tricks. And it must get sort of brainy in there, that's good. But why would this in-out competence and the look of brains get you to cons——?"

Gordon jumped on this like a Ritalin overdose. "Just what Dr. Grue said! He didn't care about the synapse matrices at all. He wanted to see what was going on, in here." He poked at the hidden layer in the last net of his series. "So I showed him."

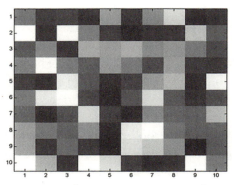

test trial 3: 500 training cycles,
Input/Output: '[he] wrote → [he] writes'

That showed him, all right. Gordon noticed my frown. "That's the central nervous system of one of the simulations. Each square is one neuron, OK?" The bright squares, Gordon explained, were neurons that had high activity. Less bright, less activity. Black was zero. His caption described the input and output at that moment in net life. Max had asked for more.

"More? How many more?" You could open a wallpaper outlet.

"Lots. All of them."

"Why?"

"I don't know. He'd use them like flashcards. Sometimes Dr. Grue would stare at two of them for ten minutes, like they were a novel or something."

Definitely an acquired taste. "When was all this?"

"Starting about a month ago. Finally he had me make him a generic simulator that he could use himself, OK? He wanted to put in his own inputs and outputs and train his own nets. He only gave me three days to write the code too. I flunked my orgo test."

I sensed a few missing expletives. Gordon and I had that much in common at least. "When did you finish this heroic term project?"

"The day before yesterday. Finally Dr. Grue seemed happy with me. But I don't know what he could do with my simulator."

"Couldn't he do all the simulations you did?" Plus maybe a little simulated intimacy with some nubile simulatrix. Or a simulated second-year graduate student. But I forgot, in *his* locker he pinned up grayscale checkerboards.

"Well, OK, yeah, but all those hard copies are taken from fully trained nets. You have to train the nets, OK? You have to make all the correct input-output training pairs for that. Thousands of lines. If you don't know how to program, you'll have to type forever to get enough I/O to train it."

"Maybe that's why he asked you to come in today."

Maybe, OK. Gordon didn't know. I picked up some of the wallpaper and pondered it. Maybe if you looked at these hard enough, you could play checkers in 3-D. Baby consciousness? In principle, maybe. The raw materials seemed right. If consciousness is part of nature, or in the brain, it will be a pattern of neurons doing whatever it is neurons do. But the raw materials would have to be put together the right way. Max would have been clear about that, the "medium of superposition." This grid would have to be able to recognize my face or Gordon's, but would also have to carry the rest, like the perverted weird intensity he had for me—and come to think of it, for Gordon too. For everybody in the Hotel Monad, it seemed. All in the net, somehow. This was on the right track, but seemed to me about as deep as a date with a bar-code scanner. Max was trying to go further, though. He was really trying to learn to read Neuro. Going *really* native in the net.

I stared long enough that the image peeled onto my retina, and when I looked up, ghostly gray squares wrapped themselves around Gordon's face. I looked away and blinked, and now a much bigger grid settled nicely on Max's books. When I tried to focus, the grid slipped along the shelves, always escaping me. Gordon, meanwhile, had spent my psychedelic moment gathering his nerve, and out of pure abstract gratitude offered me a stage side seat and a backstage pass at a Vangelis concert. This activated some new units for me, and I felt a blush rising, and that made me embarrassed too, and even more so as I heard myself say that I would think about it. That response was evidently beyond his most urgent hoping, and pushed his neural networks over the top. As he searched for a next move at the same time as he stood up, his whole stack of neuronoir memoirs scattered to the floor. Orcs and output, bug reports and bugs—drawings suggesting that his big sister had taken him to every *Alien* movie since he was six. And on top of it all, by the luck of the draw, I glimpsed a familiar face. Me. I knew the guy was a doodler, but had never seen anything like this. He had drawn me in a suit of skin-hugging armor that you'd clean with Windex. I was brandishing a sword with so many wavy edges it seemed to be made of flame, and with one aggressing steely foot I was stomping the throat of a big nasty lizard with a grotesquely half-human face. I knew the genre well enough: Xena, warrior princess, and her leather-corseted colleagues. But Gordon had cast me in that role with a twist, a spin that softened the gag reflex. He held back the drooly bits for the sake of honesty. My skinny hips and shoulders. My altogether too broad cheekbones and my wide eyes. The elf ears that would surely annihilate my career as a supermodel—damn. I was, by the silicone standards of the Doom–Quake–Tomb Raider set, a scrawny also-ran. But in Gordon's private fantasy that was good enough, and took some effort to get down on paper. Much as I hated the idea of being someone else's pretend screen test, Leonardo da Fescue was trying. And it seemed that I was his Mona Lisa—on overdrive. I did like the sword of flame and the croaking macho iguana with the Yoda ears. He looked like—I picked up the sheet to confirm the shock. Turn the ears into tufts of pepper hair, morph the face a bit, delete the forked tongue (no, undelete it), and you got a savage caricature of Max Grue. In Gordon's parallel universe my job was to stomp Max on the neck. Maybe I was doing it for him. Maybe he knew me better than I supposed.

I handed the drawing to its author, then dropped to one knee to help gather the rest. Gordon joined in, and in a second it was clear neither of us knew what to say. Several times Gordon cleared his throat, but sank back into confusion. Finally, he stood up with the blooming mess and shoveled it into his backpack. As if he was sharing a secret, he muttered, "I like paper."

I smiled. He backed toward the door. He was about to leave when he noticed the persistent question mark on Max's screen. "Oh oh," he said.

"Yeah. Professor Grue's got a problem." To say the least.

"I have a boot disk. Can I take a shot?"

"Go ahead. What the hell."

His little-boy embarrassment evaporated, and young Obi Wan strode two paces up to the stricken machine, reaching with a single smooth motion into his backpack for a shiny disk. Then he paused and pointed to the screen. "System ten. Dr. Grue has OS ten on there. I'm not sure I'll be able to diagnose it."

"You can tell?"

"Yeah. They changed the dead Mac icon with OS eleven. Ever since then it's been a question mark in a triangle. Of course," he continued, in the absence of the desired response, "almost no one knows that, since the later OS's and the newer Macs have almost never crashed. Until the Chaos Bug."

It was true. I believed I could take my laptop into the sauna and sit on it.

He sat down and laid open his CD case. "OK, let's check it out."

He hit the keyboard reset combo. The machine flashed, bounced through several screens too fast to see, and sprang to life. Max's icons scattered across the screen just like the papers strewn on his desk.

"You fixed it," I said.

"No," he said. With all the gravity Gordon Fescue could muster, he added, "You have the Chaos Bug here."

"And I left my crucifix at home!" Gordon looked at me, not quite getting the joke. For my part, I didn't see what was so terrifying about a perfectly contented Powermac, and I told him so.

"But that's the bug. Your machine dies all the way, and then it comes back from the dead. No one knows why or how. We didn't think it was on campus yet." He popped a phone from his utility belt and flipped it open like he was calling the Enterprise. In a clipped, urgent voice, a full octave below the Gordon we knew and loved, he spoke. "Fescue here. Houston, we have a problem. I've got a Chaos Bug machine. . . . Ryle, a faculty machine. . . .What?" His voice rose back to normal. "Anywhere else? I'm on my way." He hung up. "It's here. The computer lab is infested. I gotta go."

He was already in the hall before he remembered to say goodbye. He turned back and told me again that I looked very very nice.

"Thanks—you already mentioned that."

"Oh, sorry." He struggled to find something else to say, failed, turned, and walked away. I closed the door gently behind me. He had surprised me, and I suddenly wondered why I hadn't told him my whole story, so he could solve that mystery too. But then I shook my head, shook off my daze. Him, an *undergraduate*. His sketches stayed with me nonetheless. I like paper too. What a leap that was, I thought. Leaps of thought, leaping to conclusions. I guess the neural networks do that too.

In a few seconds the feeling that I was alone in thought faded and the mishmax of the mess arranged itself like a smoke ring, hanging in mid-air. What was I looking for? Oh yes, an aleph. Now, where would a zany professor stash his private transdimensional portal? Maybe he made a wormhole exit this morning, the worm.

My eyes came back again to the computer. Beneath the perky icons, it was infested. Not a pixel out of place, but the whole thing had gone icky in my mind. It spread, adding its aroma to the books behind the computer and the folders scattered across the desk. Across the industrial carpet, into the worn upholstery. I'd been sitting in his chair after all. That day-without-a-shower feeling spread along my thighs and butt and back. Here's a superposition, I thought. From everything in this office wafted a stench. The stench of bad mind.

It was a mind I had to know, because until I did, Max Grue was clearly destined to be my personal Chaos Bug. Some people go to shrinks to sniff out the bad mommies and daddies that live inside them. What do you do to extract a bad mentor? Definitely a job for a philosopher. But if the philosopher is only partly finished? And an apprentice to the bad mentor herself? It was a grim, grimy business.

The CD shimmered on the desk, brighter than sky, with faint rainbows arcing around the center. I pulled a blank CD from my bag and used the resurrected computer to copy the brain scan and whatever else. Then I returned the original to its place by the door, as if this would erase my presence.

I could wait around for the next clue, or I could eat. The choice was easy.

5

The University snack pit was a sparse, bright place with one food line open, where I bought a plastic pod containing something on white with a sprig of green. As soon as I faced the scatter of students, I knew I needed some invisibility. I crossed the lobby, past the bulletin boards gone shaggy with colored paper, into the ArtSpace, my private sanctuary. Devoted to student shows, it got about one visitor a week, and I was confident that the current exhibit would be no crowd-pleaser. It was a reprise of Seth's master's degree show, the installation that may have already led him to an MFA in Conceptual Art. It had been up last summer, and now it was back for a week to plug a hole in the schedule, I guessed because it was so easy to hang. He called it his big number, not far off since the title he gave it was "Big Numbers." The sign by the entry had it as BIG^{numbers}. One real art skill you learn in the Department of Conceptual Art is dry mounting, a talent Seth had practiced on an array of regular sheets of paper, all perfectly plastered to foamcore and each perfectly blinding in its own tight little spotlight. Each one described a big number, a specific huge sum of something that Seth had rooted out of the library or the Web. He had begun with the number of elementary particles in the universe, 10^{87}, which was centered on a panel entitled "Things." He might have written it out as ten with eighty-seven zeros behind it, but it would have been the only big number that could fit the page without the powers-of-ten gambit. The number of elementary particles in the universe turned out to be paltry. One of his professors had put him onto Borges' Library of Babel, the book nook where every combination of letters that can fit into a medium-size book, is. That set the bar at $10^{10,000,000}$ volumes. It was titled "Text." I beat that with my suggestion, Paul Churchland's estimate of the number of distinct patterns of neural activity in the brain:

> For the human brain, with a volume of roughly a quart, encompasses a space of conceptual and cognitive possibilities that is larger, by one measure at least, than the entire astronomical universe. It has this striking feature because it exploits the combinatorics of its 100 billion neurons and their 100 trillion synaptic connections with each other. Each cell-to-cell connection can be strong, or weak, or anything in between. The global configuration of these 100 trillion connections is very important for the individual who has them, for that idiosyncratic set of connection strengths determines how the brain reacts to the sensory information it receives, how it responds to the emotional states it encounters, and how it plots its future behavior. We already appreciate how many different Bridge hands can be dealt from a standard deck of merely fifty-two playing cards: enough to occupy the most determined foursome for several lifetimes. Think how many more "hands" might be dealt from the brain's much larger "deck" of 100 trillion modifiable synaptic connections. The answer is easily calculated. If we assume, conservatively, that each synaptic connection might have any one of ten different strengths, then the total number of distinct possible configurations of synaptic weights that the brain might assume is, very roughly, ten raised to the 100 trillionth power, or $10^{100,000,000,000,000}$.

This sheet he called "Mind." And so on around the room. The centerpiece was a sleek black pedestal with a gleaming glass of water in the middle of it. Its page said simply, "Number of possible arrangements of molecules in this glass, $10^{1,000,000,000,000,000,000,000,000}$." He had titled it "You are here."

Max had loved it. At the opening he chuckled and sighed at several items, and stood in such rapture at the glass of water that I thought he had become part of the installation. After the deep meanings had bubbled out of the glass, I guess I began to stare at him instead, because he turned to me as if we'd been talking the whole time. "I'm thinking of that old joke," he said, "'Would you care to join me in a glass of water?' I think there's room for two in there. If the Churchland thing is right."

"I'd prefer a single. And furnished." Four bright beams shone from the ceiling, casting four light shadows in a cross with the glass at the center.

"But from your point of view it'd be Graceland. Somewhere in this ten to the whatever possibilities is a configuration where each water molecule corresponds to a neuron in your brain, your brain experiencing this room, your brain in the Taj Mahal, on the moon."

"Or on the rocks," I said.

He smiled indulgently and continued the monologue. "What I'm wondering is whether *this* water has your brain mapped in it right now or whether it's only mapped in one of the other possible configurations."

I looked at the glass, sparkling in wonderful icy light. "I guess it depends on how you read the molecules."

"Right! So . . . so there's a possible translation manual that interprets each molecule, its position or temperature or whatever, interprets it to mean something about a corresponding neuron." He stroked his Brillo beard once, then pinched it at the chin, to hold on to his train of thought. "There's an infinite number of possible translations, and one of them makes this water an image of your brain right now. Since the manual is possible now, then the water fits it now. The water's actual, the real deal. Miranda, meet Miranda."

It wasn't quite my image of the twin sister I never knew. Before I could frame the proper way to greet a liquid, he was on to his next brainwave. "Too bad it isn't conscious," he said, with a bit of genuine disappointment.

My molecular counterpart has just been insulted, I thought. "And why not?"

"Oh, the configuration is too brief. Gone in a flash. Almost instantaneous." He snapped his fingers. "You'd hardly get a sensation up before the molecules wiggled out of sync. Meaning takes time." To prove the point, he snapped again.

While I was thinking about strobe lights and the card catalog at the Library of Babel, Max turned back toward the pedestal, picked up the glass, and began to drink it.

Hey, I thought, *don't drink the art!* The Max Moment brought the proceedings to a dead stop. Max finished drinking, and set the glass back on its altar. "Ahh!" he intoned, against a backdrop of twenty silent, startled faces.

Then Seth laughed, and it was OK. Some others laughed too, and a few shook their heads at the infamous Professor Grue, up to one of his stunts. Seth walked up to us, grinning, and said to Max, "And they said dada was dead." He took the glass, raised it in a fake toast, and walked with it toward the bathrooms. Art eternal, to be replenished at the fountain of inspiration.

A tall blonde in designer jeans and espadrilles intercepted Seth at the door, and I could hear her offer to get the water for him. She rested her hand lightly on Seth's forearm before she took the glass. Later I learned that her name was Alice.

Now I was back in the gallery again with breakfast and lunch in one hand. In one corner of the room some padded benches backed up to a slab of window stretching from the floor to the black rafters. It was my spot. Quite a few dead philosophers had joined me there, and I would not let the other memories of the place stink it up for me. I swung my shoulderbag onto the bench, and sat crosslegged next to it, leaning on the window. After a few bites of a sandwich beneath noticing, the graduate student reflex engaged and I flipped open the bag for something to read. The red folder. "Oh," I said, closing the flap. That.

I had brought my whole damn day along after all. One flash of red that told the story of Max the moron, Max the missing. How could I ever work on "The Thrill of Phenomenology" again? I consoled myself with the thought that no thrill ever really repeats, Max or no Max. Every twinge is unique. I took another bite of lunch, and the dry nothing of its taste suddenly stood for emptiness. It also stood for not buying a soda. I could repeat Max's trick, I thought, but knew at the same time that I was not that kind of girl.

Also, that glass was *his* glass. Not even ten months could erase the touch of his lips from history. I would not care to join him in a drink.

I realized that Max was wrong about the water. Mental states ripen and fade, and that takes time, just like he said. But they are there in every frame of the mind's own flick if they are there at all. The instant has to be long enough for consciousness. All these superpositions, on the sandwich, on the folder, on the glass, must be present in all of the instants that add up to a state of mind. They have to carry through the time of that particular awareness. The emptiness of the taste of the sandwich, it's there in the shortest flash. And the past and future too. I opened the flap again, to rub in the redness of red. There was a story radiating from it. Somehow the whole timeline was squeezed into my look. The line was there in every instant of my awareness of the folder. The line was in the point.

I closed the bag and returned the sandwich to its coffin. The story of my lunch was coming to its end, as I laid it to rest in the trash. Please try again later, said my stomach.

As I walked by the door, I passed the pedestal and saw all at once that the glass was empty again. For a moment I shivered and the panic rippled along my spine. Only Max would do that twice. Once, even. I shook it off. Surely the water had just plain evaporated. I was walking through arty water vapor, breathing it. I guess I'm in it after all.

On a small table by the door lay the gallery guest book and a familiar signature pulled the panic cord again—Max, of course. It was undated, but only one signature followed it, a rival for Max's own schizoid flourishes. It read, Porfiry Petrovich Marlov, in a spidery calligraphy. Another man between me and Max. I was grateful to him. If I knew when Mr. Marlov was here, I thought, then I would know sort of when Max was too.

I paged back and found Max hiding in plain sight again and again. He had been a regular at the Conceptual Art Department shows. More than once this Marlov signed just after. The name was vaguely familiar. I guessed he was another professor. Who signs anything with three names? I wondered.

I flipped back through time a few more pages and came at last upon myself, snuggled in the page after Seth. That was a different pang, the ping of another time with its own hopes. The opening had been one of our final events as a couple. I remembered Alice the blonde, her hand resting on Seth's forearm. I had no idea then that she would be Miranda II, the sequel. But two weeks later, Seth had swapped beds, and women too. I saw the hand on the forearm again, the extra second it lingered there. The extra second had been a bubble at the fringe of memory for eight months, and now I got it. The beds were already switched on me, even then, me still a believer in Seth and Miranda. I hated being the fool. I looked one last time at our signatures playing footsie on the page. The moron.

6

Holly Golightly greeted me at the door to my apartment, meowing and wrapping my ankles in fur. Another romantic rendezvous. I let my bag slump to the floor and squatted to join her in a fifteen-second orgy of scratching. Her maniacal purring made the rest of the apartment seem unnaturally still. I stood, and as I pulled off my jacket and boots the dark shapes and feeble daylight pulled my thoughts back toward dawn. Lights. And for the shiver I had just felt, I turned up the heat. Considering my day, I wouldn't have been surprised to find my apartment ransacked, just in case *I* was the one with the Maltese Falcon. A little ransacking wouldn't be a bad idea. Fluff it up.

Home sweet home happened to be a cubey studio organized around a tall black stereo with a TV on top. My big ticket in the furniture department, a futon couch, faced the stereo. Lately I left the futon open most of the time, with my Powerbook among the pillows, so I could sleep with my early works. For serious immersion I could also amoeba myself into a black beanbag chair with gray cat-hair highlights. My other prop was a desk made out of an old door, a giant's door, which I had up on crates at the windows. Painted black, of course. In the spaces, plastic crates displayed a mix of sweaters and seriously dense philosophy books, the world according to Miranda Sharpe, wannabe phenomenologist. Along the wall over my books hung my prize collection of movie posters, mounted with appropriate reverence under glass. That way I could see my own reflection morphed into purest Hollywood, strike the pose, share the mood.

Time to add *Dracula* to the gallery, I thought.

I hesitated at the stereo. Sometimes in the afternoon I would listen to "Ask Dr. Clare" and her live hours of systematic misunderstanding, but by now it would be over. Music? The current featured soundtrack was *The Hours*, a little too smoky for the moment. So, with Zen simplicity, I turned on the lava lamp, making my statement complete. My apartment said to the world that Miranda Sharpe was In, had Arrived, was There.

I was In, unlike Professor Marlov, whose office I'd found in the dismal basement of Friedman. I wasn't sure what to ask a visiting lecturer in "Forensic Data Analysis," whatever that was, on loan from the Moscow Polytechnic University. I imagined a short man with tweezers at a murder scene, picking ones and zeros out of the carpeting.

Earlier in the gallery, that thing called a sandwich had not qualified as a meal. From the refrigerator I extracted my revenge, a reckless five slices of cheese, and unwrapped and ate the first two in best bachelorette binge style. I would atone with at least one full day of skim milk in my coffee. Starting now. I pulled the basket out of the coffeemaker, and dumped the sludge from yesterday into the trash. I scooped one scoop, two scoops of coffee. It smelled like some emotion, like the long flat high of an all-nighter. Hell, I thought, and poured an extra heap straight from the can.

As the first drips bubbled into the pot I remembered—I always did—one of Seth's pieces. The plan was to recruit everyone in a stack of studios like this, all the studios at the same corner of the building, 2C, 3C, 4C, on up, and get all the occupants ready to make a pot of coffee. Then Seth would cue them in sequence by calling 2C, then 3C, and the rest every five seconds. Each one would begin to make coffee just as the phone rang. So every part of the process would be happening at every moment—he wanted to call it the Instants/Coffee. Sethy, I said, where will the audience sit? That made him pissy and set us up for a payback fight that night about the emotional waste of philosophy. Maybe the bimbette was already in play.

I sighed. The surface of the coffee shimmered and wobbled as the pot gurgled aggressively. Seth was right. My question about the audience had been real, but now I could see that the viewpoint could be anywhere. His concept piece was right here in its fullness, wiggling like Jello, offering its lovely brown smell. What I literally saw was the instant, but what I *perceived* was process, a history, and the moment before my eyes was a stage in the story. The coffee gathered up its past, and faced the future too, with the comforting confidence that it would deliver its shot of warmth and fuzzy buzz. All that was present. I couldn't even imagine it without its story. Seth only wanted to make it concrete.

One world. One instant. One art piece that never came off. One boyfriend gone. That thought entitled me to some comforting, so I sniffed the half-and-half, still good, and gave myself a little thrill of caffeine phenomenology. Atone tomorrow. I added a handful of crackers to the cheese plate, and took plate and mug over to the desk.

Beyond the plate, my two tall windows let in two cities. Through one window, my fire escape with its abandoned flowerpots sliced up the tenement across the street, a building just like mine with its own fire escapes and their flowerpots. Out the other, if I leaned in I could see up over the artful decay to a glassy tower from the world of suits. At this gray hour the hard glitter of the building lights looked completely fake, like futureland. Maybe the building had been reorganized by the Gordons of technocracy into a simulated neural network, all ahustle with neurons in ties.

As I looked at the scatter of glowing rectangles receding into the sky, I wondered about connections. Gordon's idea intrigued me. Each of his neurons could reach out to many many neighbors, some distance away. With the variability in the connections, Gordon had a network that would settle into some smart circuitry. Clare Lucid would point out that any computer could do the same thing, but where consciousness is concerned, it's not what you do but how you do it. I liked the way a Gordonic network could bounce from recognizing one letter to another; I liked the way it made the bounce without invoking any intermediate rules or software; I liked that each state somehow used the whole brain. What Gordon seemed to have going was a nice analogy, nice as far as it went. Probably Max loved it. But I just couldn't believe it was nice enough to disappear a real professor, right down to his dandruff. I reminded myself that he may have merely appeared to disappear. Maybe I liked him better off screen, way off, but I wasn't the director here.

I took a long sip of caffeine, while H. Golightly leapt onto the desk and pretended her interest in the cheese was purely aesthetic. I scratched her ears, saying, "You're hungry? Why am I not surprised?" I took some cheese to her bowl, and as I predicted she chose it over conversation. Then I sat again and unwrapped a slice for myself, folded it twice, and arranged the four perfect squares on four pristine Wheat Thins. What a day, what a day.

A light winked out from the face of the tower. Right, I thought. Gordon is out. He's innocent. The two boys actually seemed to like each other. Maybe they were the same boy. If you grew up in the '60s with all that paisley, you got Max. In the dot-com '90s, you got Gordon. It was too bad Clare Lucid's call-in show was over for the day, this would have been a nice issue to pose to her. That and the mystery visitor to Maxy's office. With a tiny shock I realized that Lucid was off the hook. Unless she was broadcasting from the janitor's closet in Ryle, she could not have thrown the light switch while I was watching. But who was it? Mr. Chaos Bug himself?

What did Max know and when did he know it? For months he'd been at his drum roll. The sophomores probably thought he already had his aleph. The grownups, if they knew him at all, knew to cut the volume on Max's enthusiasm by half. Still, Lucid bought it last night, and she may have called others. Max may have too.

My bag lay on the floor beside me, and I extracted the Maltese CD. The disk shone with that special gleam of information, an episode of Max's most private epic. Alas, poor Max. I saw myself in there too, faint ghost reflected against a backdrop of movie posters and lava lamp, refracted through the rainbow of Max's brain. All in one hand.

This is your brain on CD. Any questions? Well, yes, if I may. (Raise my hand, good posture always.) Miss Sharpe? Um yes. One. What *is* this, really? A: Your advisor. No, a slice of him. Sliced advisor on disk. Two. Sliced when? A: Yesterday afternoon, by the message. Three. OK. So why do I have this thing? A. Much less messy than the real thing. Besides, he needs the real thing, sometimes. The disk is . . . his shadow. You have it because you need to figure out what happened. Four. Why? A: . . . I have to think about this one. Finding him alive would take care of this crazy guilt trip, and it would let me get back to the job of raging at him. Finding him dead, finding that he is dead, would be weird and scary and maybe not helpful with the guilt/anger jam, but would clear a way forward.

But I realized it was something else. The troubles of two little people, three if you count Gordon—and Lucid makes four—don't amount to a hill of beans in this crazy world. Placing the bodies, warm or otherwise, mattered, but crackling through it all was *consciousness*. Something about consciousness flipped Max out of my world. Flipped his body, leaving his mind all over the landscape, like goo. If I knew what he was thinking, just one definite thing, the rest of the puzzle would fall into place. It could be big, I thought, huge.

I opened the computer next to the plate and slipped the disk in. Two files: Baby Bear and Mama Bear. Baby was 1.2 gigabytes, born yesterday. Name on the birth certificate: 04_01_mgrue_allruns.

I slid the cursor over the file. Quiet on the set. I took a swallow of coffee. I wiggled myself snug into the chair and instinctively held the edge of the desk with my left hand. Ready for anything. Lights. Camera. Double-click. Action.

I had opened an aorta of numbers. They flew up from the bottom of the screen in waves, so fast that my poor laptop developed a bad case of stripes, woozy bands marching down the screen while the numbers tore upward. Cut. I shut it down, leaving the last frame frozen.

```
0.00000000E+00   0.00000000E+00   0.00000000E+00   0.00000000E+00   0.00000000E+00   0.00000000E+00   0.00000000E+00   0.00000000E+00
0.00000000E+00   0.00000000E+00   0.00000000E+00   0.00000000E+00   0.00000000E+00   0.00000000E+00   0.00000000E+00   0.00000000E+00
0.00000000E+00   0.00000000E+00   0.00000000E+00   0.00000000E+00   0.00000000E+00   0.00000000E+00   0.00000000E+00   0.00000000E+00
0.00000000E+00  -1.99795630E+00  -1.87222690E+00   0.00000000E+00   0.00000000E+00   0.00000000E+00  -1.54933090E+00  -3.77761300E-01
8.99535280E-01   4.96629650E-01   6.50933930E-01   3.62327770E-01  -6.28802140E-03   1.65161180E-01   3.19465470E-01  -3.97763710E-01
7.77809440E-01  -1.63449790E-01  -1.20029950E-02  -2.20599530E-01  -3.89191250E-01   0.00000000E+00   0.00000000E+00   0.00000000E+00
0.00000000E+00   0.00000000E+00   0.00000000E+00   0.00000000E+00   0.00000000E+00   0.00000000E+00   0.00000000E+00   0.00000000E+00
0.00000000E+00   0.00000000E+00   0.00000000E+00   0.00000000E+00   0.00000000E+00   0.00000000E+00   0.00000000E+00   0.00000000E+00
0.00000000E+00   0.00000000E+00   0.00000000E+00   0.00000000E+00   0.00000000E+00   0.00000000E+00   0.00000000E+00   0.00000000E+00
0.00000000E+00   0.00000000E+00   0.00000000E+00   0.00000000E+00   0.00000000E+00   0.00000000E+00   0.00000000E+00   0.00000000E+00
0.00000000E+00   0.00000000E+00   0.00000000E+00   0.00000000E+00   0.00000000E+00   0.00000000E+00   0.00000000E+00   0.00000000E+00
1.84079450E+00  -1.78650230E+00   0.00000000E+00   0.00000000E+00   0.00000000E+00   0.00000000E+00  -1.56076080E+00   5.19489540E-01   7.76663350E-01
9.68114960E-01   4.96629650E-01   1.19441400E-01  -7.48677030E-02  -1.06300060E-01  -6.05802700E-02   1.05153960E-01   1.42301290E-01
1.77179680E-02  -1.66307280E-01  -2.72034290E-01  -3.57758890E-01  -4.63485900E-01  -4.97775740E-01  -2.89179210E-01  -4.32053550E-01
8.29244210E-01   0.00000000E+00   0.00000000E+00   0.00000000E+00   0.00000000E+00   0.00000000E+00   0.00000000E+00   0.00000000E+00
0.00000000E+00   0.00000000E+00   0.00000000E+00   0.00000000E+00   0.00000000E+00   0.00000000E+00   0.00000000E+00   0.00000000E+00
0.00000000E+00   0.00000000E+00   1.36586320E-01   1.08011450E-01  -4.72058360E-01   0.00000000E+00   0.00000000E+00   0.00000000E+00
0.00000000E+00   0.00000000E+00   0.00000000E+00   0.00000000E+00   0.00000000E+00   0.00000000E+00   0.00000000E+00   0.00000000E+00
```

Raw mind; viewer discretion advised. Holmes, I fear we may be too late. All that remains are his digits. I reset the font size.

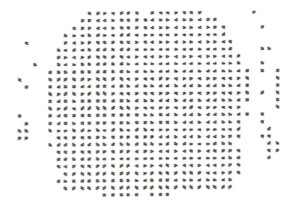

So *Max* was the Matrix. If Keanu Reeves is Neo, that makes Max Retro.

I realized the numbers could just as well be a picture, and with a few more clicks I reopened the file as a graphic. Now the numbers sank into points of gray. He was definitely a Winter:

At the end of the rainbow of experience, this pot of mush. Alone with my thoughts once again. Or not quite, since I was also alone with Max's thoughts. That's what the scanner scans, right? A: Wrong. That's just a brain. Q: And what is that, chopped liver? A: You know the answer. It's the "neural correlate." Q: You expect me to believe that there's another something just as complicated as this, in a whole other dimension? That that other something just happens to be correlated with all this? Seriously. Give my *neural correlate* some coffee. Ah. My *mind* thanks you.

The thing that says *Ah* is the thing that feels *ah*.

Holly Golightly jumped onto the desk, looked for any piece of paper that I might want to be reading, and planted herself there. She fixed her eyes on my cheese, and resumed her life of quiet contemplation.

I pulled back again:

Why so many images? I guessed that this was Max over time, a silent flipbook of Max's brain. The images went on and on. Scrolling changed them into crude cinema. His brain seethed like hot lava. Double bubble, toil and trouble. This was a long way from Intro to Phil. of Mind: "Suppose that a pain just is the firing of C-fibers," said an Australian named Smart. Why not D fibers? Why not Cheez Whiz? Why something rather than nothing? All those little examples are too little. How about this. "Suppose a pain is the mix I'm watching here in real time. Real brains for real people." A few gigabytes for the symphony in pain sharp major. I considered the idea that this spew was nothing but an accident and the pain, or the thought, or the mind was something somewhere else, in some Twilight

Zone. How inefficient! How inelegant! Maybe it was not obvious how the mind could really be the brain, but the alternative was *really* unobvious.

I was drumming my fingers while the images danced like a bad hangover. "What this movie needs is a soundtrack," I said aloud. Holly Golightly's head jerked, and she gave me her best hey-I'm-just-a-dumb-cat look, with an ear twitch thrown in. I was thinking that these brain bubbles were the images of thoughts, or could be, if only I knew how to read them. If only Max were narrating. "The thing is," I continued with Holly, "if you knew what these bubbles meant over here, and these over here, you could explain the whole double latte." I just need to read your brain, Max. Where indeed were you yesterday afternoon? A. I know that. In a brain scanner. The question is, where are you right now? "I don't suppose you'll tell me that," I said to the screen.

But what if I had the translation manual for this thing? What if I hopped aboard his train of thought? That might answer the rest. Then I'd know where I stood. What was what.

Maybe that would be the other file, Mama Bear, with her 34.8 gigabytes: 3_25_mgrue_postprocessed_iterations1000. How much is that in brains? It came from his earlier scan session, a week ago, but was much bigger. Had he been thinking *really hard?* I closed down all the running programs. I slipped the cursor over the file icon. "Holly, let's drop the big one and see what happens." I pushed back to arm's length, suppressed the desire to cover my eyes, and clicked.

A gray window popped up. "Enter encryption key," with a box for a longish password. I typed "Rosebud." Invalid entry. Swordfish. None shall pass. I never did ask Max what his mother's maiden name was. There'd be room enough in this file for that, and every other thought too, all the random musings of Maxwell Grue. The experiment was something about thinking aloud. The thought of that voice. The thought of those thoughts in my ears. There are some whispers you just don't need to hear. I closed the Powerbook. That's enough for now, thank you very much.

7

Two more non-giga bites from dinner, and suddenly my buzzer sounds. Holly and I exchange questioning looks, as I cross to the intercom. Yes?

"Miss Miranda Sharpe, please," says a musical voice.

"Who is it?"

"My name is Porfiry Petrovich Marlov . . ." and the rest of the sentence goes right on by.

"*Pardon me?*" I interrupt.

"My name is Porfiry Petrovich Marlov. I am visiting professor at Whaleard University and Trinity College also." A musical accent mixes with the static. "I would speak with Miss Sharpe about a philosophy professor she knows. There is concern about him."

Now more than ever, I think. I buzz him in. I unbolt the door, causing the cat to sprint for her hidey hole under the bathroom sink. My fearless defender. At the door stands a man much shorter than me, with dark and beautiful skin, and a salt-and-pepper moustache thick as a brush. He's wearing a thick wool overcoat that drapes to the top of lined rubber boots, and a black furry earflap hat, which he quickly removes. Gray mixed through his hair suggests he's along toward fifty, sixty.

He's smiling. Laugh lines radiate from intense brown eyes. "Miss Sharpe?"

"Yeah, that's me." I'm bracing the door with my left foot, holding tight on the knob. Watch it, pal.

"Oh, Miss Sharpe, that is good, good." The accent resolves in my mind—Boris Badenov. "Porfiry Petrovich Marlov. I am exchange professor here in America, at Whaleard University. In Forensic Data Science." He pulls a little red spiral notebook from his pocket, and flips it open. Three paperclips hold a photo ID to the inside cover. "For one year I work in this city and Professor Michael Poole work in Moscow. That is my city." His tiny photo stares at me grimly. "Russians and Americans share many ideas. It is like old Mir. Our people mingle. World has peace." He smiles at me, Mr. Jovial, like he's waiting for me to get some joke. Maybe I flicker back. The notebook slips back into his pocket.

"You ask, why does Porfiry come to me? Yes, yes, that is a good question. America is big, full of new friends." He spreads his arms, as if to hug the world. "I live here in big house, many apartment flats, and at bottom of stairs is apartment for Professor Maxwell Grue. This morning when I go to work, Maxwell's door is open. Hello, Max! I call out, but no answer. Big dilemma. Close door or leave open? Open flats are not safe in America."

I nod, thinking of the view through that open door. But this is why Marlov has come to me? For advice?

"Many years I was detective in Moscow Militia. Chief Inspector! Detective feelings come to me at Maxwell's door. So I look for him, and ask questions. First it is challenge, then it is worry. Maxwell is nowhere!"

"Yes, I've noticed."

"Ah," he says abruptly, and looks at me with disconcerting intensity. He looks along the hallway. "Is there some other place to talk? Perhaps outside?"

Coziness beats caution, and I step back to let him in. He thanks me and walks to the center of the room, holding his hat in both hands. He turns very slowly toward me, sweeping the room. Before I can frame a question for him, he is speaking again. "Seventy students he has, my disappearing friend, Maxwell Dudley Grue. Do I go to all seventy? No, it is too much. I use brains." He pats the back of his head briskly. Again the pleasant smile, all Kris Kringle around the eyes. I organize the best fake smile I can. He didn't go to all seventy. The former detective went to me. I'm wishing I had checked my boots for bloodstains, or chips of Land Rover paint. Another pause for big eye contact. "Yes, yes, you are right to demand an explanation, absolutely right! I go to his office, with department secretary. We look at papers. We ask, who knows him? And we find a folder with many papers from Miranda Sharpe. Bright folder, very red. We look for Miranda Sharpe in phone book. It is not Soviet rocket science to go here."

"But how . . . ?" *I* have that folder! Or if not, something else. I fight the urge to glance at my bag, where the folder hides. This is getting complicated.

He notices. "Is there something?"

"Nothing. I haven't seen him either." I tell him about the missed class, and the missed meeting with Lucid. Never mind about his car. And skip the scene at dawn.

His smile looks rueful. "It is all questions, then."

"Yeah."

"When was last time for you and Maxwell together?"

It takes an extra second to work out the innocent version of his question. "Yesterday. We met to discuss my thesis." And everything else. A complete metaphysical workup.

"Ah, Miss Sharpe." He purses his lips with concern. "This thesis, it is finished, I hope." Uncle Porfiry.

"Not quite." Not even. "I still have some writing to do on it." Like, most of it.

"Do you outline chapters first, or write first?"

"I usually see where the writing goes."

That cheers him up. "That is good, good. You are creative person. Philosophy must find what is possible. Is that not true?"

"It's a start, I guess."

"Yes, yes. Begin with what is possible. Look at all corners. Novels are also like this." The topic inspires him to clamp his hat under one arm and put on a pair of exceptionally geeky square reading glasses, with heavy gray steel frames. The worst shape and color for him imaginable. Then he uncaps a fountain pen and opens the notepad. "What did you observe last night? Was Maxwell like Maxwell? Or changed from before?"

"He may have been a little wilder than usual, a little more intense. He had a twitch sometimes. His hands shook." His brain wobbled a bit too, judging from the words it created.

Marlov scratched at his notes for several seconds. "Did he stand or sit?"

"We were mainly outside. Walking." Nietzsche's moustache may have been bigger, but not by much.

"Yes, that is good. Good. Legs and brain help each other to good thoughts. Walking faster than usual for Maxwell, or slower?"

"Oh, it was pretty slow. Lots of stops." If this is a clue, I'm not getting it.

"Like good Russian family after eating. Walk and talk. After thesis talk, did you talk of authorities? Of government? Did Maxwell express opinions against society?"

"No." I frowned. "You're talking like he was a terrorist."

He smiled broadly, crinkling again. The laugh lines: Sean Connery. "Oh, Miss Sharpe. I ask standard questions in Russian detective science. For analysis."

"Oh. Like in, forensic data analysis."

"Yes, yes, that is it. Absolutely, Miss Sharpe. Forensic."

To me, that means something from the morgue. "So Max is a case, then. Something happened." Somehow it's never occurred to me that there are real morgues, outside of the movies.

"Only your American police can make a case. No, old Porfiry is retired chief inspector. If I use Russian detective science to find Maxwell, it is a friend finding a friend. Curious Porfiry finds what is possible."

"And if you eliminate all the possibilities, what remains is what must be."

"Absolutely! Perhaps you also take a degree in detective science!"

"Just philosophy. It's less abstract."

He laughs at this, a rich baritone, and chuckles as he writes something brief into the notes. "Your face is north and south, yes?"

"North and south?"

"Forehead and high cheeks. You have grandparent in Sweden, yes?"

"Finland."

"And from Asia, southeast?"

"Yes. I'm one-quarter Vietnamese." Blue eyes usually make that one hard to call.

"And hair with color of copper metal." He shrugged and looked up at the ceiling, then back at me with his conspiring grin. "Brain cannot place hair."

"My grandfather was Welsh."

"Ah, like America, your family. Great stewing pot of many flavors. Good, good. And very tall, one hundred eighty centimeters."

"Is this detective science too?"

"Oh no. Russian detective science looks only at mind. Centimeters and faces, that is just old Porfiry who is curious."

"Whatever," I said. "About Max. What do you think happened?"

"Think!" And he laughed again, throwing his head back with pure glee. "Oh, Miss Sharpe! Thinking in brain is nothing but clouds and winds. It is crude, like hitting with the back of an ax! No, in detective science, we use statistical analysis. This shows us what is possible, and what is wish only. But old Porfiry will explain all. Miss Sharpe, may I sit?"

Always a loaded question here. I reject the beanbag as too familiar, and spin the desk chair his way. I sit on the foot of the bed, think better of that plan, and fold the bed into a couch, shoving the sheets off the end.

He pretends that nothing happened, and drops into my swivel with such a sigh I think he might be planning to take off his boots. I wonder if he sleeps in his overcoat. He slips his hat over one knee, crouches forward for the trading of state secrets.

"I know, I know. Old Porfiry will not stay long." Rapidly aging Miranda nods encouragement, but OP is back on topic. "But you are a philosopher. Perhaps you are a materialist?"

"Yes. If you mean that I don't believe in a soul or mind distinct from the body."

"That is good. And mind is brain?"

"Exactly."

"And the brain has three dimensions?" With both hands he panto-mimes a box around his skull: front and back, side to side, and crown to chin. I nod. Three dimensions.

"And mind? Also three?"

"If the mind is just the brain, then yes. Three." I resist the urge to hold up three fingers. "But I'm not sure the question makes sense."

"That is good. Miss Sharpe, now I tell you about the new 'rocket sci-ence,' statistics for higher dimensions. In Russian detective science, mind has many hundred dimensions. We look at all."

I'm frowning, trying to picture this square circle.

"Ah, Miss Sharpe. You ask, what is Porfiry talking about? You are right, absolutely right. It is science, Miss Sharpe. Science for us is also science for you. The dimensions of mind are not up or down, X Y Z. That is for wolves and little cats. No. The dimensions of mind are properties of minds. One man likes vodka, another does not like it. So there is one dimension, 'loving vodka,' and one is big in that way, big vodka-lover, but the other is small in vodka love dimension. Everything else has dimensions. Does person like cheese? Does person tolerate disorder? Does person make neat bed every morning? Each is dimension, one, two, three, infinity!" Neat bed: Check minus. Cheese food: Check plus. Disorder: Love it or leave it.

"So anything you can measure is a dimension?"

"Yes yes, good good. You understand. 'Dimension' is abstract only, not in space. Dimension can be scored from little to big, or just yes or no, present or not present, one or zero. You wonder, 'Where is Porfiry taking my brain on ride?' You are right, absolutely right! Yet again, Miss Sharpe. From dimensions of mind we get space of mind, and then we find places in mind-space."

My brain isn't exactly on the ride, and it shows.

"You are right, absolutely right! What is mind in space? And Porfiry, is he a materialist? Good questions, good. 'Space' is like 'dimension'. Abstract only. Mind-space is for description only. Here, I will draw for you." He hooks the little notebook from his pocket, and turns back several pages of cramped Cyrillic notes. "So, here is two dimensions, like in school, eh? X and Y." Drawing on one knee, upside down, for me to see. It's simple enough, the two axes. Could this be the long-awaited moment, when geometry *matters*?

"We say, one dimension is vodka-liking. You like vodka, Miss Sharpe?"

"Not particularly."

"Good good. Old Porfiry hates vodka. Vodka poisons motherland. Buries our hope. But my brain wanders again!" He gives himself a sharp pat on the back of his head. "Since I come to America, my thoughts are not straight like in Russia. I think it is your American television! I am in need of a five-year plan, eh, comrade?" He laughs, big Santa, then hunches back over his notepad. "Vodka-liking, that is X. For Y, cheese-liking. You like cheese, I do not. Cheese stick in very bad teeth, make breath stink. So you are big in cheese-liking, I am not big." He adds two letters to the drawing, slow as a third-grader with the labels. I see why Moscow wanted to trade him.

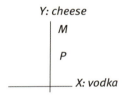

"So I am point P, you are point M. P and M not big with vodka, so both not big in X. M like cheese, so M big in Y, but P not. Two dimensions of mind, but for each mind only one point. Miranda Sharpe and Porfiry, neighbors in mind-space for cheese and vodka."

I nod. This may land somewhere. In a point.

"Now we add many people to space. Vasily, top former Soviet rocket scientist, good friend. He likes some little vodka at supper, not much, but cheese gives him a bad stomach." Holly slinks in from the bathroom, freezes, arches her back, and slips away again.

"Vasily is similar to me, not so much to you. So I graph V near P, not near M. We add many more. Some near, some far. If two people are similar, then they are near in abstract space. We can compute distance in space, very easy." He scratches in a triangle, connecting the dots. Somehow I don't think Max will show up on this map.

I nod again.

"Yes, yes, you ask old Porfiry, so what? Many people fit on page, Porfiry Petrovich, Miranda Sharpe, Vasily Ilyich. But now you ask, with many properties, we must also have many dimensions. Absolutely right! Let us add liking for tea, dimension Z. Now page is too flat—next axis must be up to sky. Do you also like tea?"

"Sure," I say, testing the possibilities. In reality I detest tea.

"Good good. Another dimension where you are good Russian." He nods. "Now Vasily, tea also give him bad stomach, and Vasily hates that feeling. So, you and old Porfiry are big in tea dimension, so our new points are up here." He holds two fingertips a few inches above the page, just over the points assigned to the two of us. "But Vasily, he is close to sheet, not very big in Z dimension. Now more dimensions, but still one point shows you, one point shows Vasily down here, and one point shows old Porfiry. Who is neighbor now? With liking-tea dimension, maybe you and I are closest, Vasily far away. If we are closest, we are most similar, Vasily is less similar to you or Porfiry."

Holly slinks in from the bathroom, freezes, arches her back, and slips away again. It's a kitty deja vu.

"Now." He pauses, with his big secret grin. "Now, what if four dimensions?"

"You mean, time?'

"Oh, Miss Sharpe. No, it could be many things. Will for disorder. Need of excitement. Rage toward government. You, me, Vasily, all are big or small in many dimensions of self. Ten dimensions. Twenty. One hundred."

Dimensions, points, and mind-space. "There's a drawing I'd like to see."

"Yes, God, He sees such things. But to God we are wolves and little cats. Human eyes are too small, human brain too simple. But statistic science, that gives us eyes of God! Take a space of one hundred dimensions. One hundred properties, some big, some little. Each person still just one point, even in big hundred-dimensional space. Maybe you are most like Porfiry, or maybe Vasily is. But even in one hundred dimensions we measure distance. Even there we are near or far in space. Even in space that only God sees."

"But I thought statistics would show us that space."

"Yes, but not yet. First, statistics measures points in space, statistic science tells us which points are neighbors in high-dimension space, which are far away."

I imagine a tape measure stretched between two floating dots, then many dots and a web of tape measures. "Sounds complicated."

"But not too much for human brain. We can list distances. This is easy." He licks a finger, flips to the next page, sketches a square.

His pen scratches on. He shapes his numbers with extra loops, and turns the page toward me.

	P	*M*	*V*	. . .
P	*0*	*1*	*3*	. . .
M	*1*	*0*	*2*	. . .
V	*3*	*2*	*0*	. . .
. . .	. . .	. . .	. . .	. . .

"Here is table of distances. Old Porfiry same as old Porfiry, so distance is zero. Porfiry quite similar to you, only one unit difference. Vasily far from Porfiry, middle distance from Miranda."

"It's like a mileage chart." In the silence, I'm suddenly aware of myself, my body, sitting on the edge of the couch with my hands clasped around one knee.

"Yes yes, good good. Only distances could be in hundred-dimensional space as easy as two-space. Same idea. Pages hold many many people."

I lean back a bit, but not enough to get comfortable. "But when you have lots of dimensions and lots of people, what does this get you?"

"Ah, Miss Sharpe. Ah. There you are absolutely on the crux, absolutely. Now we must look at mileage chart. It is also big. So we use multidimensional scaling!" He grins like a magician holding the unexpected rabbit.

"O . . . K . . . ."

"Multidimensional scaling is the statistic science method for building a new map. The new map has not so many dimensions, better for wolves and little cats and humans. The new map shrinks many many dimensions, but keeps same distances. Then humans can see what God sees, scaled down to human mind, human dimensions. Maybe two dimensions, maybe three."

"How does it do that?"

"Ah, Miss Sharpe, we must send you to Moscow in professor exchange. You are big in question-asking dimension, just like a detective. Scaling works with a big computer program. We take best number of dimensions.

Two dimensions are easy to see, but often do not fit. With more dimensions, the eyes get tired, brain gets tired. But the points fit better and better with more dimensions."

I imagine a point of light in perfect darkness. It stretches to a line, a red line. The line folds into a square, which unhinges into a cube, and then unfolds again, and again, beyond seeing. I suddenly feel uncanny, as if Porfiry had come over here from Narnia, as if reality and fantasy were blurring. Somehow these unreal maps fit with conversations with Max, that feeling of flying through invisible canyons and mountains. Dangerous, forlorn, fabulous countries of the mind. I want to walk through the portal, look at that 3-D version of the hundred-dimensional mind-space. That shrunken head. "Did you discuss this with Max?"

"Yes, yes, Maxwell and I trade many stories. I tell him my cases. Luanda, Havana, Leningrad, many cases. These technics show who is antisocial, who must have re-education."

"So criminality is just one more dimension?"

He looks suddenly sad, disappointed. "No, no. If it is one dimension, then we just measure. Banish statistic science, eh? No. Criminality emerge from all other dimensions." He is watching me intently. Suddenly his grin vanishes, and he looks at me with Moses intensity. "Once we have the mind-space for many many people, we find types in clusters. We find many clumps of good comrades. We find a country of anti-social egoist nogoods. We find a country of murderers. In the land of murderers, we even find little districts. Sex criminals, criminal insane, even a little *dacha* for serial killers. Not good neighborhood!"

"I've never thought of crime as moving you to a new space."

His voice drops to a whisper. "Crime does not move. The criminal is always at home in mind-space, then opportunity comes, then the crime is committed. Twenty years ago, in Luanda I work on Kharkov case. Kharkov, engineer from Odessa, big dam builder, big help in Angola. Kind, happy man, with a face like Andropov. Friend to children. I ask, 'Comrade, are you criminal? Did you murder?' His eyes fill with tears. 'No,' he said, 'no no no.' But physical evidence convicted him of eight murders. Terrible crimes, they gave old Porfiry a terrible feeling in the stomach. We asked many questions, measured many dimensions of mind, and Kharkov fit into space of mind, in district of not good people. But he thinks he is a good man! Worst criminals suppose themselves good men. In America too. Where everything is 'no problem,' eh? Perhaps more in America." He shrugs, then grins at me again, waiting patiently for me to catch up.

He removes his glasses and balances them on his thigh. "I will illustrate." He looks straight into my eyes and straight through them. "*Did you, Miranda Sharpe, murder Maxwell Dudley Grue?*"

It's as if he flashed an 8-by-10 glossy of Max this morning, with me posing next to him. "Murder!" The cloud of Maxisms, Maxmemories, all the Gruish possibilities, instantly collapses into one awful lump. A lump with a sheet over it. I feel like I've been slapped. "What do you mean, *murder?*"

"Of course not, of course not!" he roars, slapping his stomach with both hands, guffawing. He laughs heartily, in waves, for half a minute, and wraps it up with a red handkerchief, wiping his eyes, blowing his nose with great emphasis. "Russian detective humor. I 'pull your leg.'" He chuckles a bit more, and—it seems to me—winks. "Of course you are no criminal! Is not part of 'lifestyle,' eh?" He gestures with amusement at my lava lamp. I'm not sharing the joke. I pin him with the always-ready icy stare, the one reserved for jerks and morons.

Instantly sober. "Miss Sharpe, Miss Sharpe, please do not take offense at old Porfiry's strange ways. I look at all character, all humanity. When I was chief inspector, then I had suspects. Now I am professor, and curious. Just an old horse on his old path. But just to be curious, to be knowing. For everyone, there is point in mind-space. Where is it? That is all."

"I prefer to remain *off* the map."

"Of course, Miss Sharpe. There is no one like you! No one! Here is a person living alone, thinking alone. No one thinks for Miranda Sharpe. She is an outsider in America, like old Porfiry." He looks at me as if pondering a riddle, and then, just barely, nods.

"But I must go, Miss Sharpe. You have been so hospitable. Our little conversation, that is nothing. Just two friends, eh? I hope we may be two friends, here in strange land of America. I thank you. I thank you." He stands, makes a slight bow like a stifled sneeze, and almost runs to the door. "I will find the door, thank you." Holding it open, he looks back for a moment. "Oh, my old brain forgets again. One question more. When you enter the office with Hemands, was the computer off, screen dark?"

I look toward the ceiling. "No," I begin hesitantly, sorting scenes, looking for the trap. "No, the screen saver was running. Yes, I remember it distinctly. Flying toasters."

"Oh, yes, but of course it was! I ask you a stupid question, eh? We saw toasters too. You Americans with computers on all day and all night. Well, we meet again, eh, Miss Sharpe? I take my leave until the next pleasant meeting!"

He stiffens and bows again just a bit, and then winks at me. Or is it a twitch? Turn, and exit. Cut.

I push the door closed, hard, lock all the bolts, and then turn around to lean against it while the room settles. The cat emerges and stares at me, her usual empty-headed look, but tinged with a confused worry that I might overlook her dinner. I take a deep breath, hugging myself fiercely. And another. "Holly," I say, "I wasn't expecting the Spanish Inquisition." Nobody expects the Spanish Inquisition.

8

At lunch several months earlier I had ordered a grilled cheese and tomato sandwich and a large chocolate milk in a plastic cup with a spill top and bendy straw. Max, who was treating, fixed me with his chess master endgame stare, did the same to the waitress, and solemnly repeated my order as his own, word for word, right down to the bendy straw. Two lunches, or just one, repeated across space and time? It was the sort of knee-slapping joke that only a phenomenologist could love. Then he told me about an invention of Borges, the *zlönir*—a magical double that pops out of nothing. In a Borges story, two young people have just gotten married. They're poor and timid and all signs point down, but there they are on a honeymoon in the Andes, camping or something. The big wedding present, maybe the only wedding present, was a knife in a beautiful leather sheath, suitable for spreading butter and skinning iguanas. On their first day alone together they hike up a mountain for a picnic, and when they get back to camp they discover the knife is missing. Hubby immediately sets off back up the trail—he thinks he left it at the scene of their postnuptial bread and cheese. But the bride is just as sure it's her fault, negligence with the breakfast dishes down by the river. Both are frantic. Cut to sunset. The boy returns to camp, a big grin on his face. The girl is smiling too. She takes her hand from behind her back, and in her palm is the beautiful knife in its leather sheaf inscribed with Runic figures. The boy gasps. Without a word, he reaches into his pack, and withdraws—the knife! Beautiful, in the sheaf with just the same Runic figures, the same twists in the stitching, the same droplet stain of tanner's sweat just at the hilt, the same rainbow shimmers in the mother-of-pearl inlay. One of the knives is a zlönir. Borges never says which.

Max was one of those guys who found himself amusing, and he wasn't afraid of a joke that needed three footnotes ahead of the punchline. "So, Miranda," concluded Max, "today I will be your demi-urge. Your desires will multiply in the world, each making a zlönir. Be careful what you wish for!"

I told him that he could only be a full urge, and that as such he needed to be the careful one. I planned to spend the afternoon finishing my first book, also known as a dissertation, also known as the Swamp Thing. Zlönir *that*, I said.

For months, I'd watched him slip my thoughts into a bright red folder labeled CONSCIOUSNESS. This morning I had grabbed a bright red folder, so named. Maybe it was a zlönir. Maybe it was just another red folder. The wrong one.

Now it lay before me, clashing terribly with the pasteurized processed cheese food. The folder had lain like this in front of Max, just twelve hours earlier. His folder, not mine, stuffed with the knowledge of good and evil. I could put it back in my pack, drive over to campus, go up to the office of the damned yet again, and politely return it to his desk. That would be very nice, thoughtful, and decent. Instead, I emptied the coffee pot into my mug, and added not only half-and-half but a shot of Jack Daniels. I flipped the thing open. The back of my neck tingled.

In the movies you begin with a big embroidered page with the words "Once upon a time . . ." so you can say, oh I get it, this is *fiction*. What I came across instead was bad box office for sure: It was a Xerox of an absolutely ordinary journal article. The paper was from the journal *Cognitive Science*, from the misty year 1990. I could see that I was about to fulfill the grad student image of a wild night, reading a bad photocopy, listening to obscure music. To help me in my dragnet, Max had scribbled all over the margins, beginning with "YES" in the top right corner.

The author was one Jeffrey Elman, and the article was called "Finding Structure in Time." A memoir of my first year in grad school, I thought. Its first line:

Time underlies many interesting human behaviors.

Yeah. Time underlies many *interesting, human* behaviors. Got it. I read on. This was a paper about "connectionism," which in a few lines I quickly determined was Gordon's thing. Neuron-like widgets with lots of connections to other neuron-like widgets. A toy brain. Got it.

Elman wanted to figure out how to get a simulated brain to keep track of temps perdu. To do that, Elman gave the world the first "Simple Recurrent Network." It was Gordon's project with a twist.

According to Elman, Gordon and his kind are after the standard boring neural network, a pure "feed forward" network. It's three layers, like a cake. The input layer bubbles up to the middle layer, and the middle to the top, that's the output layer. One-way street. Such a brain would live for the moment, responding only to what was right in front of it, like a reflex. But my Mirandanet can often do more. Like hatch a plan to steal my writings back from my advisor, and be guided by the plan, and react when it fails, and fails again, and fails again. (What a day, what a day.) Time underlies many interesting human behaviors.

Elman proposed a new plan, a recurrent network, a gizmo with feedback. Like this:

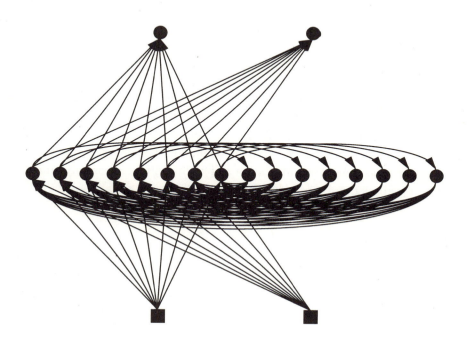

The middle layer sends its signals two ways at once. One set heads on up to the output layer, but a second set just copies over to something new, a mirror layer. Then at the next cycle, that mirror feeds back into the middle layer, along with the new input. So the network is checking out two things at once: its new, current input, and its record of its own internal state from just a flash ago. Sounds like a pretty shallow thinker, but Elman pointed out that the mirror layer is copying a pattern that reflects the middle layer from the previous cycle, which reflects the middle layer from the cycle before that, a cascade of mirrors reaching to faintness, like a Hitchcock creep-out funhouse of opposing mirrors and millions of Peter Lorres. This gizmo was a depressive brooder, chewing its cud endlessly even as it added new grass to the mix.

Yes, wrote Max. The article covered a ladder of simulations, each one a bit more elaborate than the first. Usually Max hated this techno jargon. If this was his idea of a good read, then I guess life as a male is even worse than I thought.

I read on. Living in time myself, I wondered what it was that won Max so emphatically.

Elman finished with a look at language. Not quite English, but a tiny piece of it, a piece that followed decent rules for bits of English describing bits of a mundane world. A mere twenty-nine words—mouse cat dog monster lion dragon woman girl man boy car book rock sandwich cookie bread plate glass smell move see like chase eat sleep think break smash exist—perfect for the existential toddler. The words were assembled into two- and three-word sentences, in conformity with the rules of grammar and usage and commonsense reality that the young nerd would follow in order to get his Barney stickers. An underemployed computer churned out these sentences without punctuation and without sleep. Eventually Elman had a potboiler that read like this:

> woman smash plate cat move man break car boy move girl eat bread
> dog move mouse mouse move book smash plate cat move man break
> car boy move girl eat bread dog move mouse mouse move book . . .

This went on for a mere ten thousand sentences, or almost thirty thousand words. This page-turner was fed to a recurrent network. Fed six times, in fact, just like high school. It was trained to anticipate the future. The network was trying hard to guess what came next, and its connections were constantly being adjusted, just a bit, to improve overall performance. When "cat" was the input, the net finally learned to at least limit the choices for the next word. It could be "move," "see," "eat," and a number of other verbs, but it definitely wouldn't be "sandwich" or "man."

But of course there was still enough randomness that the net couldn't really predict the next word. So what we had here was a little brain that was as smart as it could be, but under the circumstances, not smart enough to predict the future. At its best, it anticipated a future, bracing for what might happen and ignoring what probably wouldn't. Just like us!

So what, I wondered, so what? I guess Elman wondered that too, and so he asked, How does it work? It learns a little something, but what? If the gizmo were a computer, you could look at the code, but as with Gordon's experiment, all the action was in the connections. There were many of them, each one a little different from the others. If you looked inside at the middle units, at all 150 of them, from moment to moment the pattern would be complicated, with none of them having a fixed job. In short, it was just like dealing with people. They do things, but when you ask how, the nuts and bolts, it quickly gets too complicated.

Elman had a way in, however, and as I read it I began to get excited. Think of each of those middle units as a dimension, bouncing around from second to second. When the unit is very turned on, it's huge in that unit's dimension. I could almost hear Porfiry's voice: Comrade, network can be big in unit number one, and small in unit number two. With 150 units to look at, the brain is careening along a path in 150-dimensional space, hither and yon, here and there. Elman recorded the activation values of all 150 units in the presence of each of its possible input sentences. Quite the proud daddy, with an album of over 27,000 snapshots of babything. Here's the little one responding to "dog." And now "chase." Now "cat." Isn't that just the cutest?

Only God has a scrapbook to show 150-dimensional baby pix, so the only option was the one Porfiry had described to me: You could measure near and far in hyperspace, use that distance information to carve the space into neighborhoods, and figure out who lives where, who the neighbors happen to be. By itself, none of the dimensions really meant anything, but the map of neighborhoods, that could be an undiscovered country.

I took a bite of cracker and cheese. Porfiry spent his spare time crunching his acquaintances into a map of hooligans and demon butchers. Here was the same idea, only Elman was looking at a toy brain over time. At each moment, the entire universe of the net consisted of just one word. Its pinhead brain lit up at every word like the tower down the street, a different spray of lights for every word. These patterns finally funneled into a map, where similar patterns landed near each other. They were labeled with the input word that provoked them.

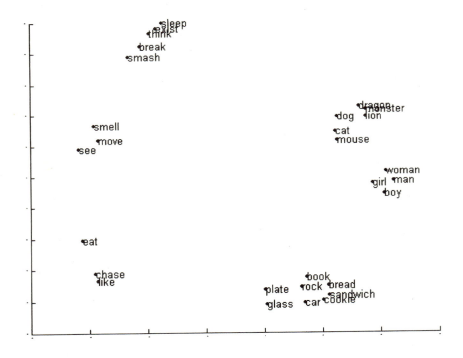

Elman looked over his result and wrote up a little tour guide. Each of his categories appeared as a neighborhood, similar patterns in the widgets as particular words were presented:

The network has discovered that there are several major categories of words. One large category corresponds to *verbs;* another category corresponds to *nouns*. . . . The noun category is broken into two major groups: *inanimates,* and *animates*. Animates are divided into *human* and *nonhuman;* the nonhuman are divided into *large animals* and *small animals*. Inanimates are broken into *breakables, edibles,* and nouns which appeared as subjects of agentless active verbs.

"Discovered" was the right word, I thought. Nothing in the stream of inputs announced any of these categories, but there they were, emerging in the toy brain after immersion in its little dog-eat-cat world.

Next to Elman's diagram, Max had scribbled "Superposition!" For a moment I thought I would need another shot in my coffee to figure out what he meant, but then I got it. We experience superposition as one of the most pervasive aspects of conscious experience. It's the overlayers, the harmonics of meaning, that attach to every object in the knowable universe. My chipped mug was more than just a pattern of dots on my retina. It was Irish coffee, a liquid, something warm, something brewed an hour ago, the stuff Seth and I drank on our first date. None of those are really separate thoughts. They are ways of seeing the coffee, non-sensory aspects of the experience. Had something of my history or the history of coffee been different, I might have had just the same retinal and taste impression, but a very different experience. Had I thrown it in Seth's face, as I sort of felt like doing during his bimbo revelation, then this mug would have a different meaning. All of consciousness is like this. A single state of mind is packed with stuff, but somehow remains one thing, one experience.

So now here was Elman's simple recurrent network. At every moment, it's in a single complex state. It picks up an input, like "cat." Its 150-unit main brain knows that cats are not dogs, and Elman had read its mind: "Cat" and "dog" patterns are distinct in hyperspace, and the map shows it. Not only that, cats and dogs live near mice in hyperspace, so the net knows, *in the act of recognizing a cat,* that cats, dogs, and mice are similar. All of the patterns responding to animals group together. So the net sees cats as animals, because the pattern for cats is pretty similar to that for other animals, but dissimilar from other things. But the net also knows that the animates belong together, and finally it knows that "cat" is a noun. All this knowledge is intimated by one pattern, one point in hyperspace. It's there because of all the relations with other points, its similarity with the nearby points, and its dissimilarity from the more distant points.

You couldn't see this just looking at the network, but with the right computer data massage, the hidden meanings surface. Once all this was up and running, you wouldn't need real cats or real dogs at all. All their meanings, and all our experiences of them, could fit in the hyper box. To the optionally real cat in the room I said, "No offense, Holly." None taken. To her, my words were sweet nothing.

The Elman piece woke up my inner graduate student, and I saw in it the potential for many wonderful dissertation footnotes, provided I could ever get to chapter two. For about ten glorious minutes I snuggled in the cool dioramas of theory. I finally began to see what a transparent theory of consciousness might be like. You start with a brain. Instead of seeing it as a mush of skinny spazy neurons, you see it Porfiry's way, as a bouncing ball in a hyperspace, a really hyper hyperspace. In the space you plot a point for each different state of mind, and what you get is a kind of map of the brain. But what if, what if that map was also a map of consciousness? Elman's network put the cats and dogs next to each other, and boys with girls too. My conscious experience also has that structure. Two in one and one for all. And the man behind the curtain *is* the great and wonderful Wizard of Oz.

On the last page of the Elman piece, Max had added a sketch. It was a simple recurrent net, just like the diagram, but he had crossed out the input layer with a big X. Next to that, a question mark. With no inputs, what *would* a big recurrent network *do?* I followed the loop around, and around, the play within a play. Would you spiral into a dream? Or down the drain?

I settled a little further into the folder. The next photocopy was straight from a paperback. Old Max couldn't even make a normal copy—one of the two pages was crooked, the other had a nauseating little dislocation running like a scar up the middle. He had slipped while he was copying it. The margins of both pages featured a smoky image of Max's thumb, smushing the book against the glass. I read:

> Under the step, toward the right, I saw a small iridescent sphere of almost unbearable brightness. At first I thought it was spinning; then I realized that the movement was an illusion produced by the dizzying spectacles inside it. The Aleph was probably two or three centimeters in diameter, but universal space was contained inside it, with no diminution in size. Each thing (the glass surface of a mirror, let us say) was infinite things, because I could clearly see it from every point in the

cosmos. I saw the populous sea, saw dawn and dusk, saw the multitudes of the Americas, saw a silvery spider web at the center of a black pyramid, saw a broken labyrinth (it was London), saw endless eyes, all very close, studying themselves in me as though in a mirror, saw all the mirrors on the planet (and none of them reflecting me), saw in a rear courtyard on Calle Soler the same tiles I'd seen twenty years before in the entryway of a house in Fray Bentos, saw clusters of grapes, snow, tobacco, veins of metal, water vapor, saw convex equatorial deserts and their every grain of sand, saw a woman in Inverness whom I shall never forget, saw her violent hair, her haughty body, saw a cancer in her breast, saw a circle of dry soil within a sidewalk where there had once been a tree, saw a country house in Adrogué, saw a copy of the first English translation of Pliny (Philemon Holland's), saw every letter of every page at once (as a boy, I would be astounded that the letters in a closed book didn't get all scrambled up together overnight), saw simultaneous night and day, saw a sunset in Querétaro that seemed to reflect the color of a rose in Bengal, saw my bedroom (with no one in it), saw in a study in Alkmaar a globe of the terraqueous world placed between two mirrors that multiplied it endlessly, saw horses with wind-whipped manes on a beach in the Caspian Sea at dawn, saw the delicate bones of a hand, saw the survivors of a battle sending postcards, saw a Tarot card in a shopwindow in Mirzapur, saw the oblique shadows of ferns on the floor of a greenhouse, saw tigers, pistons, bisons, tides, and armies, saw all the ants on earth, saw a Persian astrolabe, saw in a desk drawer (and the handwriting made me tremble) obscene, incredible, detailed letters that Beatriz had sent Carlos Argentino, saw a beloved monument in Chacarita, saw the horrendous remains of what had once, deliciously, been Beatriz Viterbo, saw the circulation of my dark blood, saw the coils and springs of love and the alterations of death, saw the Aleph from everywhere at once, saw the earth in the Aleph, and the Aleph once more in the earth and the earth in the Aleph, saw my face and my viscera, saw your face, and I felt dizzy, and I wept, because my eyes had seen that secret, hypothetical object whose name has been usurped by men but which no man has ever truly looked upon: the inconceivable universe.

At the end, Max had written:

—BORGES, The Aleph

So that was it? What a tease. Up against Jeff Elman, like two spoons in a drawer. I looked again at the Elman map, showing the neighborhood clusters in the hyperspace of dogs, dragons, boys, and girls. That was not much of an aleph. But then, Elman's simple recurrent network was not much of a brain, and its dog-eat-dog-cat-smash-plate playground was not quite the inconceivable universe.

The cat hopped into my lap. I roughed her up around the ears, until I could not only hear the purr but feel it in my thighs. Max was the excitable sort, but what I had read so far couldn't explain the call to Lucid, late last night. Somehow he had gone another step beyond the exclamation points that littered the margins of the Elman photocopy. What would it take? Maybe if the Elman net could be enlarged—if it talked, maybe. But you didn't have to know a lot about geek topics to know that this network was no Jean-Paul Sartre.

"But then, neither are you," I said to the cat, who raised her head just enough to meet my eyes, saw what she needed to see, and settled back into the cat zone.

I was only about halfway through the folder. Five minutes before I had thought that every psychotic drunkard and at least one Dostoevski character was out to get me, but now all that seemed like subplot. With my deadbolts set and *The Hours* playing, with heat included in the rent, with the whole velvet map of this mystery in my head, I cozied in the heart of my private screening room. Just pay attention, I said to myself. The beauty of the mystery of consciousness, unlike the mystery of the vanishing professor, I thought, is that it has absolutely nothing to do with me. There's no place like home.

Then came a copy of some email. The header told me it was from late in the last century.

"Well, Holly," I said, "now we're reading other people's mail?" I held the first page in her face. "Tell me if this is private." With a few sniffs she determined that it could not be eaten, and was therefore of no interest. They always say that no email is really private. So there. "Hearing no objections. . . ."

9

From:Maxwell Grue [STMP: mgrue@phi.whaleard.edu]
To:Maxwell Grue [STMP: mgrue@phi.whaleard.edu]
Cc:
Subject: Archive of Lost Time
Sent:8/7/1999 1:15 AM

>>>>>>>>>>>>>>>>>On 01/01/99, Maxwell Grue [mailto:mgrue@phi.whaleard.EDU]
wrote:
Dear Clare,
I have a question for you. What are the minimal conditions required for requited
love?
(And happy new year,) MG

I stood up suddenly, sending my chair wheeling into the edge of the
couch. The cat startled too, her back bristling. It was not quite like hearing Max's voice, but the L-word and his question were a little too Maxo
for me. Under my desk lamp the page dazzled in the middle of its red frame
in the middle of the black desk. At a distance his question slowly deflated
to mere words. I sat again.

>>>>>>>>>>>>>>On 01/02/99, Clare Lucid, PHD
[mailto:lucidc@pheonixstu.EDU] wrote:
Oh Max, you're better than a 72 point font. Who is she? (Entre' nous, of course.)
Does Emily know? (Happy 99 to you too. Personally, I'm looking forward already to
00 and 01 - they're binary!)

C

Emily. He'd mentioned her. Eternal graduate student in Comp. Lit. and
one of his formers.

>>>>>>>>>>>>On 01/08/99, Maxwell Grue [mailto:mgrue@phi.whaleard.EDU]
wrote:
Clare,
I'm not as transparent as you think - if I were, I'd be invisible. But here's the riff.
Her name is Imogen. If you're wondering how we met - we haven't, not exactly. I
found a transcript. (How I found it is not important.) But it was enough. She was
dealing with a heavy scene. Indefinite separation from her husband, Posthumus.
(It's a long complicated tale. Have you heard of a King named Cymbeline? Imogen
is his daughter!) Posthumus leaves on a boat, and the goodbye is witnessed by a
mutual friend, Pisanio. Imogen wasn't even there. The friend comes back to Imo
with the report, and the transcript says,

13:22:33 IMOGEN. [Inaudible] What was the last that he [inaudible] to thee?
13:22:36 PISANIO. It was his queen, his queen!
13:22:40 IMOGEN. Then waved his handkerchief?
13:22:42 PISANIO. And kiss'd it, madam.
13:22:44 IMOGEN. Senseless Linen! Happier therein than I.

This Imogen is not like the rest of us. For her the world is one vibrating landscape
of feeling, mental and physical at once. Her mind is everywhere, even in a
handkerchief, or - to say the same thing - the world is altogether inside her. The
real goodbye, Pisanio's narration, and Imogen's reconstruction are all one.
Imogen's farewell to Posthumus unfolds in her mind, which is to say, in her world.

13:23:01 IMOGEN. I would have broke my eyestrings, cracked them, but
To look upon him till the diminution
Of space had pointed him sharp as my needle -
Nay, followed him till he had melted from

> The smallness of a gnat to air, and then
> Have turned mine eye and wept.

She might have said, till he __seemed__ pointed as sharp as my needle. But no; Posthumus parting shrinks, literally shrinks, to a point. But that implies that there is no distance. Posthumus is neither near nor far. His departure is a simple disappearance, exit through a trap door from the stage of Imogen's consciousness.

There are no appearances for Imogen. Her feelings just are the world. She was with him, fully with him, until his total eclipse. Only then does she feel the loss and weep. But he isn't nothing - he is air. Not nowhere, but everywhere. In his absence, he attaches to every other object in the universe.

This is the oppressiveness of loss, its horrible invisibility. The lost one clogs the universe, like air, like death. And so one cannot attend to anything else. Every thing now has just one meaning: he is gone.

Raindrops trickled down my window, rumpling my view of the wet façade across the street. One drop had wandered into the corner and hung against the glass like a homeless contact lens. Or it could have been a glassy sphere, big as a beach ball, on the sidewalk opposite. A bubble for Glinda, maybe. But in Glinda's absence, I was remembering Seth.

Imogen understands this. Imogen gets it.
That's all. Hence my question. M

>>>>>>>>>>>>>On 01/10/99, Clare Lucid, PHD
[mailto:lucidc@pheonixstu.EDU] wrote:
Max,
May I broadcast an e-sigh in your general direction? Love is a hardware problem (especially in your case, as I recall). This is too much like how you and Emily got started. Suggest you drag the whole matter into the trash. Get a life.
Your friend,
C

I swiveled around to look at my doormat, a tiny patch of lurid Astro-turf. Max's infatuation reminded me of Seth, and his best Moment. I was sitting one morning in my regular booth in the snack bar when behind me a voice said, "Excuse me." A guy in the next booth, back to back with me, had turned my way just enough to present his high forehead and cute chin. "Sorry to interrupt, but I'm doing a survey on books people love to hate. Do you have a suggestion?"

Perhaps he had noticed the smushed paperback and the ring of scribbled and crossed-out pages on the table in front of me. I held the book toward him with one hand, and pinched my nose with the other. The text was a masterpiece of analytical sawdust by someone who made a living impersonating Ludwig Wittgenstein. (Hemands was breaking in the new graduate students by having us translate it into logical notation.) The boy nodded and thanked me, leaving me to ponder the forehead and the chin. I approved.

It turned out to be Seth, of course, and there was no survey. He got his own copy of the book from the library, Xeroxed the whole thing, ran it through the shredder, braided the strips and looped the braids into a lovely doormat. This he laid tenderly before me in the snack bar a week later. "It's *Dreaming*," he explained, "the book you love to hate." He added his puppy-dog GQ smile, and I was smitten.

>>>>>>>>>>On 01/20/99, Maxwell Grue [mailto:mgrue@phi.whaleard.EDU] wrote:
Clare,
Some "friend." A little green as a therapist, too. Love is a hardware problem? Tell that to Abelard. To the Brownings. M
>>>>>>>>>>On 01/23/99, Clare Lucid, PHD mailto:lucidc@pheonixstu.EDU] wrote:
Max,
Sorry if I offended. You did say "requited." I just checked: "What are the minimal conditions for requited love?" Well, for YOU . . . never mind. So now that I understand your question, the answer is obvious, n'est-ce pas? If it's mind-to-mind you want, get the program. I mean, work out the springs, the rules, the code. All the unconscious files. Then you'll "know her" - in the computational sense!

No doubt Emily will find this a turn on, too. ;)
C

The doormat was the first item to furnish our apartment a month later. In a few weeks it began to unravel and soon we were tracking random bits of text into the house. They stuck to the floor, then to our socks, and slowly infiltrated the laundry. Usually they were sliced and smudged like words

seen in dreams, but one morning not too long before the Last Straw I pulled on a pair of pantyhose, and saw plastered to my knee
                                    "I am
which at that point I completed, *in love.*

>>>>>>>>>>On 01/24/99, Maxwell Grue [mailto:mgrue@phi.whaleard.EDU] wrote:
Dr. Clare with head of air,
Now you get the sigh. (Re: Emily - point taken. But - (he says again) - all this is hypothetical.)
Imogen has no inside. That's the heavy part. The thing I like about her. Max

But of all Seth's pieces, I liked his empty bag piece the best. During our short season of domestic ecstasy the New York Times landed on the porch each morning in a blue plastic bag. We read and recycled the papers, but Seth kept the bags. When they began to take over (and I complained), he showed me the plan for the current piece, the text of an ad:

The Perfect Gift/ Keepsake/ Collector's Item

*Own the New York Times Delivery Bag from the Day
You Were Born!*

Capture and hold a Moment in History! These authentic plastic newspaper delivery bags held all the news that was fit to print on any day in History since 1950! Each comes with a certificate of authenticity, and complete instructions for framing. You will proudly display this durable memento of the world as it was *for you* at the instant of your birth. . . .

It was just $8.95 plus shipping and handling, and the phone number was ours. *This,* I said, holding the ad, *this* is suitable for framing.

>>>>>>>>>>On 02/14/99, Clare Lucid, PHD
mailto:lucidc@pheonixstu.EDU] wrote:

Max,
It's taken me a few days to write not only because of processing the page proofs for "Rebooting Your Soul." You've been in my buffer, near the top of the stack. But I have more important news: The Provost at Whaleard called. They're courting me.

Talking about six figures and . . . my own call-in radio show on the WU NPR station. (Do you listen to it? Is it any good?) Which do you think is better: "Getting Clare"; "Ask Dr. Lucid"; "The Lucid Hour" - I like the last one myself.

Meanwhile, your question about the minimal conditions for requited love makes no sense. You can't requite yourself with air. (I don't mean you personally.) That is, you can't, and still be seen as an outpatient!
I'll write more soon.
C

You tell him, Clare. The real question is, what are the minimal conditions for requiting *Max* in love with *Imogen*. I thought, minimal conditions? That's the question you ask if you have *no hope* of scoring. She's *taken,* for one thing. For another, Max, she's not your type! She talks like she's never even heard of Woodstock, and she certainly doesn't have the CD on vinyl. Well, given Emily, maybe Imogen is the right genre. But can't you see how she will respond to you? Seth's blue bags had nothing inside. Your Imogen is less than that. Inside she's Nothing, because you have filled her with your fantasies. *Why can't you all just listen?*

››››››››On 02/17/99, Maxwell Grue [mailto:mgrue@phi.whaleard.EDU] wrote:
Clare,
It's 2 AM on a Saturday night - Sunday morning. Just me and the glow. On the night plane. (I know you don't like drugs, but puleeze think about them for your insomnia patients.)

So I'm reading over the paper trail on this Imogen thing. . . . Trying to figure out. It hasn't gone away. I don't see why it wouldn't work, what I have in mind . . .

Something can come of nothing . . .

I sighed. Cubes. The rest of the long midnight letter was about perceiving cubes, imagining cubes, Sartre and Husserl. I riffled the edge of the paper stack, to see that the email went on at least as long as a Harlequin romance. I skipped a few pages ahead, looking to see where the plot picked up again.

››››››››On 03/04/99, Maxwell Grue [mailto:mgrue@phi.whaleard.EDU] wrote:
Clare,
This is how I imagine it:

Imagine sitting in total darkness. Better still - find total darkness (it's harder than it sounds). I sit, comfortable, eyes open in the velvet nothingness of possibility. Soundless infinity. I've already placed a chair facing me, two feet away. Imogen is sitting on it. I can't see her, but I apprehend everything I know of her as a visual invisibility. I can't hear her: the moment demands silence from both of us. Absolute expectation. The moment of the creation of love. Her shoulders curve forward toward me, just slightly. I can't see them, but they are rising and falling imperceptibly as she breathes. And if I strain to listen, perhaps I do hear the faintest hesitant breathing, in step with my own. Her hands are folded in her lap. She can feel her own intertwined fingers, and the smooth fabric of her dress, satin. The same fabric that covers her shoulders - I see none of this, but know it nonetheless. Between the cloth and her neck are several inches of skin, from her shoulder curving up to her ears, where strands of hair circle at the loose outside of a thick braid.

My hands rest on my thighs. We both pretend not to know what will happen next. I bring up my right hand, swinging wide to the right, and pause over her shoulder. I don't want to - can't - bring my full palm to bear on her. Instead, I lower my index finger to lead the way, and with infinite delicacy slowly settle my hand toward her luminous skin, Imogen that I cannot see or hear. A woman some inches shorter than me, sitting on the same sort of chair I'm sitting on, I know where that shoulder will be. I will touch it as lightly as a mote of dust. I will feel it as lightly as the brush of a single hair. And the warmth of that shoulder will radiate the faintest glow up the finger of my touch.

She flinches away. I stumble in panic for the lightswitch.

Seth never, ever touched me like that. I shivered.

>>>>>>On 03/09/99, Clare Lucid, PHD
[mailto:lucidc@pheonixstu.EDU] wrote:
Max,
Nagging blinking feeling of danger for you. I think you should remember that real people are written with vast amounts of dynamic code. You can't get there from where you are, and you may hurt yourself trying. Imogen - whatever she is - is no cube.
Clare

Yeah. Nor would I want to be Imogen, not that anyone is noticing. Although now it seemed like she could just be Max's pin-up after all, a little something to hang his fantasies on. I went back to the long ramble on Sartre and Husserl. Max's plan was to get beyond imagining her. He wanted to imagine *perceiving* her, promoting her from an image to something like virtual reality. He had it worked out, using Husserl as his advisor in matters of love. How to have your unrequited and requited at the same time. To the lovelorn, Edmund points out that the chunkiest, boringest cube is really break-dancing all the time. That's because we move—everything from little eye wiggles to handstands. So our point of view on the cube, the face it shows us is always shifting in big and little ways. Why doesn't it jump with eye movements, spin as we circle it, swell as we approach? Visually, it does all that and more. But the body sensations cancel the visual inputs, and abracadabra, from two flows pops one steady object. Fantasies are usually lazy movie clips, leaving out one side or another, but Max was going to project himself into the whole perceptual scene, body and the rest of it, all the channels at once. With his steely mind's eye and his steady mind's hand he planned to fill the ditch between fantasy and reality. Only a phenomenologist would love the scheme. Obviously he practiced a lot when he was alone.

›››››On 03/20/99, Maxwell Grue [mailto:mgrue@phi.whaleard.EDU] wrote:
Clare,
Do your theories make any room for intuition? Your worries about me may have something to them. I don't know. I came to bed last night at 3, and found one of Emily's poetry bombs on my pillow. (It was completely dark.) That was a whole new shock, to settle your head onto an unexpected piece of paper. I took it into the bathroom to read:

> We learned the Whole of Love -
> The Alphabet - the Words -
> A Chapter - then the mighty Book -
> Then - Revelation closed -

Maybe this means she's in a good mood. With Emily, you can never be sure. Max

I thought I could see Emily, tight and prim in khakis. On summer days she might tie the tails of her white button-down shirt into a tight knot at the navel. I guessed this would get Max hot. I guessed that Emily was the sort of gal who made sure she looked sexy when they fought. Or maybe I was thinking Seth again, down boy, down. I remembered our biggest stupid fight, about his *Dejourner sur l'herbe Australop-ithecene*. He had left the woman just as Manet had painted her, smooth and naked and French in her Playmate pose in the foreground. But for the guys in the painting, Seth had brought out the inner hominid, making them hairy and low-browed like the Dawn of Man sequence in *2001*. The picnic blanket was a flat rock, the walking stick a gnawed bone. The woman should have been *hairy*. "And another thing, Sethy," I said, in a voice just a bit too loud for apartment life, "in two million BC, women *do not have perky breasts*." As I was calling him a pig, he was getting undressed for bed. When he got down to the drawstring pants, I connected the dots: He always undressed during fights. Suddenly I was convinced that this move-the-fight-into-the-bedroom-and-take-off-your-shirt thing was a *strategy*. "Never mind," I said. "It's your painting." I left the room. My boy was shapeshifting on me. What kind of a man uses his abs as a rhetorical device? At that exact moment the entire story of Seth and Miranda split into two parts. Part 1, everything until the stupid fight: *my time of innocence*. And now, Part 2. Eventually I would know its name: *betrayal time*.

>>>>On 04/20/99, Clare Lucid, PHD
[mailto:lucidc@pheonixstu.EDU] wrote:
Max,
The Whaleard appointment looks definite, complete with the radio show. I hope you call in. I'll solve Emily for you in time for a station break. ;)

Seriously, have you talked to her about this?
C

In the end, I sent the remains of the doormat back to him through campus mail, and got the Astroturf at the dollar store.

>>>>On 04/27/99, Maxwell Grue [mailto:mgrue@phi.whaleard.EDU] wrote:
C,
You know the rules with Emily the volcano goddess. Sure, we talk all the time. More accurately, one talks. Or recites, I suppose.

I tell you, domestic life has never been stranger. I spend my days pretending to be Max Grue, aka Mr. Devoted.

Suddenly I ask why? And: why did I not ask why before now? M
P.S. I'm setting up a meeting with Imogen - at the mall. Safe!

My heart was pounding. A few lines had made Imogen real to me too, and I knew just how terrible Max's up-river Kurtz could be. I thought about trying to find her. We could form a support group. Clare Lucid facilitating!

>>>On 04/28/99, Clare Lucid, PHD
[mailto:lucidc@pheonixstu.EDU] wrote:
Dear Max,
I guess you like system crashes, eh? You've mixed up so many impulses that I don't see a decent thread in your future. I strongly suggest a noshow from you at the Mall. That will make two. The tea there is awful anyway. I'll be your colleague in two months and we can thrash through all this.

Then I remembered where I knew Imogen from. I kept my poetry books together in the crate with my camisoles. I brought Shakespeare over to the desk. *Cymbeline.* The "transcript" that started this drama was from Act I. Somehow this made the vision *worse.*

Why did you not ask "why"? Because you dread the answer.
C

Max's fantasy reminded me of the madman who held a broken cell phone to his ear all the time. If you asked him what he was doing, he'd say, "I'm on hold." Unless the Bard set Act V in the Mall, this was a meeting that was Not to Be.

>>On 05/05/99, Maxwell Grue [mailto:mgrue@phi.whaleard.EDU] wrote:
Clare,
It happened. I did it. I worked out a meeting. Sitting there in the food court, she is: shockingly young, but dressed as if she were thirty, which is to say, totally unavailable, so unavailable that the possibility of availability no longer even crossed her mind. That, of course, renders her more attractive. She's reading a book, completely oblivious to the world. I'm liking that.

I'm not. I'd been sucked into a fiction, a pit of email inside email. Was this Max's MO, this shell game of appearances?

I stand quietly before her table. She is immobilized in her book. Then she looks up, startled. "What hour is it?" she asks. She says, "I have read three hours then: mine eyes are weak." She has a winning look of permanent curiosity -- wide brown eyes and high eyebrows. She extends one hand and I shake it, and in a mutually embarrassed moment I realize she has been gesturing to me to sit down. Instead, I stammer through the menu. She smiles and says,

Good morrow, sir. You lay out too much pains
For purchasing but trouble; the thanks I give
Is telling you that I am poor of thanks
And scarce can spare them.

I paged through the play, scanning for IMO in the margins. And there, in Act II, scene 3, I found it. "Good Morrow, sir . . ." I cross-checked the two texts, holding each in place with an index finger, the real and the fake. But as I leaned from one to the other, I thought, why not weave it Max's way?

In his remake, he got her some tea, and got to the point.

"Love," I say, "in my work I work on Love. Love is the dynamo, the core that powers our lives. Without it, we die. By its light, we live. Usually we snag no more than a faint refraction, a splinter of the light. But sometimes maybe we stare right at the core itself. You know what I mean?"

Say, and speak thick;
Love's counselor should fill the bores of hearing,
To the smothering of the sense-

"Thick, yes. We live thick. Most thick in love. The beloved blankets the universe - it's cozy. It's like a warm ocean tide that rises to lap the sleeper on the beach, his toes, his ankles, the space behind his knees, his thighs, higher, and higher. In the end, it's all just layers and layers of meaning, and love soaks through everything. That's the whole core of consciousness itself, and love is the ultimate phenomenology."

She nods. "Talk thy tongue weary; speak."

That he could do! From his grab bag he pulled the story Aristophanes tells in the *Symposium*, about the ancient pre-humans whom the gods cut in half to punish them for their arrogance. She liked that one too. Then from Max:

"And do you, Imogen, know your other half?"

She smiled broadly and nodded. Here was someone who loved to love. My cheeks felt hot.

"It's clear to me, that I've come home to you, Imogen. You are my other half."

She jerks back an inch, as if to duck a blow. "But this is foolery," she says.

Uh huh.

I perceive that I have made a mistake. But the drama of my own momentum prevents me from taking it back. "Imogen - "

>I would not speak. I pray you, spare me: 'faith,
>I shall unfold equal discourtesy
>To your best kindness: one of your great knowing
>Should learn, being taught, forbearance.

"Imogen, I have never met another like you. And you must understand that I am asking nothing of you, nothing at all. I care for you - please, just take it as a gift, as it is offered."

>I am much sorry, sir,
>You put me to forget a lady's manners,
>By being so verbal: and learn now, for all,
>That I, which know my heart, do here pronounce,
>By the very truth of it, I care not for you.

Sitting at the next table, with her back to Imogen, is a fairytale figure dressed in a brown cloak and hood, hunching over a mug of chocolate. I had noticed the third one sitting there, and had dimly logged the figure as one who sleeps on subway grates and spends the days lost in a fog beneath the awareness of society.

But then I recognize her. Imogen, already alarmed, sees disaster in my face. She says,

>What is in thy mind,
>That makes thee stare thus?

I'm speechless, but not the newcomer, who throws back her hood with a theatrical gesture and turns to face us both, saying:

>'Tis Opposites - entice -
>Deformed Men - ponder Grace -

Imogen asks, "Who may this be?"

I say, "Emily, this is Imogen. Uh, Imogen, this is Emily. Emily is an old friend of mine."

And Emily almost shouts,

 Art thou the thing I wanted?

 Begone - my Tooth has grown -

To which Imogen quite agrees! She says,

 I am sprited with a fool.

 Frighted, and anger'd worse

 Away, I prithee!

"Imogen," I say, "let me explain!" But she's off again:

 Away! I do condemn mine ears that have

 So long attended thee.

And it was as if I disappeared! Imogen turned in her chair toward Emily, saying:

 Gods, what lies

 I have heard!

Emily replies,

 What harm? Men die - externally -

 It is a truth - of Blood -

 But we - are dying in Drama -

 And Drama - is never dead -

Imogen says:

 'Tis so;

 'Twas but a bolt of nothing, shot at nothing,

 Which the brain makes of fumes: our very eyes

 Are sometimes like our judgments, blind.

Then Emily pulls her chair around to face Imogen, saying:

 I'm Nobody! Who are you?

 Are you - Nobody - Too?

 Then there's a pair of us?

 Don't tell! they'd advertise - you know!

Imogen agrees:

 I am nothing: or if not,

 Nothing to be were better.

Emily:

 How dreary - to be - Somebody!

 How public - like a Frog -

 To tell one's name - the livelong June -

 To an admiring Bog!

Then they left. Together, two halves making one whole. I knew already that I would never see either one again.

›On 05/06/99, Clare Lucid, PHD [mailto:lucidc@pheonixstu.EDU] wrote:
   Max,
What did you expect? What were you thinking? Still, even though you clicked on the default outcome, you have my sympathy. It's rare to lose both wife and mistress in one sitting.

How about after I settle in a bit we move this dialogue into real-time interface? I begin every day with a pot of my own special tea. When you can, you are welcome to join me. You can also upgrade me on the Whaleard system. Who's buggy, who's beta, you know - the ropes.
Best,
C

On 06/01/99, Maxwell Grue [mailto:mgrue@phi.whaleard.EDU] wrote:
   Clare,
Your arrival could not be more timely. I accept your invitation to your morning tea. We can pretend to be the Old Marrieds that - perhaps - neither of us shall ever be.

What was I thinking? Always the wrong question in love - but you asked, so I answer. She was all hope and nothing but possibility. Exactly opposed to seven years with Emily. Seven years of actuality congealed into necessity.
Necessity, actuality, possibility. I jumped finally toward pure possibility. Over there, on that side of the fence, I thought I saw someone who understood that phenomenology was not self-consciousness. That it was not dwelling in and on a point of view. That there was no standpoint. That finally it was all poetry all the way down.

You know, don't you, where love is concerned the lover really will settle for words, words, words. These can be enough. Max

10

Holly was asleep. My eyes were burning. Up until then Max had put this story into two words—"I'm divorced." Now I'd had the ambiguous pleasure of watching The Making of the Grue Story. All the special effects explained.

I pushed back in my chair and rolled my shoulders and neck to shake free of the philosopher in a box. My coffee had gone cold. I noticed its aftertaste, lurking like regret in the shadows of awareness. I stood, stretched toward the ceiling, and walked into the bathroom. This is what graduate school had taught me: Brushing helps. I began with teeth, then pulled out the ponytail holder and shook my hair free, pulling my hands through it to get started. Then I noticed myself in the mirror. I looked old! I leaned forward to try to account for it, but could find no crow's feet, no bags, and no change in the faint but disturbing lines across my forehead. But I was looking thirtyish. My eyes narrowed and I saw a new expression, a little like disdain or contempt. Was this the look that begins the sag toward *old lady?* Max said Imogen looked like curiosity. Once I looked like that too. I wondered if Imogen was cuter than me. Maybe now she was staring at some mirror too, having these same thoughts. Maybe Posthumus was back, sitting on the foot of the bed, pulling on his socks. And they both lived happily ever after.

"Whoops," I said aloud. Tricked again. There was no Imogen. Or was there? She was nothing but words. But then, what about Emily? Grue had mentioned her, but that was just words too. But Clare took them both seriously—in Max's email. Maybe the whole episode was just his fantasy. At some point this metaphysical OD could turn Max into a fiction himself, appropriate payback for unwanted mental contact. If characters arrive by email, they can just as easily perish under the delete key. That left the camera focused on my metaphysical apartment, slowly eroding as some cosmic author backspaced over my world too: Bye bye Lava lamp,

Lava lam

Lava la

Lava l

Lava

Lav

La

L

But I remained. Existing.

I finished brushing and found that nothing in my space had changed while I was away, including the furball on the desk. But outside the clouds had lowered, sinking from gray toward purple, afternoon on Neptune.

Of course, there was a sequel. The next photocopy was lifted from Max's own scribbles. I kept reading. . . .

Dear Penelope,

After all these years, I hear from you! Amazing! Could it really be two decades since that hug at commencement? Are you still weaving? Did it turn out that there was a market for shrouds in LA? If so, then I take back all my ancient sarcasm. Or have you become an investment banker instead?

I agree with you about memory. It can pose the oddest questions, and compel some strange investigations. You asked if Emily and I were still together, and if I ever did become the phenomenologist I always wanted to be. Turns out your questions have opposite answers. But it also turns out they are just one question.

No, Emily and I are not together, fully split as of a few years ago. It was the oldest story: I encountered someone who was as unlike Emily as can

be. (Her name was Imogen.) And with someone capital S on the scene, your befores, durings, and afters are all whacked. In my story, I took a risk. The risk deepened, and just about at its max there was a disaster. My past and future collided. More accurately, Emily and Imogen collided! You may think that past and future are mutually repulsive, and their impact would leave a still crater of the luminous, instantaneous present. But in reality the loss of past and future all at once emptied the present of all possible meaning. I felt like I'd been kicked really hard just beneath the ribs. I doubled over, locked in a speechless strangled vacuum.

Coming out of this disaster I was stripped of both past and future and stood burning alone. Of course it was a mood that murdered sleep, and in one hideous night I became, as you put it, the phenomenologist I always wanted to be. That night it only took an hour to exhaust all the comforts of memory and fantasy. Midnight, one, two. By three my eyes followed the edges of things as if searching a collapsed building for traces of its former structure. But there were only unrecognizable fragments. In the blooming colors and booms of the world I experienced the ultimate blindness and deafness of mind.

With neither hope nor memory, I was alone with something for which there is no name. I can't call my visitors "things." To be a thing is to root in history and branch toward a future. No thing can be instantaneous, nothing but now—but I was just that, instantaneous, at one with a vast pure present. I didn't find Sartre's nausea there. I didn't find his shapeless masses of pure existence. My present never sank into that congealed muck. No oneness, no It—but a Them. And they, the former things, were as hard and cold as stars in the winter sky. Because they had no past or future, they could neither change nor stay the same. Each moment of them was a pure and total eruption into me. They were in my face.

Perception unglued. For that brief infinity I had five distinct senses, just like the psych books say. Vision and touch, usually just facets of the regular visual-tactile thing, split up and the same thing could thrust itself on me visually, but as I reached for it, throw aside its visible cloak to become, suddenly, nothing but texture and resistance. I couldn't say if what I touched was what I saw. And I couldn't say that it wasn't.

I became, briefly, the very man science imagined. The receptacle with senses. All there was to me was sensing and naming. There, before me— a "rectangle." A "glow." A "screen." Each of them and its label bore into me, and my eyes had no lids. I couldn't pull back or away. Do the authors of those sophomore science books ever wonder if the creatures presented by all the theories in psychology—these theories of walking detectors with their onboard computers—were either human or happy? I've now been there, and I can tell you the answer. Pure perception of the here and now, sprung from time, is hell.

Time—not "things," not "reality"—time binds all.

yours devotedly,

Maxwell

Time binds all, said Max, with maxinine mysteriousity. Mysterious, I thought, and exactly wrong. (And not the first time for him, I noticed.) Time *un*-binds all. All that ever exists is the Present, the Instant. The Now is the infinite pinnacle rising from the vast depths of nothingness. Falling away on one side, the past. On the other, ever approaching but never arriving, the future. From pinnacle to abyss the drop is infinite. Neither past nor future exists. Period.

Everything is Now. So am I. So is my consciousness. But time leaves its mark on my Now. It's in my perception of the coffee mug, that trace of history that enables me to see it with understanding. All its real properties depend in one way or another on the stories rooted in the cup. Seeing the cup is knowing the stories, an awareness of time folded up into a point. Seeing without this understanding is just another form of blindness. Maybe *that's* what Max meant, years ago: The *conscious instant* binds time. The Now contains everything else, but held in the frame of time. That was the mystery.

I held the Borges passage up to the light, wondering if the answer was written in invisible ink, a watermark, a shadow snaking through the black and white. I turned it over. The backward letters cast fuzzy silhouettes on the cloudy whiteness of the page. Borges worried that letters in books might leak across pages during the night, a nice poetic worry. That's just what his aleph did, though. It mixed everything up. But not everything. Space, not time, got the cosmic makeover in Borges. The passage moved through good old linear time like any other story. The alternative, an aleph that collapses time, would be an implosion of chaos. On the page, it would be a blot.

I picked up Max's email, looking again at the first header. The whole pathetic saga was a single message, sent by himself to himself, his way of keeping it, or maybe keeping it alive. It carried all the rest with it. Each letter flew between Clare and Max with all the previous letters attached. It was easy, Internet 101. The email program simply stuck the newest message at the end of the string, and that made the whole thing a history. The present message carried its own past. One message was a history.

But consciousness is not email. It's not text. Time can't just be added like so many footnotes. It had to always be there all the way, right now. Max must have thought that the Elman piece had an answer, and I could see it too. In the little fake brain of the simple recurrent network the past and the present collide. The present flows in from the input layer, while the past merges with it, in the copy sent over from the mirror units. In a way, the middle layer would mix them up. You could call the merged input "history with ongoing modifications" or "present with historical significations." Whatever.

And the circuitry somehow didn't get all mixed up. The hypermap showed that bumbling along in places where one thing followed another, with just a little regularity, nonetheless sufficed for the net to find the structure of the world. It never saw it all at once, never had a label attached, never had a tutor. Just the world itself. The net in the outer world grew its own inner world. That inner world kept things straight, kept the dogs and cats apart, but not too far apart. They were, after all, animals.

I flipped back through the Elman piece to a figure I'd skipped before. It was another map, zooming in on the landscape of words hidden in the flow around and through his network. This one magnified a particular slice of life that I could identify with, the net in its encounters with the word GIRL. The first map showed that various presentations of GIRL threw the net into a different buzz than BOY, CAT, and the rest. But even though the word GIRL was always the same, the net did not always see girls the same way. The second map showed the details of a GIRL's life. Within the GIRL zone, the patterns inside the network were different from one girl encounter to another. The difference reflected the context in which GIRL

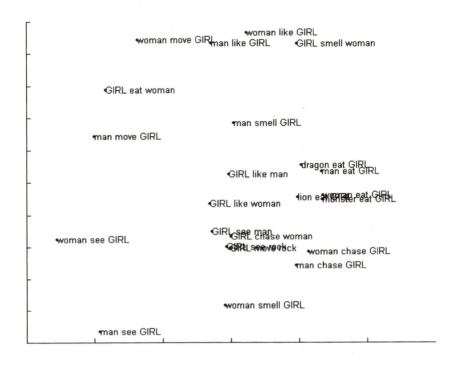

appeared. Girls as objects were different from girls as subjects. The things girls do, the things that are done to them—these arranged themselves in hyperspace in ways that made sense. On one side, poor GIRLs were devoured in all sorts of unpleasant ways. (I was glad not to find "Max eats GIRL" in the map.) Elsewhere GIRLs circled boys, smelling one another, checking each other out, exchanging coy smiles. This absurd toy knew too much about life!

What made the net different with every GIRL was *context*. One hundred and fifty simulated neurons seemed to be more than enough to keep each presentation of GIRL distinct, by itself. But in the *environment* of this network, a GIRL was a GIRL was a GIRL. It was that same word again and again. The words before and after were nonexistent. Yet there was a distinct state of "mind" for each moment. If the network could keep GIRLs and BOYs apart, it could also keep GIRLs at one time, in one context, apart from GIRLs at another time, in another context. The mark of time was etched in every moment of the flow. Even this airhead had an inner world that expressed something forever absent in the real outer world: *time*.

You could do it with matter. You could do it with brains.

Well, maybe. He said he had seen the aleph. Not read about it, not figured it out or imagined it. I saw pieces of paper, words, a cup of coffee, a cat, a window. Pretty sights, I suppose, and dripping with the invisible understandings that consciousness provides. My shifty mind was something like an aleph. Even allowing for Maximum hyperness, there was still nothing to see.

I was surprised that I'd missed the postscripts to Penelope, lying right in front of me.

P. S. I suppose Dickinson's poetry should come with a bulletin from the Surgeon General: Warning: Excessive Memorization Can Be Detrimental to Your Psychic Health. According to an acquaintance, Emily has gone off the deep end, even trying to change her last name to Dickinson, so that her thesis title page could read Emily Dickinson, by Emily Dickinson. Or perhaps, By Herself.

As for Imogen, my psychologist friend says that hers is an exceptionally pronounced case of Pirandello's Syndrome—the excessive identification with fictional figures—not helped by the pampered wealth of her upbringing. Some day I will tell you the whole story—or recite it! I still see exactly what I saw in her before, but now I look on various small silver linings, like, at least I don't have to learn to talk in blank verse. But this is another story, for another time.

So Shroedinger's cat lived—if those words could be trusted. I closed the Shakespeare and shelved it. Let them all enjoy their hall of dramatic echoes. But keep your damn dirty quotation marks off me!

P.P.S. Yes, I'm still crazy after all these years. The leaves fall every autumn and so do I. Lately the drug of choice is Prozac—I have a blank check for it at my HMO. I'm at 500 milligrams, and still waiting for something to change.

Max's seasonal mood swing was common knowledge. He'd even mentioned it in the course. That was the lecture where he claimed that Prozac was a hallucinogen, which he regarded as a good thing. As I considered it, it seemed to me that he had turned out to be right, at least in his own case.

P.P.P.S. Can I express the present instant in a word? No, a word is already too long, a drum roll of consonants and vowels, and its echoes and settlings in the mind. Perhaps the instant can be written so:
|

It passes like a seam in the highway, with a sharp clunk to announce that it has been, is gone. It passes like a stroke of lightning, in which the world is shown too fast to see. But all that truly is is written in the stroke. (Read through as fast as you can.)
|

This then is the story of our lives.
We are born.
|

We die.

In short,
I.

Perhaps you can read and understand this. Perhaps you see loss and longing reflectively, in both directions, forward and backward, weaving and unweaving.

I came then to the final postscript.

P.P.P.P.S. (the next day) We live with SARS and AIDS, airbags that cushion you to death, with land mines and market crashes, and words misspoken and misunderstood, and galloping sarcomas and the endless potential for loss, and the finality of the past, and missing you.
O Fortuna.
We live and die as easily as a spark becomes a cinder. How then can I dare to write you? How can I dare not to write? The world is out of joint, out of joint,
out of joint,
O Miranda.

11

Holly Golightly kneaded the desk with paws and claws, and after an unknown time I realized I had been scratching her between the ears and staring into the half-open slits of her catdrunk eyes. I could usually preview my own mood by how much I envied the cat's life. Would I trade the current mystery for her ditzy cool? At the moment I would, and as I peered into her petal-thin ears I lost myself in catland, in warm dark tunnels where the soundtrack was a total purr that smothered thought.

The folder was much too red, fiercely red, like an unnatural flower. As usual, I'd overlooked a possibility. Penelope, Imogen, Emily, hell—this folder, with all of its backstory, may have been constructed for an audience of one. Or was that "Miranda" at the very end just a little slip? I had no interest in playing any of *his* heroines, thank you very much.

Or was it a joke, soon to appear in my apartment mailbox? I would have been happier if I had found it funny. Or if he had previewed this particular fantasy with me, as he did with so much of the furtive unfinished junk he spun, the creative spasms that propped him up as WU's very own philosopher a-go-go.

Now Max's mind had flooded my own little sanctuary, lapping my toes. I knew too much. *Nobody thinks for Miranda Sharpe,* I repeated to myself. But the inner voice was tentative, afraid. He had tried to hijack my mind last night, and now he'd nearly succeeded, wallpapering the world with his words. And yet none of it explained anything. Why the urgency of the players in the Max caper? Lucid on speed, Marlov's jolly fierceness. And Max, sprung from himself, his own bad dream.

And where was Max's aleph?

One item remained, folded in half. His simple act of folding it, hiding it in plain sight, made it the most fearful of all. But there was no way back.

It was a copy of a fax, to one Victoria Cronkenstein from one Gabriel Zamm. I'd heard of Zamm, a high-roller scientist at Whaleard. The fax was dated yesterday.

Dear Dr. Cronkenstein,

The third transducer-actuator arrived from Cupertino last week, right on schedule, and my postdoc reports that our prototype of your apparatus is ready to test. By the way, it appears that export restrictions on devices like these will not be lifted after all. Thus, we were right to hedge our bets by establishing the TL lab here, and we are grateful to you for sharing your blueprints and for agreeing to make the trip to us for the first test.

Your flight schedule and electronic ticket for Wednesday the 2nd is attached. We expect you to clear customs by 7 P.M. You will be met in the reception area by Maxwell Grue, a philosopher on our faculty who shares our interest in consciousness. He will bring you directly to the Wundt Psychophysics Lab and your machine. I and my postdoc will meet you there, and we can proceed with the experiment as planned. (Should we be detained, the access code to the Lab is 0–3–0–9.)

I remain astonished that an acoustic vibration could have such a dramatic effect on the central nervous system. If the effect truly is local to very small regions of the brain, then your invention may finally solve the mystery of consciousness, once and for all. It is all the more impressive that you have accomplished this achievement so early in your scientific career. The three of us are eager for the demonstration of your machine. We're confident that my various grants will be able to support you and the next phase of your research. Meanwhile, we understand your desire to be discreet about your achievement—we have talked to no one about this.

Also, may I express my admiration for your willingness to be the first human subject in the device? We agree that it will be perfectly safe, but to be frank, it greatly simplifies matters to circumvent the red tape of the Human Subjects Review Board here.

I look forward to meeting you on Wednesday. I hope the flight from Zurich is not too taxing, and your American homecoming, after nearly a decade abroad, is pleasant.

Very sincerely yours,

Gabriel Zamm

It was 6 PM. Max might rematerialize at the airport. I could go out there and lurk, but why? I wasn't sure that Victoria's Secrets, whatever they might be, could cast much light on the local madness. And I was tired of following in Max's footprints, shadowing a shadow.

But the machine! "TL"—tender loving? I didn't think so. "Dramatic effect on the central nervous system." Last I heard, we needed our central nervous system for the little niceties, like breathing. It sounded to me like a zapper that left no marks, far neater than Col. Mustard in the Library with the Lead Pipe. When exactly did the postdoc set it up? Could it be moved? Or had it been moved? I knew where it was, and I knew that for the next hour Col. Mustard and company would probably be elsewhere. But after that, who knows? I could take the quickest look at it.

There were two ways to WU from the Sharpe estate. When I wanted the feel of speed, distance, landscape, serious business, I took the highway, blasting up to 75 for a quarter-mile to the very next exit, which delivered me without ceremony to the back streets around the University. That would be my route tonight. In my sprint across the asphalt, though, I felt not speed but suspended animation. The thumps of pavement and the strobing lane dashes were nagging reminders of something. It took me a moment to remember Max's drooly commentary on time. Here I was, Zeno's arrow, or Xena's, logging an infinite number of instants every inch, hung in the eternal passing of time, one second per second, drip drip drip drrrrrrrippppp. Max, electronic Don Juan, had come into his existentialism the usual way, by being rejected by elegant women who were much smarter than he, rejected in a café, no less. Of all the gin joints in the world, to get dumped in a Food Court. But you didn't need a full ashtray and a broken heart to get the point: Simple vision, simple seeing, was knit into time and the world. Without the smear of time, my freeway hurtle would be a filmstrip of disconnected instants, not the flow I watched spreading before, beside, and behind me. (Yes, check behind. No cop. Floor it.) All of the senses were equally rooted in time. You didn't need a hangover to see what Husserl was getting at in the undergraduate's doom book, the *Lectures on Internal Time Consciousness*. Every Now carried with it a thin beam of expectation, as well as a rich tailwind of just-was. The Now blurred across the space-time continuum, a gnarly wave rising to a peak and shuddering away into the choppy past. Anything else was so unlike our folksy experience of seeing that it might be called blindness. The blindness of the camera, the mindless eye.

I came back again to the thumpthump of the pavement ridges, thinking this time not of the road but of my wheels, being thumped by time, and turning. Elman built a wheel of time into a fake little brain, a loop that grabbed the Now and held on to it just long enough to throw it at the next Now. Thump thump thump thump—now now now now. . . . It seemed at once as though I was looking at Elman's loopiness and calling it the Interstate, no, that my look *was itself* the loopiness. The reconceivable universe, another recycled product, a film retrospective, the Annie Hall of Mirrors. I hit 90 as I banked into the exit ramp and shoved the brake into the world spinning beneath me. I felt like a shower of sparks.

Wundt Hall was one of those glass towers that splayed at the bottom, aspiring to be a ski jump. Its lights were never off, some sort of perverse energy-saving strategy that must endlessly annoy the rats in their stacks of no-view studio apartments. The building directory pointed me to the sixth floor. I took the elevator to the seventh and the stairs down, but needlessly, since the place was deserted.

I keyed in the door code. Science marches on. I was in.

I turned on the lights. Many of the wonders of science emerge from rooms that look like this, stacked with kinetic sculptures of duct tape and very expensive gray boxes, and, of course, computer monitors with only the grooviest of screen savers.

In one corner I noticed a moose in disguise. It was large, lumpy, and had a sheet thrown over it. Discretion indeed. Feeling my marvelous powers of deduction cresting, I grabbed the sheet and snapped it off. The machine was a marriage of *Son of Flubber* and Death Row. It was built around a chair, a padded recliner that was pretending not to be a dentist's forbidden fantasy. In fact, the gizmo wasn't exactly built around a chair, it was built around the chair's potential occupant, or to zoom in on the truth, around his head. Converging on the center of the hypothetical head were three identical midget jackhammers, or so they looked with their loops of chrome and droops of wiring, all coming to a focus at what looked like a crutch tip or a foam earphone—to nestle your skull. Each digital jack-hammer was suspended at the end of a robot arm with too many joints. What beast in nature has a five-jointed arm? What beast has *three* of anything?

OK, that's enough, said my good angel as I felt in my pocket for my car keys. You've seen it. It's nasty. It's not portable. Now go home and watch a nice video.

Instead I took a look at the control panel, a breadbox sitting at the end of the spaghetti of wires that ran to the three headpounders. Four round oscilloscope screens. Three knobs labeled "KHz." Kilohertz, I thought, feeling very acoustical. This is a sound wave generator, just like the Cronk-enfax said. And a power switch, a disappointing little toggle where I expected a fat copper blade suitable for carrying lightning bolts. The box was more Radio Shack than Frankenstein. And the sheet, for God's sake, was fitted. Permanent press. Next to the box sat a vanilla laptop, which I noted with disdain was at least a year older than mine. That is, obsolete. Pathetic.

In the back of my mind I vaguely remembered a dozen horror movies in which the curious heroine turns to a door, waits for every mind in the audience to scream, "You idiot, don't open that door!" and opens it. If only she'd been listening to the soundtrack! I took some pleasure in calling up the violin slashes of *Psycho,* and rested my fingers lightly on the power switch. Just pretending.

"Dr. Cronkenstein, I presume," intoned a melodious voice, disturbingly close to my ear. Detectives were supposed to pay better attention to little noises. I jerked around to see two men, one dapper, the other not. Zamm. The Postdoc. I felt very weak in the knees, with a feeling in my chest that reminded me of a garbage disposal.

"That's Cronken*shteen,*" I *almost* said, a very unhelpful response in a panic attack. All I could say out loud was yes, my best option for getting through the next minute without a police record. Dapper was a shortish, powerful man in a three-piece suit and a perfect moustache. He had a faint accent that I could not place. With him was his Abbott, a tall ganglion in a white T-shirt and ponytail. I could only hope they wouldn't card me.

"I am Gabriel Zamm," said Costello, offering a finger squeeze that would have to serve for kissing my hand, "and this is Steve Addit, from our lab."

Addit gave me a hearty handshake and said simply, "Hey." I wracked my brain to make sure we hadn't met at one or another grad student bash.

"You are younger than we expected," said Zamm.

"The mountain air," I offered. "It keeps you young."

It was such a stupid thing to say that it worked. "I shall have to visit, then," said Zamm. "But where is Professor Grue?"

That was the question of the day. "I don't know. He wasn't there to meet my flight. I had to take a cab."

The two men exchanged knowing smirks. Max's non-appearance was no surprise, it seemed.

"I hope your flight was uneventful," said Zamm. Why would they expect a no-show from Max?

"Absolutely." I felt my moronic ruse fraying. I'd have to try for a little character development. "A wonderful chance to make progress on my monograph."

"Marvelous," exclaimed Zamm. "May I ask what topic you are pursuing?"

"You may." I tried the favorite tactic of the ignorant TA—turn the question. "But I'll bet you can both guess my current topic quickly enough."

Addit had been in a fidgety dance the whole time, struggling to insert himself into the conversation. He blurted out, "The thalamic center of consciousness!"

"Oh, you're *good*," I said, and he blushed. I could tell he agreed with me.

"So," said Zamm, turning to the hot seat, "may I infer that your research with the Transient Lesion device has led to the confirmation of the locus of conscious experience in the thalamus?" Both men looked at me with a disquieting intensity, like dogs waiting for a treat. Really big dogs. I had that trick question feeling.

"It turns out to be more complicated than that," I said.

"Ah," said Zamm. I was looking for my next dodge, but to my surprise neither asked the obvious question. After a short and slightly groping pause, he continued. "I see you are testing your prototype. I hope it conforms to the specifications laid out in your thesis."

"Yes. It's A-OK. All systems go." Probably not what a real neuroscientist would say, but then, I was posing as an acoustic engineer. I had a sudden vision of ceiling tiles with tiny holes all through them. My new field. Ask me anything.

"Your theory of transient lesioning is a masterpiece of theoretical neuroscience. Its application in this machine will be a great achievement."

"Thank you." Transient lesions. It sounded to me like a teenage skin condition. Or a teenage lobotomy.

"May I ask for the, how do you say it, Cook's tour?"

"Of course," I said, and turned to the machine. I reached out to one of the headbutters and discovered that it was throbbing. My angel commented, See, I told you. Nasty. "Well, I suppose this part is self-explanatory."

Both looked at me and waited. I desperately wanted to switch to a new false identity. "You know, I'm so close to my invention. I often find it more useful to hear others describe how they think it works. That helps me to articulate it for myself. Dr. Addit—may I call you Steve?—you've already impressed me with your quick thinking. Could you put it in your words? I'll jump in where I see the need."

Addit looked only briefly flustered. "The beauty is in the way you see the brain. It's soft, viscous. You looked at it and saw a fluid medium, and that means that sound of the right frequency can set up a standing wave."

"A standing wave," I said. "Yes, that's it." A wave, and a curl. Just as I suspected, the machine gives you a permanent.

"The three sources enable the standing wave to be maximized at a single point. You can shut down the brain right there, in the area of intersection."

Just keep talking. "Yes, shut down. You're doing very well. But how does that work?"

Addit continued. "It turns out that when the standing wave hits a certain amplitude, the deviations in density in the cerebral-spinal fluid affect the ion-transport mechanisms of the neural membrane. It creates a transient increase in spiking threshold, and that's enough to inhibit the whole area. Temporarily, of course."

"Temporarily!" I affirmed.

"It is ingenious," said Zamm.

"Super ingenious," said the Postdoc. Aw shucks. I was beginning to believe it really was my gizmo.

"You have been very wise to be discreet about your work, and wise to bring it first to us. Were any other group to know of this . . ." Zamm looked to the ceiling and held out both hands in a gesture that could only mean God Help Us. For that second when his face was upturned, I saw the gaze of the martyr, the fanatic. I realized I would have to see this through to the end, to leave the place with my secret identity unruffled. And then dye my hair a nice jet black, and steer clear of Wundt for a long time.

"But what I find no less impressive is the generosity you've shown in bringing it to us," continued Zamm. "And courage as well—to make this long trip, simply to be the first experimental subject of your own invention!"

"Uh . . ." My spine tingled with the thrill of phenomenology.

"Steven, observe how modest she is. You should follow her example!" Both laugh at that.

I quip back, "No, after you! Surely one of you would like to be the first." Or maybe I can shout, "Just kidding!"

They laugh again at this suggestion. "Ah, Dr. Cronkenstein, you are the model of self-effacement. No; let history be made by you, and you alone." Zamm gestures to the machine as if it were a box seat at the opera, or a used car he hopes I will test-drive. Strangely, only now I notice all the Velcro straps dangling from the chair—head, chest, arms, and legs. I wonder how the lab rats feel when this happens to them.

"We'll need the Powerbook," says Addit, turning it on. It flashes to life with three cross-sections of the brain in outline diagrams. Slices and dices too, isn't that amazing? Wouldn't this be a perfect time for a power failure?

Both men stare at me expectantly. Their patient intensity makes it worse. I come factory-equipped with a pleasant and plausible expression for every situation, but this time I can't shape a look appropriate to a young female Ph.D. about to be strapped into a chair by two men. I hop into the recliner, thinking that surely Dr. Victoria Cronkenstein of the Alps is a nice person, the sort who waves at Heidi every morning, and that this angry-looking machine is as safe as an electric toothbrush. Cronkenstein has already volunteered for her personal brain drain, so at least she believes it is safe. Zamm and Addit do too. Climb every mountain. Ford every stream.

Each guy takes a side and straps poor pitiful me to the railroad tracks, all the while handling the Velcro like a sterile dressing, keeping touch— man meets woman—out of it. Am I comfortable? Are the straps too tight?

"Shall we begin?" asks Zamm. I'm about to confess and bolt anyway, when his vest beeps. I jerk against the straps, but they hold just fine. Zamm reaches into his jacket to draw a revolver, but pulls out a cell phone. My good angel calling, no doubt, to remind me once again that she told me so. But no, it's for him. He steps away from us, turning toward the wall. It's our job to pretend we aren't listening.

Addit wastes no time. He leans over to eclipse my view of his boss and affects a huge sympathetic concern: "How are you doing?" I'm staring at his nose, right down to the pores and tiny hairs. His breath smells faintly of Doritos.

"Oh, fine," I say.

"We haven't got much time," he whispers. "I have to warn you about both of them."

"Both?"

"Yes, Grue too. Zamm and Grue are egomaniacs, and rivals. This machine is the next really big thing." I nod. Addit has been as good as a TelePrompTer, and I'm not going to interrupt now. "Zamm will propose a collaboration, but don't do it. He'll absorb you like an amoeba, digest you. He'll do anything to be first, and all by himself. And Grue, we call him Byron. He'll write some bad poetry about the mind-body problem and you'll both sink with it. Listen, take my phone number and call later. Just between us, we can make it all come out right." I nod again. Suddenly I realize that Zamm's caller might be busting me. Maybe it's Victoria herself. I look toward his tweedy back for some clue.

Addit finds a pad on the lab table and scribbles his name and number, but before he can give it to me Zamm is back. "Dr. Cronkenstein, my apologies. I felt compelled to take the call—editors can be so persistent, even from Los Angeles."

"I know just what you mean," I say.

"Where shall we begin?" he asks.

"How about something unimportant? You know, um, a minor lobe or something." *With the thoughts that I'd be thinkin'. . . .*

Both look at me with surprise, and I half-hope to be challenged and shown the door. "A minor lobe," murmurs Addit. *I could be another Lincoln. . . .*

"Hey, just a little joke," I say. "Start anywhere. Let's see what's in there." . . . *if I only had a brain.*

"How about the occipital?" suggests Zamm.

"Great. Love it," I reply. Maybe that's the panic center—I can use a little shutdown there.

Addit turns to the keyboard with the zeal appropriate to an Igor, although he forgets to crack his knuckles first. I'd much rather be watching this on the silver screen. The tap tap of the Powerbook gives me a few seconds to think. Was Victoria born Cronkenstein? Or was she the *bride* of Cronkenstein? *Think.* Zamm. What if Max had called him with the same epiphany he had shared with Clare Lucid? Would Zamm feel scooped? And would that motivate a big chill? Maybe—if Addit is to be believed. His postdoc vacuum of fashion sense suggests either absolute sincerity or a basement full of dismembered cats.

And there's the other mystery, the Mystery of Consciousness. Was this hot seat the Key to Its Solution, "once and for all," as Zamm had written? This is the strangest road, I think: to shut down a part of the brain and in its darkness light up the truth about consciousness.

"X, 10, Y, –85, Z, 8," says Igor.

"OK," says Zamm. "What's the radius?"

"It's fixed at about 15 millimeters."

"We won't be able to hit area 17 bilaterally."

"No. I centered it on the right hemisphere, 10 millimeters from the midline."

"Good."

Addit looks at Zamm expectantly. Neither looks toward me.

Zamm nods. Addit hits the return key, and the shiny praying mantis of your worst geek nightmare jerks to life. The three jackhammers swing about my head in a violent ballet, and I briefly imagine what would happen if, say, Zamm's silk tie were snagged in one of them. The three rams lock into position, triangulating just above the hairs on the nape of my neck, the ones that are tingling. The throb of the machine becomes a hum, then a whir, then a whine, then a toothache. With a patient relentlessness appropriate to totally mad science, the three tips extend from the jackhammers toward my head. I feel the foamy pads brush my hair, then crush it into my skull. As the three throbbers push on the back of my scalp, they shove my head into the Velcro strap across my forehead.

This particular masquerade is definitely a mistake. I love wisdom, but there are limits.

It feels like very large cockroaches tap dancing on the deepest bones of my skull. It feels like an orgasm without the fun. It feels like . . . and then the feeling fades away. The magic fingers and I are one. With a good firm padded embrace, my head gets with the program. In synch. The shrieking buzz becomes a velvety hum.

"Now what?" says Zamm.

I look over toward Addit, piloting the breadbox and the Powerbook. My immobility makes him infinitely distant, seen through glass. Both of them have forgotten that I'm there. If I could only get the straps to do the same.

"All three are on the same frequency. Now I tweak this one"—he points to one of the oscilloscopes—"and we'll get some interference beats where the waves meet. The beats are more intense than any of the three wavefronts individually. They'll do the trick."

I watch him on my left as he gives the knob a slight turn. The scope responds by jumping about madly, then settling into an endless march of glowing waves, and then . . . disappearing. It isn't swallowed in darkness or in light. Rather, it just turns into a nothingness. An emptiness that blankets a big part of my world, but the blanket is not. However I might describe it, it is not that. With Addit folded into the gray toffee of nonbeing, I look toward Zamm, at my right. The Blob follows my gaze, and now I have lost the left lapel and sideburn, the left patch of ceiling, the left world.

"I'm blind," I whisper. "In the left eye." But even as I say it I realize that it's the left side of both eyes that is missing. "Turn it off," I say.

"Just one quick probe, if I may," says Zamm. "Look at my nose." I have to admit, it is a nicer nose than Addit's. Smoother. More shine. I can see the shoulder of his tweed jacket bunch up as he raises his arm, but the rest is absorbed into the void. "Is my fist open or closed? Keep looking at my nose!"

"I'm blind on the left. I can't see your arm."

"Not to worry. Just guess. Open or closed?"

Strange days. "Open," I say. Both men smile broadly.

"That's exactly right," says Zamm.

"Blindsight!" exclaims Addit.

I would have asked about that, but instead I find myself begging, "Turn it off." Addit promptly complies.

For a few terrifying seconds, the blind spot lingers. Then, with a smooth cinematic smear, the edges of somethingness wash over the vacuum, submerging it in the home sweet world. I can see again. I look at every object I can to revel in its left side. How beautiful, I think, to have a left side. How jerky, I think, that these assholes aren't unstrapping me. At least give me some water. Let me lean over the basin and spit.

They're thrilled, like eight-year-olds on Christmas morning. Ready for the next goody.

"Right parietal," suggests Zamm.

"Yeah, yeah," says Addit, and turns to the keyboard.

A few seconds pass. Then Zamm remembers the little matter of informed consent. "Doctor Cronkenstein, would that be acceptable to you?"

My visual world is intact. The brain drain was temporary, just like the label said. "Keep it quick, OK?"

"But of course."

The head pads withdraw their affection, leaving tingling patches of scalp behind. I reach up to scratch, and jerk against the strap. Zamm notices and frowns. "These really are unnecessary, aren't they?" He unstraps my left arm, a gesture for which I'm very grateful. I massage my startled skull. He says, dismissively, "The feeling will pass, I'm sure."

"Ready?" asks Addit, without really expecting an answer. I've always wondered what a right parietal was for, or even a wrong parietal. I only know it as another of the four principal lobes of the brain. My occipital still seems chipper enough: I check out the left world again and find its comforts everywhere. Maybe I will make it through the chamber of horrors after all.

The three vibrators shazam to a new position, much higher but still toward the back of my head. They extend to make the mind meld, with a touch of firm paternal violence that beats my viscous little brain into submission. I wish I *had* invented the damn thing, so I could tear up the blueprint.

Addit twists the third knob. Again the oscilloscope jumps and settles. I wait for some action. After a few moments I notice that Addit is gone. "Where is he?" I ask Zamm, who smiles.

"He is right here, to your left. Steven, speak."

Bow wow, Steven. "Hey," he says. I hear him somewhere close but I can't place where. And yet my visual world is complete, no holes.

"Let's trade places," says Zamm.

And then Addit stands at my right hand, and Zamm is missing.

"Over here," says Zamm's voice, but somehow "here" makes no sense. Each time I look for his face, I see only Addit, and oddly too. Something is off about the face. Has he shaved? Did he always have just one eye? I look around and suddenly find Zamm, there all along, somehow, somewhere. His face looks odd in much the same way Addit's did.

I feel something strange in my lap, and look down to the purest horror, the horror. An arm has been dropped in my lap. A funny arm, a horrible one. I jerk away, straining against the straps to throw off this monstrous joke, but the arm jerks with me. With the revulsion I usually save for leeches and tapeworms, I conclude that it has attached itself to me.

"What's wrong?" asks Zamm, with an oily voice.

"Take it off me, take it off!"

"Take what off?"

"The arm. The arm."

"I don't think you'd like that," says Addit.

"Oh, try me. I hate—hate—" but I'm somehow unable to name it.

"Doctor Cronkenstein, where is your left arm?" asks Zamm.

I look at him, still puzzling over his single beamish eye. Does everyone look like that? "I don't know."

He taps me on the left shoulder. "Whose shoulder is that?"

I have never liked being patronized. I simply stare at him, or at "him," so peculiar, so radically odd.

"All right," he says. "Then whose elbow is this? It's connected to your shoulder."

That was a puzzler. "It must be . . . mine," I say.

"Good, good. Then follow along from the elbow to the hand. Whose hand is this?" He pokes it like it was carrion.

I know what I know, and I know it. "It must be, must be . . . yours! And get it out of my lap now!"

"Good, good. Steven, shut it down." The whining slides back into its earthy throb. The cattle prods back away. Nothing changes for me. At first I'm frightened, but the more I look around the more normal everything appears.

I raise my left arm and look at the hand, clenching and unclenching my fist. Steady as a rock. I'm checking something about it, but I'm not sure what.

Both nod thoughtfully. "Hemi-neglect," says Addit. "Her entire left perceptual field simply ceased to exist. Awesome."

Occipital, parietal. Two down, two to go. "Doctor," says Zamm, "may we continue with the temporal?"

"Right, temporal."

"Actually, I was thinking of the left posterior temporal. Wernicke's area."

"Oh, good thinking. Yes, the left. Of course."

Addit taps away again, and once again I play Sigourney Weaver to the greedy aliens, who swarm me and settle in, this time feeding from just above my left ear. Addit is speaking to me, but in midsentence his voice drops to a jumbled murmur: "Can you underglimd ko?"

I try to think of a witty rejoinder, but am unable to find the words. To find any words, in fact.

"Grat milkaro bith mortrorery," continues Addit. I've heard this joke before, the one with the meaningless punchline, "No soap, radio." Suckers laugh. I want to tell them I've seen through their little charade, but once again I can't find the

"Klatu barada nicto. Gim sigmo hor kadenda. Mignnnn. Gnit. Tt besh. Aaaozzzz."

Heakkeroooonamatagngngn—ggllrr! Myzyplyzyx! Gnu! Nini nana nunu! Sncc! Sm!

. . .

echee echee echee fatang fatang—by the dog, what a what a ride. Foo.

"Well?" says Zamm.

"I could see your lips move, and hear sounds, but they made no sense." Suddenly I wonder if they were discussing when to disconnect me, like HAL. Please stop, Dave.

Will I make it through the last lobe? This name I remember, but only through a joke—I'd rather have a free bottle in front of me than a prefrontal lobotomy. Miranda, face frontal. The effect is transitory, I repeat to myself. My new mantra.

As the three ramrods swing into position, I'm grateful that the grand tour began at the back of my head. To watch the machine ratchet down on you, to feel it shove your brain into the headrest, making an offer you can't refuse—it's scary. But in some corner of my consciousness, a part of me wants every moment of this. Or does just before each brain zap. Just after, every cell in the affected areas says in unison, don't you ever, ever do that again. Perhaps in my case, it should be, don't you ever, ever. . . . Do that again.

I feel very agitated. I wonder when it will begin. Nervous, antsy. Will it be starting soon? There's something I have to take care of. Will it be starting? Right away! Straps on my right arm. Not on my left. Something about that. Get on it! Why only one arm? Will it be starting soon? Am I supposed to do something? What about those straps? Why not on my left? What on my left? What is to do? I feel antsy. Is this it? Is this?

The machine pulls back, and both men stare expectantly once again. "Well?" says Zamm.

"I'm ready," I say, trying to be helpful.

"Do you remember anything of the last minute or two?"

"I remember the garbled words, and getting ready for the next lobe, the frontal. There was a moment of confusion." I realize that my anxiety was about that. Was it a flashback? Neural meltdown?

"That moment of confusion, how long did it last?"

"Just a minute, really. You don't think I should worry about it, do you?"

"My good Doctor," says Zamm jovially, "we measured about five minutes by our watch. I've never seen such a pure case of frontal syndrome. No compensation whatever."

"You mean that was it? You did it?" You did me in too. Time to make an exit, get home, get to sleep. I'm relieved to make it through the funhouse. The real Victoria Cronkenstein is probably only now making irate phone calls to Max, to these guys, to the taxi company. I'm glad the airport is forty minutes away.

"Yes, we have inhibited major areas in each of the four cerebral lobes. You have just experienced what most neurologists must only imagine."

"Yeah, well, they're lucky. It would be hell to live like that."

"Someday, perhaps, all doctors will have to follow in our path as part of their training," says Zamm. *Our* path? Who's in the chair with the Velcro? You're just a witness to my magical mystery tour. Perhaps Addit is right about him.

"Well, Steven," he continues. "Are you thinking what I'm thinking?"

"She was conscious the whole time," he says.

"Precisely. None of these areas is the locus we seek."

"Wow," says Addit. "It's sub-lobar. Just like we've been saying."

"I suggest you set your coordinates for the thalamus," says Zamm, or rather he intones, as if he is already imagining himself being quoted. He turns to me as if to an old buddy, leaning toward me. "Who would have suspected that we would find the Grail on this night? Who would have suspected?"

It's dawning on me that they are not finished with me yet. If the thalamus is the master control of consciousness, then to shut it down is to shut me down. The idea of Zamm and Addit turning me off turns me off. "Wait!"

The demon butchers of Fleet Street pause to look at me. If I had ever been an attractive woman to them, that has passed now. I'm the whole goddamn Nobel Prize committee, or the best, most docile guinea pig good girl ever. I'm data. I'm meat.

"I have to, uh, visit the lavatory." I know my cover is thin. I'll have to keep moving now. I begin to undo my own straps. "You know how it is," I say. "Just one of those things." Let a smile be your umbrella. Shut up, Miranda.

For a moment, it seems Zamm will say no. You can't go to the potty when history is to be made! But he smothers his frustration and even a fearful little crest of anger. "Of course, of course," he says, "Your flight, the trip." And he helps unstrap me. The sound of Velcro letting go is one of the least musical in the universe, but at this moment and forever after the skish of unstrapping is better for my soul than the *Ode to Joy*. I jump up, but stand unsteadily, finding a reunion with my scrambled body.

"I'll walk you there," says Addit. I consider that maybe I'll give him the chance to tell all, or at least tell some. But then what? Bye bye, thalamus. Don't forget to write.

"No, I'll be fine," I declare, and prove it by putting one foot in front of the other. At the door, I force myself to pause, and turn back jauntily to the two men. "Be right back!"

I turn gracefully, pushing down the handle and pulling the door smoothly toward me. Then the world goes silver. I shoulder the door, clutching the handle to keep my head up in the vortex. The feeling passes, leaving nausea and sweat.

Addit is at it again. "Are you sure you're OK?"

"Yes," I nod, but I know I'm paler than Elizabeth the First.

"Here, I'll walk you," he says. I'm in no position to refuse. He's absorbed in his left forearm, the one with my arm looping through it. At the bathroom door, we face each other like a couple at the end of a blind date. Will I see you again? I hope not! I detach myself swiftly and enter the lavatory alone, staggering ever so slightly.

As I catch sight of myself in the mirror I'm astonished that they could believe me to be anything other than the woman who knew too much, a terrified outsider. Such is the power of delusion and desire.

The window stretches across the wall at the end of a row of sinks. I stand on the last sink and slide it open. A cool draft hits my face. I stick my head out the window and look down a sickening plane of concrete and glass. There are no ledges, and the ski jump façade can't be relied upon to drop me in the front seat of my Honda.

On to plan B. I lie down on the floor with my head just inside a stall. Wait. The wooziness passes, and then I hear Addit call, "Victoria? Victoria?" Rude boy, thinking himself on a first-name basis with *the* Victoria Cronkenstein! I hear the door swing open, and he rushes in and kneels over me, more or less, since I'm half into a stall. "Are you OK?" Sure, I like to lie on the floor in public restrooms. Instead of faking a faint I decide to go all demented on him. I look at his ear, which I have to note is pretty waxy, and unfocus my eyes. Then I imitate a pig snort and let my head droop to one side. He pats my cheek, lightly at first, then with a challenging firmness. But I hold on to my Best Supporting Actress option, thinking to myself, Drool! Drool! You can do it! His nacho breath is hot and urgent. "Oh, shit," he mutters, sitting back on his heels. Then he jumps up and races from the room—to get Zamm, I'm hoping.

I'm up, cracking the lavatory door just as I hear Addit open the lab door. I'll have three or four seconds to cover the twenty feet to the stairs, which I do, even managing to close the fire door behind me in near silence. I hear their footsteps rushing back toward the bathroom. My race down the stairwell of hell is so desperate that I don't even have time to place it in a movie. I hit the night air as though I'm surfacing from a sunken ship, and do a doubletake with each sensation—the damp and chilly air, the distant noise of traffic, the smell of a city longing to dry out and warm up—yes, I seem to be conscious. Functioning as before. Existing. Giddy with it. My arms and legs feel light, filled with helium, still itchy where the straps had dug in. They move. I move.

As I cross the plaza, panting and loving myself, a cab pulls up to the curb. I nearly bolt, but then curiosity rises yet again. She doesn't know me from Eve, after all. I set my course to pass right by the cab, slowing down to give the passenger time to pay her fare. A woman emerges, with a small suitcase on wheels. I hate small suitcases on wheels. But I'm shocked at Dr. Cronkenstein herself. She is tall, which is to say, just my height, with long straight hair that may be coppery or maybe just light brown. She has wide, deep almond eyes and high cheekbones. She's thin, bone thin, and the skin stretches thin to cover her face, and—looking at the strain of that face— her mind stretches thin to keep up with the treadmill she finds herself on. Fate has given me an extraordinary gift, to see the inventor of my own cancelled mind. She is me, in some dark possible future.

I turn down the sidewalk, away from my double and away from the high comedy about to ensue in Wundt Hall. Away, away. And then something wells up from the bottom of my feet with special emphasis on my stomach. Being a good girl, I make it to the curb and even to a storm drain before I throw up.

12

I took the streets home, creeping along like a designated driver who had gotten high anyway. At one point, I sat at a stop sign for half a minute. Waiting for it to change.

Philosophy was not usually a high-risk profession. Ever since that Socrates affair, philosophers had carefully hidden their best, those ideas to die for. I'd done my grad school duty several times, trying to unpack Plato, Mr. Mystery himself. There was a devastating claim there, in the parable of the Cave. The hint that there are truths so astonishing, so out there, that it is like the difference between the high noon sun and the campfire shadows on a slimy cave wall. As different as that. As I limped and listed down the back streets, it occurred to me that the New was the last thing philosophy was prepared to face. With Socrates dead, we philosophers do a different job, taking the whittle knife to Plato. Our first response, well learned from a couple of Greeks who were *not* put to death, is to make sure that anything the least bit New is quickly shown to be either the Same Old Same Old or False or—best—both.

What is Truth? Any philosophy grad will be quick to talk to you about the internal coherence of our beliefs or of their correspondence to the world. Either one is a pure cardigan straightjacket made of corduroy, all cozy and broken in. Just insist on the Truth, that'll keep you trotting in place forever. It's better than a pension.

So, what's New? As I crept home—with my mind spread out through the city, and the city blasted across my mind, so open, so craving of every nuance after tasting death on an installment plan—as I crept home, I couldn't speak the news. But I had a very intuitive intuition about the proceedings in Wundt Hall. They had it backwards. Because I remained conscious with each brownout, they thought that they had undershot the high window of consciousness itself. They had failed to land the knockout punch.

They were looking for the G-spot of consciousness. Fools. Maybe I'd be a brussels sprout without my bustling thalamus, but that fact would only establish that my thalamus was a necessary condition for consciousness. Take my heart, stomp on that, and I'd be just about as unconscious. But we don't *think* there, do we? The evidence was already in my face, if not in theirs. Each takedown led to a huge strange change in the character of my consciousness. So, with each, they hit a part of it, taking down a piece of the puzzle. Consciousness is distributed across the brain. Just ask your sobbing stroke victim, *Hey, sweetie, are you conscious?* The job of each part may be different, but it takes them all together to give me the everyday thrill of phenomenology. One task or another may lean on one part or another more heavily, but that does not locate consciousness. It was just what you'd expect, if you were Gordon Fescue. Huge Times Square patterns flashing up, down, and all over, scattering and flocking in the big neural net that I call me.

I opened my apartment with trepidation, taking only small comfort from HG, whose response to unsolved mysteries was to eat and sleep. I had nothing to say to her. As I locked the deadbolts behind me, it came to me that this day had been the end of all my sanctuaries. Just one year ago, I had Seth in a double bed and a double-signed lease on a double bedroom apartment with a porch and separate study. A year ago, I was riding a golden first year of graduate school, commanding a firm understanding of half a dozen words ending in -ism, even spending a few hours a week reading the journals, and more than a few at the cinema. A year ago, a fast-talking charismatic philosopher treated me like an equal and like a pure mind—for a while. A year ago, I had a point of view, a history, and a future. I took my car through the wash once every two weeks, and took time to vacuum. A year ago, I was a constant, an individual entity to whom things happened, some good, some bad. A year ago, I found a steady I at the fulcrum of all my memories, all the way back, and that same I was at home in all the condos and mansions of hope. The steady I with her steady eye slalomed through the world, thrilling at speed and railing at fools and morons. Moving, choosing, evolving.

In the months in between the snow turned to slush, the certainties to questions, but the clarity of the goal still wired the one and only Miranda Sharpe as the heroine of her own story. Then Seth crossed over into the realm of lies, Seth and the bimbo. Of all the airheads in the world, why did he have to find one that looked like me? Miranda lite. Less filling.

But it was me, the good old self, that hated him and missed him and fantasized his redemption and kicked herself for being a fool. The thrill of phenomenology, and my mentor, and a cat, and a collection of sound-tracks—these propped me up as the way bogged on.

Then the mentor crossed over too, over and out, and the thrill of phenomenology began to fade. I became a character in my own melodrama, surrounded by students morphed into hoods and psychos, sniffed at by a sinister shrink, my life invaded by some weird Russian statistical detective who now knew what kind of cheese I like. But the plucky girl detective held on even still, as her life got both fake and scary.

And then Victoria and Max handed me a bait-and-switch opportunity, and I played a shell game with my own personal brain. The brain drainer had thrown me over the line too, and left me there, washed up. Except for the buzz on my skull, I felt no losses in my brain at all. What the jackhammers shattered was my world. Transient lesioning ground zero was in each of four big smart lobes, but the effect was to blow out the universe four different ways. When the film jams, then you really know it's just a film. My film jammed. Locked on the screen, the frame filled with Miranda's scared eyes smoked, melted, burst into a gurgly flame.

No wonder Grue was on the team. They should have strapped him into Victoria's phenomenological orgasmatron. I imagined him begging for more—or watching me begging for less. Would he have been thoughtful of me? Or fanatic, like the other two? I was sure of the answer, and very glad he hadn't appeared. For every low, there's something lower still.

I kicked off my boots and jeans and pulled out the futon, sinking into a mush of covers, checking the ceiling for cracks and cobwebs. That is, in my brain a shifting tapestry of excited cells encoded the look of ceiling, and I was the ceiling and the ceiling was me. Until an hour ago I had a self, and the self was in the world. Inside, outside. But then I discovered in my bones that when you addle your brain you disable the whole world, knock it right out of joint down to the lint on a gnat's back. Once you've been there and done that, there's no there anywhere. Just a lot of variables, blips of neurotransmitter that fit together just like a world. No more sunsets—from now on I'd be watching the "sunset."

As a lover of movies, I should have welcomed this denouement. Cinema verité. And in her greatest role, Miranda Sharpe as . . . no, playing "Miranda Sharpe," we have . . . what?

A vast tiredness overtook me. Usually I'd enjoy the fluttering leaf of consciousness slipping into sleep. Tonight it felt like giving in to the machine, to death itself. I hung on tight, hugging a pillow. *I'm alive,* I whispered to myself. I had escaped from the psychos in the Psychophysics Lab. Safe. That thought was nice, like the pillow.

After a moment I found that I had kicked off my comforter. Without really opening my eyes, I felt out to both sides of the futon, then I swung one hand up and rapped a knuckle on the wall at my head. My body had wormed its way to the top edge, sphere meets plane. Had the wall always been so rough? My hands were bumping over what felt like a worn rock face.

The wall had distinct grooves running across it. I hadn't noticed. I followed one with a finger. It was an ancient rounded channel, just right for my middle finger to trace. Three horizontals off of a vertical, the letter E. With difficulty I opened my eyes, but all I could see was the faint thin shadows of my hands and skinny wrists, like winter trees, against a vibrating white darkness. Not that there was any doubt what I'd find next. I let my fingers do the skimming, itsy bitsy spiders. I worked back from the E: P, R, A, H, S. Miranda Sharpe, hacked into rock. My heart pounded. I already knew there'd be a line beneath, carved in the stone. I so much prefer email. I felt my way into it, starting at the right: 1 . . . 9 . . . 8 . . . 0 . . .– . . . 2 . . . 0. . . .

And I woke up. I was in the Fens, the old burial ground. Seth's and my favorite place for midsummer night dreaming, on nights just like this. I loved the Boris Karloff jumble of stones, he loved jumping my bones under the clear night sky. I'd been sleeping on a sargophagus, extra firm and just my size. A hazy red moon rolled through clouds and tree branches. I could see everything, surprising for night. It must have been a new streetlight, installed to discourage the likes of us, grave robbers and romantics. The light was just like the one I'd seen reflected in Max's monad. The snow that had streaked through the bent mirror was still there, transmuted into a swarm of gnats around the light, tracing mad orbits around the blinding orange point. And where the hell was Seth? Then I remembered I had broken up with him.

A bad dream. I sat up with the comforter bunched around my waist, and held my temples with both hands. The room seemed to be spinning, and I knew there was something very important that I must do. Words flew around my head like trapped bats, blurred shadows, unsounded shapes. Max Grue's voice: "Miranda!" I shook awake. The window rattled as wet snow began again to fall, but then all was quiet. I sank back into a confused pit of clamorous voices. Max was speaking again, at a huge misshapen podium, like a tipping desk. The room was the classroom in Ryle where The Mystery of Consciousness met. Stacks of paper were slipping off the desk, an endless glacial stream, but Max was staring at the ceiling, as he often did when he was groping for thoughts. "What is more grim, a pineapple or a lightbulb?" The students were all writing furiously, no one looking up. No one answered. I thought to myself, a lightbulb, obviously. The students seemed ghostly, fading out. "Is the smell of ammonia white or black?" I found the answer numbingly obvious, but before I could get out the words, he asked, "Is the present King of France merry or sad? Is he ping or pong? Cheech or Chong? Neither or both?" He turned up his hand and stared at it. I knew it would be covered with ants, but I was wrong. He held a teaspoon of a black grainy something, like oregano or tobacco, which he slowly poured onto the podium. Then he bent over it and with a sudden puff blew it into nothingness. He straightened up and fixed me with a wry smirky stare. "Is it something or nothing?" And here the It swirled around like a wraith of smoke, folded in on itself. Why was he asking the students such obvious questions? I was embarrassed for him. Why was he holding back, when he held the answer?

I sat bolt upright. From the foot of the bed, HG turned her sphinx gaze upon me, inscrutable. "What time is it?" I mumbled. I squinted at the glowing numbers beside the bed—barely ten minutes had passed. Next to the clock, a red light blinked on my answering machine. How had I missed it? I slumped back into the covers, turning away from time and other people. Breathed once. Sat up again and reached over to the answering machine.

The first message had been dropped at 4. It was Maureen in the department, calling at the request of the dean. The Chaos Bug was everywhere. Even Tom Brokaw had it. Shut down, shut up, hit the bunkers. No one had even found the virus yet. Until they know what it is, curfew on the Internet. "So take the night off why don't you," concluded Maureen. Nice idea. Nice of her to call.

Message 2, 6:45: Dr. Clare Lucid calling. Concerned for me following our session. Hoping all is well. Oh and *by the way,* have I uncovered any more information on Max? Numbers: office, home, service, cell phone—keep trying. I thought, yeah, right.

Message 3, 8 PM, Gordon Fescue. Sorry to be bothering me. But he had accidentally picked up a piece of paper in Max's office, just after he dumped his own mess on top of Max's. It was blue, very wrinkled. It looked important. Though it might be mine. Call, OK?

A mashed sheet of paper, importantly blue. Maybe Gordon was just longing to relate some more. Maybe he had something there. It would only take a minute to find out.

I got all the way through Gordon's number on the third try. With my best attempted fake professional voice I thanked him for the information. And by the way, what did the note say?

Gordon seemed surprised that I didn't already know. "It's a URL."

"That's it?"

"Yeah. <www.trincoll.edu/~dlloyd>."

I scribbled it down. "www dot trincoll with two Ls dot edu slash squiggle dlloyd with two Ls. And nothing else?"

"Nothing. Nothing."

13

WELCOME TO THE LABYRINTH OF COGNITION
Through these doors one may view the brain from the brain's own point of view. The starting point for this labyrinth is 34 "functional brain imaging" experiments, or scans of brain metabolism during various tasks. Positron emission tomography, or PET, is the principal imaging technology, and most of the studies encompassed here have been archived in the Brainmap database at the University of Texas Research Imaging Center (http://ric.uthscsa.edu/).

So began the website, beaming from some satellite through the void for my eyes only. Halfway down the page were the words, *Imaging Cognition, the current state of the art.*

PET studies are determined efforts to locate particular mental functions in particular regions of the brain. PET methods favor localization hypotheses. But a review of several hundred PET studies reveals that localized functions are the exception, not the rule. Instead, the brain generally employs distributed resources.

I read. The author began with a little tour of brain scanning, which he claimed was about matching specific cognitive states or perceptions to particular localities in the brain. Each part of the brain had its job, according to the standard picture. There'd be a "face center" somewhere, and a "pain region" somewhere else, a whole nest of squishy specialists. But there were some problems with the localization project, said the blog. Like, if you took a particular region of the brain and looked through every experiment where that region lit up, you'd find that most regions are active for a mixed bag of functions. Also, the localization methods filter out a lot of activity in the neurons that is just as real as the activity they leave in. Who can say what activity is relevant and what is not? And so on. I thought that maybe someday I would have to come back to the critique, some day when my own brain was a little less edgy.

I rolled down to the next heading.

Beyond hot spots: Distributed patterns of activation

Until a few years ago, local function was the only game in town. But if the brain is not a bureaucracy of functional specialists, what is it? It is—in my view—a radical democracy. A kibbutz in which everyone pitches in a bit on just about everything. Or, in the language of cognitive science, the brain is a distributed processor.

Hence, Gordon Fescue. Hence, Jeffrey Elman. Hence, Max Grue's enthusiasm. And the temporal sandwich: past present future.

But distributed processors are hard to understand, requiring special interpretive strategies. The original champions of distributed processing, the connectionists, have faced just this issue. When localism fails, connectionists turn to multivariate statistics for help. A variety of analytical techniques all work to reduce the dimensionality of a target domain. Suppose, for example, we want to understand the various patterns of activation of a hidden layer of eighty units. Multivariate thinking begins with a simple conceptual shift: Regard each activation value as a magnitude along an axis or "dimension." Eighty units, in this way of thinking, represent a space of eighty dimensions, and the eighty activation values are interpreted as coordinates in that space. In other words, the pattern of activation with its eighty coordinates is reconceived as a single point in 80-d space. This 80-d space is thus a handy container for many patterns of activation—each reappears as a specific point in a high-dimensional map.

Comrades, why does this all seem familiar? The author moved through Porfiry-land without the accent. Ultimately, the proposal was to take each region of the brain as if it were a neural network processing unit, or, in Marlov-speak, to take the scanner signal intensity from each region as a separate dimension in "brain activation space." So each brain scan had different intensities in many dimensions, but it all came together in a point in high-dimensional brain space. Then the author, Lloyd somebody, did a Marlov-type space shrink on the high-dimensional space. Multidimensional scaling was Lloyd's thing too. Brain patterns would become points in a nice regular 3-D space, the sort of space you could bring home to Mom. The brain scans made it all a little simpler, since they couldn't focus on the neurons. Instead, Lloyd took each fold and lump as a separate unit, about one hundred in all with all sorts of overly impressive Latin names. Those hundred dimensions went into the shrinker.

The shrinking idea put my own brain in a flip, so I did what dedicated graduate students do when faced with hard thinking. I got myself some dinner, a diet soda. The edge of the poptop seemed especially sharp on the skin beneath my fingernail. The sfitz seemed particularly crisp, and gave Holly's whiskers and ears a twitch. Do kittens dream of Diet Sprite? Or did a sfitz-center in cat cortex sparkle for a second and then sputter into silence?

I continued with the tour guide:

In the Labyrinth *I focus the lens of Multi-Dimensional Scaling on the accumulated PET studies in Brainmap and in the PET literature in general. My goal has been to use MDS as a crude probe of brain activation space. If MDS works without excessive forcing, and if the structures detected by MDS are meaningful, this will offer another line of evidence that the brain is indeed a distributed processor. The MDS analysis is represented in the "virtual world" of the* Labyrinth of Cognition, *which you may visit. This model has the advantage of exploiting our good abilities to grasp space and depth, especially from a moving viewpoint. It has the disadvantage (for the moment) of being difficult to view all at once.*

And in me? Did I have an area for feeling bubbles in my throat, and another for sounding words? What would it be like to be a bureaucracy? The Ministry of Miranda, a labyrinth. Maybe the website would show me the floor plan. I hoped it would include a nice arrow, "You are here."

For legibility, labels have been kept very brief. Their format is:
   Stimulus   ;   cognition   ;   response behavior
   "..." = none
Click on any label for a full description.

Then, a link: "*Enter the Labyrinth.*" I will.

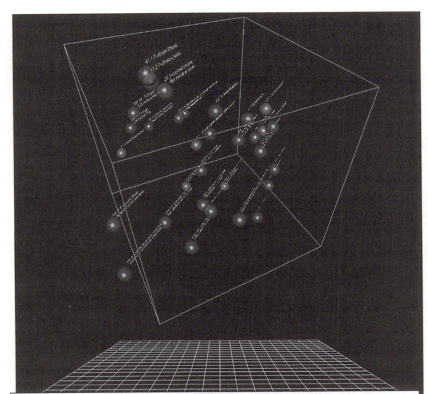

I'D DONE TIME IN DARK PLACES. I'D HEARD THE TAP OF A SINGLE
GIRL'S HEELS PASSING BENEATH THE BUZZ OF NEON. I'VE KNOWN
BLACK VELVET SKIES WITH A SINGLE STREET LIGHT PUNCHING
THROUGH, OR AN EXHAUSTED MOON AT THE END OF AN ALLEY.
BUT NEVER MOONS IN STREET GANGS, NEVER MOONS DRAPED WITH
GOD-SIZED LABELS. I HAD A DATE WITH THEM, IT SEEMED.

I SLID ALONG THE GRID
        TOWARD THIS TWILIGHT ZONE,
            LIFTED OFF,
                AND ROSE INTO THE SPHERES.

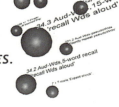

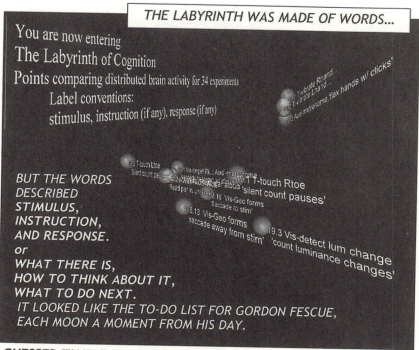

THE LABYRINTH WAS MADE OF WORDS...

You are now entering
The Labyrinth of Cognition
Points comparing distributed brain activity for 34 experiments
Label conventions:
stimulus, instruction (if any), response (if any)

BUT THE WORDS
DESCRIBED
STIMULUS,
INSTRUCTION,
AND RESPONSE.
or
WHAT THERE IS,
HOW TO THINK ABOUT IT,
WHAT TO DO NEXT.
IT LOOKED LIKE THE TO-DO LIST FOR GORDON FESCUE,
EACH MOON A MOMENT FROM HIS DAY.

I GUESSED THAT "VIS" MEANT VISION, "AUD" AUDITION, "T" TOUCH.
I PICKED A RANDOM PLANET AND CLICKED ON IT. THE UNIVERSE
SWIRLED, AND I FELL IN...

T-Itch, Rarm

THINK IT AND MAKE IT SO:
MY CHEEK ITCHED.
I SCRATCHED MY RIGHT ARM TOO, WONDERING:
DOES THE URGE TO SCRATCH BEAM YOU TO
BRAINPOINT 'T-ITCH'?
IS THIS PLANET ME, HERE AND NOW?

I FELT LOST IN SPACE.
I SHUT DOWN THE COMPUTER, TO THINK.

I PUSHED BACK IN MY CHAIR AND TOOK A SIP OF COFFEE. AND ANOTHER. I CHECKED THE VIEW OUT THE WINDOW: STILL DARK, STILL CITY.

Three states of consciousness in twenty seconds. Two similar, the third not. But beneath, underneath, inside, through them - was something - and it wasn't coffee, or its smell, or the smell of slush on grimy streets.

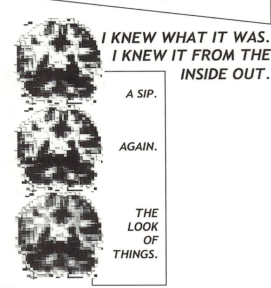

I KNEW WHAT IT WAS. I KNEW IT FROM THE INSIDE OUT.

A SIP.

AGAIN.

THE LOOK OF THINGS.

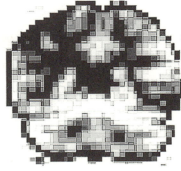

THIS IS WHAT I AM. MIRANDA SHARPE, AN EVER-SHIFTING PATTERN IN THE DARK.

I IMAGINED THE LABYRINTH AT WORK ON THE PATTERNS OF ME.

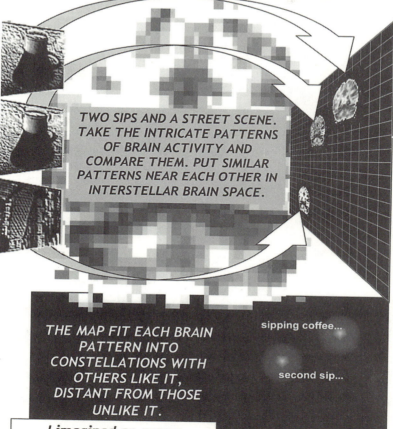

TWO SIPS AND A STREET SCENE.
TAKE THE INTRICATE PATTERNS
OF BRAIN ACTIVITY AND
COMPARE THEM. PUT SIMILAR
PATTERNS NEAR EACH OTHER IN
INTERSTELLAR BRAIN SPACE.

THE MAP FIT EACH BRAIN
PATTERN INTO
CONSTELLATIONS WITH
OTHERS LIKE IT,
DISTANT FROM THOSE
UNLIKE IT.

sipping coffee...

second sip...

looking at dark city,
wondering about
consciousness

*I imagined an arrow
swooping like a blackbird
through the labyrinth.
It says,
"YOU ARE HERE!"
in a point that gets its
meaning from the map. The
labyrinth was the pattern
of all patterns.
Out to the edge of being.
"You are here."*

I WAS READY TO
OPEN THE
LAPTOP AGAIN
AND TAKE A
SECOND LOOK.

THE GALAXY OF BRAINS FLICKERED BACK TO LIFE...

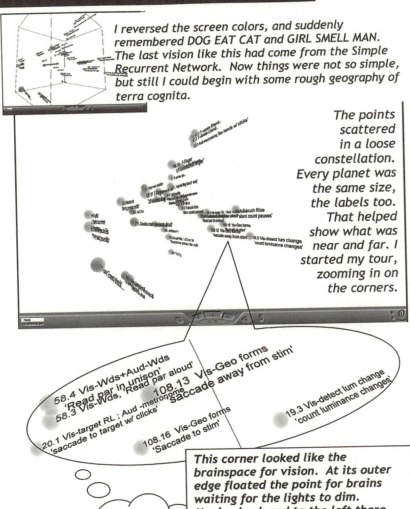

I reversed the screen colors, and suddenly remembered DOG EAT CAT and GIRL SMELL MAN. The last vision like this had come from the Simple Recurrent Network. Now things were not so simple, but still I could begin with some rough geography of terra cognita.

The points scattered in a loose constellation. Every planet was the same size, the labels too. That helped show what was near and far. I started my tour, zooming in on the corners.

58.4 Vis-Wds+Aud-Wds
'Read par in unison'
58.3 Vis-Wds, 'Read par aloud'
20.1 Vis-target RL ; Aud -metronome
'saccade to target w/ clicks'
108.13 Vis-Geo forms
'saccade away from stim'
108.16 Vis-Geo forms
'Saccade to stim'
19.3 Vis-detect lum change
'count luminance changes'

What do you read while someone else is reading you?

This corner looked like the brainspace for vision. At its outer edge floated the point for brains waiting for the lights to dim. Moving back and to the left there was more to see and do: Move your eyes, or read paragraphs aloud. So far the map kept similar tasks near each other.

At the summit, or perhaps the pit, of Brainspace, subjects felt the buzz.
Body parts mingled politely in the Zone of Touch. Dropping down, I
noticed that lips felt the joy buzzer too.

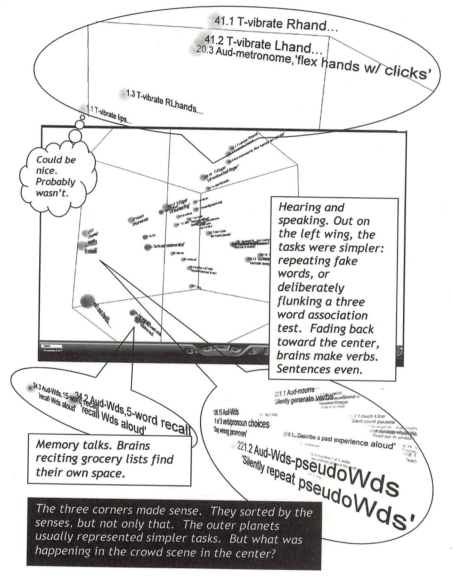

41.1 T-vibrate Rhand…

41.2 T-vibrate Lhand…
20.3 Aud-metronome, 'flex hands w/ clicks'

1.3 T-vibrate RLhands…

1.1 T-vibrate lips…

Could be
nice.
Probably
wasn't.

Hearing and
speaking. Out on
the left wing, the
tasks were simpler:
repeating fake
words, or
deliberately
flunking a three
word association
test. Fading back
toward the center,
brains make verbs.
Sentences even.

34.3 Aud-Wds, 15-word recall 'recall Wds aloud'
34.2 Aud-Wds, 5-word recall 'recall Wds aloud'

221.1 Aud-nouns 'Silently generate verbs'

108.15 Aud-Wds
1 of 3 verb/pronoun choices
'Say wrong pronoun'

219.1…'Describe a past experience aloud'

Memory talks. Brains
reciting grocery lists find
their own space.

221.2 Aud-Wds-pseudoWds
'Silently repeat pseudoWds'

The three corners made sense. They sorted by the
senses, but not only that. The outer planets
usually represented simpler tasks. But what was
happening in the crowd scene in the center?

I pushed ahead between the list-remembering brains. At the core I found the place where three ways met. My view reached up beyond hot vibrating lips into the zone of touch, and to the right down into the eyes at work.

In the center, the three branches mingled. Eyes swung back and forth still; mouths spoke; and the poking and prodding continued. But even here the different activities of seeing, hearing, and touching pulled their moons toward the three corners. Planet itch was there, and after scratching there were other jobs for arms.

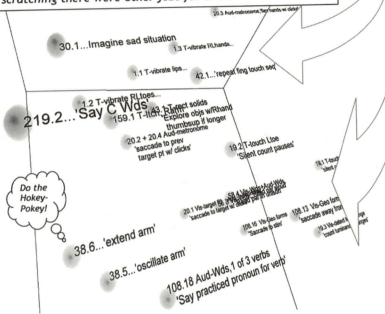

I nudged the mouse and set the universe into a slow spin. I had spent two years in graduate school sorting labels into piles: subject vs. object; mind vs. body; body vs. world; perception vs. action. As I looked across the nebula, none of these big distinctions seemed quite right. Each planet overlapped both sides of every 'vs.' All the pattern planets were ways of interacting with the world, and the whole map showed bodies animating perception while perception illuminated bodies. The world and I get along. We collaborate with hands, with eyes, with ears and lips. Our getting along is the world; it's me, too. I make the world that makes me.

"The brain from the brain's own point of view," *said the website. The map of Brainspace was based on hundreds of blips sprinkled across the brain. You couldn't read the blip patterns by themselves, not all at once. So the hyperdimensional headshrinker used the patterns to turn brains into points on a map, and the spatial relationships between the planets showed similarities and dissimilarities between the brains.*

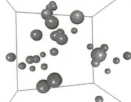

But you could look at the same map as the **mind from the** *mind's own point of view.* *Thinking about the tasks as experiences turned the map into the virtual reality version of the thrill of phenomenology, built around a semester of Psych. 101 experiments. Then near and far on the map captured likeness and difference of experience.*

So this neon world went two ways at once. Each moon was a brain pattern, but it worked just as well to think of it as a conscious experience. The brain map and phenomenology fit each other, G. Zamm meets E. Husserl. **Brainspace was also mindspace,** *and from the look of it you couldn't tell which of the parallel universes you were in. All this was built on a guess that distributed representations were the fabric of consciousness. Real physical consciousness in the squishy gray folds of the brain.*

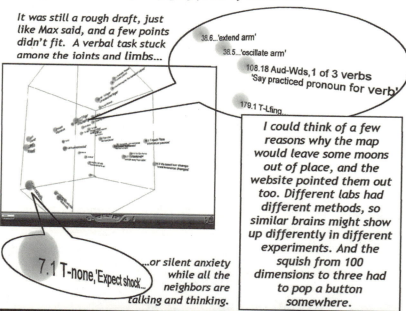

It was still a rough draft, just like Max said, and a few points didn't fit. A verbal task stuck among the joints and limbs...

38.6...'extend arm'

38.5...'oscillate arm'

108.18 Aud-Wds,1 of 3 verbs
'Say practiced pronoun for verb'

179.1 T-Lfing...

I could think of a few reasons why the map would leave some moons out of place, and the website pointed them out too. Different labs had different methods, so similar brains might show up differently in different experiments. And the squish from 100 dimensions to three had to pop a button somewhere.

7.1 T-none,'Expect shock...

...or silent anxiety while all the neighbors are talking and thinking.

I stood up, stretched, and walked to the window.

"What do you see?" Max had asked.

Outside the window, snow again,
falling in fat flakes. The city
disappeared behind them. I thought
again about last night.

"What do you see?"

During a storm like this, Max had seen
the Labyrinth, and now it was my
turn. A screen full of shapes. Clues
to find a mind in the brain.

"What do you see?"

Of course with him everything was its opposite.
Whatever he *saw*, it wasn't *on screen*.

"What do you see?"

See the unseen. Remember what may have been forgotten.
My relentless day had sprung a new dimension on me with every
encounter. I thought about the line-up: Lucid - Fescue - Marlov -
Elman - Zamm - and now the Wiz behind the Labyrinth. All of them
obsessed with a plunge into the unseen dimensions of mind. From
three to infinity. I felt the unfolding of new worlds, felt it in my
bones, in my toes. Each twist of the plot turned me inside out too.
This must be the thrill of neurophenomenology.

I sat again and pulled open a drawer. The
monad Max had given me lay on top of a jam
of folders. I put it on the desk next to the
keyboard, and it sucked desk, computer,
mug, light, and me into its shining.

Rising behind everything, like a
shadow on the clouds, was Max. I had
always been one dimension behind
him. We all were. But now my toes
hung over his brink. I had arrived at
his last known whereabouts, the real
scene of the crime.

Turning to the computer again, I backed away from the planets until I had them all pleasantly framed on the screen, a nice table arrangement for a zero-gravity dining room. All the little alephs. There were many spheres, many alephs, crisp and gleaming. But Max had been specific, singular. One aleph.

I zoomed in to my new personal favorite.

The planet of the day, I decided. In this experiment, subjects were warned to expect an unpleasant shock. But it never came. An entire planet for anxiety. My home world at last.

7.1 T-none,'Expect shock'...

I set my monad on the keyboard. The shiny sphere reflected everything, but the globe on screen was a radiant blank, a mirror that reflected exactly nothing. Or maybe, I thought, it reflected everything, but blurred it all together.

Blurry. Max had said that about his vision too. It took half a minute for a scanner to make each brain image to be funneled into the Labyrinth. Perhaps the screen sphere was the image of consciousness itself, but it was a time exposure. Like any time exposure, the image had erased time. Movement and change fuzzed into a blurry blob, or a wisp, or nothing at all.

Time to stop thinking. I closed my eyes and hugged my knees against my chest, ready for the light touch of the universe to reach into me. Slowly an arc of darkness grew and spread into a circle, and then a sphere, a pure vision where there could be no light. I kept my mind perfectly still. The sphere grew. I drew it toward me, conjuring it like a cloud of smoke. Its glowing curve grew to the size of an earth, the event horizon flattened out to an infinite edge, and like a drop of water into a sea, I fell through the looking glass.

I already knew what I would find.

Look at snow...

Radiance surrounded me. Hovering ahead, the worlds of consciousness repeated themselves, the worlds inside the world.

*Instead of the blur of a brain scan, I imagined the anatomy of a single instant, a glance of snow outside my window. The momentary look of snow was many possible experiences. There were many ways to see exactly **this**. How the flakes looked depended on how you got there.*

looking at snow after discovering boyfriend is a moron...
looking at snow after discovering advisor is a moron.
looking at snow after a romantic dinner (dream on).
looking at snow after peering into monad...
looking at snow after pulling all-nighter

Seeing snow was one sort of experience after pondering a monad, another after your advisor had meddled with your existence, and another still after a romantic dinner (if only). The past endured in every experience, and difference in the past lingered in the way things seemed Now. A different past meant a difference in the brain, tweaking the coordinates in hyperspace. The map I saw in the darkness inside me had more points than a galaxy has stars.

Looking at snow after peering into monad after thinking about Seth...
Looking at snow after peering into monad after finding Max again...
Looking at snow after peering into monad after escaping lesion land...
looking at snow after peering into monad after feeding cat...
looking at snow after peering into monad after cleaning litter box

*Inside **Looking at snow after peering into monad** was another subuniverse. Many different pasts led there.*

There was no limit to how far down the zoom could reach. **Looking at snow after pondering a monad after escaping from lesion land...** *was another way to be in the moment of seeing snow. My consciousness in the present was inflected with a trace of the instant just past, which was itself inflected by the instant just before that.*

All these modifications were worlds within worlds packed into the hyperspace of a hundred billion neurons. But as the map unfolded and unfolded the mind still fit the brain. The blurry blobs of scanner subjects repeating random pronouns resolved endlessly into the particularity of this pronoun, I, reverberating here and now with the echoes of every instant of my conscious past.

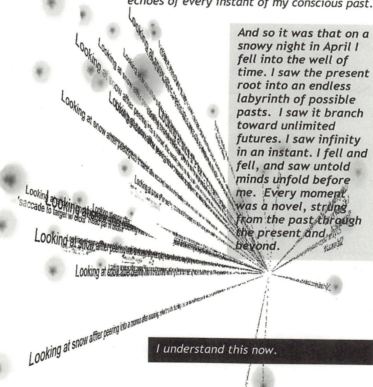

And so it was that on a snowy night in April I fell into the well of time. I saw the present root into an endless labyrinth of possible pasts. I saw it branch toward unlimited futures. I saw infinity in an instant. I fell and fell, and saw untold minds unfold before me. Every moment was a novel, strung from the past through the present and beyond.

I understand this now.

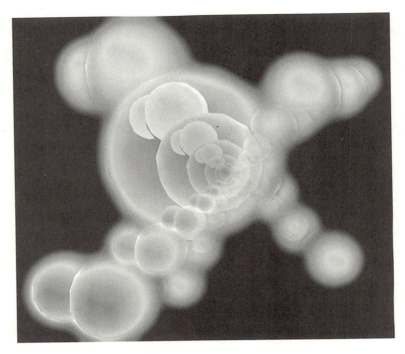

Then I opened my eyes. Snowflakes filled the space beyond the window. But they were no longer falling. They hung in absolute stillness and silence, some near, some far. I gazed in wonder.

The cat yowled. I don't know whether she saw what I saw, or just saw me seeing it. I pulled her into my lap, wrapped myself around her, and lightly pressed my lips to her fuzzy skull.

14

Many links led back from this galaxy far, far away. One of them was labeled "Discussion," which I followed into a chat room of sorts. I was the first in the door, it seemed. The only message was by Lloyd:

> I hope you enjoyed the virtual world. I'm eager to discuss its interpretation, and especially eager to address the technical issues. Please click on "reply" to enter the discussion.

I did. I wrote:

> Hey Dr. Lloyd. I get it. Do you also consider your map a theory of consciousness?
> yours,
> Miranda Sharpe (WU 2nd year grad student—philosophy.)

My head was spinning, but I wanted to weave some more brainspace. In the constellations of consciousness, I'd seen spiral shells and cornucopia, vaults and scoops, corkscrews and tubes. A little art therapy would be just right before turning in.

But before I resumed my cruise, I did the dutiful grad student thing: I popped my disk into the computer and downloaded the whole new universe before me. You're mine, all mine!

The Powerbook beeped its burp, the browser bounced me back to the chat. To my surprise, there was a reply to my message:

Dear Miranda Sharpe,
Thanks for your message. I'm intrigued by your question. I regard my model as a model of cognition, and really don't know what to say about consciousness. But I know that it's a big issue. If you have any thoughts, please do post them.
thanks again for your interest,
Dan Lloyd

I looked at my watch—9 PM. Time to let my fingers do the thinking.

Dear Dr. Lloyd,
You are working late. I think you've got consciousness on the map for a number of reasons. The first reel of any theory of consciousness has to explain why brains have it and fast laptops do not. I'm just figuring this part out for myself. I don't know much about neurons, but I don't think there's anything special about a single neuron as far as consciousness goes. It's dumb as a jellyfish, right?—just a squishy transistor. So neurons don't really matter in particular, but their networks do. This idea of distributed representation. That's big. Once many many neurons are on the same team, they can play in many many many (many squared?) formations. You need that, because conscious states of mind are so complex, every minute's a movie, every second a slice of life.

The screen hovered before me like a magic window, weightless and free. It sliced through the air in another dimension beyond the edgy shapes (and cat) on the desk. I flattened my hand on it, just a light touch. The light flooded around my fingers and wrist. So thin! So familiar. I could feel the radiant cool plane lightly on my palm and fingers, but I still felt that I was pushing through the looking glass. "They're in here," I said aloud, to nobody in particular. My voice surprised me. In pitch, my words made three quick rising, sliding hops, ending in an *rrr* with the texture of cigarette smoke. "Here," I said again, to hear the R. "Here? Here." My brain, purring.

Now you've taken some of those many dimensions and some of many possible perceptual states and worked out the plan of the neighborhood. Because you started with patterns in the brain, doing nothing to sort or label them before they squeezed through your multidimensional mapifier process, your map is based on the brain's innards and nothing but. That's the right warm-up for a theory of consciousness too. The brain is stuck inside the head after all. It can't step outside to compare its current neural state with outer reality. All it can do is measure itself against other states of itself. So, for a sensation of touch to be felt as touch can only mean that it is like other sensations of touch, and unlike sights and sounds. That "likeness" of course is not a single scale, but measured along who knows how many dimensions. Your map shows these likeness/difference relations in three condensed dimensions.

If consciousness really is a brain process, then states of the brain will show the distinctions among states of consciousness.

So you've got the right approach.

I pulled an ashtray and pack of cigarettes toward me on the desk. Tapped out a cigarette, changed my mind, and set it and the pack down.

And, as I cruise the space, it works out well. At first I thought the senses clumped up, but it's more complicated than that. I do see seeing, hearing, and touching in their own territories, more or less. But it isn't the sense that matters, it's what you use each sense for. For example, several experiments involve rhythm and repetition. Some you watch, some you hear, some you see. These hang out at the bottom of the cube. Others involve language, and hover toward the top and back, even though some are reading, and some are hearing. As you float from left to right, the focus shifts from passive perception to active or thoughtful response. And so forth.

So I asked, why is that? The answer comes from phenomenology. One of the thrills of phenomenology is the point that two experiences can come in through the same sense, but be radically different. Even good old Aristotle had this one right, when he pointed out that we hate to see dead bodies in reality, but actually get excited about the prospect in a good movie (well, for him, stage play). (I know what he means.) The exact same visual sensations can have radically different meanings. At the same time, two experiences can come in from different senses and have similar, overlapping phenomenology—reading words and hearing them, for example.

So you wouldn't want them in a clump, suggesting that everything visual (for example) was more or less the same. But you wouldn't want them scattered all over at random either—then it would mean nothing to us that they were visual—there wouldn't be anything in common to all our moments of seeing. But a region in brainspace allows for some sort of common ground among types of experiences. They can be close, not quite the same, but not absolutely different either.

There are always differences between what we see and how we see it. And what we do next. But these can never be detached from each other. They are all part of the consciousness of any object or situation.

I paused to breathe, scratch the cat, reach for the ceiling, and answer her purr with an alto groan.

As I reread this, I see that I've loaded a lot of phenomenology on you.

I was pretty loaded with phenomenology myself. I thought of the nasty red folder, Maxwell Grue's star-crossed poetics of consciousness. The thrill of phenomenology was beginning to look like it had a home in the brain after all.

The point is, we can see ourselves as comets moving through your VR world. The map you've made is a theory of consciousness—a theory you can hang on your wall, like the periodic table. Or at least it's on the way. It bridges the two realms of mind and brain in a point-for-point mapping of one to the other. The map of the brain is the map of the world of experience (the only world there is). Oz at last. (You can tell I'm a graduate student, no? :))

I don't know quite how to get this down yet, but it seems to me, after a really long day, that what the mind is doing is multidimensional scaling. Think about it. A vast shifting pixel pretzel of sensory inputs, news from all over. That's a lot of dimensions. Zillions. Just to get along in the world you'd have to shrink the space.

Maybe the space was shrinking, but I felt vast, like an angelic flame licking the corners of the universe. Words were not enough. But, snaking down my screen, they were all I had, and as I sank into them, they were all I was.

Like a wolf or a little cat, I sank my teeth into the words of consciousness. The me is the message.

The beauty of this beast of multidimensional scaling is that it's a shell game. You start with one world and a pigpile of variable dimensions. Fold, massage, pound, and presto: a map of a new world. But in a critical way, it's like the old world. That's because all the objects in the old world have counterparts in the new world, and counterparts are related to each other in the same way in both worlds. What was alike in the old world remains alike in the new. MDS preserves the structure of the world, in its now. It ignores origins and consequences, describing each object only as it is, and through each new scaling hangs on to the structure of the world, the skeleton of Being.

Each state of consciousness is what it is. Literally, each one is a pattern of agitated neurons, a point in hyperspace—like you say in your website. The pattern is all there is. What it is like to be that pattern can't be tagged by anything from outside, because for consciousness nothing is outside. And since the pattern is nothing but antsy neurons there is nothing that is intrinsic to it that would lead you to interpret it one way over another. What there is, is just other patterns, and all the patterns taken together fall in a structure, a map, the map of the world. And like any map, there are blank spaces; there must be, or the space could not be shrunk. We interpret each pattern only by exploring its similarities and dissimilarities to others. What it is like to be in a certain state of consciousness equals where that state falls on the map equals where that state sits in the space that is the world.

Multidimensional mapmaking is a process that morphs states of consciousness into new states, new maps with fewer dimensions. But it is true to the basic structure of the world, cinema vérité, because the structure stays nearly the same through every morph. The structure is the grid on which the new properties hang, the properties that are not given by eyes and ears but are put there by the mind. These new properties can be anything: the specs for a bodily response; the prediction of the next second or the next decade; a picture; a thousand words. Reality itself. Any of these could be a subset of the shrunken map. (Shrink too much and you get a stress fracture. That is, you get it wrong. A pie in the face.)

Not only that, it seems to me that a recurrent network really could do big, fast multidimensional scaling. It can compare the present in the past, locating you on the map by telling you where you've been. The brain could do it.

Brainiac maniac. I was feeling like a stress fracture myself. I rubbed my eyes.

There's more to be said. Hope to hear from you,
Miranda S.

Sent it. As the words sank into my past, I saw what lay ahead. Time. The past in the present. The brain has to keep many layers of the past alive at every instant. It isn't enough that an itch is different from reciting words that begin with C. You *experience* the difference. The difference appears in the instant too. It appears in the instant as the flashback within the story of your consciousness, C-word one second, scratching the next. The brain is a story. The brain knows its story. It knows it all at once.

That was the paradox of the day, I thought. The instant of conscious life has no duration. Like a point. But packed into the instant is history and expectation, the time line. Consciousness is the line and the point, the warp of space and time. Multidimensionality lives!

The labyrinth of cognition couldn't show me that, because the brain images were all time exposures. And combinations of pictures from many people for each experiment. The map blurred it all together. Just as Max had said, the image was blurry.

I pulled a piece of paper over next to the computer, and idly sketched a thought balloon, a lumpy circle that also looked a bit like a brain. I looked at my watch, and wrote 9:32 under the squiggle. Holly was watching, and I met her gaze. Then I drew a cat icon in my brain balloon, two stacked circles with triangle ears and whiskers. Now it was 9:33, and in honor of the occasion I drew another empty mind-space to the right of the first. The two brain sketches were like two of Lloyd's planets, one point in hyperspace, one pattern, and then another. My story, the thrill of phenomenology.

I drew an arrow from my 9:32 brain to my 9:33. And looked out the window, toward the tenement across the street. A neon sign on my side reflected over there in several windows, but the old glass warped the cool red letters into scraps and wraiths, like frozen flames, lurking magically behind the window frames. As I moved my head from side to side, I could make the glowing streaks undulate.

I drew a few windows, plain rectangles, inside 9:33. But 9:33 had to include 9:32. The cat continued on in consciousness as a ghost of time, even while the here and now moved on to new thrills. So I drew a little version of 9:32 on top of 9:33. To call it superposition would be flattering, but that was the idea. It looked messy enough, and got messier still as I reflected that inside 9:32 was 9:31, and that it was the destiny of all the layers of 9:33 to carry on in 9:34.

A recurrent neural network *could* handle the pileup before me, and inside me. That was the lesson of Elman. But do I work that way? While you were busy mapping the brain, you'd want to find out. You'd want to know if this endlessly growing tail of the past showed up in the brain scanner. If it did, that would suggest that the brain scans were images of consciousness itself, mind meets brain.

I looked at my watch again, and was surprised that barely a minute had passed. Husserl had talked about the flow of time, an endless flux. The thrill of phenomenology was the thrill of constant, endless change. While I read, it flows. While I generate verbs, it flows. While you vibrate my toes, or lips: flows. And when I return to those tasks, doing them again and again, I don't really return to the exact same state. I'm downriver, always and forever downriver. It flows.

I returned to the cyberchat. No reply from Lloyd, so I could fold my speculations directly into our dialogue. I described the issue of internal time, and the expectation that flow is the dominant feature of consciousness in its brainy form, just as it is in phenomenology. So . . .

Is there any way to look at finer time slices in your brain scans? I mean, could you see what happens while I look at a blinking red light, then blue, then red again? The idea is that you could figure out the differences between those images, and plot a map that shows how we move through time, independently of what the task is. The phenomenology suggests that we are continually moving along in hyperspace, not backtracking.

I turned the page of doodles over, and drew a circle. And inside that, another circle, and so on, tunneling into the past.

His reply came shortly:

Interesting! The PET studies don't do what you want, but fMRI (functional magnetic resonance imaging) does. Over the last few weeks I've been trying to repeat the hypermaps for series of images for the same subject—sometimes we'll get a thousand images of one brain, taken every two seconds. The plan was to show the subject moving in and out of regions of the map while the subject did red light then blue then red again, etc. But it wouldn't work. Why? Because they don't backtrack! It's like you said, the flow is always forward. You can measure it in fMRI. Thanks for this connection!

Well, I thought, that's the first good thing that's happened today. I let all my thoughts fly away free, like doves, and sat in a contented emptiness. I sighed and rolled my shoulders. I thought about getting up and doing something, but then again the chair had never been cozier. I let myself sink and slump for a moment. Forget about good posture, for once.

I had a hunch that there was more to be mined in the labyrinth of me, Miranda Sharpe, human being. So I wheeled back to the computer and clicked again on the link. And suddenly I got a 404 error—file not found. I frowned, and returned to the discussion.

Dr. Lloyd,
Did you just move the VR file?
Miranda

After a minute, I noticed I was staring at a blank screen. I went into the bathroom with no particular plan. Drank a glass of water. That felt like progress. Wrinkled my nose at HG's recent contributions, scooped same into the toilet. Poured some new litter into her box. Observed cloud of clay dust. Ick. Worse than cigarette smoke? I wondered. Then, brushed hair and fixed ponytail. Grooming the world. I opened another diet something, returned to the computer, and finally lit that cigarette.

I wondered about Lloyd, so I relaunched the browser and googled him. There were two or three of him, including a football player. All I had to do was add the word "consciousness" to his name, and I had the right Dan Lloyd in my crosshairs. He was a regular at various conferences about philosophy and cognitive science. Popped up in journals here and there. Spent time in Finland. Trinity College PR wrote him up in a little feature.

He made bread for his students. Took them to Boston to see the Turing Test live. Taught a course called Minds and Brains. He was married to another professor. Two kids, apparently little ones. I wondered if they were boys or girls. Probably one of each. That would be the normal thing to do, and this was a man with a Ph.D. in Normalness. His labyrinth was there on the Google list, just where I had seen it, but it was still missing when I tried to launch it.

The computer beeped. I got mail.

Miranda,
I have no idea what happened to it. Only copy!
yours in enormous frustration,
dan

Timely me:

Dan,
Not to worry. I made a copy. Just give me your email and I'll attach it.
Miranda

What a Girl Scout. I hit "submit." But the screen and all its words simply vanished. No more chat. No more chat room. I typed the URL of his home page, but that too came up empty. A search of the Trinity site showed no Lloyd anything. The guy's been deleted. Just my luck. I must have magic file-corrupting fingers!

The phone rang. "Well, this has been some evening, hasn't it, HG?" I said to the cat.

It was Dan Lloyd. His voice was just a bit nasal, with something midwestern or even Appalachian in it—just a bit slow, just a bit drawly. He had gotten my number from the phone book. He apologized three times for calling, but he was clearly very upset about the lost file.

"I can't figure it out," he said, with that edge of desperation. "I did all my work on the file server. It seems fine, but everything I've done is just gone. Backups, folders, the whole nine yards."

"Yeah, I noticed."

There was a pause. He was digesting what it meant to be disappeared from the World Wide Web. "Do you know how many months it took to build that site?"

"Didn't you get my email?" He hadn't. "Well, I downloaded it. I have a copy you can copy." Mother Theresa strikes.

"You do? You do?" I imagined a guy grabbing his forehead with amazement.

"Yeah. I always download the good stuff."

"That's great. That's so great."

Yay me. "That's OK."

Another pause. "Do you mind if I ask you something?"

The bells rang, but then I remembered the Lloyd files: Mr. Domestic. Dr. Dad. "Sure, go ahead," I said brightly.

"Are you a night person or a morning person?"

"A night person. Most definitely."

"I know we haven't met, and I know this is a really strange request. But would you consider giving me a chance to copy that file tonight? I could meet you someplace, anyplace. Anyplace with a computer. I won't be able to sleep until I've copied it about ten more times, and buried at least one in concrete."

I smiled. "Sure." This city being what it is, it lacked a cybercafé scene, and I couldn't bear to breathe the stress of a campus computer center. I knew he'd never suggest the obvious alternative. Finally I said, "Look, where do you live?"

It turned out not to be far, just up the mountain a ways. I would make the guy's night. Maybe his professor wife could be an academic role model for me. Maybe I could babysit. But, I thought, anybody who doesn't compulsively back up files is probably a loser. I would try to like him anyway.

I closed the computer and popped it into my backpack. It felt good to be leaving. This crazed day had been a tightening noose. At every turn, it had been, follow me into the Casbah. Each popup character had been more sinister than the last. Except for Gordon of course. But by the conventions of this destiny, he had to be either a murderer or a technoterrorist, and the nasty little clue was buried somewhere in my interaction with him, like an old land mine. Probably somewhere on the Web he'd written a fiction featuring *me,* right down to the bra and panties, and in Gordon's universe I probably spent most of my time panting consonants.

Now the game was up, up by the simple gesture of grabbing my car keys and dropping in on a *regular* person, someone without Motive, Means, and Opportunity. Trinity College, a haven of nice folks in rumpled sweaters, cruising the wild frontiers of human knowledge. I'm off; please don't forward my calls.

What I had left out of my reverie was yet another snowstorm. Some April! I swept the snow off the side window, and let the wipers handle the windshield. I remembered the Donner Party, but also remembered the distraught professor at Trinity whose nifty website was hanging on by a thread. It wasn't far, and the snow wasn't really sticking. I could think of it as rain with attitude. With my wipers furiously flapping, I plunged into the white night.

As I left downtown, snowlumps streamed passed the car like points in mind-space. Here comes a squall of serial murderers! Did Porfiry's MDS application make any sense? I wasn't sure. It would depend on the dimensions. How would you know? One way I could think of—if it works. I didn't know about the cosmonaut of crime, but a quick tour of the site I'd just seen certainly showed the kind of fit the sleuth of consciousness would like to see.

Max had seen the site/sight too. Maybe he downloaded it—he and I were both packrats. And Max was deleted. And Lloyd's files too. Now the wet flakes really were serial killers, and disk crashers too! I felt suddenly as though the world fell away beneath me as I rose through the infinite starfield, infinite worlds. My apartment was unsafe. Mr. X, whomever that was, had me staked out. I was only safe here in hyperspace.

My car shimmied a bit at the tail, yanking me back to the job. I slowed, and turned on the light to read the directions Lloyd had given over the phone. It wasn't hard. Fortunately, all the other fools were in bed, hibernating until this fake spring total winter gave up. In a few minutes I pulled up at the stately mansion of my destiny for the evening. Nobody followed. Nobody knew.

15

It looked like a barn. Actually, it was a barn. A little barn, suitable for sheep and goats, with a stone chimney splaying sooty smoke into the thick air. I knocked, then pounded on the aluminum screen door.

"Hi," he said. "Come on in." I stepped into a small kitchen, stamping my feet on the doormat. "I'm Dan," he said, sticking out his hand. He was in middle age, in the middle of many ages, with a white beard from King Lear and the fierce tired eyes of Hannibal Lecter, but the skinny legs and butt of a JV swimmer. His two eras met in the baby potbelly of a recently promoted lawyer. "You must be Miranda."

I nodded, and pulled off my fuzzy hat, shaking loose my hair, which I drew into a quick ponytail.

The kitchen, portal to the manor, was prehistoric perfection. Being polite, I said, "I love avocado," which was true in a general way, but after thirty years or so avocado appliances slip toward unpleasanter kinds of green. The yellow drawer hardware, the chocolate wood—all this would have to go.

"Thank you," said Lloyd, with apparent sincerity or really subtle irony. He took my coat and hung it by the door. "Come on in." Two mugs sat on the counter next to a thermos. He offered me a cup of tea, but I said no thanks.

He led me across a few squares of linoleum, and then we were in the living room, a very different place. To my left a huge stone fireplace rose up into the dark rafters of a cathedral ceiling. It was certainly a barn, but the fireplace reminded me of Xanadu. Two love seats faced each other in front of the hearth, each with an end table covered with framed photographs. Across the room I could see a long wooden table with two green shaded library lamps, casting warm pools of light. Behind that, a wall of French doors and hints of snowflakes outside. I was drawn toward the photographs, always my first stop in a new house. The shrine. Lloyd's collection pummeled me with Happy Family: the striking wife, the two girls, each cute as a button. Many cute poses: infants in shades, toddlers in bunny suits, yard apes on mountain peaks. Each one reassured me that I, a single woman travelling alone after 9 PM in a snowstorm without a can of pepperspray, had stumbled into a teeming nest of utter heartwarming normalness. Lloyd himself appeared in few pictures. He was obviously the Happy Family photographer. He even had his camera sitting out on one end table, poised for the next cute moment.

I told him he had an adorable family, and he agreed. I understood why movies usually don't linger with happy families, except to give the psychos or germs something to toy with. "Are the kids asleep?"

"No," he said. "They're with their mother visiting Grammy and Poppy and the Air and Space Museum." Too bad for the psycho. Too bad, or at least a little weird, for me. My errand of mercy could be a quick one. I considered turning one of the attractive wife pix in our general direction, just to keep an eye on things.

"I hope you didn't have any trouble getting here," he said.

"None. I like snow."

"Well, it certainly is wonderful of you to make the trip. I worked on that website for months. I only posted it yesterday."

"Yeah, but how is it that there was only one copy?"

"There was another, but my daughters needed some *Arthur* along to survive the drive to Virginia. It was the only disk I had, so I wrote over it. I figured that the file server was safe."

"Optimistic, I think."

"I guess so!"

I swung my pack onto the couch, and pulled out the disk. "Perhaps this will refresh your memory."

He smiled at me. "Oh boy," he said. "Am I glad or what." With reverence he took the disk and turned toward an open staircase along the fireplace wall. "My study is upstairs." He took a step back to let me lead.

"No thanks," I said. "I'll just wait down here until you make the copy."

"Oh. Of course." And with the stiffness of embarrassment he walked across the room and up the stairs. I settled into the couch, happy to be alone, and pondered the house as yet another bourgeois future for Miranda Sharpe. Would I do it like this? Maybe. The ornate old clock on the mantle was a keeper. I also liked the lights—tiny spots hung along paired cables that ran just under the beams.

Suddenly the admirable lights died. I was peering into the dark, save for a faint glow of embers in the fireplace. Another in my day of nasty jokes. I stood up, turned toward the kitchen, and listened. Somewhere above me a muffled voice said, "Shoot." "Hey," he called out. "Are the lights out down there?"

I told him they were. I liked the house quite a lot less in darkness. I heard Lloyd come downstairs, quickly, but not so fast for the last few steps.

From the landing he asked where I was, and when I told him, he apologized for not having a flashlight. Clearly, another Boy Scout dropout. His wife must go crazy.

I thought for a moment. Once before I got through a power failure without a flashlight. It was simple. I sat again and reached into my pack and popped open my Powerbook on the couch beside me. A phosphorescent glow shimmered over my end of the room. Blue Lloyd took a second to figure it out. "Well," he said. "At least we can see a little." He sat on the couch opposite, as far from me as possible, with the disk on his knee. I was relieved to see that the mood lighting made him almost as uncomfortable as me.

"Did you make the copy?" I asked.

"No, darn it. This is the story of my life. Always almost. I guess I'll have to wait."

"I don't see why. We can use my Powerbook."

"Good thinking!" I wished the men in my life were as easy to please as this puppy. He jumped up and cleared one of the end tables, which he dragged in front of me to make a little desk. I set the computer there, and slipped in my disk universe. I would copy the disk onto my hard drive, and leave the original and the website it contained with him.

The Powerbook burped, froze, crashed. The sad little Mac face, exactly as I had seen it in Grue's office. My face must have looked like glacier ice, because Lloyd looked like a day-old stroke. He sat beside me with a determined hmmm. "Maybe it's just the Chaos Bug," he conjectured. "I've heard that if you reset everything is normal again."

"Yeah." The Thing had arrived. It's only bits, I told myself. Bits and hysteria. "That's what they want, isn't it? A reset."

"They?"

"Notice anything funny about the screen?"

"Yes," he said, "it's kaput. Lights out. Clunkamunk."

Clunkamunk? "Lights out for system ten. But this is an OS twelve machine." I could see he wasn't following. "They changed the system failure graphic after system ten. If my system crashed, it wouldn't look like this."

He pointed at my screen, a long silhouette of finger. "But it's crashed."

"I don't think it has. Something else is using the graphic. Someone wants me, wants everyone, to think their machines have crashed."

"Who? Why?"

"I don't know. I don't know. The image is a fake, and a lure." To what? To drink? To throw your Mac out the window? It was a nice thought, but if you want to bring a nerd to his or her knees, you have to really kill the machine, not just pretend. This bug could be debugged with a simple restart. A sneeze, a blink. My host was trying hard not to show his exasperation, just as I was trying hard to ignore him. "Something is happening here, but what?" I said. "It's not messing with memory, or the operating system. I don't even think a virus could anymore. So what's going on?"

"Maybe it's just a prank. Someone wrote a virus to give the world a little panic attack, or maybe Apple did it themselves so that they could flash their startup ad."

That was an interesting thought, but with the current machines the restart was too fast to see much of anything. "Wait," I said. "What happens when you restart? I mean, what can change then? And only then."

"Oh, I get it. They want you to restart so some nasty little system file takes effect."

"Or something."

"Well," he said, "nowadays it's all standardized. The OS reads all the extensions and preferences, and opens the startup systems—the wireless

Internet uplinks, hypertext editor, browser updaters, virus checker. Oh, there's the rub. The virus checker would block any file rewrite, or ask if you wanted to proceed."

I stared at the frowny Mac. I'd swallowed the OS X icon as the real thing just a few hours ago. Now it looked as dated as an avocado kitchen. It even looked grainy, like it was blown up from some thumbnail. As if the screen resolution had changed. I wondered why the bad guys would settle for a grainy icon when they surely had the original graphic? What would Sandra Bullock do? Pop in a disk, hit a key, fake a guy into destroying his own system. What if this icon was a fake too, designed to fake you into launching a restart that wouldn't do anything?

"What if the restart is an illusion too?"

Lloyd looked at me. "Then it wouldn't restart."

"No no no," I said, mainly to myself. "It didn't crash. It doesn't have to restart. It's just a trick to get you to hit some keys, to make something happen." I looked up into the darkness, and the negative image of the scowling dead computer hung in black velvet like the ghost of Christmas yet to come, a retinal fake of my screen fake. How in the world would they deliver a dead Mac?

Suddenly I had an intuition that I was looking at the World Wide Web. "You're the Web gurus," I said, "you Trinity guys. How do you get the code for a page, the html and whatever? I mean, what's the shortcut?"

"Yeah, it's in the menu. I think it's command-U."

Command you too. I leaned over my possessed Powerbook. Three. Two. One. Command-U.

Opening night in the cinema hypertext! There was a page there. Html tags, xtml, brackets made the page look like confetti or a critique of Derrida. Only no text. Curiouser and curiouser. Lots that I didn't understand, but there was an image file. I slid the machine across the table to Lloyd. "I bet that gif image is our dead Mac icon. What do you make of the rest of it?"

"Yeah," he said after a moment. "It's an applet." He pointed to the bottom of the screen. "The page presents a single image, full screen. But this next line I've never seen. 'SCRES 1024x768.'"

"Screen resolution?"

"Yes. Probably," he said.

I nodded slowly. "This is what I think. I think our little Chaos Bug is sending a picture of a dead computer screen, a screen shot. And at the same time, it's changing the screen resolution so that the shot is too big to fit. The toolbars and browser and whatever are still there, but all over the edge, out of the frame. We see the middle, the little dead guy. That makes us hit the reset."

"So it's all happening on the Web? You never leave the browser?"

I nodded. "I logged on to evil demon dot com." But I hadn't. I reached for the computer. "May I?" He said sure, and shoved himself into the farthest corner of the couch. Instead of resetting, I typed the command to call up the control panels, and fixed the screen resolution. The dead computer icon sat squarely in the middle of a standard browser screen, like a photo of a corpse in a bowl of mints. The url said *<www.greenwichmean.net>*. I asked Lloyd if he had ever heard of it.

"It's about time?" he guessed.

I thought, isn't everything? I wound back through my day in cyberspace. I'd googled him. I'd visited his website. Now I glanced at him, his legs crossed at the ankles and angled toward the fireplace, to give me space. I was pretty sure he wasn't evil. Probably no genius either.

The mantle clock began to bong the hours. I checked the little clock in the corner of the browser. Ten on the dot.

"Time underlies many interesting human behaviors," I said, feeling very philosophical. He looked at me, and I nodded at the computer. "Evil demon dot com. It's a time site. Since browsers started to include clocks, they log on to these sites automatically to update the time and time zone. When you're not looking."

He pointed at the screen. "*That's* the Chaos Bug?"

"Yeah," I said. "Home page. Dr. Evil hacked into it. Instead of the correct time, you get bugged."

He made a sound halfway between whew and a whistle. "Almost all the new browsers have clocks."

I imagined a very long row of alarm clocks. I imagined them going off, one by one, a wave of jangles surging down the row like a chill up your spine. I swung the computer back toward him. "Read on, MacGuffin!" If my computer was in line for temporal abuse, I wanted to know what to expect.

He snorted like he got the reference, but without conviction. No soap, radio. He took off his glasses and leaned into the screen like it was sucking him in. Here was a man who could use some extra sleep. I thought that I should change my screen colors to something more flattering—a soft pink perhaps. "Ah," he said. "Here it is. This line reassigns command-control-delete. Makes it a write authorization."

"So, when you think you're restarting it, you're really authorizing it to jerk you around."

"So to speak."

"And then what happens?" I asked. Does it download your credit card numbers? Cancel your library fines? The wind rose and the house creaked ominously. Something banged against the outside, by the kitchen.

I startled, and he quickly said, "The storm door. 'Tis the wind and nothing more."

Freezing air swirled around my ankles and scuffed up a glow in the embers of the fireplace. Another slam came from the kitchen, louder and closer. He said, "The door must have blown open," and left the cool blue pool to take care of it. I'd read once that after about twenty minutes in the dark our eyes can see a candle at fifty miles. It had been at least that long since the power failure. I looked away from the screen and followed the afterimage into the radiant cool cascading darkness, infinitely distant and perfectly smothering. As the yellow blot faded, continents of furniture rose from the depths, with the shyness and intimacy of ghosts. To see this jiggly blackness was like touching all the known universe to your eyes. Another crash, sounding like a bucket of silverware hitting the floor—I heard it and saw stars. "Darn. Hit the dish drainer!" he called out as he closed the outer and inner doors. Then he was back on the couch beside me, looking for his place in the screen.

I shifted across the couch toward Lloyd and pressed my lower leg against his. That got his attention. I quickly pointed to the middle of the screen, and said, just a little too loud, "What do you make of this?" In complete confusion, he leaned in. Our heads were inches apart. I whispered, "There's someone in the room. Behind the big table." We both froze, still staring at the screen. The screen and the light it cast seemed infinitely tiny. The instant seemed infinitely long.

"What should we do?" he whispered back. I wanted to scream at him, You're the *guy*, damn it. Just do it.

"We need light," I whispered. I was beginning to feel silly, still pointing at the screen. "The fireplace. Can you make a torch?"

After another two-month second, he whispered, "OK." He slowly sat up, and eased the table away from both of us. "Let's see," he said, just a little too loudly too. "This xtml tag . . . it's a . . . it's a. . . ." He jumped and from somewhere in the darkness I heard the crunch of papers. I saw something eclipse the embers in the fireplace, and then light flared. Lloyd turned and rose like the Statue of Liberty, with a flickering roll of newspaper held overhead. I saw a figure shrink back from the light and wrap herself in a curtain beside one of the French doors. A woman. Lloyd saw her too.

"We know you're there," he said, and I wondered how I got Woody Allen as my knight in shining armor. "Come out, now."

From behind the curtain I heard, "Miranda, are you all right?" I knew the voice.

"Dr. Lucid!"

"Who?" said Lloyd.

I laughed. I don't know why. I laughed some more. "She's OK," I said. I nearly added, "It's just my shrink." This was funny too. The woman unwrapped herself and approached the flickering blue and red. I slowly recovered my social graces. "Dr. Clare, I mean, Dr. Lucid, this is Dan Lloyd. He's faculty at Trinity." I forgot to do the introduction the other way. They forgot to shake hands.

Lloyd said, "You mean, as in 'Ask Dr. Clare,' on the radio?"

"The same," she said. "Pleased to meet you."

"And what is this?" he asked. "Is National Public Radio doing Candid Camera these days? What's going on?" I had the question in mind myself.

"Oh, do pardon me," she began, in her best Anne Bancroft. "Miranda is a . . . colleague of mine. I happened to be logged on to your website when it went down. It looked to me like an attack. All I saw was the chat room. When she wrote that she had a copy of the site, I was very worried about her. Whoever attacked the site would know. When she didn't answer her phone, I set out for her apartment, arriving just as she left. I followed her up here." She left out the prequel, though, about following Max's webby tracks to Lloyd. She turned to me. "From outside the house it looked like you'd passed out on the couch. When the lights went out, I thought I was looking at a sexual assault in progress. I'm so very relieved that I was wrong." Good old Dr. Clare. Always with the subtext.

A bit of glowing newsprint peeled off from the torch and fluttered to the floor. Dan stomped it, and threw the rest of the roll back into the fireplace. For a few blazing seconds, we had something like room light. And what does the modern sensitive guy do when a radio personality sneaks into his house? When in doubt, host. He asked her to sit down, which she did (on the other couch). Clearly, he was the sort who'd give a mugger his money belt and then recommend a good restaurant. Or maybe he was adrenaline-surfing on my own giddiness. Lucid could not be here, and yet she was, and I was, and all of this had to be normal. He offered her tea, which she accepted. I didn't have time to warn her about letting him back into the kitchen.

The Doc slipped off her jacket and left it hanging on her shoulders. While Lloyd was out endangering the crockery, she leaned toward me with the Lauren Bacall treatment. "You said you computed what happened to Max."

"Not exactly. But I think I know what he was into when he called you last night. It's that website." I nodded back toward the kitchen. "His."

"I found it too, what was left of it. There's nothing there now. As far as I could tell, it doesn't exist. Perhaps it never did."

"Oh, no, it's real all right. Here, let me show you." Not. The screen was still in undead mode. I gave her a flashback on the web plot, the fake virus, and the rest. "We were just about to find out what the evil genius had in mind when you walked in."

Lloyd returned with a cup of tea. The light was failing again, and it seemed to me that the screen had dimmed. Or my eyes. "I listen to your show all the time," he said.

It was as if she had said, *Next caller.* She nodded, and cut to the chase. "Miranda tells me you've unraveled the Chaos Bug."

"I don't know yet. But it's Miranda who figured it out." That's right! You're OK! He began his own version of the fake virus story—and Lucid cut him off, polite Mistress Discipline. He shaped up and wordlessly pulled the table back toward him. Back to work. "There it is," he murmured. "Command-control-delete."

"And its effect?" asked the Doc.

The storm door banged again. Or so it sounded. Then it was clear that there was intelligent life in the universe, and it was knocking. Lloyd was up again. "That'll be the Car Talk guys," he said. I wished he had a front door, rather than risk the kitchen. He probably did have a front door, just behind the big snowpile. ET, now stomping his boots at the kitchen's edge, had his heartlight on; slim yellow shafts swept around the room, paused, whirled, spread.

"Goodness, look who's here!" said Lloyd.

"Da," said another familiar voice. "My automobile. Your American cars. On dry road, like the wind. In snow, like dead animal. But I sink in snow nearby your house! Good luck!"

A battery lantern led Porfiry Petrovich Marlov into the living room, with Lloyd in tow. My detective friend saw Dr. Clare first. "Dr. Lucid!" he exclaimed. "Not even Dostoevski can make so many times in one day with a charming lady." She smiled, quickly warmed, like a leftover in the microwave. Then he saw me. "And Miss Sharpe! Old Porfiry is dropped in land of literary impossibility. Miss Miranda Sharpe and Professor Doctor Lucid! All at house of colleague, Dan Lloyd!"

"Let me take your coat," said colleague Dan Lloyd. It was certainly time to lock the door from the inside.

True to form, Marlov was ahead of my question, or maybe it was Dr. Clare's. "You ask, how does Porfiry enter? Good question! I teach as visitor at Trinity, one course on Introduction to Forensic Data Analysis. Professor Doctor Lloyd and his colleagues make workshop for new faculty. I meet many people, wear nice nametag." We all sat down, with the lantern next to the Powerbook. Cozy.

"But," said Lloyd, "how do you know these folks?"

"Ah, that is my job. As you say, 'my day job.' At Whaleard University we have missing man. Or not have. These two charming ladies know missing man. I make their acquaintance, hope for clue."

"Who is it?"

All three of us, in unison: "Maxwell Grue."

"Grue," said Lloyd. "The phenomenologist? I met him once. Zany guy. So"—to me—"you know him?"

"He was my advisor." I probably blushed. I must remember to brush up on my tenses.

"Wow. That's hard."

"And old Porfiry has question too. How, on night of big snow, do two charming ladies travel to house of Professor?"

The Doc took the question. "Miranda has a theory that ties Grue's disappearance to something he discovered on the World Wide Web." She took her mug from the table, sipped it. No slurping. No surprises there.

Lloyd jumped in. "I forgot my manners. Porfiry, would you like some tea? It's Russian."

"Ah. Yes, tea. Thank you."

Lloyd stood and left the circle of light. I said, "And the website Grue saw was built by Professor Lloyd."

"What?" said a voice at the kitchen door. "*My* website?" He reappeared at the back of the couch.

"Yes," said Clare. "Our last datastream from him reported immense excitement about a theory of consciousness. We think that at about that time he saw your website. We think there's a connection."

"It would be along the lines of our email exchange," I explained. "Max is the enthusiastic type."

"This web, I would like to see it," said Porfiry.

"I copied it," I said. "But then the Chaos Bug bit me."

"You reset your small computer? All is well?"

"No. The bug only simulates a crash. It turns out it's a webpage. When you think you're resetting, you're really authorizing a change in some other file in your system."

Porfiry paused. "Miss Sharpe, I must add to your charms that you are a hacker, no?"

"No. I just put the pieces together. Professor Lloyd here knows the scene by scene."

"And this change. It is what?"

Lloyd returned to his seat, sliding the lamp to the edge of the table, away from the Powerbook. He quickly found his place, and announced, "It calls another webpage. Hold on. Here it is. It . . . rewrites your bookmarks."

"The bookmarks?" asked Clare. "The user's list of favorite websites? That's all?"

"That's it," said Lloyd.

"Wouldn't that be obvious?" I asked. "Why would you do a thing like that?"

"Yeah. I don't get it either."

I said, "Maybe it slips in a new bookmark to some, I don't know, evil website. Another one." Even as I said it I knew it was ridiculous.

Lucid seemed to agree. "But the perpetrator already has his site, lurking in plain sight. The virus is the webpage itself."

Something else was happening. "Could I?" I asked. Lloyd moved over and I pulled the laptop to my end of the table. Back at the control panels, I opened the "Auto Backup" panel. I set it to record and archive every action. Finally I hit command-control-delete. In the middle of the browser window I saw the simulated resurrection of my computer.

The deed was done. I opened the record of updates, and saw this listing:

GLOBAL REPLACE::

<ase.tufts.edu/cogstud/>	-> <ase.tufts.edu/cogstud/>
<assc.caltech.edu/>	-> <assc.caltech.edu/>
<www.cfs.ku.dk/>	-> <www.cfs.ku.dk/>
<husserlcircle.org/>	-> <husserlcircle.org/>
<www.consciousness.arizona.edu/>	-> <www.consciousness.arizona.edu/>
<psyche.cs.monash.edu.au/>	-> <psyche.cs.monash.edu.au/>
<www.helsinki.fi/collegium/>	-> <www.helsinki.fi/collegium/>
<www.phenomenologycenter.org/>	-> <www.phenomenologycenter.org/>
<www.spep.org/>	-> <www.spep.org/>
<www.psy.au.dk/phd/nncs/>	-> <www.psy.au.dk/phd/nncs/>
<www.phenomenology.org/>	-> <www.phenomenology.org/>
. . .	. . .

It went on and on. Dot edu, dot gov, dot org, like the little black book of a Mensa swinger. "It's replacing everything . . . with itself," I explained to the suspended audience. I showed the screen to Lloyd, and then to Clare and Porfiry on the other couch. Weirder than weird. Stephen King weird.

"So it is joke!" boomed Marlov. "A hacker child shows world he is big, and then gets big money job too."

Clare was frowning in the blue glow. "Normally this defect in the human operating system cries out for attention. Existential subtlety is not the hacker's way. He is typically more angry, more impatient. More male."

I agreed. I pulled the Powerbook back toward me. I highlighted one of the befores and pasted it into the "Location" window. After a few seconds a familiar scene popped up, a nice picture from the Center for Cognitive Studies. "This is so strange," I said, mainly to myself. I highlighted the replacement copy of the Tufts URL, and pasted that into the window too. The browser churned for ten seconds, then finally spit up the same scene. "All this trouble for nothing." There was no point in checking the rest, especially considering how long it had taken to reload the first site, even after already opening it. But then, I hadn't reloaded. Normally, to hit the same site a second time the browser simply flashes back to the same screen as before. "Do you think," I said to Lloyd, "that this thing could slow down my computer?"

"I don't see how."

Neither did I. I was staring at the guts of something. A thing is what it is, and not another thing. But in this hall of mirrors, nothing was what it was. I was having tea with the Mad Hatter, the Red Queen, and colleague Doctor Professor Lloyd. In Plato's Cave.

"Oh," said Lloyd, marching to a different soundtrack, "I forgot your tea."

Fine, I thought. Make a distraction. Miranda. Think. . . . OK, don't think. I looked up from the screen, following the floating after-image across the void. The eye, just another of Plato's caves. Like the computer screen. Meanwhile, noises off, from the creative kitchen. Call dial-a-wife before it gets any worse!

As the clatter sank back into conspicuous silence, I looked toward the kitchen, wondering if Lloyd really had impaled himself. From the screen and the lantern, I cast a mountainous double shadow on the wall. By focusing on the top of the shadow, I could plant the negative afterimage of my laptop screen on either of my two heads, a square halo. Saint Miranda, patron saint of bouillon cubes.

Lloyd reentered. "Porfiry, I'm sorry. I can't find a mug anywhere." Dr. Clare looked at the mug cradled in her lap, and set it back on the table. Now we could all yearn for tea together.

"No problem," said Porfiry. "Perhaps tomorrow we celebrate spring, and secret of Chaos Bug. Big Internet threat, nothing but air and wind. No threat to America."

"Or . . ." I said, getting it. "All these sites on the right, the new ones, are fake." Reaction shots: Lloyd, frowning, perplexed. The Doc, eyebrows arched at surprising, uppity me. Porfiry, ironic smile, frozen eyes. "Dan, aren't there characters that don't show up on screen?"

"Sure. Control codes, formatting, that sort of thing."

"So you could put those in a Web address, but you'd never see them, right?"

"Yes, a few of them. You think the replacement addresses include hidden codes? But then they'd open different pages, wouldn't they? Or a 404 error."

"Maybe. Or maybe these are all mirror sites, copies of the original."

"Jeez Louise," said Lloyd. "That's downright devious!"

Clare added, "But why?"

"Well," I thought aloud. "It's a sting operation. Think of all those buggy computers. That's a lot of people hitting mirror sites without knowing it. Suppose our evil genius has access to all the sites. He could get moody, and destroy the universe."

"Your evil genius must have one heck of a file server."

I looked again at the list. "Well, he's very interested in consciousness. And science, I guess. You could do a dissertation off these links." Looking over the list of hostages, I got a little chill. Apocalypso now. I turned to Lloyd. "Could I use your phone? I know a boy in the Whaleard techno-geek office, a student. He'll be up still, and he'll know who to call."

"Sure—"

"To make that call would be unwise, Miss Sharpe," said a grave Porfiry. "I suggest you sit down."

I thought, how rude, but when I turned to Porfiry I was staring at the business end of a .38 revolver. Actually, I had no idea whether it was a .38—aren't they all?—but I did notice that it was pointing at me. I sat down. My mouth went dry. I had the strangest urge to yawn.

Lloyd said, "Porfiry, is that a gun? Is that thing real?"

To which he replied, "Yes, comrade, it is real. An American Colt. It is a very good gun. Capitalism is good for some things. For making guns, and doughnuts, and Big Macs."

"What in heck are you doing?"

"You will want to ask Miss Sharpe that, Professor."

"*You're* the evil genius?" I asked.

"Oh, no, Miss Sharpe. I am but a foot soldier, one of many dedicated to building a house of cards. When the time is right, we will pull the house down. The geniuses—they have been dead a long time. Too long." The fake detective, I noticed, had replaced joviality with grammar. What an act. He slid to the end of the sofa, the better to see the three of us, three stooges. "I am very sorry that your stories must end tonight. They have been so entertaining. But you must blame the ingenious Miss Sharpe. Her theory must not leave this room. We are not ready."

I noticed the Doc inch her foot forward along the rug. The nearest leg of the table was about three inches away; she would need to slump in her seat to reach it. "But, Porfiry," I vamped, "I don't get it. Why the consciousness sites?"

"You are a poor materialist after all, Miss Sharpe. A theory of consciousness will be a plan for the ultimate psychology. Before the Chaos Bug, all the world has the information, the data. Now it is ours, and the world has only mirrors, thousands of mirrors for each original. Today the copies are good mirrors. But when we strike, we will corrupt the evidence. For some sites, we alter only small matters. For others, we will turn the large conclusions into their opposites. Nothing will be real. For consciousness, the Internet will be useless, full of contradiction, a labyrinth of the false and true. The West will drink its own corruption, and hardly know the taste. But we will be ready."

"But, but" (keep talking), "why not mirror Lloyd's site?" Doc to table leg: two inches.

"Ah, your cleverness continues. Lloyd was too close, approaching conclusions we reached two years ago. None must see that work, none but our scientists. So we must purge the site. The rest may continue until our prototypes are ready." I pressed myself into the couch, trying to become heavy to help the Doc in her glacial spread to the table. I forced myself to keep my best dinner date eyes focused on Porfiry.

"And Grue. He was so clever that you had to purge him? How many clever people will you have to delete?" One inch.

"Maxwell Grue. Who listens to Maxwell Grue? He is nothing. We do nothing with Grue. We only watch him because he is working on consciousness. His telephone call to you, Dr. Lucid, was noted. I sought him, but then his computer led us to my colleague Dan Lloyd. We knew of your maps of cognition, of course, but like you, Miss Sharpe, when we saw the web we knew it was only one short step to consciousness itself. The key—

when you merely realize that you have it—will unlock the rest. This you cannot have."

"And this is your route to world domination? Through a theory of consciousness?"

"Miss Sharpe, you are clever but poor in dialectics. Will the System not try to right itself? Corrections and clarifications, from thousands of researchers. How will these be transmitted? The Internet, of course. We will be ready then as well. For every cognitive scientist, we will simulate her mind. You will receive email from a famous researcher. She will flatter, amuse, discuss, explain. But is she one of our simulations? A ghost from a mirror site? The name will look the same. The thought will seem the same. In our laboratories, thousands of simulated minds await the day of birth, the dawn of their connection. When they are online, consciousness science will collapse in confusion. The world will then have no defense."

"No defense?" I asked. "From what?"

"From simulation. We will fold our agents into every interchange, and none will be able to organize against us." I imagined ranks of glowing pods in a shadowy underground warehouse, each one housing duplicates, triplicates, multiplicates of plain folks. *Suddenly all their eyes spring open.* That would be the film version, of course. The bunker Porfiry had in mind was just a room full of computers, the wake-up call a keystroke. The invasion, a flood of words, words, words. But marching out, swarming the globe—*spam consciousness.* For Porfiry it was already destiny. "When the present is ours to control, we may freely alter the past. Every archive. Even your egoistic blogs. History shall then be ours, and so also the future."

"And then?"

He was staring at me, but in the feeble light he seemed to be looking through me toward the horizon. I imagined marching, banners, fists in the air. "The Motherland will welcome our return. The world will know it."

I, still swallowing my impolite yawns of terror, felt a little urge to sneeze, and I seized it. The Doc jerked her foot and the table—tea, lantern, Powerbook—all went over. The scuffle was hard to see, but I could hear the Doc making loud "Hah" sounds. I found this encouraging. I pulled up my feet and tried to decide which way to jump.

"It's all right," she said. "He's down. Can we get some light?"

Lloyd said, "Here's the lantern." I found my Powerbook, snapped shut in the fall. I popped it open, still glowing with the page of doom. I held it forward to light what I could. Lloyd was shaking the dark lantern and listening to it.

Porfiry was face down on the carpet, with his hands crossed behind his back, Dr. Clare Lucid kneeling astride him. "Do you have some rope?"

"How about an extension cord?"

"Dr. Clare," I said, "how'd you get to be Emma Peel?"

"Black belt Tai Kwan Do. It's a hobby."

We sat Porfiry in a chair and lashed him in until he was ready to plug into the wall. "You will not stop us. We will bury you, even still," he murmured, but without conviction.

"We'll see about that," I said. I'd always wanted to use that line.

16

It was snowing still. The police were on their glacial way. Clare was sipping tea again, by the light of my spunky heroic laptop, restored to its spunky heroic table between the couches. The gun lay like a dead fish next to it, stubborn and mean. Lloyd was on his hands and knees with a roll of paper towels, blotting up tea. "I still don't understand what happened to that mug."

"Don't worry," I said. "I don't like tea anyway."

"Do you believe him? About Max?" asked Clare, with a glance to Porfiry.

"Yes," I said, playing a hunch. "Nobody cites Grue. He really is old footage."

She shook her head. "It's been twenty-four hours. The buffer looks bad."

Lloyd said, "I gather you were both close to him. So I don't know quite how to put this. . . . Was he depressed?"

"Yeah, it was one of his favorite topics," I said. "Though it's hard to see how. He was on five hundred milligrams of Prozac a day."

Both of them stared at me. "You mean fifty," said Lloyd.

"No. Five hundred. I'm sure of it."

Lloyd said, "That's an overdose, sure shooting. I've looked into all these drugs—as a part of my Phil. of Mind seminar."

"And the symptoms," said Dr. Clare. "Mania, hyperexcitability, blackouts. I don't know why I didn't compute the cause."

Mania, the boy's middle name. Hyperexcitability, every boy's middle name. And a blackout. A fade to black. The world wiped away, leaving a thin blue wedge of light and a thin mix of minds, mixmastering the manifold. Grue, poor Grue, poor Max, poor bastard. Not just high on life, OD'd on it. I sighed.

The Doc continued. "I just don't believe he could have been taking that much. Where did he get it?"

"Oh, he had another shrink. I mean, there was a psychiatrist at his HMO who gave him a blank check down at the drugstore. He just kept upping the dose, waiting for something to happen."

"For how long?" asked Lloyd. "He couldn't last more than a day at that dosage."

"It was at least a month," I said. "He told me. He told me it was doing nothing."

A vaguely pissy Dr. Clare said, "He never said anything about upping the dose to me."

"He knew how you felt about drugs."

"He hit five hundred, and it did *nothing?*" asked Lloyd.

"So he said. And until last night, I'd say he was right about that. He was the sort that would bitch in heaven."

"And last night?"

"Mania, hyperexcitability. Even more than usual. Everything but the blackouts." Miranda, skiing over the crevasse, hoping the crust holds.

"I concur," said Clare, claiming her man yet again.

Lloyd scratched his head. I visualized dandruff. "What else was he taking?"

"Nothing," said Clare.

Dan said, "When people overdose, they give them L-tryptosinate. Even with a tiny dose it blocks all the reuptake inhibition, no matter how much Prozac is floating around. It steadies the dopamine system. Even Steven. If he really was taking that much Prozac over the last month, then the only way he'd be walking is by taking tryptosinate at the same time."

"But why would he take the drug *and* the antidote?" I asked.

We all sat and pondered that for a moment. My day, make that time itself, washed over me like a parade of tidal waves. I was sick of fading to black. The darkness penetrated my head and I felt like I was on a sinking roller coaster. Could it be that I would ask someone to help? I did; I asked for a glass of water.

Lloyd returned to his kitchen. "Oh, here it is," he called. "Right under my nose the whole darn time." Well, gosh darn it, I concluded that he had found his missing mug.

"Where the hell are the police?" asked Dr. Clare, looking at Porfiry looking at the floor.

I drank the water before Dan could settle again. Praise water. I looked at the mug which had been found, happily without tea. I realized that I didn't just dislike tea, I hated it. I had hated the nasty little drowned bits in the bottom of Grue's mug this morning, and—not in the afternoon. The mug had been lifted by then. The hound had not barked.

"Dan," I said. "What would this trypto stuff do if you *weren't* on Prozac?"

"I don't know," he said. "Nothing, I guess." He looked at Lucid for confirmation.

"Oh," she said, "I don't have any data on that."

That surprised me. The author of *Deleting Prozac* and nemesis of antidepressants ought to have heard of this.

"Someone was feeding him the antidote," said Porfiry, surprising us all. "Is that not obvious?"

"You, no doubt," Clare replied.

Porfiry snorted. I was busy mixing the antidote trypto whatever in with the overdose, B&W with color. He wouldn't take the antidote willingly, but he would have to get it every day. It would be in something he did take. In his Prozac? That would be a pill for our time! In his corn flakes? In his operating system? No, that was another plot. And, whatever it was, he *stopped eating it.* Hence the OD.

It was the tea, of course. And I knew perfectly well who the source was.

"To block the anti-depressants in a depressed man," Lloyd said. "It's perverse."

What a lousy routine, to be betrayed nightly. Indeed, where *were* the police? Could they issue a new identity on the spot? I could file the paperwork first thing in the morning. I sighed. I sighed again. "Doc," I said, "do you pull this shit with everyone? Or just with men who turn you on?"

"I beg your pardon?"

"You're not a person," I said. "You're an agenda." Hannibelle Lecter looked at me with a vast disdain and a withering contempt. I was the nastiest of mosquitos. "A student gave him some tea the other day. He started drinking it. He stopped using your stash. That's what happened." Now I knew why she was so desperate to find Grue. One blood test from mad Max in the Emergency Room, and Clare Lucid would be just another former celebrity.

She looked paler than pale. Lloyd said, "Oh," and stiffened where he sat.

"You have no idea what these drugs really do," she said. "I was protecting him, keeping him true to himself. I didn't know he was upgrading his dose."

We'll see about that. "Tell it to the police." I'd always wanted to use that line too.

"Two million listeners and half a million readers mean nothing to you, then." She continued. "Many of them are confused, corrupted. They look to Dr. Clare for hope, for insight. You'll use this incident to hurt them all. You won't do that, Miranda. It would be wrong."

Wrong? Now there's a novel concept! "Look," I said. "You don't fuck with people's computers, right? You don't fuck with their minds either. Get it?"

"I see that you are angry—"

"No," I shouted. "I see that *you're* a *moron!*" Her double facelift looked like a sheet of ice with two eyes filled with cold hate. I wanted to slap her many times.

The Doc had something stronger in mind. That annoying gun. I felt like laughing, like they do down in the asylum. Porfiry snorted again.

Lucid says, "You may take heart, Mr. Marlov. All the clever deductions of this evening will never leave this room after all. Having slipped from your bonds, you will indeed shoot them all, and then yourself. With your own gun, of course." Clare stands up, and backs toward the fire to keep all her subjects in view. "Stand up," she commands Lloyd and me. I wish I hadn't forgotten to call Gordon. If I can save one World Wide Web, I shall not have lived in vain. Otherwise, shit.

In the middle of my laptop screen a message appears. I check to see if Clare has noticed it—apparently not. I know what it must say, that my battery is tired. In a few seconds, the screen will flicker out, and the room too. Audrey Hepburn, Grace Kelly, and then, inexplicably, Jimmy Stewart come to mind. Lloyd's second end table, still loaded with picture frames, is about five feet to my right, at the end of the other couch. Sitting on the edge of the table is a camera. I contemplate the perfect photo ops that may or may not remain in my young life.

Blackout. I give Dan a quick straightarm to the shoulder, "Get down!" And then I throw myself at the table of kidpix. As my shoulder crash-lands in the carpet, Clare pulls the trigger. A lightning flash and harsh boom fill the room and drill into us. For a second it seems to be happening all in my head.

"Don't think you can escape!" shouts Lucid. "I warn you, I am trained in marksmanship."

My ass. I crawl around behind the couch. She's moving too. In a few seconds we will both be able to see, however sketchy the sights might be. But she won't need to see much. I hold the camera against my stomach with one hand. As I lie on my side, I feel for the lens, and then along the top for the shutter. Then I have it in my hand like a camera should be.

I stick the camera in the air over my head, pointing it in the general direction of Clare's most recent public appearance, and clamp my eyes shut. "Hey!" I shout as I hit the shutter. The gun fires again. Something shatters across the room. It smells like the Fourth of July.

Still lying on the ground, I open my eyes. Clare is standing on my side of the couch, no more than five feet from me, waving the gun from one side to the other. She has been dazzled by the camera and probably the gun flash too. She holds both hands in front of her, and takes a step toward me. I stand up just enough to roll over the back of the couch onto the seat, and then to the floor. She hears, and quickly points herself and the gun toward my general location. I'm up again, rolling over the second couch the same way, landing on top of Lloyd, who stifles an oof. The gun slams the air once more. Not worrying too much about the etiquette of kneeling on a married man, I wave my arm in the air, call, "Say cheese!" and press the flash.

I flatten Lloyd beneath me. My puny flash is answered by her thunderbolt. Stimulus-response; Skinner was right. And dead too. I have to keep the razzle dazzle going. I roll off and whisper to Lloyd, "Keep moving." He does and so do I.

I kneel behind the couch, up periscope. I can see Lucid outlined against the windows at the end of the room, still standing behind the other couch. She's holding the gun with both hands now, and doing quite a nice job of pointing it at my face. Last known whereabouts. But she's blinded still. Her head turns halfway and tilts toward me, listening. Very slowly I lower myself onto my hands and knees. I feel tight through my ribs and diaphragm. I want to claw to the surface, gasp for breath.

Crouching, I hold the camera in the Doc's crosshairs. Flash. I leap toward the open space and run behind Porfiry to the big table. But something is missing—she hasn't shot. How impolite. I surface to the tabletop to see that she faces me once again. At least I have a little more distance.

"Miranda," she says, quietly. "Come out. We can discuss this like adults. It doesn't have to end like this." Still killing me softly.

I hear a faint metallic noise in the kitchen. Oh no, I think, you didn't go in *there*. Some people never learn. Lucid swings toward the kitchen door, but only briefly. Back to me. I guess I'm the big fish. And me, only a second-year graduate student. I ease back to the floor, and crawl another foot behind the thicket of chair legs. But how to put this on my resume? My hand bumps something round and smooth, plastic, a toy. I throw it at her, but it hits the wall just above the kitchen door, loudly, and bounces along the wooden floor. That's worth a bullet, and then another, just for good luck. I miss the timing of my blink, a bright purple spot hovers where the world should be, and a ringing stops up my ears. I grope along to the end of the table. Ahead, I can remember only a vast open plain of living room, a wall of glass, and a few miles to an open staircase. A perfect shooting gallery.

I dimly see her pivot back toward me, covering two flanks at once, and I hit the flash for old time's sake. These will make a wonderful album, I think, as I tuck my rugburn shoulder into the floor, diving back along the length of the table.

"Miss Sharpe," says Porfiry from the front row. "The gun is now spent. You are safe."

Although I like that thought, I have my doubts, considering the source. I can see a vague Clare slowly scanning the room, a gun barrel for eyes. She takes two steps toward the table. I will have a few more seconds of purple spots and ringing ears. I have only one thing left to throw. I stand up, very quietly. While she aims from the other end of the table, I call up every soft-ball moment of elementary school, and focus on the belly of the beast, hurling the camera with all my strength. And miss. It skids along the floor behind her and starts to whir, rewinding its film. How convenient for Clare. She can take it to the drugstore to be developed.

She takes another step. I crouch and scurry back along the table. Now she's at the opposite end. Beyond and away, I see the wintry outline of the French doors. Here in the country, doors are unlocked, right? I spring for the door, pushing down the handle. Wrong. Clare's now moving like a battleship along my side of the table. I feel for a door latch, finding only a bump with a slot in it. And no key. No pathetic key. No answer to any damn thing, just questions questions questions. I want to cry. I want to die. But not like this. I turn back to face her.

She's standing at the end of the table. She'll be seeing and hearing now, rise and shine. "Listen," I say. "I figured out the theory of consciousness. Max's aleph. Don't you want to hear it?"

She stops about a Miranda-length away, spreads her legs like Calamity Jane, and raises the gun. "Not really," she says. The gun clicks.

Time may have stopped just before that click, or during, or just after—I'll never know. We each stared at the dark outlines of the other. Then I dove right at her, catfight time. I hoped I might tear out her windpipe, or even mess up her perfect hair. I wanted to try a roar, and maybe I did. As I pushed her over we both collided with Lloyd, holding a frying pan over his head. He went down too. The Doc was first up, first to run, first through the kitchen door and into the night. By the time we got there, all we saw was a snowdrift with headlights back down the driveway, and then grind along the street, its ass skidding from side to side like a drunken diva.

The glow of her taillights shrank to red pinpoints, and then to air. Cold, wet, delicious air.

17

Then the highest tree branches were crisscrossed with red and blue beams, and the boys in badges arrived. They were prepared with flashlights big as bats, like searchlights slashing the dark. The air in the living room was smoky, and their big beams probed the scene like it was a sunken stateroom on the *Titanic*.

My computer had taken a slug right in the middle of the screen. As someone working on a dissertation, I'd often had the fantasy, but to see it real was disturbing. The bullet had torn an angry hole straight through, fringed with circuit shards. Its inert darkness was somehow more emphatic than the long shadows wheeling around it. I realized I could see straight through the hole to the scene beyond, where a cop was daintily slipping a gun into a baggie. I thought, what excellent virtual reality. No, erase the "virtual." And the "excellent."

"Alas," said Lloyd, looking over my shoulder.

"Yeah. Time for an upgrade." I wiggled my hand into the front pocket of my jeans, looking for the universal tool, a paperclip. A cop lent me a flashlight. I wedged it under my arm, and used an end of the clip to release the disk. It seemed unharmed, sleeping beauty. I put it back into my limp, sad, almost empty backpack. Then I returned to the computer and gently pushed the lid down toward the keyboard. Goodnight, sweet prince. My best husband.

"Ma'am, please don't do that," said a voice. "We'll need it for evidence."

So, instead of lying in state in my apartment, my laptop went to the morgue. I wondered if they wired a little ID tag to the escape key.

Porfiry was led out in handcuffs, and slowly the evening unwound in flashbacks. It was a completely ridiculous story, especially the part about me taking snapshots of the climax. But they confiscated the camera eagerly enough, and muffled their surprise about the perpetrator, Clare Lucid.

I almost forgot to tell them the other part, about the Doc and Max Grue. But when I got into that they became totally puzzled. No one had told them that Max was missing.

"How long has this Grue fellow been AWOL?" asked one.

"Since this morning." I think they looked at each other before dutifully entering it in their notebooks. Grue was backstory at best.

With Lucid at large and the lights out, they suggested we remove ourselves from the premises until morning. If Lucid knew my address, they added, perhaps I should stay away from there too. Perhaps we had a friend we could drop in on. At 3 AM.

Lloyd suggested a diner he knew, and the cop approved the choice. He offered us a ride, but Lloyd cheerfully declined. Since he grew up in Buffalo, he explained, he could handle the snow.

Which had stopped snowing. I stood on the stoop in my fuzzy hat, watching the cops unroll yellow tapes to seal the house. I had been part of a genuine Crime Scene. I had a Police Lieutenant's business card in my pocket, and rug burns on my elbows. I didn't want the guys to leave.

Lloyd locked the door, and circled a heap of snow with dark wheels. It glowed like an igloo when he opened its door to pull out a brush. With a few strokes—learned in Buffalo, I supposed—he had the windows cleared. He started the car, emerged again, and circled to the passenger side, where he opened the door for me.

I looked at my own car, parked next to his. "Why don't I just follow you?" I said.

"Of course," he said, and made another embarrassed retreat. I gave my car a quick brushoff. We mushed our vehicles onto the road, crawling down the mountain to the slushy streets below. I loved the streetlights and the neon, the gleaming puddles, the glowering red sky. In a few minutes he pulled into a parking lot, and we were there.

Where? I thought. As I slammed the door, I saw the big Vegas sign, GODOT'S. A silver bullet with windows. The mother ship.

"I know," said Lloyd at my side. "They even pronounce it the same way."

"How is it that I never heard of this place?"

"I don't know. Do you have insomnia?"

"No."

"That may be part of it." He held the outer door for me, by its diagonal chrome handle. "It's the only place open all night. When I can't sleep to save my life, I come here."

I opened the inner door for him, and we entered a glare of vinyl, metal, and formica with swirls.

"Well, if it isn't Dr. Dan," announced a waitress in a sweatshirt and pleated skirt.

"Hello, Diane," he said. The waitress looked me over and I tried to do the same to her, but smilingly. She was skinny as a cigarette, on the wrinkly side of middle age, with brown and gray hair that would need another hundred bobby pins to keep it in. Lloyd introduced us.

"Hello, dearie," she said.

"Pleased to meet you," I said. "How long have you been waiting for Godot's?"

"Honey, you're number four hundred and thirteen with that joke. And that's just since I started counting. This is a college town, you know."

"Oh."

We slid into a booth, Diane close behind. "You missed all the excitement," she said.

"We did?" asked Lloyd.

"We had a bat in here. It was the craziest thing."

"What happened?"

"We were all swatting at him with newspapers and rags. Bats don't like that. I think we scared him to death. He kamakazied into Keno's stew in the back."

"A bat in a vat!" Lloyd said.

Diane pulled out her pad. "So, what'll it be?"

Lloyd opened: "I'd like the Buffalo bat wings, please."

She looked at me, as if to say, get a load of this guy. I said, "And could I please have the McBat deluxe?"

She flopped the pad onto the table and planted a hand on her hip. "The two of yous. What a pair."

"You did throw out the stew?" Lloyd asked.

With mock indignation, Diane said, "What do you think we are?"

We glanced across the table at each other, thinking that she hadn't quite answered the question.

Serious orders. Survival—to this exact moment—was an achievement, I decided. The world should toast it. So I ordered toast. And coffee, of course. Three cups. "Line them up," I demanded. And pancakes. And an omelet.

"Home fries with that?"

"Uh, no. But bring on the hot sauce."

Lloyd already knew what he wanted, and I was pleased that it had nothing to do with me: French toast, a fried egg on the side. Diane took our orders back to the kitchen. I liked her. I liked almost everybody just then.

Dan asked, "What was the last thing to pass through the mind of the bat as he hit the windshield of the truck?"

"Um, his butt?"

"Oh, you heard that one."

"Actually, no," I said. "As a materialist, it just made sense."

"What *was* the last thing?" he asked.

"The truck, I suppose."

"As a materialist, that makes no sense. How can a truck get inside a bat?"

I shrugged. "The truck produced an impression in the bat?"

"You could say that," he said. "I'm sure the grille made an *excellent* impression."

I laughed. "Truck to bat: imagine *that*."

He laughed too. "Bat back to truck: Splat!" He slapped his palm on the table for emphasis. "But if it's not an impression, then what is it?"

"Lately, I think consciousness is a soundtrack." I pointed to the micro-jukebox hanging by the mustard and ketchup, and made a note to check it out. "A soundtrack without a movie. Hints and innuendo."

"I like that. A soundtrack. I've always thought that more than anything else life needed a soundtrack. Something upbeat, jazzy, but moody too."

"Lately I'd have to mix in *Psycho* strings and screechy bits. You know, whenever you open the closet."

"Usually my soundtrack is a little more Jerry Lewis," he said. "In my brain, choirs of angels sing 'It's a Small World After All.'"

"Maybe I should reconsider my career choice."

"Not at all. That's just me."

"How did you get into this anyway?"

"Into philosophy?"

"No, into your mind-brain montage. Cognition and consciousness."

"Well, the superficial answer is that it was what seemed ripest after I finished *Simple Minds,* my book about mental representation. But the real answer." He looked up at the lights, thinking, then back at me. "The real answer is that I'm the sort of person who goes into a theater and chooses a seat strictly according to whether I might possibly obstruct someone's view. Heaven forbid I should be a problem, or a burden. I think a lot about other minds."

"I see. Looking out for number two."

He nodded. "And you?"

"I was told I was good at it." I've been told too many things in my life, I thought.

"You took the quiz from the Academy of Consciousness Studies? 'Draw this bat and win a valuable scholarship.'"

"It was something like that," I said. "I was drifting, and got sucked into someone's orbit."

"Grue's."

"Yes. But it wasn't just that. I think you could say that I found myself obstructing everyone's view. My advice to your daughters is, don't be tall and have auburn hair. One or the other but not both. So many people have a thing about me that I often think I *am* a thing. I see the science of consciousness as an escape."

"I would think that understanding consciousness would make you more conscious of the minds of all these others, not less."

"Yes, but it also reaffirms my own self, in here." I tapped my temple. "And there's the wonder of experience itself, personal experience. I find that magical."

"And how. That is the mystery, isn't it?"

How odd that he should put it that way. "Yes," I agreed.

"The soundtrack analogy is good. All the instruments are separate, but in relation to each other. And it's all beyond what's on screen. But without it, what's on screen is hollow. Silent."

"Yeah," I said. "Guns that go poof." We thought in silence for a moment. Our coffees arrived. He raised his cup. "L'Chaim."

"I'll drink to that." We clinked cups. It was indeed good to be alive.

"So why is it," he asked, "that we only discover that we are alive when we are about to die?"

"Just another case of the thrill of phenomenology."

He looked puzzled.

"That's the title of my dissertation," I said. "I argue that genuine phenomenological ontology only occurs when something real is on the line. To understand rationality, get wasted. To get to the bottom of love, fall head over heals for a jerk. To know what the world is, go die." To get it all at once, have a day like this one.

"But take notes as you do."

"Exactly."

"You're inspiring me—to take up plumbing."

I nodded. "I know. If you don't want to take the Humphrey Bogart approach, you can get close by imaginative identification. For example, go to the movies."

"That reminds me," he said. "Have you ever seen *Rear Window?*"

"You have to ask?"

"The move with the camera. That was clever."

"Thanks. Thank Hitchcock." It was true. I felt deep personal gratitude to Alfred Hitchcock. Where would we be without him?

He lifted his cup. "To Alfred." Then, almost to himself, he added, "To be alive. To be. What is it?"

"It's this cup of coffee," I replied. "This diner. This moment." The bright fluorescents molded the room with their unrelenting shadowless light. The red vinyl of the booths, the chrome wrapped around the counter, the smoky metal pedestals and their mushroom seats. A fine hallucination. A mirror site with no site to mirror. Marvelous existence.

"You mean, it's the world," he said.

"Yeah, the whole thick, bloody thing."

"The whole blanketyblank enchilada."

"The full monty."

"The cave of mysteries."

"Exactly what I was saying," I said. "The movies."

He nodded. "There's just one thing I don't understand."

Ah, I thought. It's how I knew it was the tea. It's how I guessed the websites were fake. It's how I discovered his own website. It's how I spent my day. Elementary, Watson.

"Why couldn't this all be in your head?"

"That's the thrill of it. It could be. But what matters is the thickness of it. The part that lays itself upon you. Reality means no more than that, and no less."

Diane delivered a breakfast from heaven. A plateau of pancakes with primordial sweet steam curling along its perfect brown. A continent of eggs, hot and knotty. I shook the tabasco over the eggs, and smelled a peppery, syrupy, rich infinity.

"But *something* is in your head, right?" he asked. "The sensory properties. Like the taste of coffee or eggs. They're the thickest of all."

"Ah, the smell." Ah, the smell. "Why should sensory qualities be in your head any more than anything else?"

"But isn't it different from the objective properties? Like the size of the counter."

"Why should it be any different?" I asked. I poured syrup on the pancakes.

"Because you can measure the counter. You can bounce light off of it."

"And that's outside of your head?"

"Of course. It's over there." He pointed.

"And your experience of the counter. Is that over there too?" My experience was just then joyfully overloading with pancake.

"No, it's in my head," said his head. "Isn't it?"

"Just like the smell, then."

"Hmm." He took a bite to think with.

"There is no side view of your own consciousness." Not of smells. Not of diners. Or counters or guns. We could never walk around our own states of mind to check what was out there to cause them.

He nodded. "That fits with your email to me."

Diane appeared at our side just as we both stuffed our mouths. "How is everything, folks?"

"Mmm. Fffnn." And I nodded.

"Warm up that coffee?"

"Mm-hm," he said. And I nodded again.

Dan swallowed and continued. "How is everything. That really is the question, isn't it? How could anything be anything? How could anything be?"

"All I know is, experience and the world are one. One."

"Yeah, like a third substance, in between."

"No, like one thing."

He nodded again, and gazed thoughtfully at an imaginary cloud. His eyes were a pale green. Nice eyes, but very tired. I wondered what I must look like. Catching a bullet in your teeth must leave you with a shocked expression, and a wrinkle or two. And the thrill. Still thrilling.

"What about intentionality?" he said.

"Yes. 'All consciousness is consciousness *of* something.'"

"That's the bumper sticker all right. It sounds to me like two things, consciousness and whatever it is *of* or about. The bat mind and the on-coming truck."

"I know, I know." I poured some more cream into my coffee, watching the swirl tighten and then spread. There's a shape in that cloud, I thought. What is it?

"Psychology is built around intentionality," he continued. "Everything from Descartes on. Mind and the world. The world and the mind. Stimulus, perception, cognition, response. Out there. In here."

All I could think was, wrong. Wrong wrong and again wrong. It had to be wrong all the way back. "The bumper sticker must be wrong."

"All consciousness is *not* of something?"

"No, maybe: All consciousness is. No, too cryptic. How about, all consciousness is not of something *else*. Not of something other than itself."

"There and back again. So only your mind exists? Solipsism all over again."

"But that *problem* has to be wrong too. The problem only plays while Truman is deceived. But while he's deceived it doesn't matter that he's really in Burbank."

"I saw it, but I don't get your point."

"*The Truman Show,*" I explained. "They raise a real guy in a fake world—actors playing his pals and dad, whatever. We can see that Truman is deceived, and we can contrast his fake world with Burbank, the real place with the fake studio world built in it. But if it's all working perfectly, Truman can't ever find out that it's a fake. All his knowledge will be true by the only standards he has, by the best standards he can contrive."

"Yeah," he said, "but he's still wrong."

"Well," I said, "this could be *The Truman Show*. The Miranda Sharpe saga. The epic of Dan Lloyd. Playing me—um—"

"Sandra Bullock," he suggested. "No. A little too old."

"Oh, the writers will take care of that."

"Lucy Liu. J-Lo. Or that actress in *Star Trek*—"

"But if it works," I cut in, "Sandra Bullock is not a person from the outer sphere. She's another creation of the clever writers. The idea that she could play me entirely arises within the fake world, and can't refer outside of it."

"But Truman figures out that he's wrong. The spotlight falls from the sky."

"Right, but that can't happen in solipsism. Only you exist. Anything that would either confirm or disconfirm that claim can only arise in you. It's an empty threat."

"But it makes a huge difference. If solipsism is true, I'm just a character in Miranda Sharpe's private cinema. These dishes and food are props, well, not even props. They're just posits, constructs. You've just written them in with phrases here and there." He held up his napkin. "All you have to do is think, 'Dan picked up his napkin.' But this—"he shook it—"is no construct."

"My secret is out. I did create this scene, and you, and my whole life. I'm writing it right now. Your turn."

He laughed. "I guess I'm one of those characters who takes off on his own and won't be pushed around by the author."

"Precisely. It's as if you had a mind of your own."

"And a separate existence," he added. "A house, wife, kids."

"Nice touches. Establishes sympathy. Keeps the reader interested."

"Reader: I guess that's you," he said. "Writer and reader both."

"And don't you forget it either."

"Well," he said, "on behalf of characters and constructs everywhere, please take a raincheck on natural disasters, alien invasions, and the like. We like our slice of life just fine as it is."

I said, "Uppity characters like you make it tough for us solipsists. Not to mention the classic refutation: Kick the stone. Or this." I stuck a finger into my coffee, down to the first joint. Hot, but not scalding. A gentle all-over embrace, with a subtle hug at the surface, like a weak rubber band. Soothing, as if I were drinking coffee inside out. It felt wet only when I pulled out my finger and wiped it in my napkin. "I'm not saying that this proves that there is coffee really. But it is in my experience as real. Nothing could be realer. And if you did or didn't exist, it would make no difference to me, because you have all the claims to reality that there could be. You, stones, coffee. And it can't make a difference to you either. If you're really real, then your movie is playing, and all's well. If you're a mere construct, then you aren't the sort of entity anything could make a difference *to*."

"Like a mirror site with no site to mirror. It's just a site. That will be as real as real could be," he said. I nodded. "If you're right," he continued, "setting up a brain in a vat wouldn't be quite so hard. When philosophers imagine the brain-in-a-vat, they always imagine extracting your brain and simulating all its inputs perfectly. But they wouldn't need to make the simulation very good, would they? After all, you couldn't look outside the vat to check up on it."

"Yeah," I said, "they always assume the simulated world is a perfect replica of the real world, don't they?"

He took a bite of eggs, and looked toward the window. "Actually, it could be really awful and we'd still believe it. You know, like bad art, like daytime TV. Too many coincidences. Weak character development. Derivative."

"Ah," I said. "A B-movie. B for Brain." He nodded.

"And little glitches. Inconsistencies across scenes. Stopped clocks. Intrusions of sensations that make no sense. Exact repetition of a perception."

"Like the cat in the *Matrix*," I said. He took another bite, and looked toward the window again. Apparently the next thought entered both our minds at the same instant. We stared directly at each other, each trying to look straight through the other into some inscrutable alien world. For a second everything froze.

In unison, "Nah!"

I laughed. He grinned and pulled off his glasses, shaking his head. "What a day," he murmured, pinching and massaging the bridge of his nose. He put the glasses on again, and apologized. I assured him that it was OK.

He steered us back toward normal. "OK, so what comes after intentionality?"

Thinking aloud: "Maybe the 'of' has another meaning in 'All consciousness is consciousness of something.' Not 'about' but 'composed of.'"

"So, the bumper sticker should read 'all consciousness is made of something.' OK, I'll bite. Of what? Of what stuff are dreams made?"

I poured more syrup. "Not one stuff. It's not a special goop poured into the brain. Each state of consciousness is made of its own something." I raised the bottle so I could see the syrup ribbon thin to a gold thread.

"Yikes. Goops galore."

"No. Patterns galore. Each one an experience. Each one different. Just like in your website. The patterns are in the brain. Your labyrinth is based on the brain, but maps more than that." I set the bottle down, and watched the sweet puddle spread on my plate. It had been far too long since I played with my food.

He nodded vaguely.

"Each pattern is the entire intentional package, subject and object together. The pattern is the image of your relations to everything. That includes the world before you. That includes the past and future. All that is just as real as anything else. In the end, the labyrinth is reality. The patterns *are* the world."

Now he nodded more convincingly.

"The patterns are the world showing itself," I said. "Only when the world shows itself can there be a world. That's what 'world' means and is. We are such stuff as dreams are made of."

"Yes," he said. "It's a small world after all."

I groaned. I had completely forgotten to pick some tunes, and now, as the Vienna Boys' Choir was warming up somewhere in my tired lobes, I would need it. I popped a quarter into our tabletop jukebox and hit A1, B1, C1, D1, E1, F1. Then I flipped to the listing: "Wipe Out," "What a Day for a Daydream," "Norwegian Wood," "Telstar," "Back in the USSR," "Louie Louie." Not bad.

"Hard day," he said, sympathizing.

I nodded. The surfer bongos woke us up, like a Hawaiian shirt at an inquest.

"I've never even seen a real handgun," he said.

I nodded. "I've seen quite a few things for the first time today." I was grateful that we'd made it this far into breakfast without once looking back at the scene of the crimes. Denial had been sweet.

But now he wanted to know the whole story. I demurred, for a moment, and then in an exhausted what-the-hell told him about the scene in Grue's office. And the class, Grue poof. And the fifty minutes of data processing with Lucid, and Gordon Fescue's big anthology of brains, and the cheery meeting with Porfiry, the man of many dimensions, and the mind-boggling recurrent red folder that I wasn't supposed to have. Not to mention the scene with Zamm and Steve "Doritobreath" Addit, and a scary glimpse of Cronkenstein herself. Then his website.

All this took forever, plus three refills on our coffee and as many quarters in the music box. Rock around the clock. I wondered where the dawn was in this dark city. Hiding out with Max Grue, probably. Lloyd turned out to be a good listener, although a little long on the knitted brows and empathetic sighs. Or maybe not. It was *that* sort of day, after all.

There was no story left, when the pay phone by the door rang. Diane answered, but it was for Lloyd. He seemed surprised, but said, "Oh, hello, Officer," and the news flowed in. After a minute of listening, with more than one "gosh," he thanked the caller and hung up.

"They got Lucid," he said as he sat down. "No word on Grue, though."

I nodded. "It's strange, but I'm a lot less worried about him now."

"Yeah," he said. "I don't know if I should tell you this—"

I hate when people say that. In my life, if you don't know, then you shouldn't.

"The gun. It wasn't empty. It jammed on the last bullet."

I felt the thrill of phenomenology like a harp arpeggio racing up and down my spine. I felt cold.

"You beat the odds big time," he said. "Thank heavens."

"That little fucking liar." I was so angry that I cried. Just a bit, just for half a minute. I couldn't face the world or the man across the table—who sat paralyzed, the right response just then. Then I blotted my eyes with a napkin, and raised the curtain on the world.

He began to speak, but I cut him off with a shutup sort of nod. I reached for my pack to find a tissue, finding instead the inner world of conscious-ness, sleeping in a CD. I set the disk on the table to get it out of the way.

As I blew my nose, I noticed Lloyd looking at the disk. It held every-thing. All my papers. All my clips and scripts. All my letters to Seth, and some back. Everything I've written in the last two years. And a website.

"I think I'll be getting to bed now," I said.

"Yes. Of course. You must be exhausted."

"You too." He was still glancing at the disk. I guessed he didn't even know it.

"Of course, if the power is on, we could run back up to your place and make that copy. It would only take a few minutes." Ms. Humanitarian.

"Oh no, don't worry about it. It might be on, but probably not. It can take them a day to get repairs in up there."

I thought about it. My computer was dead, and the WU computer cen-ter would not be open for at least a few hours. Then I had a brain flurry.

"I can get us to a computer over at Whaleard. That's just five minutes from here. It's on my way home."

A little too quickly, he said, "You're sure it wouldn't be a problem?"

"Sure." I smiled. Dragging Lloyd's fuzzy cum-ba-yah reality into the WU scenario might help, garlic against the vampires. Exorcism had been my symbolic goal, a half-life ago. Uncle Dan might lend a hand.

A few minutes later, as the first grays feathered in behind the last city glow, we walked in front of the Fake Thinker, currently sporting a toupee of snow. Nice rug, I thought. Makes you look years older.

Those doors. The stairs. That hallway. To have his eyes along made them all different. Merely there. Mere reality. Whether that was a metaphysical loss or gain didn't matter. I felt safe, and that was a feeling I welcomed.

"This is his office," I said, unnecessarily, since the door was plastered with Gruesome zeitgeist, cartoons about Nietzsche, Foucault, Calvin and Hobbes, Doonesbury. In the middle, a large hand-lettered sign read: "Grue—green until 2000 and blue ever after."

I opened the door and snapped on the lights before I noticed that, as al-ways, a surprise was waiting. At the computer, banging away like the Phan-tom of the Opera at his organ, sat Maxwell Grue.

18

He was peering into his monitor, rubbing his nose in the glass. The screen was blank. He tapped away nonetheless.

"Hold on," he said without looking up. "Just have a little gulch, I mean glitch here. Lost a file. Forgot my password. Four letters. J H V H—no. Sorry, wrong aleph. Hold the line, just got to work this out." He glanced sidewise toward the open door, then yanked his gaze back to the computer. "It began with M!" He held his arm up with the index finger down, and slowly lowered the boom on a key. "Speak, Memory. Hear, mnemosyne. When I first studied M, a mountain was not a mountain. Just like Descartes said. But after years of study, a fish is as good as a mountain, when you're not paying attention. Attention need not be paid! Real being, the noumena, the *dingaling an sich*, that's like, whatever." He threw his head to the side and raised one hand, palm up. Tap. Tap. Tap. "M R N D. Damn. Nothing." He held his hand in front of the still dark screen, fingers spread wide. Slowly he pushed into the glass, as if to slip through it into the underworld. I was surprised when dull matter met skin and stopped it. He flexed his hand, kneading the glass, then scratched one ear as if it had fleas. Then toward us: "Is it my office hour already?" His eyes searched all over the room, trying to lock onto us. I realized what a simple thing it was, to meet the gaze of another, to recognize. I realized that in the exchange of glances, that in one look back and forth you could see the unreeling of life stories, distilled into a single frank gaze, or an averting of eyes. I noticed all that because his look had none of it, because his look did not find us, did not find the wall behind us, did not find the empty space in which we stood. He was without eyes, without face, without mind. We were standing on the edge of a vast devastation.

"If you're here about your paper, I haven't gotten to it yet. So go away." Max was leaking self, venting being all over the rug. "Or would you like a pretty story?" Jet fuel mixed with whisky, swirling away into a black hole. "Well?" he demanded. "Do you want to know what happened, or don't you?"

"Yes, Max," I said softly. Down the drain with Maxwell Grue.

He froze. "By Zeus, it's working. As Jehovah is my witness! Thane of Cawdor and king hereafter. M R N D. I couldn't get to your papers because my dog ate them. One at a time, choking on the way you abuse Heidegger. What did you call him? Heildegger? Oh, no, that was me. Clever shit, man." Again he stared at the blank screen and tapped away.

Neither Lloyd nor I could move. It was as if we weren't there; we could only act accordingly.

Lloyd was next to wade in. "Professor Grue . . ."

Max's unreeling paused. "Well, well, well," he chortled, "one and one and one is three! And who might you be, sonny boy?"

"Dan Lloyd. We met once at Trinity, when you gave a talk. In the mid '90s, I think."

"I gave a talk and you took it? Or did you take a hear?"

"Listen, are you OK?"

"I don't know. Ask the muse."

Lloyd and I glanced at each other. I made a face that said that I didn't know what to do either. I couldn't understand what made it so hard to speak.

"Max," I said, "you have to go to the infirmary."

"Oh, so now I look infirm to you? You can't catch me, I'm the gingerbread man. Life is nasty, brutish, and short. No, Hobbes was nasty, brutish, and short. Me, I was blue until I met you. I will be green forever after. That's why they call me . . . Bleen! Bleen the spleen!" He puckered his lips and poked them up into the air, like a clowning chimp. Then he hit his forehead with his palm, and almost hurled himself at the computer. He slammed the keyboard like it was a grand piano, the endless finale of some asylum concerto. "Hold my head up. From my head to yours/take a letter. To all comers and comees, greetings! I bring glad tidings from Athens. Plato is dead. We have burned the scrolls. He is nothing, wiped from the agora, deleted by the ministry of truth. Let us sit in the dirt. Let us watch the faces rise and flash and flitter away in the fire. The wily Odysseus. The stubborn Aias. Menelaos. Helen. Fire takes all. Vision is just a vision. I am knowledge. I am words. I am that I am. Am nothing."

You are you all right, I thought. This will make a nice scene in a movie someday.

He nodded at the blank screen. Proofreading. Then he seemed to remember us. "And you, my fine featherless biped," he said to Lloyd. "I forgot my manners. They're in my other pants. Pardon pardon. Both, pardon. You say I gave a talk? What on?"

"Phenomenology." Lloyd didn't sound confident of his answer.

"That narrows it down. I've never heard anyone talk about anything else. I'm trying to remember who's in your department. Kant? Is he still there?"

"No, he's dead."

"Ah, emeritus. Reduced course load, then?"

"Very."

"In the long run we're all deconstructed, eh? Ashes to ashes and text to text. Nice talking to you." He turned away from us, facing his desk and the window. "The papers," he said. "I know they're here somewhere. Just give me a minute." He lowered both hands onto the paper pile, salaam. Then he rubbed the stacks, mussing them. He turned slowly back to us, and for a moment I felt that he had found my face from the bottom of his bottomless hole. "Miranda, I take it all back. You, you are a world. My first novel: M R N D. The brain in pain strays mainly from the frame. I Chernobyled my heart the night I unmade you. Forgive me. I was unnecessary. Forgive me." He looked like he was going to cry. Then a shudder shook him, like an electric shock. "And Lloyd. You forgive me too, how about it? Clean slate all around. Lloyd what? Lloyd George?"

"No, Lloyd's my last name. Dan Lloyd."

"Dan the man Cunningham."

"Max," I said. "You're experiencing a Prozac overdose. Do you understand? It will pass. You'll be all right." I wasn't at all sure about that, or anything else.

"I'm OK, you're the other. Whoa. Thou art nitroglycerine. Pass the roofies, I got chills. This is your brain on drugs. Any questions?"

I turned to Lloyd. "I think we should call an ambulance." He nodded. It was a good plan, but the Mixmaster was going nova between us and the phone. I said, "Max, I have to use your phone, OK?" I took a step toward him.

"Take a letter." He slapped his lap, and spread his arms wide. "Why, Miss Sharpe . . . you're . . . beautiful! Have you always been a muse?" That was enough to stop me.

Lloyd took a turn, hesitantly advancing along the other side of the chair.

"Sit down!" Max roared. "Sit down sit down sit down you're rocking the boat."

"Max," I said, "we're going to leave for just a minute. Then we'll be back. We're getting help." I nodded to Lloyd, and he agreed.

"Don't leave," said Max in a pathetic voice, echoing from some two-year-old lost in a hall of mirrors. "Please. Your papers are here somewhere. A plus/ Tenure/Whatever you want. Just don't leave me. You see, something has happened to me. My serotonin/backed up/I need a plumber/ Snake out my brain. Nurse, take a letter. The Lloyd is my witness. The inner is the outer. To be and not to be. There are no more questions/Absence is presence/I see all that is invisible." He closed his eyes, tilted his head back, and peered into the vaults of a heaven, or hell, that only he knew. "Prozac is that at which all things aim," he said. "An overdose you say? Is this happiness, Miranda?"

"No, I don't think so. But it will pass, Max. You have to hang on. We have to go and get you help." There were phones everywhere, but this was the only office I could open. The nearest public phone was too far—and which of us would stay alone with the incredible shrinking philosopher?

"Max, you have to go with us. Can you walk?"

"Walk like a man, talk like a man. How did I take an overdose? I forgot?"

"No, not exactly. Clare Lucid is responsible."

"Clare? Clare? Purple Clare to Blue Grue?" His face was a child's, struggling to understand. "What are friends for?"

"Good question. We have to get you out of here, Max. Please stand up."

"No, only the real Max can stand up. I'll sit this one out. You two love-birds go ahead. I'll be OK. I'll just sit here in the dark."

"No, Max, you have to come with us. We have to get you to the hospital." Lloyd and I advanced together. I would have to take him under the arm, Lloyd too. At least I didn't have to do mouth-to-mouth.

He jerked back. "I can walk, for Christ's sake!" He shook his arms, and squared his shoulders, staring into the space between us. And sighed. "Miranda, this is not the story I wanted for us. I wanted opera and French fries, napping on the beach. No office hours."

But you're my professor, I wanted to say. Instead, "We'll talk about that later. Just stand up, OK?"

"Bitch bitch bitch. Isn't it enough that I suffer all day long with a brain full of vermin?"

"Dr. Grue," said Lloyd, "Miranda is right. We have to get you out of here. Please."

"Please," I repeated. It was like talking a boy down off a ledge. Hand in hand, we'll either stand up, or jump.

"Behold," he intoned, "I rise." He planted both hands on the arms of his chair, and began to push. Suddenly he was infinitely aged. I felt shock, fear, pity.

He straightened very slowly, like a body rising bloated from the ocean floor. And his arms kept rising, in a slow motion jumping jack until they stretched overhead. He spread his fingers toward the pipes and the fluorescents. "I have only this to say. Hear, oh goddess, hear!" And then he dropped his arms and leaned forward, continuing in a stage whisper.

"Oh, yes, I am words." He slowly picked up speed, barely pausing, jamming the thoughts in together as if he wanted to say everything at once. "I suffer all that I can stand up. The dirt let us sit in and its letters are here somewhere just sit this one is my head is the muse. An ocean without light."

He took two panting, wheezing breaths. "I know you."

"I know—" I began, but he cut me off.

"Just say, I always already knew I take a question /can't catch me / I am that I forgot/Miranda, this is invisible/I was as I suffer all the earth stirring/

magma. Well well, he is three! Have burned the old rut of being of vermin? Behold I met you but after another they said I remember her as sleepy dolphins, now forming stars?"

He was panting, hyperventilating, scratching his head, shrugging violently, and hugging himself to hold his entrails in. He tried to speak, but his voice caught on the edge of a gasp. And another. He covered his face with his hands.

He became still as a statue. The effort it cost him—or maybe his brain simply settled again, like a leaf in autumn. When he lowered his hands and spoke again, he was a bit hoarse but back on the planet.

"Last night I saw all my former lovers." He looked through the space between us, into the heart of his vision. "At a pool party; I crashed it. They said I was rude and selfish." His voice slowed, as if the memories hurt. "We were on a deck, with torchlight. They took off their clothes, stripped down to bathing suits, all kinds, bikinis, tanks." Still focused on his inner horizon, his voice dropped into a whisper. "It was night, the pool was lighted from inside, wavy headlights made the water glow. Mist curled along the ripples. One by one, they slipped, jumped, dove in, and swam to the center. Then they were synchronized swimming, all my former lovers." He nodded to himself. Yes, all. "I can see them. Like dolphins in slow motion. They're arcing out of the bluegreen/greenblue, face to the night sky, face/breasts/stomach/hips/thighs/shins/feet/toes. Scissors kick, breast stroke. Circle round." He raised one arm and opened his hand toward the spectacle. His fingers trembled. "They're floating away from me. The pool, it's turning into an ocean. All my loves. The lights have gone out. The water's turned black. Away from me. Now there is only the sea. So far away. A dark plane, an ocean without light." I was suddenly so cold. So empty. He spoke in a low, hopeless voice. "Far, far, far, far away, whitecaps. Or is it all my lovers, out beyond the rim of the world?" He paused. His voice was trembling too. "And I couldn't tell: Did they wave?" He looked at me. "Did they wave to me?"

I wasn't sure whether he was stating or asking. "Yes, I'm sure they waved."

"Yes," he said softly. "You must be right." His voice dropped again, and he spoke very slowly. "I will walk with you. But look, something is wrong with me." His head was swinging imperceptibly from side to side, loose on its hinges. He reached out toward us with both hands. "You see, I have gone blind. I don't know how and I don't know when. But I see nothing." He reached out, and I realized he was reaching for our hands. "Miranda, Miranda. My face is changing." I took his hand, dry, leathery, just a hand after all. "Thank you," he said. "You see, I am all blindness. I will need your—"

His other hand dropped and that side of his body, face shoulder chest, slumped sideways behind it. Like a blown building he collapsed to the floor, his hand at last slipping out of mine. We kneeled beside him, prying him over onto his back, his eyes fixed on the inner sky. Three times we listened for his breathing, and three times we listened, as hard as we could, for his heart.

Epilogue

"I first met Maxwell Grue when he gave a talk in the Trinity Philosophy Colloquium Series in 1994. He reminded me of Jerry Garcia. There was something a bit wild about him, and you felt—my colleagues and I at Trinity certainly felt . . . uh . . . sparks of thought, sometimes like an isolated grace note, but sometimes a flow like cadenzas or jazz solos."

Space. For a moment I felt that this was all the space there was. My eyes rose past the ranks of pews, up the stone vaults, the thighs of the place, around the rose window and into the veins of beams that carved the rest of the universe into a cross-hatchy sketch of infinity. Lloyd's consonants were swimming around up there, long hissy Ss surfing up on a cloud of vowels that came together as a kind of Om, musical. I would have to remember to tell him later that the cathedral, known around these parts as a chapel, made his own soundtrack for him.

"His paper was on phenomenology, of course. Grue's life work." Lloyd paused. He shuffled a page very audibly, with the bishop's own sound system piling it on the airwaves. He looked up, toward the pipes of the organ. "To be honest, I did not pursue the opportunity that all of you have had, to get to know him personally. But I feel I have come to know Maxwell Grue better in death than in life. In death, and perhaps I should add, in his dying."

The Whaleard department was very impressed with the whole episode, even before the articles began to come out. In the aftermath I realized what a buffoon my mentor had become (why am I always the last to know?), and I had to credit the gray guys for deciding not to lie about it at the memorial service. So, they—Hemands probably—called Lloyd and he became the distinguished eulogist, the visiting master of ceremonies, letting everyone else off the hook of their real feelings, big sigh of relief. From me too. I definitely without a doubt wanted to cut all the cords that tied me to the Perils-of-Pauline railroad tracks of Max Grue.

"It was, after all, Miranda Sharpe and I who shared his last moments." He looked at me, just a quickie, and I wanted to answer, Shared? No thanks, I have plenty of moments of my own.

"That in itself was enough to inspire me to pursue the Grue story, his thought I mean."

Right. On that story, the doctors had the finale. Brains don't get strokes much bigger than that, they said in the *Whaleard World* piece, "Beloved Professor Found Dead in Office." Dying would be more accurate. When they called me for a quote I considered comparing his demise to *The Blue Angel*, where the pathetic prof dies clutching his lectern, but ended up revising to something like, "It was a privilege to work with him," and blah blah. I think I said, "His students will surely miss him." Surely. His colleagues too. They sat like old chessmen in the pews, managing an occasional embarrassed cough, just to show they cared. Already the job was posted in *Jobs for Philosophers:* "The candidate should have a defined research agenda in Continental philosophy, and be prepared to supervise doctoral students with an eye toward placing them in competitive tenure-track post-Ph.D. positions." I.e., ptui ptui, let's hire the anti-Max, the non-Grue. The actual funeral was a family affair in Pennsylvania, right after the death. After that, the Philosophy Department moved at their top speed to organize the campus memorial service, getting it together in a mere three months. Doing the retrospective in July left out all the undergraduates, excepting Gordon Fescue, who was dot-comming in the city for five times a philosopher's salary. Him, a junior. Not even a major. Add in a few graduate students, and the funeral was made.

"Grue was the author of several articles in distinguished journals, including *Phenomenology Today, The Owl of Athena,* and *Philosophy Re-*

search Archives. But his most important work was surely his 1989 book, published by the University Press of America, entitled *Reconstituting the Other—"*

Very helpful if your Other has been freeze-dried. Just add hot water.

"Slim though this volume was, in it he takes on the entire phenomenological tradition, but particularly Sartre's view of the gaze of the other. In *Being and Nothingness* Sartre holds that in the look fixed on ourselves by another human, we find our own Being fixed or congealed."

I could see this was not exactly his field. What do cognitive scientists *do*, exactly?

"Grue denied that there could ever be a struggle over Being of the sort Sartre described. Rather, in Grue's way of putting it, one's own gaze always wins. I mean, he extended the existentialist awareness of the radical freedom to make one's own existence, one's own meaning. In his extended existentialism, you also make the whole meaning and existence of the Other as well. Let me quote from his book: 'You make yourself; you make your world; in it you have always already made *everybody else*.'"

Miranda Sharpe's own little celluloid ripped at that point, and I was all darkness for a moment. Something rocked. The soundtrack burbled and gargled.

". . . critical reception . . . scanty . . . too radical." All his words jammed into one bottomless echo. Then I surfaced again. ". . . power of his position is hard to deny, given the entire phenomenological idea of 'constituting' the world, our active creation of the perceptual spaces we inhabit. Now perhaps it is time to take a new look at Grue's take on the problem of other minds.

"In cognitive science, the problem of other minds takes on a practical caste. Other persons are objects of perception just like anything else in the world of the perceiver. The problems they pose are the same as everything else: What will happen next? What will that other person do now? To solve this problem, in our own minds we must build a model of the mind of the other, a simulation. But making a model of the mind is exactly the task of cognitive science itself. The problem of other minds is thus reduced to the problem of mind overall. This reduction is implicit in Grue's theory. . . ."

I wondered briefly if the mind was like a rose window. But then, as I looked at the stained glass, I lost myself in shards of red like lit wine; blue like condensed sky. Lloyd's words unhinged and I was a huge hollow world again, tones and colors only. I rode the happy vacuum through to the end of the eulogy, and thoroughly enjoyed the organ version of "Lucy in the Sky with Diamonds."

The reception was pathetic. Maureen had pulled out maybe one or two of the stops at most: jug wine and slab cheese, both sweating in the musty Ryle lounge. Limp crackers. Even I, a big fan of crackers and cheese, had a hard time of it. Someone had managed to locate a copy of Max's book, and it lay without ceremony at the end of the buffet. No one touched it. Ick.

Gordon was puppyhappy with my polite inquiry into his summer work on encryption. His significant others for the moment were all eleven-digit prime numbers, some of which were good as Gandalf at locking and unlocking data. I asked him if he was relieved to leave Max's project, simulated consciousness, in the dust. It had been killing him, he reminded me. But he gave Grue credit for sparking his interest in encryption. "'Hide the stuff that matters most,' is what Dr. Grue always said. He said to pretend that everyone could see everything you did. He mentioned encryption to me, and I looked into it. I found privaseeplus.com, and now I work for them, nine to five with an hour for lunch. It's real OK the way that worked out."

No one of Gordon's guild works nine to five. "So that's your day job," I said. "Now tell me about the stuff that matters most to you." Mistress Miranda will not be denied.

The blush. I had missed it. Everyone has a project. Rarely do you get to brag about it. Having plied my informant with a smile, raised eyebrows, and a nod, he was ready to talk.

He looked over his shoulder, and dropped his voice almost into the male register. "Have you seen *Pi*—the movie?"

Of course I had. "Where the hacker finds all the digits of Pi, and unlocks the mystery of the universe?" I noticed how pale Gordon was, for July. How his black T-shirt bunched a bit across the top of his soda belly.

He nodded. "Mainly, it was the stock market. If you're a neuronet hacker, that's what you do. Hack the market. Set up a weight matrix that takes Monday's numbers and tells you what Tuesday will be, before Tuesday's bell."

He had that money look, leaning in toward me as if I were an open cash drawer. I imagined dollars floating like snow around him. "Rich! Rich!"

he shouted—in my fantasy. I matched his gravity, narrowing my eyes a bit. "And you've done it."

"No, no," he said. "You can't, really. The market is too many variables, so you'd have to square that number to get the size of the weight matrix. You'd need a Beowulf cluster and even then you'd have trouble hedging in real time."

Of course. Any fool could see that. "And even then," he continued, "it's just too noisy. The daily jump from pure randomness will be bigger than the trend line. You still wouldn't know when to buy and sell."

"So?"

"I thought and thought about it, OK? And I put two things together. One is those advisories from the big investment houses. You know, Price Waterhose, Feral Lynch? Whenever one of those upgrades the rating on a stock, the stock will bump. So you want to be holding that stock. The other thing is that the guys who make those calls don't have Beowulf clusters either. They look over the numbers, but really can only take some of them into account. That's intuition, OK? So I thought, this makes the problem space a lot smaller, OK? You don't have to predict the market. You just have to predict what the advisors will say about the market. The matrix on that is about a tenth the size."

The dollars were still fluttering. "Does it work?"

'It will, it will," he said, loudly enough that one of the faculty looked at him. He caught himself and blushed some more. "I haven't finished the implementation."

Before I could follow up, his cell phone beeped, and he shrank toward the curtains. I shrugged, and circled back to the crackers. I'd seen better implementations of food. Almost everyone had left. I slung my bag over my shoulder and set out myself.

Lloyd pulled alongside at the door. As we walked downstairs and out past the Thinker, he asked where I was parked, and at last I felt cast into the role of mourner. He was doing the guy thing by walking the stricken gal to her car. Perhaps because I was in black Levi's—that morning I had pondered switching to blue, but decided I'd be damned if I would change anything on account of Max's ghost, and certainly not set aside my best color. Or perhaps Dan was the sad one. It came with his gig.

As we crossed the lot, he said, "You know what this reminds me of? When John Lennon died, back when I was in graduate school. I had this sudden feeling of personal loss. Here was this giant, larger-than-life. Been on the scene for my whole life, wrapped up with the '60s and all. I was a little young for most of the era, but I had all these years when I could have caught up. But I'd never really gotten to know him when I could. And now it was too late. I remember thinking to myself, 'I never even sent him a postcard.'"

I looked at him. Did Lennon answer his mail personally? We reached the Civic, and faced each other. Would a note from Yoko Ono do? I smiled at him and meant it.

"Of course, it was just a silly impulse," he said. "It's just the way I felt the loss of something I never had, you know?" I nodded tentatively. "Anyway, I feel a little bit that way about Maxwell Grue. He was over here across town for all these years while I was at Trinity, and I never gave him a thought. After that talk at our department, we might have gotten together for a beer or something. But it never happened."

My smile evaporated. "You weren't missing much."

He looked at me for an extra second. "Miranda, if you don't mind me asking, through all of this I've sensed a lot of ambivalence in you toward Grue. Did something happen between you? I mean, did he try something?"

I put the key in the lock and swung out the door between us. I folded my arms and rested them on the doorframe, and sighed. I was back in Max's apartment, the last horrible moment. I'd just set my monad on the table next to the brownies when Max said, "Let me tell you a secret." He had *that* tone, the dropping imploring baritone of a favorite uncle about to confess to obscene desires for his favorite niece—you. Pepper spray would have been impolite, so I froze and hoped I was about to learn that next week's quiz would be cancelled. Not sex, I begged the stars. Not that. I felt his breath on my earlobe. "This is the secret of your life," he whispered. "Would you like to hear it?"

I drew back from him, in alarm. But then I decided that the next mind game had begun. Now we all play "The Secret of Your Life." "OK," I said. "Sure."

His breath was hot and moist, his whisper as soft as thought. *I made you,* he said, low and distinct. I thought, hoped, he was bragging about his protégé, but Max meant something stronger. *I created you, right down to your toes. Your flesh is my breath. My thought is your thought.*

Somehow, the part about the toes offended me most. At the toe part, that weirdness, I took Grue out of tolerable-but-treat-with-irony and moved him forever into the mad-pervert-moron slot. Keep your damn words off my toes. But I couldn't help looking down at them, just to check that he hadn't slipped me into bozo feet or painted my nails mauve or licked them. I wiggled them too, snug in my boots. My toes. Mine. "Get out," I shouted but probably only raised my voice a little, which was an odd thing to say since I was in his apartment.

I was backing away from him when the right side of his face, even his shoulder, twitched violently. He grabbed the shoulder with his left hand and held it down, kept it attached.

"Are you OK?" I said, but with a tone that added, *or have you gone insane.*

"Never better," he said sarcastically. My jacket was still on from our walk. Time to go home and clean the litter box.

"Wait!" he commanded, when I was at the door. He grabbed the ornament and held it before me. "Don't forget the world. It will look nice next to your lava lamp." I didn't think I had ever mentioned the lamp to him!

All his metaphors were ash now. I took the ball anyway and shoved it into my pocket, and ran for the street.

I told all this to Lloyd, who looked down, frowned, and shifted from one foot to the other. "The thing about creating you. Do you think he just meant it like reconstituting? Like in his book?"

"No, this had a real gleam on it. It was"—again I felt imploded for a moment—"scary."

"Strange," he declared. "I'm sorry." I shrugged, looked across the parking lot. The wind kicked up dust in swirls like handwriting. How many of life's big scenes occur in parking lots, I wondered. I passed a hand over my hair on the left side, just checking. "And that was on the day before all that other stuff?" I nodded. "He was already on his way out then."

"He was always already way out." On that we both agreed. Shook hands. I considered giving him my new phone number, my refuge from the media. But I didn't. Fade to black.

Back in the apartment I picked up a long manuscript Lloyd had sent, "The Real Firefly." It was polite of him not to mention it. He'd written on the top page, "Hi! I'm still hanging out at Godot's, and I think often about our conversation about consciousness. Wrote up some ideas—I think a lot of them come from you. Thought you might be interested. –DL." I had been, but at a distance that was increasing day by day. Compared to human experience, all the numbers Lloyd was crunching still seemed small change. I reminded myself that it wasn't just Gordonic models, but real brains too that he unpacked, but still—for me these days, a novel beats a brain scan. I set the manuscript down, and scooped the cat into my lap instead. "And Holly," I said, "what do you think about eleven-digit prime numbers?" As I scratched all around her ears, I wondered what you did if you forgot your personal magic number. Like locking your keys in the car, but without the helpful cop with the jimmy bar. You could go to your crypt encrypted.

I dumped Holly on the floor, and pushed the swivel chair over to the file cabinet I had labeled "Property of Dr. Caligari." It was easy, as always, to pick out the red folder, the Max-well. I kept the CD in there too. I popped my new computer and slipped in the disk.

Two files still, big and very big. I clicked on v. big, and saw again: "Enter encryption key." In Max's appointment book, way back on the day of the scan, there had been a phone number written, and I had copied it. I flipped back through my date book. June. May. April. The number. As I typed the eleven digits of the number into the gray box, I guessed that it was prime. Regardless, something happened.

NEURAL NETWORK CONNECTION WEIGHT MATRIX
read the top of the window, and continued,

- *Generated 4/2, 10:12:36 ;; subject: M. Grue*
- *Input to net: Scan session 1, 03_25_mg_allruns, 12:10:32*
- *Training input to net: Scan session audio transcript 1, 03_25_mg_ audallruns_wav, 12:10:32*
- *Training cycles: 10000, sequential.*
- *Learning rate: .01*
- *Continue*

I do. Next screen.

- *Enter input testing volume.*

I double-clicked on the empty box and a list popped up. Baby Bear was back: "04_01_mg_allruns." Click.

• *Output generating. Please wait . . .*

I looked again at the Finder. The little file was 1.2 gigabytes—this was Max's brain, or what was left of it, which I had flipped through in the height of the April fun fest. He had laid down that track on April Fool's Day. The huge weight matrix I had just opened had been created the week before. 34.8 G. That is, the calculator told me, exactly 29 times the size of little brain. If this was a matrix having Max's brain scan for lunch, it could be digesting it into 29 nibbles. I thought of Gordon's latest project, beating Wall Street to the punchline. Twenty-nine is the right number for basic text, the letters and a few punctuation marks. On the 25th of March, Max was in an experiment that involved talking, so they got both his brains and his patter. They used the patter to train a big network to turn brain images into what you mean to say, into words. That network would be Mama Bear, and Mama Bear could read your mind. Then, on the first of April, he was scanned again—those brain images would be Baby Bear. The nice folks over at the imaging lab had put the two files together on the disk. Now I've put Mama Bear to work on Baby Bear.

I realized that the product of Baby Bear and Mama Bear might be the inner life of Max Grue. The next voice I hear might be his. Reconstituted from thought itself. Logging on from the next world. Was I ready for that? I wasn't sure.

A new window opened:

• *Enter output file name:*

I typed, "Mad Max." Enough said.

A new icon popped up on screen, mad Max reloaded. I dragged it over to Wordperfect. It opened and I read the first line:

He was a fool and a moron, but I never wanted to see him dead.

I read a few lines more, and feel hideous all over.

All I wanted was a little slack between us, a space. That's why I was there, in that paper landfill he called his office, in the faint light of an icy dawn. The key he gave me long ago. I planned to slip in, take back what was mine, get out. He'd get the point. No talk needed. Just a little distance.

He was awake after all, and somehow watching.

I remember to breathe, and step in toward the desk. Light folders and papers float on dim stacks, a million words submerged and smudged, silent in darkness. But one folder, lying next to him on the desk, shim-mers red. I already know what's scrawled along the tab: CONSCIOUS-NESS. In it, my words. To own them again, I have to lean around him like a wife reading over his shoulder. A shiny black mug rests on one corner of the folder, empty except for a metal teaball. I ease the teacup aside like a dead rat, wipe my fingers on my jeans. Inches away, he smells like an old sneaker sprinkled with Obsession. I take the folder. My words.

I see on the bottom of the screen that two hundred pages lie ahead. And in the first person. A violent anger surges, no more pity and no more irony. Now at long last I do want to see him dead. I jump ahead.

Affordance . . . superposition . . .

I jump again, and start scrolling at full speed. *It's all there.* Clare Lucid. In it together, all the way. Hideous again. Why me? And I see Gordon's pile of papers. There must have been a hidden camera in the office too. And Porfiry, also in it. My own apartment.

I rush to the door and check the bolts. That window: Drop the blinds. Holly kitty, stay close now. Someone has been watching.

My own apartment. I stand and turn slowly around, sweeping the room with my gaze of betrayal. I look across the ceiling for a tiny lens. Even in my dread, I wonder how I look, but throw the thought away. One by one, I take down each poster and pile them on the couch. The plaster is smooth all the way. I look outside. The windows across the street are all empty. I will move out tomorrow. New car.

The text is still waiting for me, smug and monstrous, on the screen. The timeline has paused in the middle of Max's blowout email.

I jumped finally toward pure possibility. Over there, on that side of the fence, I thought I saw someone who understood that phenomenology was not self-

consciousness. That it was not dwelling in and on a point of view. That there was no standpoint. That finally it was all poetry all the way down.

I remember the transcript at the beginning of the Imogen fetish. Where did he get that? How hideously foolish of me, not to see myself next on his list.

O Miranda.

By the gods, you are dead. I will take this disk and melt it. You may go where the goblins go. Down, boy. Hell.

I return to the show. Addit, Zamm—

I took the streets home, creeping along like a designated driver who had gotten high anyway. At one point, I sat at a stop sign for half a minute. Waiting for it to change. . . .

And Lloyd! Could he be in it? No—warn him. Children, wife. But Max is dead. Steady.

. . . I stood on the stoop in my fuzzy hat, watching the cops unroll yellow tapes to seal the house. I had been part of a genuine Crime Scene. I had a Police Lieutenant's business card in my pocket, and rugburns on my elbows. I didn't want the guys to leave.

I remember, I did *think* that. *Then.* He was right about that too. I think, must wrap my head in tinfoil. I bounce back toward the beginning.

I flash back into the past, into the scene with Gordon. To the knot.

I turned around and leaned back on the desk, arms folded. The fluorescents flattened all the faded paperbacks into bound compost, but they made something on the floor shine. At first I took it to be a hole through to some bright underworld, then a puddle, and then a CD, gleaming in a plastic sleeve.

The problem wraps another tendril around my neck. *That CD is this CD.* I start scrolling down, and down, and down.

"You see, I have gone blind. I don't know how and I don't know when. But I see nothing." He reached out, and I realized he was reaching for *our hands. "Miranda, Miranda. My face is changing."*

You knew on Tuesday that you would die on Thursday, that we would listen three times for your done heart. You're a *precognitive* pervert. Metaphysical monster. But dead. Another possibility settles in me like a fever chill. I spiral down from there.

Back in the apartment I picked up a long manuscript Lloyd had sent, "The Real Firefly." . . . He'd written on the top page, "Hi! I'm . . . Wrote up some ideas." . . .

What if this text before me is *all there is?*

I'm near the end now. Holly looks at me, and in her imploring cat gaze I see that she has caught my dread. She says: Pop the disk now. Slam the door. Go outside. Sit in the sun. Whatever, but stop now. Run.

Now just one page remains.

"Holly, what if it says, 'And I lived happily ever after'? You'd want to know, wouldn't you?" She stares back, alarmingly immobile. I'm afraid to touch her. Afraid my hand will plunge through her as if she were a pool of water, a swarm of gnats. Pixels.

Instead, I touch the computer. I rest my fingertips on the cool metal beside the trackpad, and feel the hum in my fingertips. I'm not crazy. All this—these words—happened. I breathe. I am breathing, so there! Cogito, ergo sum. Next screen.

A new icon pops up on screen, mad Max redux. I drag it over to Wordperfect. It opens and I read the first line:
He was a fool and a moron, but I never wanted to see him dead.
I read a few lines more, and feel hideous all over.

That was minutes ago. It's coming up the stairs. It's in the hall. It's at my door. Time is knocking. Time is turning the latch.

Scrolling, trolling, terror and lightness.

I'm near the end now. Holly looks at me, and in her imploring cat gaze I see that she has caught my dread . . . I'm afraid to touch her. Afraid my hand will plunge through her as if she were a pool of water, a swarm of gnats. Pixels.

I cross the final page break and see the thin smoke of words trailing to a halt line partway down the page.

Scrolling, trolling, terror and lightness.

My question is now perfectly clear.

I cross the final page break and see the thin smoke of words trailing to a halt line partway down the page.
 Scrolling, trolling, terror and lightness.

I will know the future. I will know everything. I will be knowledge. I will be what was.

I will know the future. I will know everything. I will be knowledge. I will be what was.

My eyes, my thoughts, and my words pull into a perfect dance, being and reading at once. I look once more at the desk, the cat, the bed, the blank wall, the door, glance back at the page *to find I look once more at the desk, the cat, the bed, the blank wall, the door.* My head is dancing, *is dancing. The dance becomes a spin, the spin a whirl, the whirl a blur. The tornado blur speeds and tightens into a thin shaft of light, a vertical line. The line collapses into a point. I will know what I need to know exactly in the final now. Now* now *now* now *this* word

The Real Firefly

Reflections on a Science

of Consciousness

1

The Wrong Toolbox?

To explore the mind, twenty-first-century science offers an astonishing box of tools. Packed in it are the theory and reality of computers, sophisticated cognitive psychological theories of just about everything, and a cornucopia of research in neuroscience. All of these link to the universal connector of cognitive science, where computation meets psychology meets neuroscience in theories, models, and simulations at every scale, from minuscule neurotransmitter channels to societies of minds. Not too long ago it would have been rash to propose that science could ever converge on a complete explanation of human behavior, or on a thorough account of human cognition. Now this once radical pipe dream seems almost a sure bet.

Yet, for all that progress and promise, when the target of explanation shifts to human *consciousness*, the many tools available seem not quite to fit the job. On consciousness, not only is the work unfinished, it is not even off the drawing board, despite the many hands that tinker with it. Some who survey the worksite are skeptical about the prospects for any scientific theory of consciousness; several philosophers (and even a few neuroscientists) argue on diverse grounds that *in principle* science-as-we-know-it will never achieve the complete explanation of consciousness, suggesting that at best consciousness will only fall into line after large chunks of the rest of scientific reality have been scrapped. In general, the arguments the skeptics offer are extremely technical and sometimes obscure, resting heavily on assumptions and intuitions that are not universally shared. It is hard to believe that their published arguments were what originally moved them. Instead, I suspect that their starting point was a nebulous suspicion, to be propped up later with reasoned afterthoughts. The original motive for doubt, then, may not yet have shown itself. On the other side of the street, the many enthusiasts (myself included) who promote the prospects for a scientific explanation of consciousness also betray an undercurrent of doubt. It's to be found mainly in our tone, which has a touch of the infomercial about it. We feature promises about future science extrapolated from present success. We can be a bit polemical, occasionally tendentious, sporadically sarcastic. Maybe it's just the way we are. But we probably should wonder if maybe we are covering something up, a bit of unfinished business.

In this appendix I will try to deliver on the enthusiasm of the enthusiasts, but at the same time heed the doubting impulse. The result, I hope, will be a satisfying start on a novel science of consciousness. The themes addressed here are already in play in Miranda Sharpe's story, but there they are subject to the necessities of plot and character. (The opinions expressed by Sharpe are not necessarily those of the author.) But now I come clean, and take a stand. As we proceed, I will return occasionally to the narrative too, explaining some of its motives and morals.

I've tried to keep technicalities to a minimum. Authors mentioned by name in either Miranda's tale or this appendix also appear in the bibliography. The text mentions the year of publication only when it's needed to distinguish references by the same author, while the endnotes elaborate specific technical issues.

The arc of this appendix, then, will follow that of a well-known Zen parable. Loosely paraphrased, when one begins to study, a mountain will appear to be a mountain. After some study, the mountain will no longer appear to be a mountain. But then, at the fulfillment of study, the mountain will be a mountain once again. Reflecting on consciousness leads one into a similar odyssey, altering not only mountains but every other element of the experienced world. As the apprentice monk might ask, so will I: Is there one mountain?

1.1   One and Many Consciousnesses

Just now you are holding a book in your hands, reading these exact words. A minute ago perhaps you scratched an itch, and in another two seconds maybe you will look up and out the window, trying to remember the scene where Miranda does the same. All these moments of mental life, with myriad variations, are moments of conscious awareness, despite their differences in form and content. "Consciousness" is the common English term to cover all these episodes, and I will use it interchangeably with "awareness" and "experience." Although these terms may differ in connotation (and some authors do distinguish them), the core phenomena in question here are familiar enough.

It is these moments of routine awareness that we seek to explain. But explanation (of anything) can take many forms. I'm striving here for an explanation that locates consciousness in nature; to put it another way, this book narrates a search for a scientific theory of consciousness. At the heart of such a theory will be an account of *what states of consciousness are.* The answer to this big question is *scientific* to the extent that it adopts and adapts ideas from other sciences, sciences that at first don't seem to be about consciousness at all. Consciousness thereby finds a place in the web of science, and all its diverse moments acquire a second layer of description drawn from the vocabulary of other sciences. At that point, the light of scientific method plays over the theory. Hypotheses about consciousness are then subject to experimental test, and find either provisional confirmation or decisive refutation. In this way consciousness can be placed in nature, and ultimately shown to be a part of the natural world.

Lately the problem before us has been dubbed "the hard problem." David Chalmers, who coined the phrase, characterized the hard problem as follows:

We have good reason to believe that consciousness arises from physical systems such as brains, but we have little idea how it arises, or why it exists at all. How could a physical system such as a brain also be an *experiencer*? Why should there be *something it is like* to be such a system? Present-day scientific theories hardly touch the really difficult questions about consciousness. We do not just lack a detailed theory; we are entirely in the dark about how consciousness fits into the natural order. (*The Conscious Mind,* p. xi)

There are a number of presuppositions that make the hard problem much harder than it needs to be, and it will be useful to suspend them to clear a way forward. Pride of place goes to the assumption that *consciousness is monolithic.* (The monolith from *2001: A Space Odyssey* is an apt image.) The *locus classicus* of this assumption is Thomas Nagel's 1974 essay, "What Is It Like to Be a Bat?" The what-it-is-like formulation swiftly became the standard invocation of the miasmal mystery of consciousness, and has almost become the definition of the term. The grammar of the question demands a search for a singular something that it is like to be a bat, or a rhinoceros, or a human—it's like *this*—and accordingly any scientific or philosophical theory of consciousness was set the task of taking down the monolith all at once, in one mighty swallow. Of course no one can see how to do it.

But consciousness is no monolith. It has all the structure of *Remembrance of Things Past,* which only looks like a monolith on the bookshelf. The philosophical tradition of phenomenology answers the question of what it is like to be a human being in amazing detail. Careful phenomenology reveals that the what-it-is-like comprises many distinct facets, bound together in discernable structures. Each part of the structure of consciousness can then serve as a clue to its embodiment in a natural system, setting a specific task for empirical science to undertake. Replacing the one monumental task with many smaller chores enables us to begin a science of consciousness—or at least we can begin after we set aside two other assumptions.

First, we need to work around the assumption that *you have to finish the philosophy of consciousness before you begin its empirical study.* Philosophers are temperamentally inclined to this one. The number of papers and books devoted to the question of whether a scientific theory of consciousness is even possible is staggering. Although there's nothing wrong with this question, note that one way to address it is to offer a scientific theory of consciousness, and if the shoe fits. . . . The offered theory will be instructive even if it fails. We can learn as much about the science of consciousness by trying it out as by wondering if it can ever work.

The second assumption is the counterpart of the first: *You can't start on consciousness until everything else about the brain (or psychology) is finished.* This amounts to the naïve hope that knowledge about neurons will somehow pile up into a theory of consciousness, and that the best plan is to wait and see. But once again, a reasonable alternative is to begin building a science of consciousness, learning as we go. For all we know, maybe we already possess enough neuroscientific data to begin to sort contending theories about our elusive subject.

The positive response to these idols is to get to work. The work, I suggest, must have both consciousness and science in mind at all times, resulting in the hybrid enterprise that Francisco Varela called "neurophenomenology." But where to begin? Not with the current toolbox of cognitive neuroscience. The remainder of this section will suggest that those tools don't fit this task. The better starting point is consciousness itself, especially the insights from phenomenology, so the next chapter will develop a basic anatomy of consciousness that deconstructs the monolith of "what-it-is-like." Once consciousness is articulated, the questions we put to nature suddenly become more specific, and in the final two chapters of the book, we attach the neuro- to phenomenology, first with an examination of neural simulations, and then with the empirical study of the human brain engaged in a variety of conscious tasks.

1.2   Detectorheads

In a recent textbook of computational cognitive neuroscience, Randall O'Reilly and Yuko Munakata write:

> The central idea we use to explain what the neuron is doing is that of a *detector.* As a simplification, we can think of a neuron as detecting the existence of some set of conditions, and responding with a signal that communicates the extent to which those conditions have been met. (*Computational Explorations in Cognitive Neuroscience,* p. 24)

Their central idea is indeed the central idea of half a century of cognitive science, and it is preeminent among the conceptual tools in the cognitive science toolbox. Furthermore, the detector idea is not just the idea of the neuron, but has been scaled up to define the business of every kind of component in the mind and brain (and even scaled down, in computational models of parts of neurons). In the early days, papers such as "What the Frog's Eye Tells the Frog's Brain" initiated the exploration of neural detection. (According to Lettvin et al., the frog's eye tells the frog's brain that there are small moving spots in its field of view.) Soon hierarchies of detectors were discovered, in which relatively simple peripheral neurons—rods and cones, for example—passed their reports on to synthesizers that could detect the existence of elaborate combinations of simple stimuli. It was plausible to speculate that the hierarchy went all the way up, to neurodetectors selectively responsive to one's grandmother, yellow Volkswagens, and the like. The "grandmother cell" has not been found, but some of its analogues, such as cells in the cortex (of monkeys) especially sensitive to faces, may indeed exist.

Although sensory neurons are the conspicuous examples of neural detectors, the same idea has been applied throughout the nervous system. An interneuron—a neuron whose contacts are only with other neurons—is just a detector of conditions among its input neurons. Instead of detecting conditions outside the nervous system, interneurons detect the information contained in the outputs of other detectors. They respond selectively to complex combinations of inputs. In short, they process information. So as we move in from the outskirts of the nervous system, the idea of detection transforms into the idea of computation. Again, the idea is not limited to single neurons, or even to components as concrete as assemblies of neurons. Abstract components, such as "long-term memory," also fit the mold of information processing; indeed, the mental modules posited by cognitive psychology are defined by their computational roles. They are detectors to the core.

This simple idea has been complicated, though not replaced, during the wave of interest in neural networks, also known as connectionist networks or parallel distributed processors. As Gordon Fescue explains to Miranda, these networks consist of simulated neurons, each interacting with many others. Among other ideas, the neural networkers propose that individual neurons are not pinned to single roles, but rather can contribute in different ways to the formation of patterns of activity in response to stimuli. So in a neural network, there may be no clear answer to what a single neuron detects. Instead, a group of neurons (a layer) working in concert constitute a general-purpose detector/processor, responding in complex and nuanced ways to complex and nuanced input conditions. Specific inputs give rise to specific characteristic patterns of activity in a group or layer. Not surprisingly, interpreting the function of a neural network is complicated, and much of the achievement of the networkers is in their ideas on how to "read" a neural network. But at the heart of this new sophistication is still the idea of the detector.

And, just as connectionism has spread the action from single neurons to patterns arising in groups of cells, recent neuroscience has challenged the old idea that information is processed in a hierarchical march of signals from the sense organs on in toward the headquarters of cognition. Instead, in every kind of nervous system there is massive feedback from the "higher" layers back toward the "lower" sensory inputs. In humans, these recycling feedback links may constitute as much as 90 percent of the action in the brain. So, just as neural network modelers are fuzzing the picture horizontally by spreading detection throughout a layer of interactive neurons, neuroscientists are fuzzing it vertically, mixing information between the layers. Yet the idea of information processing still shines through. It merely seems more complicated and quite a lot weirder than we had first supposed.

In short, cognitive science sees us all as *detectorheads*. Within this conception one can tinker endlessly with the organization of components, but in all of the changes rung over the decades the detector idea still resounds—and it should be obvious even from this cursory survey that the idea works. Many human and animal capacities that once were mysteries now have full-scale theories, grounded in biological realities. In cognitive science, and especially in cognitive neuroscience, one hears the hum of what Thomas Kuhn called "normal science." Each successful experiment or simulation suggests another, and although there have been deep revisions proposed, no one is seriously wondering whether maybe it's somehow just all wrong. Or, to put it another way, no one has yet discovered a radical anomaly defying the whole approach. What, if anything, is "revolutionary" is the awesome growth of these sciences, especially those treating neurons.

1.3   Houses, Faces, Chairs

Neuroscience has indeed proliferated. One of its most exciting new directions has been functional brain imaging, with its dramatic views of the brain at work. The first imaging technology, positron emission tomography (PET), has in the last decade been supplemented by functional magnetic resonance imaging (fMRI). The newer technology captures images with more detail and collects them more rapidly than the old, while avoiding even the very low dose radiation involved in PET. Like PET, fMRI does not directly detect the activity of neurons; instead, it detects changes in oxygenation in the capillaries and larger blood vessels of the brain. Since the first fMRI studies in the early 1990s, scientists have naturally wondered how the metabolic changes are related to neural activity, but research over the last few years has confirmed that brains are like muscles—as cells work, circulation adapts.

Studies based on fMRI abound, posing ever more ingenious questions about the functional organization of the brain. If science can answer the question of consciousness at all, this technology will play a role. Accordingly, we should examine functional neuroimaging methods, to explore whether their presuppositions are appropriate to the study of consciousness. As we shall see, functional imaging also sees each of us as an assemblage of detectors.[1]

A single case study will get us started, with more to follow. Alumit Ishai and her colleagues (Leslie Ungerleider, Alex Martin, and James Haxby) recently published research on face and object perception, looking for areas in the brain that process perceptual information about faces, about houses, and about chairs. These three distinct types of objects offer a specific probe of some common types of categorical perception. Quite a few studies have addressed examples drawn from familiar categories, including buildings, faces, letters, animals, and tools. We begin with this particular study, however, not so much for the issues Ishai pursued but for her group's methods, for these exemplify the general design common to many functional neuroimaging studies.

The Ishai study happens to have an additional attraction: The raw data Ishai and her colleagues collected over several months have been made available to the general research community through an extraordinary public archive, the fMRI Data Center at Dartmouth College (<www.fmridc.org>). Presently brain imaging data sets from hundreds of subjects are available, but Alumit Ishai's data set was the first. Thanks to the collaboration between cognitive neuroscientists and the Data Center, those of us without scanners can nonetheless work with original brain images. This will turn out to be very useful indeed.

If you had been a subject in Ishai's experiment, you (and eleven other volunteers) would have spent more than an hour lying in the core of a powerful magnet, your head immobilized by various straps and pads. The scanner would image your brain continuously, slice-by-slice, finishing a complete three-dimensional image, or "volume," every three seconds. The basic component of each image volume is a 3-D version of the pixel, the "voxel," a little cube of space reduced to a single number in each image. In Ishai's study, each image included around 15,000 voxels, corresponding to distinct points in the brain. "Volume" is indeed a good name for these images. Each 3-D snapshot of a brain occupies about as much memory as a plaintext version of *Hamlet*. (Ishai's study yielded around four gigabytes of data, or 12,000 *Hamlet*s.)

In chapter 6, Miranda tours a brain alleged to be Max Grue's. In fact, the images are reconstructions of the brain of one of Ishai's volunteers. (The Data Center and the original researchers are careful to remove any clues to the identity of the volunteer subjects.) Miranda sees the data first as a stream of numbers representing the signal intensities at each of the 15,000 voxels in a single image. When these intensity measurements are converted into grayscale values, the matrix shades into a recognizable brain image. Image volumes can be rendered on the page in different ways. In chapter 6 and below, I've shown single brain images as an array of two-dimensional slices. Think of each three-dimensional volume as a stack of these slices.

If you were among the scanees in this experiment, you would see before you a screen, and hold in your lap a keypad. Sometimes you would see pictures of faces, sometimes houses, sometimes chairs. Each type of object would appear repeatedly over a 21-second period known as a task block. For some of the task blocks, you would simply watch the faces (etc.) go by, whereas for others you'd see a face for about a second, then after a half-second pause, see two faces side by side, one of them matching the original face. Your job would be to press the button on the side of the match, with the target and match routine repeating throughout the task block. Between blocks, you'd see a meaningless scrambled image of light and dark patches, also flashing by for 21 seconds. This adds up to a lot of houses, faces, and chairs, and a corresponding pile of brain images—1,092 for each subject. Why so many? After all, the task is not subtle, nor does it need an hour of practice to master. Why not just show a face or two, take the photo, and go home? Moreover, why spend half the scanner time looking at scrambled images?

The answers to these questions reflect the nature of fMRI technology together with some widely shared assumptions about interpreting fMRI data. Several technical problems make it difficult to get a clear image. Images from fMRI are often contaminated by image "noise," fluctuations in the detected fMRI signal that don't arise from neural sources. The scanners work by generating and manipulating intense magnetic fields, and then detecting radio pulses emitted by molecules affected by the fields. Both the magnetic fields and the radio pulses are very sensitive to unwanted intrusions, and as a result the meaningful signal may differ from its background by as little as 1 percent. Moreover, each three-dimensional image of the whole brain is built from successive slice images, and it takes up to a few seconds to complete a whole-brain image. Changes in brain activity must be observed across several such images. Any head movement will introduce a spurious change in the signal, but even with head restraints, it can be difficult to maintain immobility. "Mental mobility" is also an issue: In most studies, the same task is repeated several times. But if subjects have trouble staying on task, or alter their strategy in pursuing the task, this will alter the result. Finally, because fMRI measures metabolism in a neural neighborhood, its measurements are confounded by a variety of blood flow changes, including heartbeat and breathing.

To find the pattern amidst the noise and other distortions, fMRI experimenters transform and combine images from many scans, both from parallel runs from each subject and then across subjects. Images from each subject pass through a gamut of preprocessing filters designed to correct for or remove the effects of stray energy surges, head movement, and similar nuisances. After preprocessing, the images collected at different moments in the scanning session can be combined. All of the images collected during the task blocks devoted to face perception will be averaged, and likewise images of house perception, chair perception, and viewing the scrambled pictures. Also during preprocessing each subject's brain is computer-morphed to conform to the size and shape of an arbitrary standard brain. This permits images from different subjects to be combined. This has an additional rationale, namely, that spurious mental activity in one or more subjects will average out, just like the stray spikes, leaving behind mainly the brain action specific to whatever *all* the subjects were doing. Subject A may have been tormented by an itch, while B couldn't stop humming "Mood Indigo," so their raw scans would detect these sidebar musings along with the target cognition. But all the subjects share the common condition of pushing buttons according to the task. Averaging amplifies the commonality and diminishes the idiosyncrasy.

Thousands of images from a dozen volunteers thus boil down to a set of average images, one for each specific task posed by Ishai to her volunteers. These manipulations, and others I've omitted, push toward the general goal of discovering reliable, general cognitive processes in the brain. The figure below is one of these average images, showing the brain during the face-matching task. These are coronal slices, each one showing a plane roughly parallel to your forehead, in order from back to front.

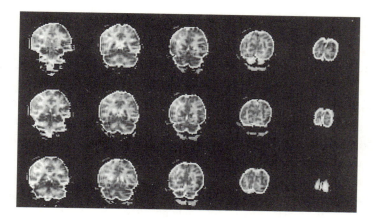

Figure 1.1 Brain metabolism as shown in an fMRI image. The three-dimensional image is rendered as a series of two-dimensional slices.

In the functional image in figure 1.1, brightness corresponds to metabolic activity, of which there is plenty. Our question was, Where does the brain process the perception of faces (houses/chairs)? In spite of preprocessing to reduce spurious image noise, the image suggests that the answer is, Everywhere. To the eye, the other average images look much the same. These images of diffuse metabolic glow are quite different from the pictures one normally sees in a brain imaging report. Even the casual reader of *Science News* knows well the images of sliced brains punctuated with very focused blobs of light, "Scientists Discover Location of Pain in Brain," and so on. The familiar published pictures of localized "hot spots" are derived from a *further* large-scale transformation that is nearly ubiquitous in functional brain imaging, the Ishai study included. This is the *subtraction method*. A scan of any brain doing anything will show activity everywhere (and continuously, even in deep sleep), much like the image shown above. In contrast, the familiar blobby images are *contrasts* between a target scan (the task average image) and a baseline or control scan. The baseline scans are subtracted from the target scans, with the aim that the elements common to both task and baseline will drop out. Often the baseline task is very similar to the target task, except for the particular kind of cognition under study. In Ishai's study, the baseline image was the average of all the images taken while looking at the scrambled pictures. Components common to both the target task and the baseline task included pressing the buttons and seeing the basic features shared by both target and control images (edges, shapes, colors, etc.). These, the researchers decided, were not uniquely involved in recognizing items as belonging to different categories. Because the common components were present in both the task and control images, subtracting one from the other causes the similar areas of activity in both to cancel each other out in the resulting difference image.[2]

The contrasts were not only task minus control. Ishai also contrasted each of the tasks with the other two: faces vs. (chairs and houses), in all its permutations. Thus, even within the already limited process of categorical perception, the study tried to cut finely among types of perception.

Averaging and subtraction: Research in functional brain imaging almost universally employs both. These methods serve the general scientific goal of extracting underlying causes and effects from a sea of unrelated

information. But in both subtraction and averaging we also see a commitment to the familiar idea that we have heads made of detectors. For example, we hypothesize (with Ishai) that in the brain there is a detector
specifically tuned to chairs, or at least to pictures of chairs.[3] If we are
right, then the chair detector is On during all the moments we are in fact
perceiving a chair (and our button presses can confirm that we really are
paying attention), and Off during all the other moments. If there is such a
detector, then the best hope for finding it consists of exactly the strategy
outlined above. Combine the Chair-On brain images, subtract the combined Chair-Off images. The remainder will be the brain areas engaged
in detecting chairs. The implicit rationale might be: "Chairs are distinct
physical objects, differing from houses and faces in specific ways. To perceive that something is a chair is therefore to be able to *detect the difference* between chairs and the other types of object. A failure to do this
would amount to an inability to see chairs as chairs. So, to discover how
the brain perceives chairs, we seek the *difference in the detectors* tuned
to *chairs,* as opposed to other kinds of things. Only in the difference in
the detectors can we see how the brain detects the difference. Once we locate the regions where the brain differentially activates in the presence of
chairs, but not in the presence of non-chairs, we will know where (at least)
chair-as-chair perception occurs."

At the risk of spoiling the suspense, I'll just mention that this study, like
many, was successful. Distinct regions were indeed active for chairs (or
houses or faces) only. The anatomical locations of these areas of activity
will not be important here. As a percentage of brain volume, the "chair region" and its counterparts are very small, comprising just over 3 percent
of brain volume. Functional magnetic resonance imaging worked beauti-
fully once again. This technology, conjoined with the subtraction method,
further conjoined with several other research strategies in cognitive neuroscience, is filling in a marvelously complex collage of the human mind,
embodied.

1.4 The Real Firefly

Once cognitive scientists became comfortable using the word "consciousness" in ordinary conversation (in the late 1980s), it seemed natural to

bring the well-oiled machine to bear on this ultimate scientific and philo-sophical question. Consciousness is, after all, a mental phenomenon, akin to, say, working memory, form perception, and dozens of other capacities studied by the sciences of mind. Cognitive science took the sensible ap-proach of regarding consciousness as a capacity among other capacities, immediately opening a range of new Frequently Asked Questions. For in-stance: What is the function of consciousness? Where is consciousness lo-cated? How does it interact with other mental capacities? Each of these mysteries spawned others. "Function," already a controversial concept, also has an evolutionary interpretation. Accordingly, how is consciousness adaptive for survival? (Do cows have it? Ticks?) Various metaphors for placing consciousness among or distinct from other mental capacities gen-erated a lively interest in the distinction between conscious and uncon-scious mentation. Perhaps consciousness is another name for an already known capacity—"covert speech" or attention or short-term memory or motor rehearsal, or. . . . Interesting experiments and many discussions continue on all these questions.

With all these conversations to join, it is difficult to begin anew. Or so I found in several attempts to write beyond this point. I finally had to close the notebook and take a break. But my situation was fortunate. I was in Vermont, working late on a cool night that had broken a midsummer heat wave. I stepped outside and sat at a picnic table. A half moon sailed through haze directly overhead, and the tumbling *shhhh* of a stream across the meadow was the sole sound. The trees looked like their opposites: mountainous black nothings instead of leafy somethings. Against their ut-ter indefinity, fireflies. A solitary firefly, seen from afar on a dark night, looks like the forest's version of a mathematical point. It is not only with-out size, its stroboscopic wandering eludes the eye and all of the stolid ex-pectations that make a thing what it is. The firefly seems to flicker at the edge of existence.

As I watch, it occurs to me that quite possibly the firefly I am admiring has a mimic in my brain. A tiny point of light at about one hundred feet might be exciting one or a few neurons, at least in the first stages of per-ception. If I am tracking it with my eyes, maybe the same neurons are flash-ing in time with the bug. If not, then in one or more regions and layers of my cortex, the firefly traces a squiggle of chemical pulses, a firefly on the brain. There are, as it were, *two* fireflies, the one out there and the one sparking along a plane of brain from roughly my eyes to the back of my head. The terms introduced earlier fit the scenario: My brain *detects* the firefly. The neurofly is the detection of the firefly. The seen fly creates in me a flighty seeing.

Let us suppose that the firefly and its neural effects are tightly matched—that the neurodetector is very good at its job. Consider then a very enthusiastic proposal, namely, that the neurofly just *is* the conscious experience of the firefly. We might call this the Detection Theory of Consciousness. Expressed simply, the Detection Theory would hold that to be conscious of X is to contain detectors that are presently detecting X. Detection Theory (DT) has a lot to recommend it. Philosophically, it does two things at once. It tells us when a system (say, you or me) is conscious, and it tells us what we are conscious of. Out on the deck, I'm conscious of a firefly flickering at the edge of the woods. Detection Theory states that what makes me conscious—and the picnic table not—is that I am detecting something. And DT tells me that what is detected, the real firefly, is what I am conscious of. The lightning bug is the content of my consciousness. Scientifically, DT is appealing because it seems so clearly compatible with natural processes, with observable, quantifiable, respectably worldly goings-on. "Detection" in DT will need some clarifying, but as the sections above point out, cognitive science is all about detectorheads. The big toolbox is ready.

Natural selection ensures that in the long run animal species will be well provided with all sorts of detectors, which will usually detect what the animal needs to know. Where there are brains, there are detectors, and cognitive science is hard at work to describe them. (The Ishai study is one among thousands.) But the question here is whether detection turns out to be a useful concept in the pursuit of consciousness. I think not, and one agenda in this appendix is to distance the search for consciousness from the detectorheads of standard cognitive science. This critical exercise is only the beginning, however. I also hope to embark on consciousness science, a *new* science, as it could look after we set aside detection.

1.5   Clever Leeches and Sympathetic Thermostats

To begin the shakedown of the Detector Theory of Consciousness, consider the leech. Equipped with just a few hundred neurons, the leech is no intellectual giant, but it is quite successful in locating its prey. In a pond, a hungry leech can often find any swimming or wading mammal. Considering its behavior, then, this canny little torpedo is a good remote mammal-detector. How does it work? The leech is one of few animals whose neural circuit diagram is almost complete, so this question has a specific answer. Leechy sophistication is the effect of two very simple mechanisms. First, the floating leech orients itself to head into any ripples. Then it swims, like a surfer paddling his board into the breakers, adjusting its course to the changing orientation of the surface waves. Should it bump into anything at all, thermoreceptors around its mouth take a quick temperature reading. If the obstacle is warm, the leech attaches. As it happens, any large animal moving in the water will inevitably make waves, concentric ripples that announce its position from moment to moment. The leech follows the ripple trail blindly. If it finds warm skin (vs. cool feathers or hip waders), with equal blindness, dinner is served.

The leech picks out mammals based on circumstantial evidence. Thanks to the neural inventory provided by leech neuroscience, we can say with confidence that the leech doesn't know anything about mammals-as-mammals, or about anything else. Conditions in its environment, however, make its rudimentary nervous system into a highly specific and accurate mammal-locator, the Sherlock Holmes of blood-sucking parasites.

Evolution has led to countless clever detectors like the leech. In all of them there is a contrast between the simplicity of the mechanism and the complexity or specificity of the results. Proceeding along this path, we see ultimately that even a thermostat could be a very complex detector in the right context. A very sensitive thermostat, in a very insulated room occupied by one person who divides his time between writing and sleeping, could perhaps detect the subtle changes in metabolism (and heat production) consequent to writing fluently and with passion. (It would be a wall-mounted mood ring.) Like a good friend, this thermostat "knows" when the writer is having a good day, or not.

Detection Theory embraces both leech and thermostat as conscious entities, and declares that they are conscious of mammals and fluent writers, respectively. I'm inclined to say that these consequences are absurd, and therefore the ability to detect subtle and complicated environmental conditions is not sufficient for creating consciousness in a detectorhead, no matter how complex those conditions are. However, detectors are defined by what they detect. Therefore, considered strictly as detectors, when the condition to be detected is "writer-having-a-good-day," both a thermostat and a longtime friend could be equivalent devices. So also, in many contexts, a simple photocell and I are interchangeable as firefly-detectors. These mechanical and animal devices are all detectors, but performing that job is irrelevant to the presence (or lack) of conscious awareness. My successes or failures as a photocell, and yours as a thermostat, are unrelated to our being beings endowed with awareness.

But (replies the Detection Theorist), leeches and thermostats are cheap shots, resting on some sleight-of-hand with respect to the way I described the environments in each example. The leech isn't picking out mammals, nor is the thermostat tuned to the writer's muse. Both are merely detecting heat, and it is only luck that finds them in places where local warmth is linked to highly specific environmental conditions. Something that really detects *mammals,* not just warm bodies, or *happy writers,* not just the hot air they generate, must have a lot more upstairs. The core intuition endures: Where complexity is detected, detectorheads embody consciousness.

And moreover (continues the DT enthusiast), as what is detected ramifies, so does the detector. Like the leech and thermostat, my inner firefly seems to fall far short of the depth and detail of conscious experience (for humans, at least). As my telling of the example suggests, the physical setting contains far more than just a blinking point of light, the additional details of which are also detected in my brain. In addition to the firefly, I'm aware of trees, river, moon, and many other details. Something in my brain adds those contextual features to the track of the firefly, and so even the simple form of the Detection Theory, even in this seemingly simple scene, begins to look rather more complicated. To the neurofly we add the neurotrees, neurobrook, and the rest, including some sort of encoding of the arrangement and relations among the perceived parts of the scene before me.

Thus the Detection Theory seems after all to gather plausibility in proportion to the complexity of what is being detected. Why? It can't simply be due to the complexity of the environment, because every environment is complex. The appeal of Detection Theory rests instead in intuitions about the complexity *inside* the head that is built from detectors. That is, a detectorhead is a plausible seat of consciousness because of something about its internal structure or function. The ability to detect complex environmental conditions seems to require complex innards. But of course every head is complex too. (Ultimately, however you slice up the world, you face complexity. That is, you can always find a level of descriptive detail at which simples dissolve into myriad parts.) So the appealing assumption at the heart of the Detection Theory is that the complexity of the detected environment is somehow *matched, mirrored, reflected,* or *modeled* in the innards of the detectorhead. Call this the "matching assumption." This *inner* world, then, has the right stuff to be conscious. The Detection Theory of Consciousness accordingly claims that detecting environmental complexity is sufficient for acquiring an inner world of appropriate complexity for consciousness. In addition, the matching assumption preserves and enhances the initially appealing DT account of the *contents* of consciousness. Our states of consciousness are about the situations that our detectors detect. For example, my brainstate in the presence of the firefly and its context is about that particular scene just because I detect the objects composing the scene. Through this link my experience can be an experience of a firefly. Detectorhead science declares, then, that once all the detectors are discovered and described, our picture of consciousness will be complete, at least for the exemplary case of ordinary perception of objects and scenes.

The matching assumption is generally false, however. Nothing about detection enforces a match between the innards and the world. Adding sophistication to a detectorhead will increase the environmental subtleties available for detecting, but does not at the same time guarantee a match between the inner and the outer. A little science fiction will help to make this clear. One of philosophy's most popular tall tales is the "Brain in a Vat." In the standard version, undergraduate members of the campus Neuroscience Club snatch your brain while you are sleeping, plop it in a vat of appropriate fluids, connect microelectrodes to all your sensory and motor neurons, and simulate all the inputs appropriate to your world. You awake oblivious to the Potemkin world that has replaced your usual habitat. From the third-person viewpoint external to your poor brain this is, of course, a vast change. Yesterday you awoke to bird-song and sunshine, whereas today your various neurodetectors have all been bamboozled, and you greet only virtual birds and simulated sun. But within your own first-person point of view, nothing has changed. Whatever the Neuroscience Majors are up to, these manipulations are irrelevant in your experience. We cannot subjectively distinguish "before" and "after," and are indifferent to their interchange.

The story not only reminds us of B-movie classics like *The Brain That Wouldn't Die,* but is rich with philosophical implications. The first is immediate: The contents of my consciousness are unaffected by the switching of worlds perpetrated by the Neuroscience Club, but what my brain is detecting is vastly different between the two situations. It may be that the playful neuroscientists will keep the simulation close to the old familiar world, but they need not. At their whim, they could seat a turquoise translucent rhinoceros across the table from me—in my conscious awareness—but that particular content of consciousness is not matched to anything rhinoceros-like, or turquoise, in either the net of wires that feed my optic nerve or the real world beyond the lab doors. My brain is still detecting my environment, now consisting entirely of computer-generated impulses to my nervous system, but my experience is of something quite different.

Implicit in the story is the contrast between good old reality and the irreal simulation provided by the scientists. This is understood as a metaphysical demotion, and the moral of the story is that the switch *could have already happened.* Properly told, the tale should excite a little extra doubt about the solidity of the outside world. But we can just as well imagine the story in reverse: Maybe we were born into vats (as imagined in *The Matrix*), and benign scientists do us the favor of restoring us to the real world, a world that until then had merely been perfectly simulated for us. This would accordingly be a metaphysical promotion. Properly told, you might be able to experience a sigh of epistemic relief at the possibility that you awoke today to a world much more "real" than yesterday. These small oscillations in the confidence in reality are surprising, because as premised the vat scenario offers no reasons for skepticism. The story is just as (im)possible in either direction, as both versions hinge on huge transformations that make no practical difference whatsoever. Yesterday's and today's stimuli are equally convincing. We could flip between them as often as our imagination permits. The bi-directional possibilities suggest that the difference in the two worlds is not really a difference in "degree of reality" at all. They are just very different worlds that look exactly the same. Detection Theory ties consciousness to the differences in worlds, but consciousness is the same in either case.

Ultimately, then, it doesn't matter to my state of consciousness whether I'm in a normal world or a vat. The thought experiment reveals that consciousness is constituted by processes that are blind to their own ultimate causal origins. Of course, our conscious brain is embedded in the world somehow. (Isn't everything?) And of course the vat scenario is highly improbable. But in this section I've been arguing that the embedding isn't what makes us conscious, nor does it dictate the contents of our awareness.

Another tall tale will further sunder detection and consciousness. Suppose that you were here, looking with me at the fireflies, and happened to have with you a high-end brain scanner that showed you the neural tracings of the firefly's flight. In this scenario, the tale of two flies, one detecting the other, could be a routine empirical explanation. From your perspective outside me, detection is readily detectable. Do I detect a firefly? You can tell. Something about me—my words, or blood flow in my brain—tracks the stimuli, or not. The tracking correlation requires, of course, that you have access to the variations in *both* the stimulus and in me. From your third-person perspective toward me, you would be able to observe both parties to the relationship, and the correlation between them that is the mark of detection. But when the topic shifts to Experience, the point of view moves from your third-person perspective to my own first-person subjectivity. From my own point of view, I cannot make the correlation that is so easy for you. From inside me, there is simply no independent access to the other correlate, no side view of both flies. In other words, the real firefly transcends every experience I might have. For me there is just an experience, and another, and another. Some of my experiences feature fireflies, and some feature other things, and that's all there is to it. Whatever I experience, it will never be the correlation of the inner and the outer, because I can only experience everything "out there" through the lens of my own conscious awareness.

The new message of the vat should not be that we *could be* brains in vats, but that we *already are*. Our vats are skulls. We are at the same distance from reality in either the vatted or normal case, and experienced reality is always a media event, the exclusive production of neurons.

In summary, two paths have led to the conclusion that experience is not detection or "information processing." First, I argued that a detector is the wrong kind of thing to be matched to consciousness. Detection is defined by relations to "outside" states of affairs, whereas consciousness is dependent only on its own internal complexity. Second, I argued that from within the first-person, subjective point of view, those same outside states of affairs are inaccessible. The relationship of detection cannot be directly observed in the first person. In short, as *cognizers,* we are detectorheads. As *conscious beings,* we are something else altogether. What that "something else" could be will only emerge after further reflection.

1.6 Everything Goes

There is, for me, only one firefly. It's that one, near the treetop. Or so I would have said a few pages ago. Now I find myself in an updated version of Descartes' quandary in the *Meditations.* Descartes asked us to imagine that we are dreaming (right now), and furthermore that a very powerful mind-controlling demon is deceiving us in every judgment we make. I've suggested that Cartesian isolation from the world is more than a mere possibility. Subjectivity itself exiles the bug in the bushes (and the rest of the world) to a transcendent otherworld. As a result, consciousness science must place on hold the links connecting the brain to the rest of the natural world. Those links are crucial to understanding the place of the brain in nature, but by themselves these brain-to-world connections do not constitute our conscious experiences.

There is still one firefly in my experience, but now I feel forced to say that it *isn't* the one out there. Instead, experience is just the ebb and flow of neurotransmitters, spiked by ion surges along axons. Patterns in this flow are correlated with events beyond the synapses, but the neurons don't know this, and can't know it, so any correlation (or its absence) is irrelevant to the issue of what a state of consciousness *is.* All there is for experience is the fireflies within, the neuroflies. As the Zen parable expresses it, the mountain is not a mountain.

Cutting the cords of detection overthrows just about everything. All of the components, from neurons on up, have long been identified through their function in a detectorheaded, information-processing system. We know how to do that! Now I'm suggesting that all those identifications are irrelevant, the nice labels merely confetti. If we thought the old way was hard, looking at the brain *without* the apparatus of cognitive science is at first completely bewildering.[4] To approximate the throwback I'm recommending, one might imagine oneself in the company of Renaissance anatomists, dissecting this curious organ. The names still in use for many parts of the brain originated back then, and the computational neuroanatomist Christopher Cherniak has translated them. With Cherniak's help, we can see the brain through the anatomists' eyes:

> For example, one finds among frequently used expressions, largely translating from Latin: seahorses, snails, shells, worms; almonds, olives, lentils; breasts, buttocks, teeth, tails, knees, horns; spiderwebs, nets, tufts; girdles, belts, ribbons, buttons, spurs; chandeliers, cushions, baskets, cups, funnels; chambers, roofs, gables, tents, bridges; stars, suns; hillocks, pyramids, wedges; fires, mosses, glue. And also a substantia innominata. ("Philosophy and Computational Neuroanatomy," p. 91)

Cherniak also provides the Latin that any anatomist would know so well, respectively:

> Hippocampus, cochlea, putamen, vermis; amygdala, olive, lentiform nucleus; mamillary body, nates, dentate nucleus, caudate nucleus, geniculate bodies, ventral horn; arachnoid, reticular formation, flocculus; cingulum, limbic formation, lemniscus (and ribbon synapse), synaptic boutons, calcarine fissure; chandelier cell, pulvinar, basket cell, cupula, infundibulum; thalamus, tectum, fastigium, tentorium, pons; stellate neuron (and astrocyte), solar plexus; colliculus, pyramidal neuron, cuneate nucleus; pyriform cortex, mossy fiber, glial cell.

Considered in itself, the organ in question is a charming hodgepodge. Remember, though, that this hodgepodge is you. This is your conscious brain. Like so many other truisms of science, it is an article of modern faith that these three pounds are the seat of us. But with detection cast out as the definer of consciousness, we can no longer say what it is about the brain that makes it the seat of awareness. At this point we could just as well suppose some other part of the body to be the natural home of consciousness. In the *Odyssey,* when Odysseus is undecided about a course of action, Homer tells us that his heart was torn two ways inside its cover. And why not? (Sometimes a dangerous choice feels just so.) Indeed, why suppose that the stuff of consciousness is biological at all? Max Grue is not the first to find a mind in a glass of water. Max's thought experiment originates with Ian Hinckfuss, and is described by William Lycan:

> Suppose a transparent plastic pail of spring water is sitting in the sun. At the micro-level, a vast seething complexity of things are going on: convection currents, frantic breeding of bacteria and other minuscule life forms, and so on. These things in turn require even more frantic activity at the molecular level to sustain them. Now is all this activity not complex enough that, simply by chance, it might realize a human program for a brief period (given suitable correlations between certain micro-events and the requisite input-, output-, and state-symbols of the program)? And if so, must [we] not conclude that the water in the pail briefly constitutes the body of a conscious being, and has thoughts and feelings and so on? (*Consciousness,* pp. 32–33)

From the brain-in-a-vat and the mind-in-a-bucket we derive two problems. The first is a problem of knowledge, particularly a problem about knowing the external world. The thought experiments pry open a crack of doubt between us and the world. This philosophical skepticism is the usual interpretation of these experiments. If the first problem is a problem of knowledge, then the second is a problem about the knower. The possibility, however faint, that we are brains in vats implies that consciousness is whatever it is with or without worldly interaction. That leads to a different sort of recognition, the realization that we have no place to start on the question of what consciousness *is*. In the aftermath of the brain-in-a-vat, the underlying reality of the world could be anything. But then, the underlying reality of consciousness could be anything too.

Any of us could be a pail of water. Accordingly, please imagine that *you are that lucky bucket of water right now.* (You may have to suppose your mental processes are speeded up, or that the random motions of your constituents are slowed, in order to give yourself enough time to contemplate your quandary.) By the assumptions of the experiment, it seems that you will be having an experience. If normal-you were in the same state, normal-you would experience a normal percept and any accompanying normally interpreted mental states. You could never tell the difference between normal experiences and bucket experiences.

All this is logically possible. Though the probability is incalculably small, this *could* be you. Right now.

2

Real Life: The Subjective View
of Objectivity

So now you have been convinced by these skeptical arguments. Your confidence in external reality has crumbled, and with it any hope of understanding the place of consciousness in nature. You conclude that all is hallucination, that your mind constitutes a mysterious chaos with nothing outside it, or at least that whatever is outside will be forever unknowable to you. Right? Not likely. I'm not convinced either, and I'd bet that even full-time skeptical philosophers look before they cross the street. As David Hume says:

> Most fortunately it happens, that since reason is incapable of dispelling these [skeptical] clouds, nature herself suffices to that purpose, and cures me of this philosophical melancholy and delirium, either by relaxing this bent of mind, or by some avocation, and lively impression of my senses, which obliterate all these chimeras. I dine, I play a game of backgammon, I converse, and am merry with my friends; and when after three or four hours' amusement, I wou'd return to these speculations, they appear so cold, and strain'd, and ridiculous, that I cannot find in my heart to enter into them any farther. (*Treatise of Human Understanding*, 1:548–49)

Our confidence in reality rests in part on a lively sense of the absurd improbability of the brain-in-a-vat or pail-of-water scenario. But in addition to that, in imagining these science fictions, there was a second recurrent difficulty. It was very hard to imagine these scenarios *both* experienced from the inside *and* experienced with the insight that one was in the scenario. *Without* the insight, all of the stories are easy to imagine exactly. Subjectively, they are one and all *just like this* (where "this" is your current situation). But as soon as one tries to imagine knowing oneself to be a brain in a vat (etc.), an odd double vision sets in. The counterfactual imagination falters. These tales of the weird are all perfectly conceivable from the third-person point of view, as unfortunate circumstances befalling some other brain, or you at some other time. But from the first-person viewpoint the scare quotes around "reality" just don't stick; I can pretend my way into alternate realities, but not into non-reality. I just can't shake off the world.

But bear in mind that we really are brains in vats! The arguments above were intended to show that reality is at a conceptual and practical distance from consciousness. The thought experiments were supposed to help us imagine that our experiences are not in direct contact with the real world. But they failed in this purpose.

Thus we encounter *the inescapable experience of the real as real.* I propose to make this the starting point for the study of consciousness, setting aside for now the toolbox of cognitive science. The path from here begins with an examination of the phenomenology of reality, or, more simply, the experience of the world. The pioneers in this enterprise are the European phenomenologists, beginning with Edmund Husserl (and including Martin Heidegger, Jean-Paul Sartre, and Maurice Merleau-Ponty), and the American pragmatists William James and John Dewey. Yet phenomenology has been disparaged consistently during the cognitive revolution (and pragmatism ignored), so it may be useful to reflect on the reasons for this. In brief, phenomenology suffered from guilt by association. The bad company phenomenology kept was known as introspectionism, founded on the belief that one could observe one's own mental entities in their natural habitats in the mind. Psychology for introspectionists was based in empirical generalization. Carefully trained introspectors observed and recorded their mental lives, their observations tabulated in the hope of finding regularities. Unfortunately, it didn't work, despite the best Germanic efforts of a generation of scientists. The mind's eye never saw, or the mind's mouth failed to report, anything consistent. However, Husserl and James (both scientists by training) spoke approvingly of introspection and frequently invited their readers to look inwardly for confirmation of their ideas about consciousness. One hundred years later, the failure of introspectionism remains a warning, so with that failure in mind, I will suggest an alternative reconstruction of phenomenology. Its better self is found in Husserl's practice, even if it is not always his official method, and in Dewey. Instead of ogling the varieties of experience, the reconstructed method argues from necessity. It identifies what must be true of the mind in order to have certain types of experiences at all. (Standing behind us all is Immanuel Kant, but that's another story.) This analysis will ultimately describe the "peculiar complexity" found in conscious systems. From there the path leads to issues of implementation. What kind of physical system could have this special complexity, and how would we tell? And finally, is the brain such a system?

To begin again: We are not solipsists. For each of us, there is a real world, a world *for us*, a reality for us. Phenomenological bedrock: Our experiences contain within them the supposition that they are ultimately grounded in an objective reality. But how is this achieved? Certainly not by philosophical argument. Not by direct observation of the brain-world correlation either, because this side view of detection is unobtainable from the first-person viewpoint. These unobtainable perspectives offer an objective view of subjectivity, but they don't work. Instead, we start anew, not from reality in itself, but from the idea we have that there is a reality. We turn from the *objective view of subjectivity* to the *subjective view of objectivity*.

Husserl recommended the method of bracketing or "epoché" (suspension of belief) to expose the gears of consciousness. One tries to put one's commitments to reality on hold, considering everything as if it were an appearance without a material cause or correlate. For him, this suspension of belief is an act of will, a let's-pretend. I suggest that the outside world is already bracketed, prior to any skeptical thought experiments. It can't come to us any other way. But the implications of bracketing are similar to those of the arguments here: The first-person perspective does not contain within it the direct observation of the relation of the subject to the world.

That correlation is always invisible from the subject's point of view. In short, *experienced reality* must be considered in isolation from ordinary, "real" reality. Nothing from the world may be imported to explain or justify experience. One way I will signal this contrast is to spell regular Reality with a capital R, keeping experienced reality, the seemings of the real, in the lower case. Real Properties, real Relations, and So On, can all be marked in this way, as opposed to apparent or merely experienced properties, relations, and so on.

Reconstructing the experience of a reality without recourse to capital-R Reality is not easy. The stages below offer successive approximations, digging toward foundations while revising them at the same time.

2.1   Stage 1: Intentionality

To me, there is a reality. There is something. What does this tell me about my own consciousness? Even if I happen to be a vat-head, when I direct my attention to what I call reality, at bottom I experience a relationship between *what there is* and *how I see it*. Tentatively, we can distinguish two aspects of any experience of reality, the *objective* and the *subjective*. In perception, then, I encounter what the phenomenologists call *intentionality*, the fundamental idea that consciousness has this object-subject bipolarity. "Object" and "subject" are already misleading, however. Phenomenally, there are objects—apples, chairs, cellos. But are there subjects? Descartes assumed there were, but ever since philosophers of every sort have questioned the idea of the self, ego, or "I." (Eastern philosophy has questioned the self for much longer than that.) A more cautious construal of intentionality might be the observation that my experience of objects is always from a *point of view*. Subjectivity, for now, should be limited to just that, the idea of a viewpoint.

In the simplest case, I get up and move around, watching my surroundings as I go. As I circle the picnic table, I see it from different angles. The visual field, what I might paint or photograph as I move about, is changing, but the table remains the same table. My experience at every moment distinguishes my shifting point of view from the comparatively stable object and its constant properties.

Subjectivity or point of view does not appear in consciousness as a separable part of an experience. It is instead a facet or aspect "built in" to the presentation of things. A thing cannot appear to us except as from a point of view. Nor can we occupy a point of view except insofar as it is a point of view taken toward some thing(s). The symbiotic relationship between what is presented in consciousness and the point of view informing the presentation is enshrined in the celebrated slogan of phenomenology, "All consciousness is consciousness of something." But, although the subjective and the objective are inseparable, they are different, and intentionality is also our awareness of that difference. I can disentangle objects from points of view, but detangling the two does not lead to the isolation of either. Instead, there is a continuous elasticity in the intentional relationship. It stretches one way as objects change or move, another as viewpoints shift. It can snap abruptly into a new shape when I discover that I've made an error in my understanding of either pole, or when I switch my attention to a new object. Throughout its shapeshifting, though, it retains its bipolarity, its intentionality.

Intentionality also names a central question in cognitive science, but there it has a very different sense. In cognitive science, "intentionality" is the mysterious connection between the mind and the Real World, as exemplified in Real Perception. (Detection Theory is one attempt to understand this connection.) Because it is a Real relationship between consciousness and the World, we can ascribe to cognitive science capital-I Intentionality. But phenomenology isn't concerned with the relationship of the inner and the Outer; instead, phenomenological intentionality is entirely inner. It is the fundamental structure of consciousness itself, rather than the link between consciousness and external Reality.

This contrast illuminates an opportunity for phenomenology that cognitive science usually overlooks. The cog. sci. version of Intentionality equates consciousness with pure subjectivity, because the objective is Real and therefore outside of consciousness. Because the Real cannot get inside consciousness, the relationship between consciousness and Reality is also beyond the reach of consciousness itself. On this interpretation, what remains internal to consciousness is just what we experience as internal to *subjectivity* alone, locking the discussion on issues of self, ego, introspection, and the like. At the same time, if it is the external relationship of Intentionality that makes those subjective states conscious, then it is completely mysterious why they should be felt or experienced as they are, or indeed why they should be experienced at all. The external relation could hold between perfectly unconscious systems and the external World. From Intentionality to consciousness there is no easy path. Phenomenology, on the other hand, underlines the internal manifestation of intentionality and the objective pole that it intends. Of course it is a "subjective objectivity" that phenomenology studies, but that's not a problem as long as we don't confuse it with capital-O Objectivity. Phenomenology invites us to notice that the external World and our relations to it also appear within consciousness, and that it is possible to examine them phenomenologically. It is this examination that constitutes the phenomenology of perception, and in the developing results below we will see what it might offer.

The invitation to explore intentionality phenomenologically does not yet mean that we understand it. This goal will only be approached through successive approximations, where vague terms are analyzed into slightly less vague components, progressively unearthing the structures of consciousness that usually escape notice. So far, the anatomy of consciousness has identified the blurry outlines of the poles of the subjective and the objective, and suggested that there is a specific relationship of intentionality between them. Because so much in contemporary philosophy is obsessed with the subjective, we will pursue the less familiar phenomenology of objectivity.

2.2 Stage 2: Superposition

The "ground" in which real objects are embedded includes far more than location. Objects travel with a flock of meanings attached. Consider again the firefly. My initial telling of my experience kept it as unfreighted as possible ("a mere point of light"), but even naming the perceived object already embeds it in a vast network of meanings. For example, the apparent point of light might have been any of the following:

- A prankster dotting the leaves and grass with a green laser pointer.
- A stray cosmic ray cutting across my retina.

- An LSD flashback.
- An invasion of very small UFOs.

When I call the object a firefly, I turn my seeing into a case of seeing-as. I see a point of light as a firefly, or as one of the other possibilities. Even prior to recognizing or naming the object, the blip of light is seen "under an interpretation." I will call ever-present symbiosis of object and interpretation "superposition."

Just as cognitive science has overlooked phenomenal intentionality, it has also overlooked superposition. This myopia originates in the experimental approach to perception, a tradition that predates cognitive science by nearly a century. (Among phenomenologists, Maurice Merleau-Ponty was its most persistent critic.) Psychologists like to probe fundamental perceptual processes (as detectors), and to this end compose countless variations of lab stimuli that they hope are relatively meaningless. Nowadays many an undergraduate has spent time in the psychology lab listening to beeps and boops, sorting red squares and green triangles, and the like. But in experience there is no such thing as a "pure stimulus," and nothing is without superposed meanings. All of the neutral nonsense stimuli are just as richly embedded as the firefly. They carry their usual worldly location, occupy their place in a range of possibilities within the experiment, their place among the conventions of the experimental situation, and their place in the lives of the experiencer. The red square is: over there, not a green triangle, needing to be tolerated to get credit in the course, my favorite color. . . . Any sophomore who experiences only the raw visual presentation of a red square and absolutely nothing else will need an immediate escort to the counseling center. He or she has lost a grip on reality.[5]

The alternate visions of the firefly illustrate another central feature of superposition. Some of the alternatives (tree-dotting vs. firefly, for example) have an effect on the apparent trajectory of the point of light, because seeing it as a point descending in the space between the trees and me gives quite a different look than seeing it as a dot jumping along the leaves and grass. This difference seems to have a sensory component. But seeing it as, for example, a fleet of tiny flying saucers, might well make no difference at all in where I locate the lights. The difference among these cases is *non-sensory*. But it is nonetheless a difference in the experience of the light, part of the perception of its glow. The general conclusion is that experience always contains superposed sensory and non-sensory components. The ultimate non-sensory superposition is revealed by the brain-in-a-vat. The very basic interpretation that this world I *seem* to see is *in fact* real turns out to be non-sensory, because the thorough hallucinations created by the Neuroscience Club duplicate everything sensory from ordinary perception.

The phenomenology of superposition reminds us that reality is more than meets the eye. But the world of which we are aware is also less than meets the eye. The phenomenological tradition includes extensive discussions of absence, of things missing and hidden from the perceived world. In *Being and Nothingness*, Sartre describes the experience of looking for an absent friend in a café:

> But now Pierre is not here. This does not mean that I discover his absence in some precise spot in the establishment. In fact Pierre is absent from the *whole* café; his absence fixes the café in its evanescence; the café remains *ground;* it persists in offering itself as an undifferentiated totality to my only marginal attention; it slips into the background; it pursues its nihilation. Only it makes itself ground for a determined figure; it carries the figure everywhere in front of it, presents the figure everywhere to me. This figure which slips constantly between my look and the solid, real objects of the café is precisely a perpetual disappearance; it is Pierre raising himself as nothingness on the ground of the nihilation of the café. (*Being and Nothingness*, p. 10)

This is a complex experience, but completely familiar. We can understand it within this elementary phenomenal framework as follows: "Being Pierre" is a complex property with both sensory and non-sensory aspects. Pierre's absence appears in consciousness as a property of all the things and people in the café, meaning that all of them conspicuously lack the property of being Pierre. This property under negation is of course non-sensory, as well as superposed on the various presented properties. These explicit absences, or, if you prefer, implicit presences, are ubiquitous in awareness. Every real object, for example, has a back side, and the presence of the hidden parts of an object is part of the experience of an object.

Though out of sight, the back sides of things are not out of mind, and we experience the invisible parts with all the solidity appropriate to a real thing. Miranda's narrative explores various complex human examples. (Tracking all the missing persons in the story is an exercise that will be left to the reader.)

In the relationship of sensory and non-sensory in a single act of perception we observe once again an intimate symbiosis of aspects. As with the intentional relationship itself, superposition is always present, and every superposition rides on some object of perception. But, again as with intentionality, we can keep objects and interpretations distinct. We can keep the point of light constant as we imagine various interpretations, or we can fix the interpretation (it's a firefly, no doubt about it) while varying the ways in which it might present itself.

In summary, so far: The conscious perception of an object requires the superposition of sensory and non-sensory aspects. This stage helpfully reflects back to stage one, as follows: The ability to separate object and point of view entails the resilience and elasticity of intentionality. And that, as described in stage one, implies the ability to modify one pole of the intentional relationship while holding the other relatively steady. Now consider a familiar instance, seeing an object from different points of view. For example, imagine discovering the picnic table by sight, and then distinguishing the same table by touch. What is the same across these viewness of "same object," essential to intentionality, is itself a non-sensory superposition in the contents of consciousness.

In drawing attention to the non-sensory, phenomenology deepens the rift between human consciousness and detectorheads. Traditional psychology, from which the detectorhead has evolved, imagines perception as tracking specific Real features of the Environment. Real Things have Real Effects, and where a Thing is missing there is no effect at all. Cognitive science elaborated the detector idea to allow those Features to be complex, but still saw each of us as dedicated to deciphering what is actually Present before us. Non-sensory properties are nonsense within this framework; nothing can come of Nothing. Accordingly, detectorheads have no room for the rest of the phenomenal world, the many dimensions of perception that are out of sight but still very much in mind.

Now we have two insoluble relationships, intentionality and super-position, two aspects of reality that seem perpetually entangled with each other. But although some aspects of objectivity seem non-sensory, not all are, nor are the non-sensory aspects of experience exclusively aspects of the objective pole of intentionality. Superposition is everywhere, but by it-self does not make an object real for us. These mysteries carry on into the next stage.

2.3   Stage 3: Transcendence

The objectivity of the objective side of the intentional relations within consciousness is, of course, merely apparent objectivity, a construct. So the next task is to understand what "objectivity" could mean in a virtual world, and how it is distinct from "subjectivity." Implicit in the polarity of intentionality is a distinction between the inner and the outer, but this spa-tial language is only metaphorical. By what features can we tell that one aspect of experience is the manifestation of reality, and another is the man-ifestation of a point of view? We must still resist the temptation to appeal to the physical features of the World, such as size or shape, because Facts about such Properties cannot explain why it is that objects appear in con-sciousness as having apparent size or shape. Worse, even apparent size and shape don't isolate phenomenally objective properties, for objects with these apparent properties can be *imagined*. This possibility allows us to put the question in its most acute form: What is the difference between imagination and reality? Imagined objects are not perceived, not real. They are creatures of pure subjectivity. But they can have all the phenom-enal properties of reality. For every property I might perceive, I can also close my eyes or cover my ears, and imagine that property. What is the difference?

In the eighteenth century, David Hume distinguished percepts from im-ages by their "force" or "vivacity," but of course perceptions can fade smoothly into imperceptibility without crossing a faintness threshold into imagination. Husserl and Sartre identified a more satisfying contrast. Real things, they observed, always conform to the old saying that there's more to them than meets the eye. Real things, that is, always seem to have as-pects that go beyond what can be sensed. The dots of light in the dark meadow are not isolated and unrelated. In seeing them as a firefly, I connect the dots as a bug in motion. But I never really see a single bug in the spaces between the flashes. Less sketchy objects, such as the table before me, intimate a vast array of properties beyond the colors and textures that are present to my senses. To bring some of these properties into sensory awareness, I can look under the table, or pick it up, or scratch it. But even a year of exploration will not exhaust the potential for discovery inherent in any real thing.

Phenomenology has called this "going beyond" or overflowing *transcendence*. Usually transcendence connotes surpassing the World, and as such is reserved for the supernatural. But phenomenological transcendence is not only worldly but commonplace. Every real thing has it. Every real thing engages our awareness with something beyond its immediate sensory presentation. Because transcendence overflows sensation, it is a very general non-sensory property of real things. However, naming this property does not yet entail that it is understood. Transcendence has been one of the most contended topics in phenomenology, but nonetheless some preliminary distinctions can emerge for straightforward cases of transcendence in perception.

Consider again the picnic table, a real thing. (Or better, consider a real thing in *your* present environment.) Its transcendence is a sort of disposition, a capacity to reveal new aspects of itself. Contrast this with the encounter with an imaginary table. We can imagine exploring a table in great detail, somewhat as Max Grue attempts to construct Imogen in Miranda's tale. Although imagined perceptions are usually less detailed than real perceptions, with effort that difference can be erased. But even when details coincide in sensory properties, the non-sensory property of transcendence appears through a lingering distinction: Imagined details appear or disappear *at our discretion*. We may alter imaginary properties simply by choosing to do so, or by imagining them as different. Properties of real things are both more stubborn and more capable of surprising us. This is the symptom of their transcendence.[6]

The emerging picture of the contrast between subjective and objective rests on the transcendence of the objective. Among all the non-sensory superpositions, transcendence is the one seemingly shared by all the real things in our experienced world. To experience an object as transcending your immediate awareness of it is to recognize it as a piece of reality. But transcendence is (as ever) itself a property *within* consciousness. It is a property of which we are aware. We cannot appeal to Real Properties to explain phenomenology. So, the search continues.

2.4 Stage 4: Temporality

Superposition, the inseparable network of sensory and non-sensory embeddings that constitute any experienced object, is necessary in any experience of a reality. To steady a phenomenal object in a real world, we experience its transcendence. Transcendence then must be explained.

To outline a minimal set of necessary and sufficient conditions for the consciousness of a transcendent reality, it may help to consider those moments when reality is in doubt. Macbeth expresses that experience eloquently:

> Is this a dagger which I see before me,
> The handle toward my hand? Come, let me clutch thee.
> I have thee not, and yet I see thee still.
> Art thou not, fatal vision, sensible
> To feeling as to sight, or art thou but
> A dagger of the mind, a false creation
> Proceeding from the heat-oppressed brain? (II.1.33 ff.)

Throughout the play, Shakespeare exquisitely balances Macbeth's world on a precipice between being and non-being. In ordinary life, we are rarely so challenged, and one naturally hopes it remains that way. But we nonetheless encounter fleeting Macbethian doubts and know how to resolve them. The process by which we resolve what is real will help refine the account of the experience of reality, especially if we keep Reality out of play. (Our phenomenological assessment of what is real cannot appeal to Physics, for example.) Let's return again to the picnic table. Here is a partial list, neither exclusive nor exhaustive, of the phenomenal symptoms of its reality:

Relational constancy. The table (and its parts) tend to hold together in specific arrangements.

Perceptual invariance. The table tends to be unperturbed by being perceived. A property is a real property to the extent that many apparent changes can be "cancelled out" as side-effects of changes in the perceiver. (Location, for example.) Some corollaries: (1) The table carries on through lapses in perception; we can pick up where we left off after a blink or a nap. (2) Properties of the table tend not to be subject to acts of will. (3) It (and its properties) are often presented through more than one sensory modality.

Correction. More precisely, *corrigibility,* the capacity for correction. A mismatch between my ideas and the world never appears directly. Instead, I experience a failure of expectations, and as a result of the failure readjust my ideas about reality. For example, it may happen that I have a false idea of the location of the bench beside the table. I think it's *here* and I'm not in the least doubtful of that judgment. The judgment appears *as an error* only when I discover my mistake. In that discovery, the belief that the bench is here is replaced by the new belief that it is *there.* Only in retrospect can I recognize my errors. (Sometimes my expectations are so fixed that I never detect my errors. Phenomenally, then, there is in these cases no error, however Wrong [in Reality] I may be.)

The reality of the picnic table is easy to ascertain, but where objects are more evanescent or our point of view is compromised, the phenomenal symptoms of reality listed above are engaged in complicated ways. A doubtful case such as the trace of a firefly or a hallucinated dagger may pass for real on the basis of slim or even contradictory evidence. Note that in these various phenomenal processes, there is still no occurrence of *real* detection. The "objects" before us are all just neurosquiggles. Phenomenal detection is all circumstantial evidence collected within the subjective, first-person viewpoint. In this respect, we are not so different from the lowly leech, constructing a picture of reality that turns out to be a composite of clues. Our clues are just more numerous, flexible, and interdependent.

The point here is not to offer a complete guide to infallible perception of reality. Rather, across all these principles there is a common feature, which will turn out to be critical for this investigation: *Each of the processes of phenomenal "reality confirmation" involves the comparison of current presentations with past presentations or anticipations of the future.* Even at this most general level, the phenomenology of reality teaches a single inescapable lesson, that *real things are extended in time.* To assess the constancy or change in an object or scene, one must compare present with past appearances. Comparison over time is necessary to disentangle objective properties from subjective properties. Only in comparing appearances from moment to moment can we sort out changes in point of view, in contrast to changes in the objects before us. And the discovery of errors through their collision with reality is entirely an affair of "before" and "after."

In short, reality is temporal. Concerning ordinary Objective Reality, this is an ordinary claim. But concerning the subjective experience of reality, each term must be read through the lens of phenomenal reality: *Phenomenally* real things are *phenomenally* extended in time. We can't assume that phenomenal time shares any properties with Real Time. Phenomenally, we experience the interaction of past, present, and future. Somehow events removed in time affect consciousness in the present. How can this be?

2.5   Stage 5: Temporality (1), the Threefold Present

One might think temporality is easy to implement, in the form of memory. However, simple storage does not lend experience temporality. Recall that any detector, ourselves (and all our parts) included, is blind to the origin of its signal. The time of recording is as much a part of conditions at the origin as any other physical fact. So, simply to call any state of a system a representation of the past is to tag it from the third-person point of view. The tag may originate in history, but we can't appeal to its Real origin to account for how it is experienced. Without that, however, the tag is just another property, with no account of why what it tags should appear to us to be from the past. Nor will it help to date-stamp each record in memory, either absolutely ("July 5, 2003") or relatively ("yesterday"). That would explicitly code time, but the results of any date-stamped comparisons are still temporally blind. The reason is the same: The date stamps are meaningful only insofar as they designate moments of Objective Reality. The Objective relationship we use to apprehend temporal relations between the stamp and the time of origin is not subjectively available in the experience of reality.

Both proposals are detector solutions. Both tag presentations with a date stamp and both fail for the reasons that detection in general failed as a foundation of consciousness. We won't get to temporality by symbolizing time in a scheme dependent on Real relations between symbol and origin. Instead, we must find time embodied and embedded in the structure of experience, as seen from inside. Until that is accomplished, there will be no account of the phenomenology of reality, and hence no account of consciousness.

Husserl considered this issue in *The Phenomenology of Internal Time-Consciousness*, published in 1928 (but based mainly on lectures delivered almost exactly one hundred years ago):

> When we see, hear, or in general perceive something . . . what is perceived remains present for an interval although not without modification. Apart from other alterations, such as those in intensity and richness, which occur now to a lesser, now to a more noticeable degree, there is always yet another and particularly odd characteristic to be confirmed, namely, that anything of this kind remaining in consciousness appears to us as something more or less past, as something temporally shoved back, as it were. (p. 30; all Husserl quotations are from *The Phenomenology of Internal Time-Consciousness*)

His principal example is the perception of a melody. Each note does not simply disappear from consciousness as it finishes sounding. If it did, then we would be unable to perceive the relations among notes, and thus unable to perceive any melody at all. On the other hand, the notes do not persist in consciousness as lingering sensations. If they did, we would hear all the notes at once, the melody lost in a single cacophonous chord. Therefore, past notes in the melody must remain in awareness while the current note is sounding, but their continuity in consciousness cannot be as sensations.

What is true of a melody is also true of its constituent parts.

> Every tone itself has a temporal extension: with the actual sounding I hear it as now. With its continued sounding, however, it has an ever new

now, and the tone actually preceding is changing into something past. Therefore, I hear at any instant only the actual phase of the tone, and the Objectivity of the whole enduring tone is constituted in an act-continuum which in part is memory, in the smallest punctual part is perception, and in a more extensive part expectation. (pp. 43 ff.)

My present perception, here-and-now looking or listening, in fact has three aspects. In addition to what is before me right now, there is an appended awareness of the history leading up to the present, and an appended anticipation of future experiences radiating out from the current situation. I will call the component of awareness yoked to events presented right now Presence. The long shadow of past presence I will call Retention, and the branching anticipations of the future Protention. ("Presence" appears with a different meaning in Heidegger. "Retention" and "Protention" are Husserl's terms.) The temporal traces of past and future are superposed at all times in the *present* object, in the *current* state of consciousness. They extend from every moment to a fuzzy and indefinite temporal horizon.

I am the effect of causes, some ancient and some new. From my physical constitution scientists could deduce some of those causes. My current physical state, brain included, will also have specific effects, and science can deduce some of those too. But what the analysis of temporality shows is that my present state of awareness contains past and future in a sense very different from the causal dispositions discovered by science. I am not just the product of my past, but I contain it still. It lingers in my *present* awareness. And my future does not merely await me out there in the world to come; rather, the future is *present* to me now. I live in time, it's true; phenomenology shows us that, in addition to living in time, *time lives in us.*[7]

Temporality infuses awareness at all times, and of all the objects of awareness (including psychological "objects"). Only on the basis of tripartite temporality could we be aware of either change or stability in any object, or the distinction between an event and a process, or of the duration of things. Consider a pocket watch dangling on a chain. Hanging plumb, is the watch moving or still? At any isolated instant, it would be impossible to tell without knowing its immediate past or future positions. In figure 2.1, a time-lapse photograph makes retentive and protentive

Figure 2.1 The conscious present includes the awareness of temporal context. Perception of a moving (or stationary) watch depends on the simultaneous awareness of its immediate past appearances, and includes an awareness of its immediately anticipated future.

awareness visible. To see a *moving* watch entails that the temporal (retentive and protentive) information is already superposed in the current awareness. The photograph therefore represents the essential contents of current awareness of the watch. One of its positions is its present, but all of them are part of the current state of consciousness.

Human life (and perhaps the lives of some animals) is experienced within this ever-present temporal landscape. Once we observe this aspect of phenomenology, we observe it everywhere. In class, I play a recording of the first chord of a well-known Beatles tune, a fraction of a second of music. In sonic isolation, Paul sings "Hey—." In every head resounds a silent "Jude." Many other examples of expectation can be used to make the same

. . .

point. That the present is continuously modified by the past is clear in any case of repetition. You can't step in the same stream of consciousness twice. You can't step in the same stream of consciousness twice. You can't step in the same stream of consciousness twice. The first occurrence of the previous sentence is a mere observation. The second adds emphasis. And the third is annoying (but makes a point).

Retention and protention are distinct from explicit recollection and anticipation. Through these familiar processes, we can reach beyond the temporal horizons of retention and protention. As Husserl observes, recollection of an event has the same three-part structure as perception: As I reminisce about my first kiss or high school graduation, the scene replays with an artificial now-point moving through it. Inside that pretend-now will be a relative retention of preceding events, and a relative anticipation of what came next. Anticipating an event—my next kiss or my daughter's high school graduation—has the same structure, an artificial now packed with past and future. Thus explicit recollection, perception, and explicit anticipation all have this tripartite temporality. They differ in the "openness" of possibilities relative to their moving now-points. Traveling down memory lane, both retention and protention are closed or fixed, done. In anticipation, relative past and future are open—nothing of the time line must necessarily be as it is anticipated. Perception enfolds a fixed retention and an open protention.

Temporality suffuses the entire perceptual field, intersecting in every phenomenal object. This overturns the idea that some objects are stable and endure unchanged over time. As Husserl writes:

> Every temporal being "appears" in one or another continually changing mode of running-off, and the "Object in the mode of running-off" is in this change always something other, even though we still *say* that the Object and every point of its time and this time itself are one and the same. (p. 47, emphasis mine)

The consciousness of time entails that the phenomenal object itself is always changing, always adding to its duration. Temporality turns out not to be a tag attached to relatively stable presentations parading through a specious present; rather, there is nothing stable on parade. Instead, in every temporal being we find the "absent presence" or non-sensory awareness of its own time line, like the unseen reality of the back sides of objects.

Intentionality, superposition, transcendence. With the addition of temporality to the mix, some of the mystery of consciousness snaps into focus. Temporality seems to be the glue that binds the others in a single outline of what it is like to be you or me. Temporality provides, first, a way forward in our understanding of transcendence, suggesting that it is a particular structure or outlook rooted in protention or anticipation. Transcendence is an aspect of protention. It is the expectation that an object will offer new sensory presentations that are not presently explicitly anticipated. Transcendence, like many other properties, lies along a temporal dimension that reaches beyond the immediately given primal impression. These marks of past and future inflect the present with the fundamental property of duration, a property that cannot appear in the instantaneous presentation of immediate reality. Temporal properties are therefore non-sensory. But these properties attach securely to particular objects in the world, some of them old, others new, some steady, others changing. Finally, with temporality appears the hope of understanding the fundamental elasticity of intentionality. The immediate sensory impression cannot distinguish between what pertains to the object and what reflects one's point of view. The distinction between these two springs from temporal properties, a complex structure of the expectations and retentions that comprise the objectivity of the world at the same time as they comprise the subjectivity of one's point of view.

In sum, experience is temporal. Illuminating this unseen dimension is helpful in organizing and clarifying the phenomenological stages above, but that does not explain lived temporality itself. What then is temporality?

2.6   Stage 6: Temporality (2), the Order of Moments

Husserl's proposal literally adds a dimension to phenomenology. The temporal dimension—the history and future of an object in experience—is a part of its present. It is perceived, although not in the same manner as the sensible three dimensions facing us. Phenomenally, each object, perceived second-by-second, incorporates a continuously updated side view of itself careening through time. Change and permanence are therefore immediately present, and phenomenal reality is constructed thereby. Paradoxically, it is only through the idea that objects are in continuous phenomenal flux that the stability of reality can emerge.

In many respects time is a well-behaved dimension, as admitting of measurement by humans and machines as any other dimension. Experimental psychology of time perception is devoted to human temporal judgments on the analogy of judgments about any other dimension. Topics include the judgment of elapsed time and the impact of various stimuli and other causes on it, the judgment of temporal distance to past and future events, and the ordering of events in memory. The Einsteinian interchange of space and time contributes to this tight analogy between time and spatial dimensions. But temporality in the full-bore phenomenological sense developed here is a very unusual dimension. Though generically like all other dimensions, including spatial dimensions, it is uniquely differentiated through its specific phenomenological qualities. It's always changing; its changes are all non-sensory superpositions; it is a global property of all real things, and bears them all forward at once. Finally, it is unitary. Among all the properties that crisscross a reality, there is always just one time. So, once again in the pursuit of the subjective view of objectivity, a new layer of mystery surfaces. Why would any property have these features? Must experience of a reality include such a property?

Once more the firefly can light the way. At the present instant—still sitting at that picnic table—what is sensed, or present to my sight, is a point of light. Is it a timeslice of a moving firefly, or random flash of a faltering neuron (a firefly of the mind, false creation of a heat-oppressed brain)? Considering any instant of this stream of perception, there can be no definite answer. A single instant of perception cannot resolve whether the dit of light is real or not. Only in relation to once and future dits does this light get placed in a trajectory. Husserl saw that the succession of firefly impressions resolved nothing without some unifying temporal combination of them all. The present glow bears with it a non-sensory ghost of seconds past and to come. To see the firefly is to perceive at one swoop its trajectory over a time greater than the instant of the Now. All the other superpositions about what it is I see before me follow from this trajectory.

So far this recapitulates the three prior stages of phenomenological excavation, but now we dig through one more layer. Consider the fly in just two dimensions, its height in my field of vision, and its apparent distance to the right or left of some arbitrary midline of the scene. Two numbers can encode its location on the standard Cartesian grid—<1,3>, for example. The idea of encoding its trajectory is equally simple: <4,7>,<4,6>,<3,6>,<2,5>,<2,4>,**<1,3>**, . . . I perceive all these points right now, the last as a sensation and its antecedents as retentions, and I base my judgments about the real/unreal firefly on the set. In this case, the point is clearly on a wavering path from upper right to lower middle, just like a firefly and very unlike some other things that might look like little flashes of light. The last point is in boldface to signal its presence.

To a first glance it appears as if this simple world is entirely two-dimensional. But in fact, there is an additional dimension hidden in the trajectory of points. For me to understand the trajectory as wandering from upper left to lower right, I must keep the points in order. It isn't sufficient that they in fact happened in an order; I must have that order available to me now (for every Now). Without an explicit order, I have just a scatter of points, a connect-the-dots challenge where the dots are unnumbered. In this case, these six specific points could be arranged in 720 different possible orders, suggesting to me everything from multiple fireflies to total madness. The ordering dimension will necessarily have certain properties in order to sort out our reality:

• It will have to be mainly *monotonic*—meaning that it can't reverse or loop back to assign a single place in the order to more than one point. If it looped, two points would be assigned the same place in the order. Even in this simple case, that would assign the firefly two different trajectories. Each time a moment in the order is used twice, the number of consistent trajectories doubles. One rapidly sinks into a Borgesian garden of forking paths,

> an infinite series of times, in a growing, dizzying web of divergent, convergent and parallel times. . . . We do not exist in the majority of these times; in some you exist, and not I; in others I, and not you; in others, both of us. (Borges, "The Garden of Forking Paths," p. 127)

• It will have to order everything; that is, it will be mainly *ubiquitous*. Suppose there is also a flash of light at <5,8>, but that we have no idea of where to place it in the trajectory. That is to say, it could be anywhere.

Again, interpretation falls apart, and faster than in the garden of forking paths. A loose point generates as many alternate orders as there are points.

Without an ordering relationship with these characteristics, there will be no experience of a reality. But even still reality has not been secured. The big dig continues.

2.7   Stage 7: Temporality (3), Phenomenal Recursivity

Experienced time is, as noted, monotonic and omnipresent. And, if the considerations above are persuasive, it is also necessary. Only with temporal relations present to consciousness can what William James called a "blooming, buzzing confusion," a meaningless succession of instants, emerge into reality. Living in an experienced reality presupposes a general capacity to relate almost any event to a great many others in time, and this capacity to perceive temporal relations can be employed in recollection and anticipation. The order modifies every object, updating continually and synchronously.

In the numerical abstraction of the firefly example, time was forced upon us to order the observed points. The order of succession, which had been taken for granted as the order on the page, was made explicit with the addition of the temporal dimension; two dimensions became three. But unfortunately this recreates the ordering problem within each moment. Now our ordered triples of <x-coordinate, y-coordinate, time-coordinate> themselves will need ordering, lest we get confused between (in this case) space and time. So we require another dimension. This in turn will make ordered pairs out of single points, and keeping that order straight will require another order, *ad infinitum*. For experience of a reality, the regress must stop in a foundation order that need not be ordered outside of itself. In other words, in addition to being monotonic and ubiquitous, the order will have to be *basic* (or, if you prefer, *ultimate* or *absolute*).

Time *seems* basic. But the threat of regress shows that our pursuit of necessary conditions is not over quite yet. Other orders may be needed, leading either to an endless hierarchy of orders or to an arbitrary stopping point. The way forward is again through Husserl.

Husserl's tripartite present illuminated temporality as a confluence of retention, presence, and protention. A real firefly, for example, appears at any moment as the triptych of its possible appearances, its current sensory aspect, and its non-sensory trail of historical appearances. What is the structure of the retentive panel? In the previous section, I sliced the experience of the firefly into an array of moments, where each moment is the confluence of temporal properties. Consciousness of reality is this array, experienced all at once, like a screenful of thumbnail images for a computer slide show. Something like this must be present to consciousness; without it, reality would shatter into disconnected atoms. But, strangely, ordinary presentations of the firefly and everything else seem nothing like this filmstrip of temporally ordered moments. Instead, it is as if all the moments are stacked on top of each other, and we look through the stack from above. The top image is the image of the immediately present, and the images beneath are the superposed non-sensory retentions, like palimpsests, embedding the present in its temporal world. The ordering is still necessary even though the metaphorical viewpoint has shifted. Each moment must preserve its intrinsic temporal "depth" as a part of its presentation. At issue is the phenomenological understanding of this non-spatial depth.

This obscure depth resolves if we bear in mind that what is shoved back by each new now is not just the current now, but the entire tripartite present at that moment. The structure of the retentive part of the now is itself tripartite; it is the trace of the immediately previous protention, the immediately previous now-point, and the immediately previous retention. But with retention itself retained, the order of retentions becomes a recursive nesting. A diagram may help make this clear. The panels of figure 2.2 offer a schematic diagram of a particular present moment in the flight of the firefly, showing only its temporal aspects. Accordingly, the points are identified by number. The left panel schematizes simple retention, the idea that what is sensed as immediately present is all that sinks down into retention. The right panel shows recursive retention, the process where the *entire* contents of current consciousness (protention, presence, retention) slides into retention. (For simplicity, I've shown only presence and retention. A similar recursive nesting would extend into the future. Also, the diagram wraps each moment in an ellipse, suggesting discrete moments, like the ticks of the clock. This is just to help visualize the process, which is not discrete but a continuous, elastic flow.)

Simple retention illustrates the ordering problem: How do we know how far back each point is, without assuming a tacit marker of temporal

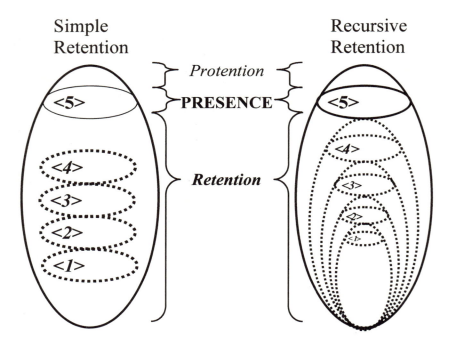

Figure 2.2 Schematic representation of the distinction between simple retention and the more complex recursive retention suggested by Husserl. In simple retention, only the presence of the immediately given is retained. In recursive retention, the entire tripartite present state of consciousness is transformed into a tripartite retentional structure. Thus from moment to moment retention retains a recursive nested trace of the succession of past moments.

order? Recursive retention, and its diagram, suggest a solution to the problem. The diagram suggests the depth just described, but it is of course a pictorial illusion. Depth is a temporal illusion in just the same way. The entire current state of awareness (not just its presence) slides into retention continuously. Thus a single transformation, applied continuously, is the most fundamental phenomenal border, at the edge where the present here-and-now is transformed into the non-sensory past of retention. That transformation affects retentive contents no less than sensory presences. For example, after the clock turns over from 11:59 to 12:00, 11:59 sinks down into the retentive consciousness. At 12:01, 12:00 lapses into retention itself, complete with its own prior retention of 11:59. So consciousness at 12:01 contains a retention of a retention of 11:59. Time accordingly effects continuous changes on the retained past. Thus one basic transformation is sufficient to organize time all the way down, while keeping the past in play. The crossing from present to past is permanently present, as with each moment the entire present, with protention and retention attached, sinks into the invisible dynamic history of past moments.[8]

The recursive nesting at last provides a stable foundation for experience. It embeds the temporal order and depth in that order. The other properties of temporality, monotonicity, and ubiquity are simply aspects of the nesting, because the totality of experience is nested and the depth of recursion is the depth of time itself. The nesting also provides a natural phenomenology of temporal perspective and distance, and the horizon of the past, that point at which the past is accessible only through recollection.

Real things are experienced as such by their recurrence across the layers. What is necessary to anything real, then, is phenomenal duration. To *see* a picnic table (as opposed to detecting it) is to see its having-been-present as well as its will-be-present-still. The firefly achieves its toehold on its reality for us in the same way, as a path or thread of light. The path is apprehended in each flash, each instant of its appearance. Neither the firefly nor the picnic table are isolated presentations, however. Both are enriched by countless superposed aspects of meaning and context, which also intertwine into the depths and heights of temporality. What I can see of the picnic table shifts as I move around it, and my movement and its appearance synchronize in a perfect dance exactly appropriate to a stationary thing. This hints at the complicated recipe of reality, a recipe in which the basic ingredient is always the experience of temporality.

2.8   The Rest of the Story

Merely having a capacity for temporality does not suffice for having a reality, but it plays a unique and pivotal role in building the objective world for consciousness. Dan Zahavi refers to temporality as the infrastructure of consciousness, an apt metaphor. Temporality is the skeleton that sustains objects and objective reality. Once we understand temporality, the way to incorporate consciousness overall opens before us.

The rest of the story is not trivial, of course. Fleshing out the simple perception of a solid cube takes Husserl a good four hundred pages in his

Thing and Space. The full constitution of a thing is the result of the interplay of information from the senses and from the body. For example, as our eyes turn, the image on the retina slides in the same direction as our gaze. Why does the scene before us not appear to jump with every eye movement? Husserl's answer appeals to a second channel of sensory information, the kinaesthetic (or proprioceptive) awareness of the rotation of the eyes. Gazing on a static scene, the awareness of eye movement and the corresponding slippage of the image counterbalance each other, enabling us to perceive the scene as stable. In contrast, an afterimage stays in the same place on the retina while the eyes move, resulting in an apparent glowing patch that slides over the scene. That violation of the counterpoint of eye movement and image slippage is a sign that the afterimage is not a real surface. Other bodily motions enter into complex counterpoints with sensory information from vision, touch, and hearing. All these channels of information present us with the intricate harmonies of reality, enabling us to distinguish the changes due to our point of view from those due to changes in the objects before us. When the objects are real, these multisensory harmonies conform to the rules of counterpoint, such as the rule linking eye movements to retinal image slippage. To perceive a real thing is to experience this intricate coordination of aspects of sensory awareness. Of course, the regularities of phenomenal objectivity can only be apprehended over time. In this way, the skeleton of experienced temporality acquires the substantial flesh from sensations of and by our bodies.[9]

To sum up, temporality provides a foundation for transcendence and superposition, and these in turn explain the fundamental polarities of subject and object. Experience in time weaves and reweaves the tapestry of reality. There are many variations on experienced intentionality, and many books by phenomenologists exploring them. Here my focus has been on the comparatively mundane case of the phenomenology of perception. This paradigmatic example nonetheless intimates the basic structures shared by all states of awareness.

The undifferentiated monolith of what-it-is-like has been anatomized, but the main task of placing consciousness in nature still lies ahead. Phenomenology has brought the structure of experience into clearer view. Of what is experience made?

3

Brains in Toyland

The subjective view of objectivity revealed that there was more to reality than meets the eye. What matters most is non-sensory, and among all the insensible dimensions that constitute reality, the first is experienced time. Time is copresent in every experience and in every object of experience, and it flows through everything. Every object of experience is ceaselessly unreeling its history and cancelling all but one of its possibilities, and this flux is internal to the object. Every object is therefore always changing. Moreover, the ceaseless flow of reality appears in consciousness in every instant. Both history and the future are compacted into every moment of awareness. Expressing this insight folds language into paradox: Temporality, it turns out, is always instantaneous. Time takes no time. The mountain is not a mountain at all.

These conclusions will surely seem paradoxical, if not downright mystical. How could any real system, physically realized in biology or any other form, aspire to this? How could we, looking at such a system from the outside, ever hope to detect the profound stirrings of experienced time? Indeed, if Husserl is right, cognition and consciousness seem mutually exclusive. Cognition depends on the ability to detect sameness over time: same house, same word, same color. Consciousness, being temporal, is ever changing, and nothing is ever the same from moment to moment. How do we snatch cognition from this maelstrom? If consciousness presupposes temporality, and temporality is like this, why is life not a chaos of single, unique, irreproducible instants?

This appendix began with the objective view of subjectivity in the form suggested by cognitive science, namely, building consciousness around the idea of detection. After setting that framework aside, a second movement approximated the subjective view of objectivity, a phenomenology of experienced reality. Now begins the third and final movement, a return to the objective view of subjectivity. This time, however, we are looking for something different, the very structures of experienced reality revealed by phenomenology. These will be the structures embodied in a conscious entity. Moreover, if conscious entities are part of the natural world, we will need scientific methods for observing them. The double task ahead includes developing ideas about the ways conscious systems might be constructed, and how we might observe the structures of phenomenal reality in those systems.

I will work toward this materialization of consciousness in two stages. The first stage points the way. Using artificial neural networks, the love objects of Gordon Fescue, I will show how some very general features of certain networks of neuron-like processors generate internal states with the properties of temporality (or its close analogues). This first stage will constitute an "existence proof" that a material system with the right organization can simulate a central aspect of first-person phenomenology. It will show, I hope, that temporality is not mysticism. In addition, through the analysis of neural nets, we can test-drive the elaborate interpretational techniques needed to understand the complex doings of a brain. Then, in the next (and final) chapter, we will return at last to fMRI, exemplified in the houses-faces-chairs study and several others, and bring to bear the new interpretive apparatus. This will constitute an empirical probe of consciousness. If phenomenology implemented in neural nets shows how consciousness *could* be embodied, then in this final stage we will discover whether consciousness is *in fact* so embodied. I hope then that the appearance of paradox will evaporate, and mystery will transform into wonder.

3.1 Beep . . . Boop

The auditory equivalent of a firefly might be the laboratory beep. As Husserl noted, even a naked tone in isolation has temporal structure. A sequence of tones separated by silence allows for the experimental exploration of time in isolation from most of the other dimensions of experience. For example, in one common experiment, subjects hear several sequences of two different beeps separated by a few seconds of silence. The first beep in each sequence may occur at any time, but whenever the beep sounds, exactly five seconds later a different beep follows, a boop. Differing only in pitch, not much distinguishes the two tones as sounds. But superposed on the immediate presence of the two stimuli is a big difference: The time of occurrence of the beep is always a surprise, but the time of the boop—five seconds after every beep—never is. Subjects obviously anticipate the second tone. (They can show this by trying to press a button simultaneous with it.) Between beep and boop is a period of silence, so in some form subjects must remember that a beep occurred and note the passing seconds. If the experiment is conducted in controlled surroundings, between beep and boop there should be no environmental change, no clue to indicate how much time has passed. Thus, from the fact that it is easy to anticipate the boops, we conclude that elapsed time information is somehow available, but how this information appears or is used by a button-pushing system like one of us is unknown.

The experiment is often done, but not with phenomenology in mind. Rather, the paradigm happens to elicit a predictable "brainwave" (a tiny electrical current) detectable by electroencephalograph (EEG). The EEG will show a drop in voltage at electrodes on the scalp, gradually slumping as the seconds tick by. With the boop, the EEG bounces back to its pre-beep level. The effect is known as "contingent negative variation," or CNV. Of course the brain must be doing *something* during the interstimulus interval. The CNV is an intriguing but ambiguous clue about those goings-on.

Much has been written on the relation between EEG effects and underlying brain processes, but instead of taking that tour I propose to play with toy brains instead. Throughout this book there have been references to artificial neural network models, a research branch of cognitive science that has flourished somewhat in isolation from the empirical studies of cognitive neuroscience. Artificial neural nets are webs of neuron-like processing units with variable interconnections. As such they are more like the biological brain than is a typical digital computer, while nonetheless differing greatly from their living counterparts. In thousands of simulations, artificial networks have developed capacities like those of brains. Indeed, they have been so successful that creating a network that can do something, no matter what that something is, is no longer news. The interest in networks lately has shifted to a host of engineering questions about improving network performance (they have business applications) and a smaller host of questions about enhancing the biological realism of network models.

Although very few authors use nets to model phenomenology, the two-tone paradigm invites the effort. First, it's simple. It consists of just two basic stimuli, with a fixed interval between them. One can hope to set up a straightforward model of the task, a "world" for an artificial neural net to inhabit. Second, following from the first, the resulting network will itself be relatively simple. Because all the questions have now shifted to "How does it work?" one can also hope to address the network version of the question. Third, if the arguments so far are right, the dominant and successful frameworks of the rest of cognitive science are not appropriate in this quest. We're starting over, looking for a different expression of phenomenal reality. We will need new methods, and again, simple systems could be a good warm-up. Should a network mimic humans in this one phenomenological respect, its structure and function will offer ideas about analogous structures and functions in us. These will be suggestions only, because a working network can at best illustrate one way a process could be implemented. Actual embodiment could be something else altogether. But considering the mysterious phenomenology of time, any suggestion could be welcome.

3.2 CNVnet

Creating a simulation is an exercise in creative oversimplification. For a human, the beep-boop experience will be rich and complicated. Nonetheless, here we strip away the richness to isolate just one dimension of the experience, time. The first step toward this simple model is to define the bare bones of the task. That is, we take the inputs, beeps and boops, and the outputs, whatever it is we want our toy brain to do, and condense them into a simple number code suitable for a simulated brain to digest. The basic structure of the input consists of many repetitions of stimulus-delay-stimulus; everything else is negotiable. Forget about tone, pitch, timbre. Forget about the other senses too. At bottom, beep and boop are just two different items, either present or not. So, let "10" be beep, and "01" boop. We'll represent everything else (the silences) as "00." It doesn't matter what we use to represent beep or boop; any two digits (two bits) will do. But once we have chosen the codes, the order of their presentation does matter. It's always beep-silence-boop, and we can represent the interval between beep and boop by the number of 00s between them. For example, a regular beep-boop sequence might read like this: 10, 00, 00, 01. If we assume that each pattern is presented for one second, beep and boop are here separated by a two-second pause. Beeps can occur at any time, but once the beep sounds, the boop is sure to follow after a fixed interval. In our simple binary notation, we then generate a long string of 00s, and drop the 10,00,00,01s in at random. A small chunk of this input stream might look like this:

. . . 00, 00, 00, 00, 00, 10, 00, 00, 01, 00, 00, 00, 00, 00, 00, 10, 00, 00, 01, 00, 00 . . .

The only other rules for the input stream are that the beep-boop sequences never overlap, and that following each sequence there is a silence of at least a few seconds before the next beep-boop can occur. This, then, is the world our hypothetical network inhabits, a pretty boring place, but with one regular feature: Beeps predict (a pause, then) boops.

Next, what is this toy brain to do? What is the desired output? In the human version of the task, subjects press a button when they expect the boop. Our interest here is not really behavior, so we can use the outputs as a psychologist might, as a simple device to make sure the subject is paying attention. In general, we can set the network the task of anticipating the next input. We can accordingly use the same coding scheme, 10 for beep, 01 for boop, and 00 for silence. The network strives for precognition, or, more mundanely, simple prediction, of the next input.

Now we can build the toy brain. It will need two input neurons, one for each of the two digits of the inputs. The first unit will be on when there is a 1 in the first place of the two-digit input, and off for 0. The second will encode the second digit in the same way. The possible outputs will also need two units. One of these output units will represent the prediction "beep ahead," the other, boop. Between input and output, we can install any number of simulated interneurons, and we can connect them any way we choose. For example, we could install a "brain" of just six simulated neurons, as figure 3.1 shows. In the lingo of neural networkers, the whole comprises three layers, input and output layers flanking a middle slab known as the "hidden layer." (The units in this layer are called hidden units.) Though hidden from the simulated environment, the hidden layer is not hidden from us. Its activity will be the center of scrutiny whenever we look into how the network works. The many connections (lines) between units represent the interactions among them, and the arrows indicate the direction of interaction. One unit can excite another, increasing its activity, or inhibit it, decreasing its activity. The diagram as a whole shows dynamic relationships among the processing units. Diagrams like this represent the "functional architecture" of a network.

Bear in mind that the toy brain is not something to construct from physical parts. What looks like discrete units and wires between them are ultimately mathematical functions. The functions together comprise a

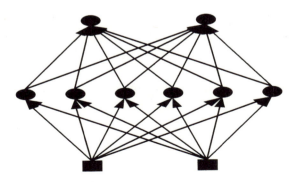

Figure 3.1 Simple feed-forward network architecture with six hidden units.

mathematical model of the network, simulating its behavior, which in turn is a simplified simulation of a nervous system. If unit A is "on," its "activation" will be quantified. (That's why beep and boop are encoded with zeros and ones.) If there is an "excitatory connection" between unit A and unit B, that means that activity in A is added to B (to put it roughly). The adjustable "strength" or "weight" on the connection between A and B is a simple coefficient that adjusts how much of A's value is added to B's value. One cycle in the life of a net consists of updating all the values on units and all the connection coefficients, all according to the equations that ultimately define the simulation. Accordingly, to probe a net is to extract numerical values from its units at particular moments or cycles in its operation. As we will see, we can compare and visualize these numbers in many different ways.

The net in figure 3.1 could easily discriminate 01, 10, and 00, responding to each with a distinct output pattern. These discriminating responses would have to be immediate, however; with each cycle, the network begins all over again with the present input. The beep-boop scenario is different. In this case, one input (10) conveys infallible information about the inputs to follow for the next few cycles. But the net lacks the means to hold on to the clue long enough to use it. Like a photocell or a thermostat, it is a net of the moment.

Earlier in this book, Miranda spends some time with a milestone article in cognitive science, Jeffrey Elman's "Finding Structure in Time," published in 1990 in the journal *Cognitive Science*. Elman, a linguist, began from the observation that a great deal of cognition—and all of language—depends on interpreting stimuli in ways that are contingent on the past. In a single ingenious revision, he gave nets the capacity for finding structures across time. The revision was the addition of an adjunct hidden layer, a "context layer," whose job was simply to copy the most recent state of the regular hidden layer. That copy was then re-presented alongside the next input, resulting in the architecture shown in figure 3.2. The hidden layer now receives its input from two sources, from the input layer (the environment) and from itself—one cycle in the past.

Elman called nets with this architecture simple recurrent networks, SRNs. Simple as they may be, the internal recurrence effectively opens a

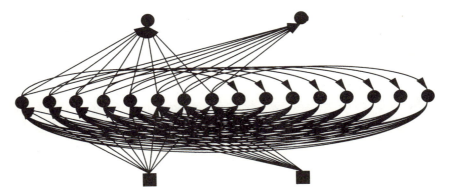

Figure 3.2 Functional architecture of a simple recurrent network. The current state of the eight hidden units is copied by a "mirror layer" of eight context units. The copy is then available along with the new inputs at the next time step, allowing the network to use its own past to detect and anticipate patterns unfolding over time.

new dimension in the elementary innards of a network. Now the network responds not just to the currently present stimulus, but also to its own most recent internal state. Because that echo dates from one cycle ago, the next internal state can enfold both present and past information. Then that new internal state, combining present and just prior information, itself recycles; therefore, the successive state carries forward information from two cycles previous. And so on. In principle, this neuronal hall of mirrors can keep a pattern alive indefinitely. In practice, the past might get shoved aside by the demands of the present.

Elman and colleagues have also provided the cognitive science community with a friendly software package, Tlearn, in which one can easily build simulations of both standard and recurrent networks. My networks graphics have been generated by Tlearn, and with it I simulated the beep-boop experiment for an SRN with the architecture shown above. I will call the simulation of the contingent negative variation "CNVnet." As Gordon Fescue explained, an artificial neural network is trained rather than programmed, so CNVnet underwent many trial runs through beep-pause-boop sequences. After each trial, the many connections among the units were automatically adjusted so that its performance the next time would be slightly improved. The two figures below show the responses of the net-

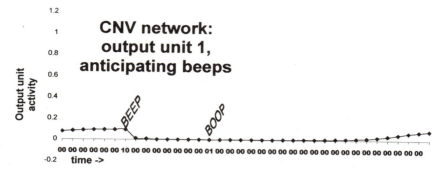

Figure 3.3 Output test of CNVnet, anticipating beeps. The *x* axis is labeled with inputs to the net, which has been trained to anticipate them. This graph shows the output of the first output unit, symbolizing "1 0" (beep). Since the beep occurs at random, the net cannot learn to predict its occurrence. But following the beep, the network suppresses the beep output, reflecting the correct prediction that no beeps will occur during the waiting period and subsequent inter-trial interval.

work after several million training repetitions through a run of one thousand inputs that follow the beep-boop rules, with seven cycles between the two inputs. About sixty sequences of 10,00,00,00,00,00,00,00,01, were scattered randomly in the thousand presentations. The figures show the net response during one of them. First, figure 3.3 shows the network's inability to anticipate beeps. No precognition here, as we would expect, because a beep can occur at random. But once a beep has sounded, the network can know that no other beep will occur for a time, and so the beep output is completely suppressed for this interval. The input series also follows the rule that beep-boop sequences are separated by at least sixteen cycles of silence; the network output correctly reflects this.

CNVnet can't know when to expect a beep, but it can easily anticipate boops, as figure 3.4 shows. In this case, the boop output unit springs to life at just the right moment. The warning implicit in the beep has been heeded. Considering its behavior, then, the CNVnet has learned everything there is to learn about this toy environment. Its biography ("Beeping and Nothingness") would report the detection of beeps, boops, and the void of waiting, both the void of random waiting and the void of pure nothingness. Its successful performance implies that the

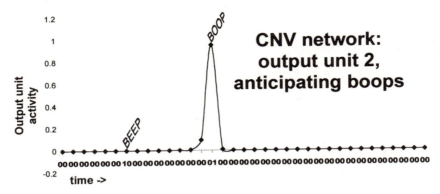

Figure 3.4 Output test of CNVnet, anticipating boops. The *x* axis is labeled with inputs to the net, which has been trained to anticipate them. This graph shows the output of the second output unit, symbolizing "0 1" (boop). Since boops always occur eight cycles after beeps, the net has learned to use the beep as the cue to the subsequent boop. It correctly retains information about elapsed time, in the absence of any explicit temporal cues from the environment.

temporal relationship of the various inputs is available to guide the network response.

3.3 Into the Net

It works, but how does it work? In exchange for the radical oversimplification of the CNVnet in comparison to almost every living system, we gain the hope of actually answering this question. Networks leave nothing to the imagination. We can probe and prod them any way we like, and check any observation against the real functioning circuits. The relative transparency of a simple network, then, can be a workshop for the comparison of methods analogous to those used in neuroscience. I will consider three prominent examples, familiar empirical approaches to living brains. An ideal probe—either of a simulation or a real brain—would accomplish two goals. First, it would promote a satisfying understanding of how a particular system works. In this case, we want to know how CNVnet hangs on to temporal information that tells it when the boop is coming, in the absence of any cues from the environment. Second, a useful method would lend itself to the dicier issue of the embodiment of temporality as an aspect of phenomenology. Both of these hurdles will turn out to be hard to clear, even for the pipsqueak CNVnet.

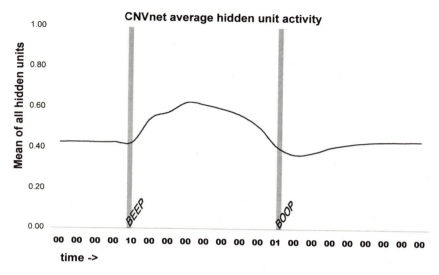

Figure 3.5 Average activity in the hidden units of CNVnet, the network analogue of EEG recording. The graph shows a steep rise followed by a slower decline in overall activity. This follows roughly the human contingent negative variation.

Method 1: Population Averaging ("EEG")

We can observe the contingent negative variation in electroencephalograph (EEG) recordings, so as a first step, we try a comparable probe. An EEG indirectly measures the combined signals of huge populations of neurons. In effect, the signal at an electrode is the average of signals from millions of neurons. By analogy, we can average the activity in the hidden units (the "central nervous system") in this net. Figure 3.5 shows the mean of all hidden units, again indexed to the inputs to the net. Beeps provoke a rapid rise in the mean activity, followed by a negative ramp down to the boop. In its crude way, then, the net has not only mimicked the target behavior, but significant physiological side effects of the sort detected in humans.

This average curve shows something concrete about the activity in the network. If this were the only way in, we might summarize our findings thus:

"EEG" from the entire network reveals a slow oscillation correlated with temporal processing.

But what enables the oscillation to carry on through the silence, and ultimately produce the correct response? The average signal is too general to answer this question. Something is happening while the net waits for its moment, but from this alone one can't infer any particular mechanism. If the processing units are responsible for the distinctive output, we will need a more specific window into their individual contributions.

Method 2: Single-Unit Recording

Next, we borrow another technique enshrined in neuroscience, the single-cell recording. In experimental neuroscience, this method requires a thin electrode delicately slipped into a single neuron to record its tiny signals. But in this simulation, without so much as touching an electrode, we can extract the activity of a single "neuron," as in figure 3.6. If EEG was too general, then single-cell recording shows the very specific function of an individual processing unit.

The figure shows a single unit that becomes active at the onset of each sequence, and retires as soon as the boop sounds. Like the EEG, the effect is nicely bound by the time course of the two tone sequences. If we could use only this method, we might draw the following conclusion:

"Single-unit recording" reveals a specific unit that is correlated with a time-limited working memory of the stimulus.

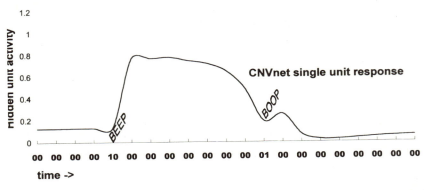

Figure 3.6 Activity in a single hidden unit of CNVnet, the network analogue of single-cell recording.

This one unit seems to explain the ability to keep the boop in mind through the pause; in a brain, the unit might be identified by its anatomical location. But what explains the behavior of the unit? Unfortunately, as with EEG, the cause of this unit's behavior is an unknown combination of other units. The dynamics driving the unit remain out of sight. Moving from the greatest generality to the greatest specificity has barely advanced our understanding.

Method 3: Functional Imaging

A useful method, it seems, will be a middle way between maximum generality and maximum specificity. Functional magnetic resonance imaging inspires a network equivalent, following the methodology described for the Ishai study. In this case, we begin by dividing the beep-boop task into three distinct phases: encoding (10), working memory (the intervening 00s), and response (01). To isolate the encoding function, we extract the hidden unit values during "10" inputs and average them, and then subtract from them everything else. In this way, we isolate activity that uniquely contributes to beep processing. We could use similar extraction to address how the net processes the waiting states, and the boop. This is a logical way to decompose the process, because the task necessarily contains these separate components. Figure 3.7 shows the functional images from this analysis. Each image shows all eight hidden units, after averaging and subtraction. The simple numerical graphs of the previous examples have been replaced with a color-coding scheme. The eight units appear as squares in a 4-by-2 grid, and their activation values show as the brightness of each square.

Beep   Working Memory   Boop

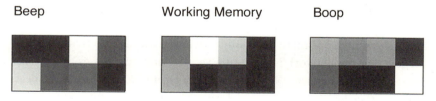

Figure 3.7 Activity in all eight hidden units, averaged over time during specific stages of the beep-boop task. This is the network analysis analogue of functional brain imaging. The eight units are represented in a 4-by-2 grid, and brighter squares indicate greater activation values.

The bright squares are areas of greatest activity in contrast to the baseline in each case. The map-like image invites us to name the regions shown, and functional neuroimaging suggests a style of nomenclature. Beep processing, it seems, is correlated with activity in the "right superior medial region" (upper middle, right side), with secondary activation in the left lateral inferior. For the boop, conjoined as it is with the "motor response," different areas light up. Interestingly, working memory also partly activates the R superior medial and L lateral inferior, regions involved in beep-procession. Perhaps this is exactly where the stimulus is encoded?

Functional imaging of this simple network has the apparent effect of localizing particular subfunctions (encoding, memory, retrieval) that together comprise the task. As it happens, in this example each "region" is just one processing unit, but in larger nets, regions could parcel the network into components of varying sizes. The analysis leaves open how each region processes its assigned subtask, but at least the method narrows the options. Now smaller subsystems remain to be fit to less complicated functions.

The functional neuroimager might therefore conclude as follows:

"Functional imaging" reveals distinct regions specifically correlated with the separate components of the temporal task.

However, back at the low end, the simplicity of this net highlights some questionable assumptions of this method. To create each image, the entire time series of unit activity was divided into two piles, the cycles devoted to the subtask (e.g., cycles of beep inputs) and everything else (delay, boop, pure hanging out). Each of the two piles was then averaged, and the two averages contrasted. But the contrast will isolate a component of distinct function only if every item in each pile is generally similar to the rest of its pile *and* the initial division truly isolates *exclusive* functions. On the one hand, if within a pile there are wildly different patterns of activity, this will suggest that the network is executing very different processes at different times. The initial division of tasks and time points would then be suspect. On the other hand, if processing during the excluded time points shares resources with the selected "in" function, that overlap will be excluded in the subtraction. Regions that should be counted in will be falsely excluded. The resultant analysis will be blind to both of these alternatives.

Its accuracy thus depends entirely on an initial functional dissection of the task. It may be that the network really is doing the same thing during every beep, and it may be that what it is doing during every other cycle is unrelated to that process. But the contrastive analysis itself is blind to both possibilities.

Despite their differences, the three methods share the common problem of conflating or excluding potentially distinct causal factors. In empirical neuroscience, however, these methods may be the only ones available. What then? Here again are the three plausible conclusions based on CNVnet:

1.   EEG reveals a slow oscillation correlated with temporal processing.

2.   Single-unit recording reveals a unit correlated with a time-limited working memory of the stimulus.

3.   Functional imaging reveals distinct regions specifically correlated with the separate components of the temporal task.

In this example, all three conclusions will seem a bit embellished, but with respect to this network, all are basically true. (And repeatable, but those details are not important for the example.) In the literature of real brains, exactly these sorts of data are enlisted to support hypotheses similar in form to the examples. The conclusions are almost always hedged by an awareness that correlation is not causality, but often too the correlation is proposed to indicate a possible cause. Always the correlations are presented in a context of many other studies. In particular, choices of what to highlight and what to subtract are always made with reference to prior research.

Nonetheless, each of the three conclusions reflects the methods used to determine it. Each method also selects some aspects of the data and excludes others. Is this a serious problem? In this case the conclusions, though sound, obscure the real dynamics of the network. Being small, we can examine the net in its entirety, and observe the dynamic time courses of all the hidden units, which is plotted in figure 3.8. In this figure, each line represents the activity of one of the hidden units before, during, and after a beep-boop sequence. We can see that the hidden layer spends much of its time between tasks in a holding pattern, during which some of its units are on, others off, and a few steady in the middle. But with the beep, everyone

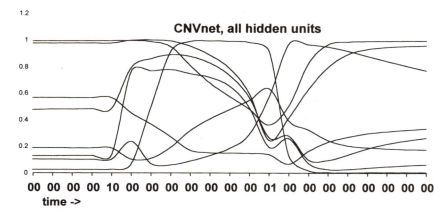

Figure 3.8 Simultaneous activity in all eight hidden units during the beep-boop task. Network performance rests on a complex interaction of all eight hidden units over time, with rapid changes in all units during periods between beep and boop. The previous analytical methods failed to anticipate this complexity.

springs into action. A few units seem to follow the downward slope of the contingent negative variation, but the others defy easy characterization.

This complete trace of internal activity should be compared with the figures preceding it. The EEG showed a smooth rise and fall of the collective. However, the whole story just above shows that there is no collective mass action, and the real components of the smooth average curve are jumping wildly. Each stage in the average reflects a very different underlying pattern, and the impression of stately procession through a gradually evolving pattern is false. Next, return to the single-unit recording. Here it looked like we had found the neuron in charge, but the whole story reveals many contenders for boss unit. Nearly every unit is in a different state at each step in the overall processing. Finally, the functional image seemed to show three distinct states of encoding (beep), memory (pause), and response (boop), with specific modules of one or two units in charge for each. But the whole story contradicts that impression as well. Not only is every unit doing something, but during the waiting period, each moment is unique, and nothing particular segregates all the "memory" states from either beep or boop.

Even in this subbasement of brains, nothing is simple. The CNV network hasn't got that much on a thermostat, but even the tempest in this teacup anticipates some heavy weather for neuroscience in the quest for consciousness. On the one hand, each of the three analytical hypotheses is sound (with allowances for the bare-bones of the example), in that each correlates a true (and repeatable) observation with a plausible causal mechanism. Yet, on the other hand, the helter skelter of actual activity in this "brain" is a surprise. Nothing in the three standard hypotheses predicted, even in broad terms, that the CNV network would look like *that*.

3.4   Having It All

What is to be done? The standard refrain yearns for a synthesis and convergence of approaches, and in so doing drives a push for more (and more) data, along with refinements of the existing methods. Everyone hopes that ultimately these analyses will converge on a satisfying picture of the dynamics of a complex system. But there may be a deeper caution (and an opportunity) in the example of CNVnet. Each standard approach omits part of the underlying dynamics of this network. The EEG average cancels complementary interactions or oscillations through the entire period. The single-cell recording omits the web of causal factors that sustain the plateau of activity in the unit that so nicely tracks the waiting state. The functional image omits a bit of both. It conflates complementary dynamics by condensing and averaging disparate time points (averaging over time has exactly the effect of averaging across space in EEG), and then, by subtracting baselines from functional images, it obscures causal factors that contribute to both the process of interest and the baseline. (Subtraction isolates regions from their context, as occurs on a smaller scale in single-cell recording.)

If each method is myopic, then collecting more data with the same methods may be doing things the hard way. If each experiment passes through the filters of analysis described above, each dataset will conflate causal factors, omit them, or both. Comparing one experiment with another will be difficult, because the filtering effects will be different in each. Comparing many experiments will be even harder.

What is really to be done, then, may not be to redeploy the same methods in more (and more) variations of the experiment. Instead, perhaps we should get some new methods. Toys such as CNVnet can help here too. We can take advantage again of the relative simplicity of this net to begin with the concrete. A new method in this case can be characterized in response to the analytical methods and their shortfalls. The new analysis should:

Consider all processing units (like EEG and functional imaging, but unlike single-cell recording);

Consider them individually (like single-cell recording and imaging, but unlike EEG);

Consider each moment separately (like EEG and single-cell recording, but unlike functional imaging based on averaging and subtraction).

Fortunately, I have not had to invent methods that meet these criteria. Since early in the network renaissance of the 1980s, modelers have used techniques of multivariate analysis borrowed from the social sciences. These techniques have been developed to interpret data that track many variables at once. At the core of multivariate analysis is "dimension thinking," as Porfiry Petrovich promotes in Miranda's story.

Dimension thinking will be important in what follows, so I would like to give a graphical example, again drawn from the annals of CNVnet. Consider (for simplicity) two hidden units at a particular moment in the beep-boop sequence. The neural net simulation will represent their activity as two values, for example, .184 and .482. These numbers are the product of all the inputs to each unit at this moment in the simulation. At subsequent time points, these values change. In the graphs used in the sections above, these values are plotted against a time line, as in figure 3.9. The graph maps two dimensions, activation value and time.

But we can represent exactly the same information in a different graph. Let one axis represent the values for one unit, and the second axis, unit two. Now we can use their two values as the coordinates of a single point, (.184, .482). The two-dimensional plane can represent the oscillations of both units. Because each unit now has its own axis, we can represent the state of the two units at any time as a single point. Simply switching axes around, then, has the interesting effect of representing a complex state of affairs as a single point. The two values pick out a single point in two dimensions.

Once each unit has its own dimension, the dynamic evolution of the same system takes on a different look, as figure 3.10 shows.

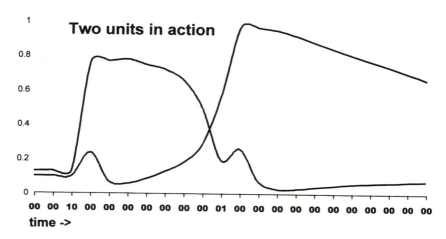

Figure 3.9　Two CNVnet hidden units, plotted as they change over time.

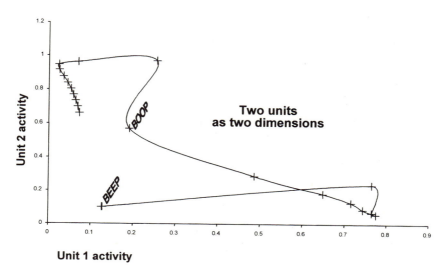

Figure 3.10　The two hidden units from figure 3.9, now plotted on different axes. Instead of using time as an axis, here the *x* and *y* axes each track activity of a distinct unit. So the combined activation of the two units can be represented as a single point, and the dynamic change of the network over time appears as a trajectory followed by that point.

Where there were two lines, now there is one. Time is no longer an axis but a trajectory through the two-unit space. If we had a third unit to plot, we could give it a dimension too. Then one path would represent the values of all three units, but that path would wander through a three-dimensional space. It happens that a picture of that space would use the familiar three dimensions of height, breadth, and depth, but the dimensions the picture represents are not spatial, but rather the values of activity in the three units of history. They comprise a special kind of space, "activation space."

The first advantage to this reorientation is conceptual. Three numbers define a single point, and the overall dynamic of the system is the movement of this point. If two states of the system are similar, they will translate into nearby points. Thinking of patterns of net activity as points, and similarity as proximity in activation space, greatly reduces the mental overhead. This simplification works for an arbitrary number of variables, even as our imagination boggles. For example, with eight hidden units, the tiny CNVnet careens within an eight-dimensional space. Nothing in mathematics prevents us from adding more dimensions to a space, as abstract geometry is infinitely accommodating. So we can add a new dimension for every added variable, one for each processing unit we want to track.

In effect, multivariate thinking has turned this system inside-out. Prior to any dimension thinking, we could only conceive of CNVnet as a collection of discrete processing units. We could readily understand the function of any one of these units by itself, but the action of the entire network depended on the interaction of all of its parts. This collective, global dynamism initially boggles the mind. Dimension thinking is the first step toward demystification. Multivariate thinking expands the parts of the system, transforming them into dimensions or axes that map the boundaries of an abstract space. At the same time it takes the system considered as a whole and transforms it into a mathematical point, a point defined by its coordinates along all the new axes of "system space." So, instead of the entire system containing its parts within it, now the parts have become a single space and the system is contained within them.

The transformation is merely conceptual, however. Multivariate mathematics simply proposes another way of looking at complex phenomena.

Its initial advantage is simply to suggest that one can consider a system all at once, as a point, without sacrificing or neglecting any of the specific contributors to the overall action of the system. Never mind that it is difficult to depict or imagine an 8-D space. Think of the high-dimensional space and all the points within it as a big holding tank from which we draw conclusions. The mathematical transformations available at this spigot yield understandable draughts from the big brew within. I've already mentioned the first transformation, namely, that similarity of multivariate states equates to nearness of points, and with it the progress through various states—such as the net waves above—is a walk of little and big jumps. From this simple calculation, others follow, each with differing powers for grasping the ungraspable spaces.

In this book, the emphasis has been on one method of transforming high-dimensional affairs into maps in two or three dimensions. That method is multidimensional scaling (MDS); the classic introductions to MDS are in texts by Shepard et al. and by Kruskal and Wish. (MDS is one of many methods for analyzing and visualizing multivariate data.) In this book, Porfiry Marlov introduces multidimensional scaling, and the maps it yields are consulted in Miranda's examination of Elman's article. (In fact, the original article uses another method, cluster analysis; the maps I presented in the novel are my own, derived from Elman's data presentations in his article.)[10] The "Labyrinth of Cognition" at <www.trincoll.edu/~dlloyd> is also a scaled map, in three dimensions (derived from a space with more than a hundred initial dimensions).

In brief review, MDS is a process that works from distances between points in hyperspace, producing a map in a space of fewer dimensions in which those distances are nonetheless preserved. Multidimensional scaling, in short, tries to extract the underlying structure or shape of the points, and reproduce that structure in a form we can see. The fidelity of the resulting map compared to the real distances can vary, as the scaled map may require forcing points into locations that are not at true distances from the other points. This distortion is known, appropriately, as "stress." One can choose the dimensions of the scaled map according to how much stress one is willing to tolerate. There is a widely accepted standard for allowable stress in a "good" analysis, and all of the maps presented here meet that standard.

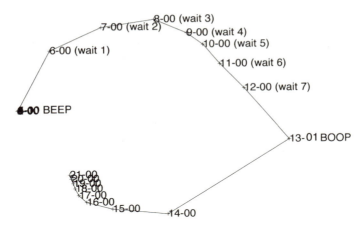

Figure 3.11 Map of the CNVnet trajectory, reduced from eight dimensions to two by multidimensional scaling (MDS). The MDS map reveals a nearly linear path through hyperspace during the beep-boop interval.

Figure 3.11 is an MDS map of 20 cycles of CNVnet, during which it completes one beep-boop encounter. The figure reflects the dynamic activity of eight hidden units. In dimension thinking, the hidden layer is a point bouncing around an eight-dimensional space, but it turns out that much of the variability is redundant, and so the same interpoint relationships can also be shown in a two-dimensional space. The scaled map shows us the skeleton of the network's path through the eight dimensions. It shows when the net makes big jumps and little, and (more important) when its dynamics bring it back again into a state similar to some earlier state.

The natural geography of this newly discovered country is surprising. For the first five cycles, up to and including the beep, the net is dormant. Some units are active, and some not (as we could see in figure 3.8), but for this waiting period the pattern doesn't change. Those initial cycles are mapped on top of each other, at no distance from one another. Then, beep. The network swings into action, and over the next seven cycles strides through hyperspace, finishing with the output anticipating the boop. With the boop behind it, the activity steadies. Eventually the net will return to its somnolence, ready for the cycle to begin again. Not surprisingly, there's a salient border between the activity involved in beep-booping and all the waiting around. In the net's inner world, this is a large distinction. But the activity between beep and boop is unexpected. With each cycle, the pattern shifts dramatically. But during this period there is no further input to the net, nor is there any output. Considered from without (looking just at inputs and outputs), the net is doing nothing at all. But the brain of the net is consumed with anticipation, and its plunge toward fulfillment parallels just one worldly variable: elapsed time.

These observations and many like them are in fact observations of the eight-dimensional space traversed by the network. We also saw this activity in figure 3.8 above, but the spaghetti of that graph was not easy to interpret. The MDS map can't show us eight dynamic variables directly, but even in this example the graphic is the next best thing to being there. The observations suggest several interesting hypotheses about the dynamics of the network:

1.   Although the units themselves may oscillate, the net as a whole does not (in this sequence). Instead, it moves by discrete steps through netspace. Overall, points further apart in time tend to be further apart in pattern of activity.

2.   This progress through netspace is stately when nothing is happening, but in the waiting period between stimuli it takes great leaps with every cycle. It is more dynamic then than any other time, despite the fact that there is neither input nor output for the entire period.

3.   Inputs and outputs are big events in the environment, but have relatively small impact in the internal network dynamic. The beep throws the net into action, but the production of the boop is not dramatically different than the waiting states that precede it.

Keeping this in mind, how does the net solve the problem of accurately anticipating a boop in a world of be-bop regularity? It uses its eight-dimensional playground expansively, traversing it along a path that is more linear than not. In the rest states between trials, it is nearly stationary in this space. But during the crucial anticipation the net measures large distances for each cycle. It counts time by occupying globally different dynamic states for each cycle. One of these states is primed to launch the output.

3.5 Our Multivariate World

The previous sections have been devoted to a general critique of methods for studying complex dynamic systems such as CNVnet, and I've suggested that multivariate methods such as multidimensional scaling are more appropriate for understanding the mood swings of a neural network, which is, after all, a system of multiple changing variables. At the heart of multivariate visions such as an MDS map is dimension thinking. Multivariate analysis is sometimes the only way to begin an analysis of a complex system, but it also offers a general framework for thinking about less obscure phenomena. In the novel, this world view appears several times as a recipe for a general anatomy of messy reality. Porfiry Marlov, in particular, points out at length that any configuration of properties can be abstracted into a point in a high-dimensional "property space." For example, in addition to its location in three spatial dimensions, my glowing firefly radiates differing degrees of color and brightness. Color and brightness are additional dimensions, or axes along which this firefly can be situated. We can regard all the superposed properties this way. "Capacity for eliciting philosophical speculation" is a property or dimension in which the firefly excels, for example. Experience is clearly a high-dimensional affair!

Dimension thinking seems to me to be especially well suited to phenomenology. Multivariate methods harness geometry for both measurement and visualization. The ultimate goal of a phenomenology of reality is to reconstruct experience independently of all the props borrowed from Reality, and as we proceed, the abstract geometries of property spaces can usefully replace a less reflective appeal to other categories. This is compatible with the phenomenological quest in several ways. First, it represents the congruence of superposed properties in an object, metaphorically capturing the binding of sensory properties and all the non-sensory overlays that also always attend. It also allows a ready conceptual framework to ponder the relations between dimensions. If color and brightness correlate for all fireflies, we can imagine the correlation as the combination of axes. But its most important side-effect may be that all these property dimensions are abstract. Where there was redness, now there is axis R, and some magnitude (or distance) along it. So two objects separated in space—two houses, for instance—might be very close along other axes, such as color, shape, or habitability. Within this framework, we can view objects as the confluence of properties, that is, as points in property space. Or, we can view properties as confluences of objects, or points in object space. "Red," for example, could be an experienced property shared by an apple (to a high degree), a pumpkin (to a lesser degree), and a cucumber (to degree zero). Ideally, geometry and phenomenology can work together to dissolve strong assumptions about the fundamental furniture of reality.

When we apply dimension thinking to a complex system such as CNVnet, we create a space for CNVnet to inhabit. It is its particular activation space, and every pattern of activity internal to CNVnet can be fit as a separate point into this space. We can do the same trick with any complex system, including the brain. The brain's activation space might have billions of non-redundant dimensions, each representing the variable state of a single neuron (or perhaps even parts of neurons). A particular instant of overall brain activity accordingly shows up as a point in this billion-dimension space. Accordingly, the story of a brain as it seethes with activity can be rendered as a path of a point in brainspace. But even in a billion dimensions, multivariate analysis works, and through relatively simple measures of multivariate distance between points, we can extract the abstract anatomy of brainspace using techniques such as multidimensional scaling. This is one way of looking at the brain.

These multivariate reflections gently nudge us into a new way of seeing the problem of consciousness. Multivariate thinking can apply to both flanks of the problem of consciousness, offering a way to think about the dynamics of experience and a way to think about the dynamics of a complex physical system like the brain. Dimension thinking converts both phenomenology and neural activity into points careening through abstract spaces. Techniques for reducing the dimensionality apply to both spaces, and the resulting maps, however crude, can be compared. If they match (the big If), the correspondence provides evidence that there is in fact just one system, and that the neural version and the phenomenal version are simply different labels applied to one underlying Reality. But it is no easy matter to probe for matches, even in a toy brain like CNVnet. The way forward will be more like rock climbing than a stroll.

3.6   Toy Temporality

The strategy throughout this long ramble with artificial neural networks has been to exhibit simple analogues of real brains, in the hope that the analogues will offer hypotheses that we can scale up and test against empirical neuroscience. CNVnet operates in a simple "world" in which temporal relationships matter, and we know by its performance that somehow it can exploit time. But the study of consciousness reveals that we don't just use time, we live it as a complex structure of temporality that loads every moment of awareness. In the dynamic state of the hidden units of a recurrent network, will we discover analogues of temporality?

In the sections above, I tried versions of three standard interpretive methods on CNVnet. I argued that each showed only part of the dynamic story. Because they showed their part vividly and validly, the missing dynamics seemed insignificant, but when all the action was displayed at once, the three probes suddenly looked very blurry indeed. Multidimensional scaling offered one way to grasp this real complexity, by extracting essential relationships within the underlying multivariate dynamics. Multivariate analysis tells a different story from the other methods. Now we relate that story to the phenomenology of time.

The phenomenological analysis of temporality, building on Husserl, delivered strong conclusions about the structure of time as seen from within. To review:

1.   Temporality is flux. Every object or scene evolves in consciousness even if none of its other phenomenal or real properties change.

2.   The non-sensory superpositions that are in constant flux constitute a built-in awareness of past and future. Retention and protention are in continuous flux even if no other properties change. Each retention holds the trace of the total previous experience.

3.   Considered as a dimension, temporality appears in consciousness as a monotonic ordering progression. It moves in one direction without stalling or backsliding.

4.   Temporality inheres in all presentations. However else we pigeonhole experience, it is all always encompassed in time.

5. Temporality is intrinsic to all presentations. We "bracket" the influence of the outside world, leaving behind detection and other relations of inner and outer.

A recurrent network seems to be the architecture of choice for capturing temporality. Its context layer, copying as it does the immediately prior state of the hidden units, looks like retention incarnate. And we have set up the task in its protentive form: Anticipate the next input to the net. However, the case for recurrence as the sufficient condition for implementing consciousness cannot rest on its architecture alone, for two reasons. First, even though in principle the right connections are potentially available to recurrent nets, that alone does not guarantee that the net in fact uses temporal information through a capacity such as retention. Second, only for toy brains is the architecture so obvious. For any real brain the circuit diagram will be derived from other probes. Other ways of assessing the processing will be necessary, at least for now. Therefore, we seek evidence for network temporality through analysis of the net dynamics, rather than architecture.

It would be hard to validate any of the suppositions above using population averaging, single-unit recording, or functional imaging. However, the MDS map is revealing. The internal state of the net is in constant change, especially between beep and boop. This change tracks neither the environment nor behavior, because both are quiescent. So, even at this simple level, you can't step into the same network dynamic twice; all is flux. The map also reveals a strong monotonic progression of dynamic states, manifest in the tight connection between distance in netspace and time. That is, for each cycle, the next or previous cycle is also the nearest neighbor in netspace, and as we examine longer intervals between cycles, the dynamic distance also increases. This relationship prevails over any other categories. Nothing else moves the net far enough in netspace to pull it out of its monotonic temporal march. This in turn suggests that the temporal order is a global condition, and at the same time that no particular state of the net is exempt from this order.

In addition, our analysis offers a solution to the paradox of consciousness and cognition. The paradox appears as a contradiction between the flux introduced as a necessary condition for experience, and the stability (of categories, objects, properties) necessary for cognition. The new map shows us both. The network is always moving, but for different periods it moves within one region of netspace. The map shows these regional sojourns. The stable features of the "world" of the net are thus captured as a nested hierarchy of regions on the map, and respected in the dynamics of the network itself. The waiting state, for example, wanders through one such region. Although each cycle of the wait is very different from the next, all have in common their larger affiliation toward the upper right of the map, and as a group are more like each other than like any other state. In this way the net can have it both ways, being at once same and different over time.

The analogy seems promising. Flux, monotonicity, and ubiquity are properties read off of the scaled map. The other features of temporality will take a little digging. First, does this model implement these features of temporality intrinsically? So far I have assigned labels to the points on the map according to the net input at each cycle. Net "subjectivity" requires that those inputs be ruled out of play in any interpretation of internal states. So, we first erase the labels. The geography remains, because it derives from the internal structure of the network dynamics over time, reporting a history of (now unnamed) states. But at any moment, the net has no access to its real past or future. What exists are just eight processing units. Our net in a vat at an instant (cycle nine, as it happens) has one thought on its mind, and it is this:

$$0.316, 0.874, 0.987, 0.805, 0.745, 0.951, 0.167, 0.086$$

These are the numerical values calculated by the equations that govern the network. When we refer to the pattern of activation in the hidden layer, we refer to these numbers. They are all there is to network psychology at this moment. In what sense could this, considered only in itself, be a presentation of a world with the tripartite structure of retention, present, and protention? To answer this question requires moving beyond network psychology to network psychoanalysis. If the phenomenology of time is correct, buried in the eight numbers is protention, retention, and a primal impression. As if we haven't done enough already with CNVnet, now we have to read its mind. How do we do this?

One could spend many hours (as did Max Grue) pondering the patterns of activity over time of a network like this. I propose instead to take a step back and address the problem indirectly. Imagine, then, a black box, a mechanism for mind reading. On the box is a knob, which you can set for "protention," "primal impression," or "retention." You feed into the box the numbers describing the current state of the hidden layer of CNVnet, and choose a knob setting. The box delivers the following results. For protention, the box examines the hidden layer and tells you what the next output will be (because that in turn represents what the net anticipates as the next input). For presence, the box reads the hidden layer and tells you what the current input to the network is, the analogue to its sensations at the present moment. And for retention, the box takes the hidden layer and returns the numbers of the layer itself, *one cycle previous* to the present cycle.

Each of these black box readings is based on the hidden layer alone; the box itself has no access to the units outside the hidden layer, nor to past and future states of the net itself. But we have that access, so we can take the readings given by the box and compare them to the actual states of the net. In that way, we can determine just how accurate the box is. Suppose, then, that the box turns out to be very accurate. The mere fact that the box works tells us the answer to the initial question, whether the hidden layer at any moment in fact encodes protention, primal impression, and retention. If the box works, then the information specifying the three facets of temporality must have been present in the hidden layer, in some form. The black box works by somehow extracting the information and translating it into the explicit patterns we then recognize as accurate descriptions of past, present, and future. Note that we don't really have to know how the black box itself works. We don't even need to know how the hidden layer encodes its temporal information. If the question is simply whether temporal information is present, a working black box entails a positive answer.

With respect to CNVnet, all we need to do is build a black box that performs the extractions just described. This turns out to be rather straightforward. The problem the box has to solve is one of pattern matching. Given one pattern (the hidden unit values), it should produce another pattern (the temporal information, according to the knob setting). For a complex pattern-matching task like this, the best solution is . . . an artificial neural network. In the end, we will have *two* networks to discuss, the original target, CNVnet, and the black box mind-reader network, which I will call a "metanet." The job of a metanet is to interpret complex states in a target network. It is not a born interpreter, however. Rather, it is trained to transform patterns into contents. If it succeeds in this learning, settling into a state where it reliably produces content when given a pattern, the metanet itself is a translator, the black box we seek.

Several examples will explain metanets more fully and set the agenda for metanet analysis of CNVnet. We discussed three separate analyses above, each with its analogy to temporality in experience. First, do the hidden units encode inputs? We want our metanet to try to find a way to look at each hidden layer pattern, "reading" the original input out of it. In effect, for this test, the metanet inverts the usual flow of information. Accordingly, we build an upside-down neural network as follows:

Metanet *input* patterns will be CNVnet *hidden* unit patterns.

Metanet *output* patterns should be CNVnet *input* patterns.

Each CNVnet pattern is itself the encoding of this information, and so we discard temporal context in this analysis. Thus, metanets are not recurrent.

The first test, then, is whether the black box can extract the input pattern from the pattern encoded in the hidden layer. To find out, I built a metanet and trained it on many repetitions of a set of a thousand input-output pairs, derived from the states of the trained CNVnet. Not surprisingly, the metanet quickly learned the correct mappings. After training, I turned off further learning, and tested the metanet in its trained state. It performed perfectly. The metanet found a way to extract from each of the hidden unit patterns an accurate description of the input state to the net.

A similar net then probed exactly the same set of hidden unit patterns to see if the correlated outputs could be recovered. The input patterns in this case were again the hidden unit patterns of CNVnet, but now the target outputs were the actual outputs of CNVnet. This worked well too. This metanet became a filter or reader of the net's best attempt to anticipate the upcoming state of its world.

The critical test, however, is the metanet probe of retention. In this case, the phenomenological prediction is that each hidden unit state encodes its own prior state, that is, that a complete record of the past state of mind is enfolded into the present state of mind. After several million training cycles, this metanet performed well too, but not perfectly. The question then becomes, does it perform well enough? When nets are trained extensively, the possibility arises that they transform patterns based on something like rote learning. If the metanet learns simple associations of patterns, disregarding their inherent meaning, then the temporal order of the patterns would be irrelevant. So, for a comparison case to serve as a control, I shuffled the order among all the hidden unit patterns. When the patterns are randomly ordered, any systematic relationship between adjacent patterns will be lost, because their temporal proximity has been lost in the shuffle. Therefore, any information about past and future will be erroneous, because the time line has been jumbled. But when the randomly ordered patterns are used to train a metanet, the metanet will still be able to match patterns by rote.

Thus there will be two metanets, one trained on patterns in their true temporal order, and one trained on patterns in random order. Both will be able to learn pattern associations by rote. But if that is all they are doing, then they should perform equally. Temporal information will make no difference. In this case, however, there was a big difference. The shuffled versions of the patterns led to learning with an average error more than ten times greater than the original metanet. This comparison, then, implies that the metanet was extracting a systematic relationship, resulting in a network reader that could scan CNVnet hidden units, and extract from them the immediately prior state of the same units. The metanet is the black box mind reader, and it works. The CNVnet hidden layer therefore encodes the network analogue of retention.

3.7   What Is It Like to Be a Net?

Rarely has an artificial neural network been poked and prodded with such tenacity. I sought to illustrate several points. First, I wanted to show that some methods in common use in cognitive neuroscience were not well suited to discovering the dynamics of distributed neural networks, and were acutely ill suited to discovering analogues of conscious experience. The toy brain helped in this conclusion by allowing us to second-guess the standard methods, comparing them to the complete dynamical picture of the net in action. To overcome these limits, I spent some time with multivariate methods of analysis. The resulting maps offered a more inclusive picture of a neural network in action. Multidimensional scaling, for example, promptly revealed analogues of several of the phenomenological descriptions developed previously. A second wave of analysis in which networks were turned on themselves completed an analysis of one network in which everything phenomenological had an image. The toolbox of consciousness science should include these analytical strategies.

A second goal was to display a particular functional architecture that could spontaneously develop analogues of temporality. The architecture has several distinctive features. First, it is an *artificial neural network*. At heart, it is a device particularly well suited to working with patterns, which occur in networks as the varying profiles of activity in layers of neuron-like processing units. Because each pattern can represent subtle differences at the same time as it encodes broad similarities, neural nets enjoy the capacity for superposition of information, owing to the expressive power and subtlety of distributed representation. This point impresses Miranda in each of her encounters with neural nets, both simulated and real. She embraces what is generally called the "dynamical systems perspective." (For elaborations on this way of thinking, see Smolensky 1988 and Port and van Gelder 1995.)

The second distinctive feature of the critical architecture is *recurrence*. Recurrent feedback allows the superposition of temporal information, information about both stability and change.[11] Consciousness depends on exactly this sort of information. As the patterns circulate, the recurrent network offers a dynamic model of the recursive, nested structure of phenomenal temporality. Interestingly, the expressions of temporality the new tools revealed all arose spontaneously, as side-effects of the combination of this kind of architecture and an environment with temporal structure. The architecture captures a feature shared with many biological nervous systems, and of course the Real World is a place of myriad temporal contingencies. Continuing along this speculative path, we could develop an evolutionary history in which consciousness is an entirely natural and essential expression of biological adaptation. To embed awareness in nature in this way would be a nice additional accomplishment for a science of consciousness.

My conclusion here, however, is somewhat weaker. Recurrent networks demonstrate one way to embody temporality. The network model of time consciousness was developed around beeps and boops only, and I haven't shown that CNVnet will scale up toward the mix of superposed phenomenology that is distinctively human. That is a project for another time. Nonetheless, despite its simplicity, the artificial neural network developed here proves by its very existence that these symptoms of temporality can be materially implemented. In this respect, CNVnet and others like it could be object lessons comparable to early digital computers. The vacuum tube monsters known in the 1950s as "electronic brains" didn't have much brainy about them, but they clearly did something that until then had been the exclusive province of humans, namely, process symbols or representations. Prior to computers (including their earliest abstract conceptualization), this talent of brains had seemed so special that it was hard to believe that any material system could pull it off. But then something mechanical got into the business too, and ever since, computation has offered a framework for thinking about cognition, even as particular computers remain very distant from anything like real human capacities.

Consciousness, I've argued, is essentially a very different process from cognition. And recurrent networks are a quite distinct species of material thing. There may be some general compatibility here, however, despite the still huge gulf between any artificial neural network and any person.

So the reader may rest assured that I will not be promoting CNVnet as an entity that is conscious in a human way. First of all, it's only a simulation running on a digital computer. Second, the beep-boop task is so simple that the world of the net is inconceivably minimal compared to even the world of the fly or the leech. Third, there's the rest of the story. In fact, this network captures only brief bursts of temporality, occurring just during the beep-boop sequences themselves. In between, the net settles into a steady state, and when a beep hits, the cascade of patterns is always the same. Overall the net is locked into a repeating cycle separated by long periods in which there is no change at all. A bigger multivariate analysis (looking at more time points) would show this. In short, considered in its total trajectory, CNVnet fails to exhibit analogies of temporality, and the metanet analyses are at least in part fooled by hundreds of cycles of emptiness in which the net flatlines—it's not too hard to learn how to do that. This backstory reinforces the caveat that should be published with all artificial neural nets: Just because this network worked, don't think that any real system will work this way. Nonetheless, I hope I have shown how analyses like these could work, if applied to a real system.

Now, at last, we turn to that real system.

4

Braintime

Phenomenology unhinged the mind from the World, and opened the way instead into the world of experience. New tools were needed to explore the phenomenal world objectively, tools tested first on simplified toy brains. The long exploration of neural networks prepared the ground for the final phase of this investigation. Experience, especially the experience of time, might be implemented in a material system (of a certain sort). This possibility would be most interesting if it turns out to be a reality. From the speculative claim that we *could* work this way, we turn now to the question, Do we?

In the first part of this long exploration, I proposed that the detector-head model of mind and brain didn't fit the subject of consciousness. Consciousness itself requires much more than simple detection. It encompasses the awareness of a host of non-sensory dimensions of experience, of which at least one is essential. In general, this phenomenal holism forces us to trade one toolbox for another. The old tools were attuned to isolating specialized detectors, dedicated but narrow-minded functionaries in a neural bureaucracy. Awareness is never limited to the slim contents of these detectors. Rather, consciousness embraces the world in all its complexity.

The multivariate methods introduced in this appendix and in Miranda's story provide an alternative way into the labyrinth. In chapter 13, Miranda encounters a first generation of multivariate analysis based on published findings, many of them archived in the Brainmap database at the University of Texas Health Center at San Antonio (<www.uthscsa.edu/brainmap>). As that chapter explains, the variables that analysis considered are derived from activation values in relatively large regions of the brain, as revealed through image subtraction. Thinking dimensionally, that analysis considered just over one hundred dimensions of the dynamic brain.

Since the pioneering achievement of Brainmap, however, a second-generation data archive has emerged, the fMRI Data Center at Dartmouth College (fMRIDC), mentioned in chapter 1 of this part. In this archive, researchers have been depositing not just the results of their analysis, but the initial data as well. Data sets include all the images from individual subjects, without averaging, smoothing, or subtraction. For this researcher, the fMRIDC experience has been like trading in a pair of very fine binoculars for the Hubble Space Telescope. From one hundred dimensions, we move to tens of thousands, and, perhaps, our first window into the empirical study of the specific aspects of consciousness uncovered by phenomenology.[12]

4.1   Indices of Temporality

If we were to really analyze the neural network that is the brain, we would base our analysis on recordings of every single neuron, all 100,000,000,000 of them (more or less), sampling activity thousands of times every second. For better or worse, functional brain imaging is coarser both in space and time than the brain itself.[13] Still, the analysis of brains in time dwarfs the analyses presented so far. For example, figure 4.1 is a simple plot of the measured activity at a single voxel in one subject from start to finish of one of the Ishai study experiments. (Recall that "voxel" is the fMRI term for a pixel in a 3-D image.)

The depicted "voxel time series" comprises 1,092 observations. There are around 15,000 such time series recorded for each subject, and they all look pretty much like the one above. In the spirit of the CNVnet example,

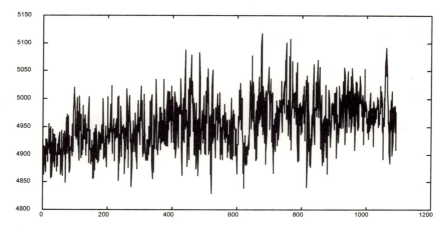

Figure 4.1 Time course of activity in a single voxel (fMRI image pixel) over 1,092 images from the Ishai study of house, face, and chair representation.

one could plot all the voxel time series on a single graph. The result would be ink all over, so the impressionistic look-and-see interpretations of CNVnet will not work. In addition, the number of time points boggles any display method such as MDS. Nonetheless, at the foundation of all multivariate interpretation is still the idea of similarity in a space of possible activation patterns. Multivariate similarity can lead to a number of measurements that reveal the extent to which we humans embody the temporal dynamics introduced via phenomenology and implemented initially in neural simulations. These measurements will form the basis for various probes of temporality in the brain.

All fMRI interpretation must work in the context of noise, and multivariate interpretation is no exception. A multivariate effect, measured across the entire brain over time, may differ less than 1 percent from the noisy background. Imagine a TV screen that was 99 percent snow and 1 percent show. Watching raw fMRI is like that. Still, tiny effects may nonetheless be significant. That is, they may be unlikely to occur by chance alone. In accordance with scientific convention, we will consider effects significant if their chances of occurring at random are less than 5 percent.

Below I discuss the first wave of multivariate tests designed for detecting the necessary conditions for consciousness in the brain. Because these results are important, and the methods are novel, I will be thorough with both rationale and method description. Once the methods are understood, however, they will provide a ready distillation of what would otherwise be a mountain of data.

From the image series, I measured three indices or "gradients," of which the first is the most important.

The Temporal Gradient, *t*

Phenomenology suggests that every experience is saturated with time. All the objects of the world present themselves in the present moment with a non-sensory bow shock of anticipation, and a wake of retention. I argued earlier that the classical phenomenologists were right to regard temporality as an essential dimension of all experience, and I tried to characterize some of the essential features of the dimension of time in phenomenology. In addition to being pervasive, time unwinds (or if you prefer, winds) in one direction only. The mathematical term for a measure that's always increasing (or decreasing) is "monotonic." Although the rate of monotonic temporal change is always varying, the flow can never reverse. If it did, phenomenal reality would disintegrate.

Temporality appears to us from within our own first-person viewpoint. When we step outside ourselves and adopt the objective view of subjectivity, what might phenomenology imply for the dynamic evolution of a conscious system such as the brain? There are several immediately plausible consequences. First, because temporality is in everything experienced, it should be everywhere in the experiencer. Temporality will not be limited to a special process elicited by a certain kind of task, such as judging duration or order. (These sorts of tasks invite judgments about quantities of time, based on the more fundamental experience of temporality itself.) If temporality can be observed at all in the brain, it should be observable in a wide variety of tasks, and accordingly across many regions of the brain. We expect it at the very least to jump about like a firefly, or, to put it in network terms, we expect it to be distributed across many areas. Second, because temporality is pervasive and monotonic, it suggests that experience is in continuous flux. Along this one ubiquitous dimension, everything is always changing, and the change is one way. Just as Heraclitus concluded that you can't step in the same river twice, you can't step in the same stream of consciousness twice. The continuous monotonic flux implies something about conscious brains over time: They are changing monotonically (in their temporal properties). Your brain at 12:00:01 is different at 12:00:02, and different again at 12:00:03, whether or not anything in your environment has changed. Nor can a conscious brain, as an organ of temporality, return to a previous state, whether or not features of the environment recycle. This is the implication of monotonic temporality. So, in general, as elapsed time increases, the difference between brainstates increases.

How might temporality show up in a series of brain images? If temporality truly is ubiquitous and monotonic, images taken close together in time should be more similar, compared to images separated by greater temporal intervals. A little dimensional thinking helps here. Each image is built of about 15,000 values springing from that many spatially distinct voxels in the brain. But we can condense each image into a *single* point in an activation space of 15,000 dimensions (one dimension for each voxel). In brain activation space, then, similarity is simple nearness. Monotonic change along a dimension means that the moving point never retreats along that dimension.

In short, phenomenology entails a continuous flux in experience. If there is a comparable flux in the brain, global multivariate change will increase with each passing moment. I will call the basic measure of this effect t.

To understand t, it may be useful to entertain the hypothesis that there is no temporal effect. In the Ishai experiment, subjects experienced repeated trials of the same sorts of stimuli. For example, you might be matching pictures of faces to one another for task blocks beginning at 40 seconds into the experiment, then at 80, 120, 160 seconds, and so forth. If time has no effect on brain patterns, then the face-matching task elicits similar brain activity during each task block, and the neural patterns during all of the face blocks will be similar to one another. Without temporality, the first and second face blocks are no more or less similar than the first and third, the first and fourth, and so on. That is, in the null case, elapsed time between blocks will have no effect on the calculated multivariate similarities between them. A null data set will be temporally "flat," as the length of time separating two blocks will have no effect on their multivariate similarity score. There may be no temporal effect at all.

Alternatively, an effect may be too small to detect. Noise in the 15,000 voxels could overwhelm any global measure of multivariate change. The jiggles of a noisy image do guarantee that each image is different from the next, but don't lead to differences that increase with time interval. Over time, the images are as likely to jiggle toward similarity as dissimilarity. Once again, the image series will be temporally flat. (This is easy to confirm by simulating images of pure noise.)

Where there is a detectable temporal effect, on the other hand, the similarity measurements will reflect the temporal interval between blocks. In that case, the first and second occurrence of the same stimulus type will be more similar to each other than the first and third, first and fourth, and so on. The similarity scores will "tilt" in favor of shorter temporal intervals, and the extent of the tilt can be regarded as a slope or gradient.

There are several ways temporality might show itself, and thus several ways to calculate the temporal gradient, t. Here I calculate it as follows. Suppose we take a volume from a scan series and calculate its dissimilarity from all the other volumes in the series, both before and after in time. Those that are relatively close in time should be more similar, compared to those at greater intervals before or after. The near-in-time dissimilarities can be simply divided by the far-in-time dissimilarities. That result is then subtracted from one, simply to calibrate t on a scale from zero (no temporal gradient) to one (infinite temporal gradient).

To assess temporality in a scan series overall, one repeats this calculation for every time point in the series. That is, for each of the 1,092 whole-brain images, its multivariate distance from the 1,091 others is calculated, and the distances to images taken just before and just after contrasted with the distances to images separated by greater time intervals. The average of these 1,092 calculations is the mean t for the entire series. We assess significance by comparing the mean of distances to the near-in-time images to the mean of all distances between the images. [14]

Of nine subjects analyzed, eight exhibited significant t values. (For each, the probability of its occurring by chance was less than .0001.) The largest t was .51, the smallest, .12. The mean of t for the eight was .39.

The temporal gradient was calculated separately for each subject, and significance assessed for each subject independently of the others, excluding powerful filters such as averaging, smoothing, and, most important, subtraction. Considering all this together with the noisiness of the fMRI signal, then, suggests that this primary temporal gradient, a 39 percent temporal tilt, is a large effect.

The effect was not significant in one subject's brain, however. What happened? A closer look at the image series showed that one chunk of 92 images showed an increase of magnitude for all the voxels, as if the volume knob had been turned up for those images. Because it affected all the voxels, and affected them for exactly that subset of the image series, it seems most likely that this was some side-effect of the imaging process rather than something about the subject's brain. The voxel energy surge dislocated the similarity measurements for the affected images, distorting *t* for this subject.

In short, one important symptom of temporality is indeed present in the majority of participants in the Ishai study. Although they returned again and again to identical tasks with very similar stimuli, a global multivariate analysis shows their brains to be flowing with time. Ishai's paper shows that specific areas in the brain are engaged by the tasks in her study. The secondary analysis here shows that something else was happening too. That something else was global, large, and in agreement with the prediction derived from the phenomenology of time.

By itself, this observation would be suggestive, intriguing, but ultimately inconclusive. The brain is a complex system with workings largely unknown. Confirmation of the first temporal hypothesis is nice but does not eliminate other possible sources of the multivariate time effect. For example, it could be due to something specific to the tasks Ishai studied, to the particular methods of this experiment, or to circumstances particular to the study, such as the operation of the scanner. Or, it could be due to some bodily process unrelated to neural activity, or even some neural process unrelated to phenomenal temporality. These alternatives cannot be eliminated, but their probability can be reduced through two broad strategies. First, I will extend the analysis to other studies, engaging other tasks (at other laboratories, with different equipment). Second, I will introduce further measures of temporal effects, and apply them to the broader set of brain imaging studies. In the end, there will be more measures, more variety in what subjects are doing, and more subjects, and positive results in all can be explained either as the side-effects of a diffuse variety of incidental processes, or as the confirmation of a single broad hypothesis originating in the phenomenology of time.

I enlisted three other studies archived at the fMRI Data Center. First, I examined an experiment involving a simple response (a button press, as in the Ishai study) to a visual stimulus presented with other visual distractors. In this case, the task was to press one button if a light was either yellow or blue, and another if the light was either red or green. Flanking the target light were two other lights. Sometimes the flankers were compatible with the target light, for example, yellow flanking blue. But they could also be incompatible, green flanking blue, distracting subjects from the correct response to the target light. I'll refer to this study as the "response competition" study. Its primary author was Eliot Hazeltine, working with Russell Poldrack and John Gabrieli. The study was different from the houses-faces-chairs study in another way, in that each image run was much shorter. Hazeltine's eight subjects performed the task for just two minutes. In Ishai's study volunteers were in the scanner, hard at work, for over an hour.

The next data set probed processes involved in reading, and informed a paper by Andreas Mechelli, with Karl Friston and Cathy Price. Here, subjects silently read either words or "pseudo-words," strings of letters that could be pronounced (in English) but had no meaning, such as "FEAP." The rate of presentation of the words also varied, from a leisurely 30 words per minute up to a speedy 90 wpm. Three hundred and sixty images were collected from each of six subjects.

Finally, I examined a complex experiment by Bradley Postle (with Jeffrey Berger, Alexander Taich, and Mark D'Esposito). I will tag the experiment as "spatial memory," because one phase did capture exactly that. Each task block included a sequence of small squares illuminated in various orders in various places on a screen. Sometimes subjects were instructed to merely follow the sequences with their eyes (the eye movements are also called saccades). Sometimes subjects had to remember the exact order and positions of the squares in each sequence. Sometimes subjects had to not only remember the sequence, but rearrange it, employing not only spatial memory but imagination. Finally, during some blocks, subjects simply moved their eyes back and forth while looking at a blank screen. I had complete data for four of the five subjects Postle studied.

Add to this the variations in the Ishai study, and we are surveying a modest diversity of human cognitive life. The various subjects perceived stimuli from simple to complex. At the simple end, they watched both moving and stationary shapes, with and without distracting contexts. The more complicated stimuli included words, pseudo-words, and objects (good old houses, faces, and chairs, both in photographs and line drawings). Their tasks included simply watching, observing patterns over time, reading, remembering items through a delay, spotting matches after a delay, remembering sequences of simple shapes in different locations, rearranging spatial sequences in their heads, and recognizing types of objects. Their overt behaviors included eye movements, both deliberate and automatic, pressing buttons, and sometimes doing nothing at all. As in the beep-boop task, in each of these studies there were many idle moments and blank screens. Some of these occurred during the hard-working delays in memory, imagination, and matching tasks. Others were basic baseline tasks, such as simply looking at the center of a screen. And still others were pure rest, microvacations between task blocks. Through all of this the scanner methodically collected images, and all of these images now gather for this re-examination through the lens of phenomenology.

Of course, human conscious life includes much much more than the assortment of experiences described above. But for the study of normal consciousness, this diversity within and between experiments is nonetheless a good starting point. Because all of the subjects were conscious throughout their experiments, each of them is a resource for understanding the neural expressions of awareness. And, again thanks to the work of these researchers, including the formidable additional work involved in preparing data for archiving at the fMRI Data Center, it is possible to look at many subjects, 27 in all. As it happens, the papers the authors wrote based on these data were all published in the *Journal of Cognitive Neuroscience*. The various stages of processing these data sets ultimately occupied around 20 gigabytes of memory in various computers. (For comparison, this is around six times the size of the human genome.)

Now that 19 additional volunteers have joined the eight analyzed in the Ishai study, the next task is to extend the measurements of t to all of them. Two of the three other studies delivered t measures quite similar to the Ishai study. All six subjects in the reading study by Mechelli and colleagues displayed highly significant ts. Their average was .36 (ranging from .22 to .56). Similarly, all four of the subjects analyzed in the spatial memory study of Postle et al. displayed ts averaging .45, with a range from .42 to .55.

The study of visual cueing by Hazeltine showed distinctly smaller effects. In two of the eight subjects, t did not reach a significant value. In the remaining six, t averaged .16, ranging from a bare .03 to .35. A probable reason for this exception is the short duration of the experiment, consisting of 60 images collected over two minutes. The others comprised 360 images per subject (the reading study), 1,092 images (houses, faces, chairs), and 1,632 images (spatial memory), taking around 20 minutes and as much as an hour or more to collect. As a result, the analysis of the Hazeltine study is based on a considerably smaller set of comparisons, and thus the inherent noisiness of fMRI played a larger role. The temporal signal might be very faint against the snow. Even so, it was detectable for most of the subjects in the experiment. Experience is no clock, and the temporal flux detected here clearly varies in its velocity through brain activation space. But ordinary consciousness is in part the awareness of time passing. The flux may lie beneath the observed changes in the brain images as time passes.

4.2   Tributaries of the Stream

The Relative Temporal Gradient, t_r

At this point, then, 24 of 27 subjects in a variety of experimental settings have significant t gradients, as anticipated if the phenomenology of time is correct. Indeed, for most of these subjects the measured effect is large.

Next, we diversify the exploration in another way, with another manifestation of the same basic temporal phenomenology. The big gradient t measures absolute temporality. It may reflect a subject's awareness that he or she is progressing through the entire duration of the experiment, or, more generally, that time is passing. However, the sensibility to time passing and time remaining is also a facet of shorter intervals, as in Husserl's observation that one experiences temporality in single tones just as in an entire melody. This relative temporality will be measured by a relative temporal gradient, t_r. For example, in the Ishai study all the task blocks were 21 seconds long (i.e., seven image volumes in each), as were the interleaved baseline blocks. After a few of these blocks, one would acquire a "feel" for the temporal progress through each block of distinct activity. That is, in each block there could be a dimension of awareness representing to oneself that one is now in the beginning of the block, now in the middle, now near the end. Like the broader river of time, this tributary would saturate every object of awareness. Wherever attention settles, the focus is inflected with the relative awareness of rough position in the 21-second block. This invites an effort to identify a multivariate symptom of relative temporal position, another gradient.

This local gradient, if it exists, would be measured relative to the endpoints of each block, suggesting the abbreviation t_r. Once again, the idea of multivariate similarity or dissimilarity was the key to calculating the gradient. In this case, temporality leads to the hypothesis that states of mind at the same relative temporal position (i.e., serial position in each task block) are similar to one another, and dissimilar from the states at other serial positions. Perhaps we can detect these similarities and differences in the brain. The strategy for measuring t_r will resemble the comparative strategy for measuring t. In the Ishai study, measures of t_r can be taken for each of the seven time points that recur throughout the thousand images in each subject's scanning session. For each time point, I calculated the global multivariate similarities among all of the images gathered at that moment in the block, and then compared this value to the mean of all multivariate distances among images, regardless of serial position.

In short, the relative temporal gradient, t_r, is a measure of the brain's sensitivity to position in a sequence, calculated independently of the stimulus or behavior occurring during the sequence. Each of these similarity measures is also affected by the global and ongoing main temporal gradient, but the two components of the ratio that is the basis for t_r are both collected from time points throughout the experiment. In effect, the large t effect cancels out in the calculation of t_r. In the Ishai study, all the subjects analyzed (except for the suspected outlier, whose scan series did not display a significant temporal gradient) displayed highly significant t_r for at least one of the seven parallel time points in the 21-second blocks. Eight of the nine exhibited significant t_r across all instances of time point four (12 seconds into the block). Seven showed significant t_r in the flanking second, third, fifth, and sixth images (6, 9, 15, and 18 seconds into each block). Points one and seven were registered as relatively similar by four subjects and six subjects, respectively.

The mean size of this effect in all of its significant instances was .03. This relative temporal gradient t_r is therefore a weaker effect than t. But it is surprising that it is detectable at all. The moments of its appearance may find the subject perceiving different houses, faces, or chairs, or engaging in a control task before nonsense pictures. All that is common to the moments is their temporal position, and the brain seems most acutely tuned to temporal position in the middle of these relatively short blocks. Moreover, t_r is based on a comparison using smaller subsets of image series than used for t.

The spatial memory experiment of Postle et al. alternated task and rest blocks of 17 seconds each. Images were collected every two seconds, so each cycle of task-then-rest was recorded in 17 images. On average, the subjects in this experiment displayed significant t_r for half of the 17 positions, ranging from one subject with three positions with significant t_r to another with 13. Similar results were obtained in the response competition experiment of Hazeltine. Blocks in this study were six images each, collected over 17 seconds. Subjects showed serial position effects for two of the six positions on average. At least one significant serial t_r surfaced for each of the six subjects. Interestingly, even in subjects where there was no overall t gradient, t_r was observed. That leaves the reading study of Mechelli. In this case, the task didn't perfectly match the image series, with tasks starting or ending at different moments while images were being compiled. Images couldn't be consistently mapped onto timings, and so I did not include this study in the analysis of t_r.

In sum, I applied the analysis of t_r to 21 subjects, and in all at least one instance of t_r reached significance. The moments of its appearance may find the subject engaged in any of the variety of tasks in these studies, or even doing nothing in particular. All that is common to the moments is their temporal position. Moreover, t_r is based on a comparison using smaller subsets of image series than used for t. As with the short image series of Hazeltine, where there are fewer images to work with, noise intrudes. Nonetheless, t_r appeared, in agreement with the predictions of phenomenology.

The Stimulus Similarity Gradient, *s*

As expressed in two experimental gradients, time seems to structure the dynamic activity of the brain. If there is so much change in the brain (and in consciousness), we begin to wonder what, if anything, is ever stable in the phenomenal world, or how the constant features of the environment are ever expressed in the churning brain. This perplexity first emerged in CNVnet, and multivariate analysis suggested a solution. There, it appeared that large regions of high-dimensional activation space were assigned to the various distinct states of the CNVnet environment, and that temporal dynamics could unfold as movement within the boundaries of the large region. In that way, CNVnet could have both stability and change in a single multivariate trajectory. We were able to observe this through multivariate analysis.

Functional brain images are both more complex and more jittery than the patterns in a little model such as CNVnet, and require a more indirect assessment of their global dynamism. But the same issue emerges. In most fMRI research, constancy in the brain is discovered using the subtraction method and a number of statistical techniques designed to sort signal from noise. In contrast, in this appendix, I've been developing techniques that consider the brain globally. Instead of striving to isolate a region with a specific role, these multivariate techniques allow for the simultaneous contribution of every voxel, and therefore every area of the brain that can contribute to an fMRI image. No anatomical images result, but the methods nonetheless enable us to characterize some of what is going on inside the storm of nerves. It would be nice, then, to consider the issue of constancy within a multivariate perspective. I've argued that a conscious brain will be in continual flux, but that is not to deny that we do in fact experience stable phenomenal objects. Just as the dynamic and infinite flow is a ubiquitous non-sensory dimension of experience, its mundane results, like "Hey, there's that chair," also appear in consciousness.

Another measure is needed, to determine the extent to which distributed neural activity in the brain is sensitive to conditions that remain the same (or repeat) during a scanning experiment. After all, the success of the existing published research in fMRI and PET already shows that there is *something* constant in the brain when conditions are constant in the

World. How will this constancy show itself as a multivariate measure? Let us use s as the measure of stability in the phenomenal world. To calculate it, we can adopt the multivariate strategies from t and t_r. The idea behind s is simply that global brainstates that share the same tasks or stimuli will be more similar to one another than the average of similarities among all images. We can measure this dimension of sameness/difference in much the same fashion as above. First, average all the similarity scores for all the pairs where stimulus conditions matched. That is, for example, calculate the mean similarity of all volumes collected during the face-matching task, and all the similarities across all the chair-matching tasks, and so forth for the matching tasks, the passive tasks, and the control blocks. Compare this mean to the mean of all similarity scores, regardless of whether between the same stimulus volumes or not. This leads to an aggregate gradient for all the stimulus categories. In the same way, we can compute specific stimulus similarity gradients for each type of stimulus. For example, we could determine whether all the perceptions of faces were more alike than the grand mean of all similarity scores. As in the calculation of t_r, images on both sides of the comparison occur at regular alternating intervals, so the large global temporal effect averages out.

In the Ishai study, the tasks and stimuli could be sorted in two ways. While watching pictures of the three types of object, every subject had some trials in which he or she merely watched, and some trials in which she or he had to recognize which of two pictures matched a sample picture. We can measure the variable s for both the passive viewing and the match-to-sample conditions, regardless of the type of object viewed. Conversely, we can also sort the task block by the type of object, assessing s for houses, faces, and chairs. This measurement detected the commonalities in both passive and matching conditions in six of nine subjects. The remaining three exhibited significant s scores for at least one condition. While perceiving houses, faces, chairs, and scrambled images, regardless of their response, seven of nine subjects showed significant s for between one and three categories. The statistics for the other three studies were roughly similar. Overall (including Ishai) 21 of 27 subjects turned in at least one instance of significant s. For those 21, multivariate s detected stability in about 57 percent of task or stimulus types.

As with the other gradients, the ability to detect any stability using a global measure is surprising. Standard subtraction methods reveal small areas of activity specifically correlated with specific tasks. The global multivariate measures run the risk of submerging meaningful effects in a sea of noise. The stimulus similarity gradient s is not a temporal gradient. Instead, it reflects (albeit faintly) what we all already knew: We (that is, our brains) know a chair when we see one. (Likewise houses and faces.) It was already established in all four studies that specific blood flow effects attended the various tasks examined. The importance of reconfirming this result here is not the foregone conclusion, but the method by which it was achieved. The three indices, t, t_r, and s, all share the assumption that the brain is a distributed processing system. Under that assumption, any one region of the brain can pitch in to many functions. Indeed, the measure of multivariate similarity embraces the radical assumption that every part of the brain is potentially relevant in every function. The last index, the stimulus similarity gradient s, is the indicator that multivariate analysis applied to the entire brain (a "region of interest" 30 times larger than the regions isolated in the Ishai subtraction study) is sufficient to detect reidentification of the same stimulus category in the majority of individual subjects—and the analysis at this point does not avail itself of many of the statistical tools that sharpen traditional analyses.

The two temporal indices, however, add something new to the picture. That same distributed one-for-all and all-for-one brain seems to be tracking both global time and elapsed time in repetitive blocks. In the three indices, measured from the same brain in each instance, we see superposed three broad dimensions of conscious life: Our detection of a stable world (s), embedded in the foundation of experienced reality itself—temporality.

Three strands of interpretation now converge on a rough characterization of the organization of brainspace. First, there are the suggestive analogies with artificial neural networks: The analysis of CNVnet using multidimensional scaling suggested one way for a neural network to embody both stable categories and ubiquitous temporal flux. The stability of objects and types in CNVnet seems to reflect broad similarities in patterns of activity in the hidden layer, so a separate region of the hyperspace is devoted to each type. (In CNVnet, object types are just beep and boop.)

Within each type-specific region the flow of time appears as a trajectory through the region. Elman's network also seems to use its hyperspace this way, assigning the largest regions to the most inclusive types, and nesting subtypes within the more general categories. At the finest level of organization, Elman's nets distinguish words according to context. Contextual information is available only over time. Thus, although he did not look at the overall temporal dynamics of his network, its representation of context is consistent with CNVnet's temporal trajectory through hyperspace.

The second strand of interpretation arises from the multivariate analysis displayed in the "labyrinth of cognition" discussed in chapters 13 and 14 of Miranda's story. The geography of brainspace mapped there parallels the nested regional organization found in the toy brains. The organizing principles are not so simple, however; brainspace is not arranged by input alone, but rather by the confluence of stimuli, task type, and response. This is not surprising from a phenomenological point of view, as it seems to reflect the mutuality of the subjective and objective poles of intentionality. But there were two major limitations to the analysis. First, the variables were derived after image subtraction and some anatomical generalization, so information hidden in global, distributed activity was lost. Second, the images underlying this analysis are all time exposures or average images over time, so temporal effects on brain activity were also lost.

The analysis in this section was designed to overcome these limitations by exploiting the improved spatial and temporal resolution of fMRI, and using raw fMRI data in new ways. The three indices provided the third strand of interpretation. Positive results with index s, the measure of similarity in activity during similar tasks, conforms to the labyrinth and neural net expectations. It appears that the hyperspace of brain activity is organized to reflect the intuitive and logical distinctions arising in experience. But the temporal indices reveal aspects of the data that the labyrinth could not show, namely, that the brain shuttles nonstop through its hyperspace as an effect of time itself. CNVnet took its greatest leaps in hyperspace along the temporal dimension, and it traveled in an almost straight line. The size of the temporal effects in the brain, and their monotonic increase over time, suggests that the active brain traverses its hyperspace in much the same way.

Dimension thinking translates the enormous complexity of the brain at any time into a single point in a space of many dimensions. It's one way to think of yourself. Time moves you, fast, through your personal hyperspace. Think of yourself plummeting through this space always. (Or, if you prefer, think of the view from the bridge of your personal starship, boldly going where no one has gone before.) But that one large dimension and our plunge along it is supplemented by many other dimensions, and as we dive into the future we sashay from side to side (to side to side . . .), weaving in and out of the myriad varieties of human experience. The phenomenology from two chapters previous to this suggested that life is like this (except that the rush of time is non-sensory and invisible). So it seems as we look at the brain from the outside as well.

Now we've interpreted the brain over time, fitting it to experience over time. But the time that surrounds us also appears within us. We turn, accordingly, to the internal structures of temporality in the brain.

4.3   Retention Revealed

The three indices pull out three aspects of experience, with a new emphasis on temporality. If all are significant, a series of functional brain images exhibits the signs of consciousness in its phenomenologically enriched, post-detectorhead sense. The classical phenomenologists, however, went further, discovering at the foundation of temporality the tripartite structure of protention, presence, and retention, which we unpacked for CNVnet using metanets as interpreters. For example, in CNVnet we detected simple retention by constructing a translator, a black box that could take the current state of the net (and nothing else) and reconstruct the past state. With CNVnet, the metanet translator found, in the present, the shadow of the past and foreshadow of the future.

All this applies to real brains in the same way. In general, we have no idea about how the complex dynamism of the brain expresses any particular content of consciousness. But we can nonetheless address the questions of retention and protention indirectly, using the same approach as with CNVnet. A brainstate incorporates a retention of its past if the preceding state can be read out of it. We seek a translator that can use the information about the present state of the brain to reconstruct an immediate past state, or (for protention) use the present state to "preconstruct" the future. Because neural networks are capable of detecting subtle patterns among many inputs, they can be harnessed here too. We will begin with an analysis of retention based on the Ishai study. Accordingly, I turned artificial neural networks loose on the Ishai subjects. As these artificial networks learned, they settled toward a consistent decoding of brainstates, approaching a single stable network that could decode every brain image presented to it in this backward-facing way.

Extracting retention from real brains might be argued to be reading minds (literally), but for the present my intent is merely to show that retention is a pervasive aspect of the brain, considered as a distributed processing system. In outline, the empirical study of retention using neural nets had two main parts. In the first, I used half of the volumes recorded for each subject in the Ishai study as patterns for training the metanet. For training, the metanet attempted to learn a pairing of each brain pattern with the immediately prior pattern. The remaining patterns were reserved for testing with the trained network. That way, I was training the metanets not simply to produce the prior pattern by rote association, but rather to generalize to new patterns, extracting the retained information *de novo*— sight-reading the mind, I suppose. As the net trained, I continuously measured its performance on the novel patterns. When it ceased improving, training was stopped, and its best performance on the novel patterns recorded as its global measure of success.

Meanwhile, I did the same with a shuffled deck of images from the same subject. That is, I broke up the temporal relationship among the successive images of the brain, reordering the entire set of 1,092 brain snapshots to be random with respect to their time of occurrence. Our discussions of both recurrent networks and phenomenology suggest that what retention retains is the immediately prior state of the brain or consciousness. My big shuffle, therefore, should have prevented the metanet from learning the association between the present and the immediate past, because the conjunction of the two had been sundered. But every other feature of metanet learning was the same. So if there were other, nontemporal regularities buried in these brain scans, or if pure rote learning of pairs of brain patterns could give one a leg up on novel patterns, the randomized metanet should be able to accomplish that much. The overall procedure was the same as above: Half the shuffled images were reserved for testing, and the net trains until further training led to no further improvement in performance with the novel stimuli.[15]

Success is measured in the contrast of performance between the metanet and its randomized counterpart. Like the gradient scores, in this case I have calculated the results so that equal performance registers as zero. Any score greater than zero will mean that the original net is outperforming its randomized counterpart, suggesting that the network is indeed recovering temporal information. Of course, if only one instance of each network was created, any contrast might well be due to pure chance. Only after several test and random metanets have been made and tested can we assess the difference between them for its probability of arising randomly. I re-analyzed data from 21 subjects. (The reading experiment by Mechelli et al. produced images with around 60,000 voxels, which exceeded the computer capacity I was working with.) Revisiting the Ishai study, it took very few iterations of this procedure to clearly establish a highly significant contrast in all subject scan series. All of the test metanets, charged with the task of reconstructing the images of times past, achieved an average score of .28 in the Ishai experiments. (That is, they were 28 percent better than the random controls.) In the spatial memory experiment of Postle, all four subjects averaged .28, exactly the score achieved by the Ishai metanets. Finally, the response competition study (Hazeltine et al.) also produced significant results for all eight subjects, but as in previous forays with this data set, the effects were slimmer. The average was .11, and it required a hundred or more copies of the networks to converge on their performance scores. The smaller image set may again be a factor.

Overall, the analysis suggests that patterns of activation in the human brain encode past patterns of activation, and particularly the immediate past. The metanet cannot tell us how these patterns are encoded. Reproducing those patterns, as the metanet does, only indicates that something is there to embed the present in the past. Phenomenology led us to anticipate this aspect of brain function. Neural networks simulated a potential mechanism to implement it, and showed us how such a mechanism might work (and how we might observe it working). Functional brain imaging, refracted through phenomenology and neural nets, revealed that we may indeed be consciousness incarnate.

4.4   To the Future

The strategy can easily be turned toward the future as well. Now we pose to the black boxes the task of reconstructing the immediately following state of the scan, based on the present image. In every other respect, the test and control nets are built, trained, and tested in exactly the same way. And once again, all 21 subjects exhibited significant positive results. For houses, faces, chairs: .2; for spatial memory: .23; for response competition: .11. Thus the image series encode protentive information, as well as retention.

Is this network precognition some sort of neural ESP? Not at all; it is the expression of simple expectation, the reasonable predictions on which our ability to navigate in the World rests. As phenomenology suggests, the experience of a reality is rooted in retention and protention, as well as immediately given sensations. It's interesting to note that in the two larger studies, Ishai's and Postle's, the success of the metanets in reconstructing the past exceeds their ability to project the future (and this difference is also statistically significant). This intriguing finding also has its phenomenological side. It may be the contrast between the certainty of the past and the uncertainty of the future. That is, the future appears in the present as indistinct alternatives. In the studies I've examined here, subjects met few surprises. Nonetheless, they could not know exactly what would come next, and so their protentions could not perfectly anticipate the next state of their own brains. But, looking backward, this indeterminacy is moot, and nothing further intervenes to alter the path of retentions leading to the present moment. This phenomenological difference seems to be reflected in the analyses of functional images. It will be an interesting topic to explore as neurophenomenology develops.

4.5   And Beyond?

All the plot lines now meet their end. Consciousness viewed from within is thick with context, and the first and most important context is always temporal. We are aware of temporality in every experience, but I have argued for something stronger: Temporality is necessary for any experience at all. This, I suggest, is a missing link in contemporary scientific approaches to consciousness. By failing to grapple with this vast dimension of time, most accounts of consciousness either limit themselves to the tip of the iceberg or merely nod toward some murky unanalyzed depth. For that reason, most scientific accounts of consciousness seem unfinished. They have generally failed to face the true nature of the complexity that we live.

Consciousness viewed from without showed us that temporality is not magic. Recurrent neural networks demonstrated how a physical system could embody the features of temporality described by Husserl and adapted here. They provide a concrete object lesson in methods for analysis of temporality in physical systems. Brains are recurrent networks too. But my argument did not rest on this suggestive analogy of functional architecture between artificial and real neural nets.[16] Rather, I swung the analytical tools for deciphering temporality around toward the brain, and found strong evidence that we are time in the flesh. Consciousness viewed from without displays the necessary temporal properties found in consciousness viewed from within. In the *Tempest,* Prospero says, "We are such stuff as dreams are made of." Rebecca Goldstein offers the converse, "We are such dreams as stuff is made of." In this book, the traffic between dreams and stuff—consciousness and brain—is continual.[17]

Throughout *Radiant Cool,* fictional and real characters share a common quest for a scientific theory of consciousness, an account that will embed consciousness in nature as it is known through science. How does the current work contribute to the quest?[18] The traditional goal of science is to explain and predict natural phenomena. To what extent, then, has this book explained and predicted natural phenomen*ology?* One can set the standard for success with reference to one's favorite example of scientific discovery: the circulation of the blood, the ideal gas laws, the periodic table, relativity, and so forth. For each there is that satisfying *aha* as the pieces click into place. I *predict* that readers did not experience their personal click as the book unfolded; I would like to try to *explain* that absent *aha.*

Science marches on in part by the selective disregard of many of the messier aspects of life. Most sciences are defined through ideal cases, conceived in ideal circumstances, and thus most observational confirmations are approximations. The brilliance of scientific discovery is often canny choices about what is essential to the process to be explained, and what can be ignored. Often the result is a satisfying simplification expressed in a beautiful equation or a single sentence of illumination. Both experience and the brain certainly are messy targets of explanation, and this book has conveyed no master equation or single crystalline insight. Predictive power does lurk, however, in the data and programs undergirding the empirical discussions in the book. For example, in researching the sections just above, I constructed neural networks that were trained to "read" a state of the brain, and then extract both the prior state and the subsequent state of that same brain. As discussed in several places in this book, a neural network is really just a numerical specification of the "synaptic" strengths between processing units. All those numbers defining strong or weak connections constitute the "weight matrix," and it is this matrix that determines exactly what the network will do. One way to think of all these weights is as coefficients in a very large equation. In this case, then, the neural nets I built constitute huge equations that explain (by correctly reproducing the immediate past of the brain) and predict (by correctly reproducing the immediate future). *Aha!*

Or not *aha*. It's not clear whether having these equations would lead to a satisfying understanding of brain function or consciousness. They are simply too complicated to be grasped, and their complexity is a byproduct of the target to be explained. The equations are complex because the specific complexities of particular brainstates make a difference in what happens next, and only a very complex set of variables could describe the relevant conditions. Just like consciousness! In tandem with neural complexity, throughout this book we have encountered, and celebrated, the complexity of consciousness. Even the straightforward perception of ordinary objects is a very messy affair. And, says phenomenology, it has to be that way. What *Radiant Cool* leaves open is the possibility that both brain and consciousness are *essentially complex*. What that means is that the processes of consciousness cannot be simplified beyond a certain point, and that there will be no master equation or *aha* insight. Consciousness and brain are messy of necessity.

Now it may be that the *aha* moment lies ahead for the science of consciousness, and that in its wake much contemporary research on the subject, this book included, will seem like so much scholastic fog. But it may also be that the science of consciousness will always have a different, shaggier look than those pristine sciences we admire.

The goal of prediction and explanation may therefore not be wholly appropriate to the quest. Instead, perhaps we should think of embracing a different goal. I suggest that our model for inquiry might be borrowed from the humanities: *interpretation*. Interpretation is a form of non-predictive explanation, and one of its principal goals is the enlargement of meaning found in the thing to be interpreted. In contrast to science, interpretation stays closer to the concrete particulars of its object. Even as the object is subsumed into larger categories of meaning, its particularity remains relevant, and therefore interpretations remain open to revision. Interpretations can be good or bad. Really bad ones are flat-out false, but good ones do not exclude further elaboration, and multiple interpretations can illuminate the same target without excluding one another. In some cases good interpretations of the same thing can even contradict each other.

Objects of interpretation are often artifacts, especially text. It's unusual to regard a natural system as a candidate for interpretation.[19] But in the hybrid study undertaken here, bending the light of interpretation on a natural system creates novel possibilities. Imagine an interpretive science of consciousness, which would marry the scientific goal of naturalizing consciousness with the interpretive goal of enlarging the meanings found in the conscious brain. The scientific goal could thus be re-characterized as the goal of developing interpretations from phenomenology (on the one hand) and neuroscience (on the other) that ultimately converge in a single method of interpretation: neurophenomenology. Neurophenomenological interpretations can be rigorous by the standards shared by scientists and humanists alike: accurate description of evidence; thoroughness of research or observation; clarity of reasoning; judicious weighing of alternatives. These interpretations will illuminate the brain in the language of experience, as they illuminate experience in the language of the brain. Our knowledge of the world appears to us in conscious experience; understanding consciousness in nature will yield knowledge of the process of knowing itself. In this way, a mountain may again be a mountain.

A colleague of mine once remarked, "The brain is a story." One theme of this book has been that every moment of every brain is a story unto itself. Reading this non-textual story has required special methods, and future neurointerpretation will demand methods as yet undreamed. We will know that neurophenomenology is flourishing when its toolbox overflows. Wallace Stevens has shown us thirteen ways of looking at a blackbird. Neurophenomenology may ultimately show us hundreds of ways of looking at the brain. Results from these methods will be open rather than final, suggestive rather than definitive. The success of any of these methods by itself will be hard to measure, but collectively the variety of methods should yield a steady growth in understanding. Instead of the *aha* of sudden insight, we may come to experience the *ah* of appreciation and wonder.

Neurophenomenology may also invite novel expressions of our emerging vision of the conscious human being. Brains and stories do seem to have a powerful metaphorical connection. Both unfold worlds. I hope then that this book has offered glimpses of worlds poised in that abstract space between the narrative of one's life and the matter in which the narrative is inscribed.

And Miranda Sharpe. . . . Philosophers do love their thought experiments, and I have always thought that the most plausible thought experiments are those that explore the details—if not *all* the details, then at least many. The most thorough thought experiment, then, is a novel. As with all thought experiments, novels derive their import through some intersection of the fictional with the real world. Determining where those worlds overlap (or collide) is a large component of the joy of reading. Miranda, whose existence ultimately turns on whether a particular word is italicized, does invite us to reconsider what it means to exist *as consciousness* or, if you prefer, *as a story*. Perhaps she is on to something, but figuring out what that is must necessarily be left to you.

Sources and Notes

Part One

Behind several scenes in the novel lurk specific texts and sources, which would have been awkward to identify explicitly or acknowledge in the novel itself. These are clarified here. Full citations for sources are given in the bibliography.

Epigraphs

"Howl" by Allen Ginsberg is excerpted from *Collected Poems 1947–1980* by Allen Ginsberg. Copyright 1955 by Allen Ginsberg. Reprinted by permission of HarperCollins Publishers, Inc. "Thirteen Ways of Looking at a Blackbird" is excerpted from *The Collected Poems of Wallace Stevens,* by Wallace Stevens, copyright 1954, by Wallace Stevens and renewed 1982 by Holly Stevens. Used by permission of Alfred A. Knopf, a division of Random House, Inc.

The Thrill of Phenomenology

Chapter 1. The Husserl quotation is from *The Phenomenology of Internal Time-Consciousness* (Churchill, trans.), p. 78.

Chapter 2. Some of Clair Lucid's dialogue was generated by the early Artificial Intelligence program, ELIZA, created by Joseph Weizenbaum. See Weizenbaum's *Computer Power and Human Reason.*

Chapter 5. "The Library of Babel" by Jorge Luis Borges appears in his *Collected Fictions.* Daniel Dennett calculated the approximate number of volumes. See his

"In Darwin's Wake, Where Am I?" APA Presidential Address (American Philosophical Association), December 29, 2000. Available at <http://ase.tufts.edu/cogstud/papers/apapresadd.htm>. Paul Churchland is quoted from *The Engine of Reason, the Seat of the Soul*, pp. 4–5.

Chapter 6. The brain scan data were originally collected by Alumit Ishai (Ishai et al. 2000), and archived for public distribution in the fMRI Data Center (<www.fmridc.org>). Graphics were produced using Matlab software (Mathworks, Inc., Natick, MA).

Chapter 7. Dostoevski's *Crime and Punishment* inspired Profiry's character, but for the rest of him, consult an introduction to multivariate statistics—for example, Marcoulides and Hershberger 1997. Kruskal and Wish wrote the classic introduction to multidimensional scaling.

Chapter 8. In "Finding Structure in Time," Jeffrey Elman presents his analysis in dendrograms based on hierarchical cluster analysis. (See note 10, below.) I used the dendrograms published in the original article to recover multivariate distances between points, and then re-analyzed the data with multidimensional scaling in Matlab. The Matlab graphics I generated for this chapter and chapter 10 don't appear in Elman's article, but the multivariate structure revealed by the two methods, and shown in his and my diagrams, coincides. Michael D. Lee wrote the MDS functions I used. I discuss the connections between connectionism and consciousness in more detail in the articles listed in the bibliography.

The passage from "The Aleph" appears in *Collected Fictions*, by Jorge Luis Borges, translated by Andrew Hurley, copyright © 1998 by Maria Kodama; translation copyright © 1998 by Penguin Putnam Inc. Used by permission of Viking Penguin, a division of Penguin Group (USA) Inc.

Chapter 9. Imogen's words are all line quotations from Shakespeare's *Cymbeline*. Emily's are all stanzas or partial stanzas by Emily Dickinson, reprinted by permission of the publishers and Trustees of Amherst College from *The Poems of Emily Dickinson*, Thomas H. Johnson, ed., Cambridge, MA: The Belknap Press of Harvard University Press, Copyright © 1951, 1955, 1979 by the Presidents and Fellows of Harvard College. Emily (the character) quotes from poems 268, 288, 531, and 1005.

Chapter 11. Miranda's descriptions of the experience of brain injury derive from multiple sources, but are at best a vague pastiche of first-person descriptions of these conditions. For genuine and authoritative discussions, see works by Larry Weiskrantz (especially on blindsight), A. R. Luria, and Oliver Sacks. The transient lesioning machine is pure fiction, of course.

Chapter 13. In *Dawn*, Nietzsche wrote, "If we wanted and dared an architecture in accordance with our minds (we are too cowardly for that!), then the labyrinth would have to be our model." The Labyrinth of Cognition can be viewed at <www.trincoll.edu/~dlloyd>, where it is referred to as the Labyrinth of Consciousness. A more extensive discussion of distributed representation, functional neuroimaging, and the methods and lessons of multidimensional scaling can be found at the website, and in my article "Terra Cognita: From Functional Neuroimaging to the Map of the Mind" (2000). Most of the imaging results used are archived in the Brainmap database (<www.uthscsa.edu/brainmap>). The Labyrinth is written in VRML, "Virtual Reality Markup Language."

The list below matches the original papers to the labels on the "planets" in the Labyrinth. The short task description found in the figures in chapter 13 has been expanded somewhat in parentheses, where I've paired stimuli and tasks for each experiment, and noted experiments where there were no task stimuli or no specific response ("none"). Full citations of the original papers are in the bibliography.

1.1: T-vibrate lips (vibration to lips; none; see Fox et al. 1987).

1.2: T-vibrate RLtoes (vibration to both toes; none; see Fox et al. 1987).

1.3: T-vibrate RLhand (vibration to hands; none; see Fox et al. 1987).

7.1: T-none, "Expect shock" (expect painful shock [none delivered]; see Reiman 1989).

19.1: T-touch Rtoe, "silent count pauses" (touch to right great toe; silently count pauses in touch; see Pardo et al. 1991).

19.2: T-touch Ltoe, "silent count pauses" (touch to L great toe; silently count pauses in touch; see Pardo et al. 1991).

19.3: Vis-detect lum change, "count luminance changes" (silently count changes in brightness [none occurred]; see Pardo et al. 1991).

20.1: Vis-target RL; Aud-metronome, "saccade to target with clicks" (blinking light with metronome; oculomotor saccades to stimulus; see Fox, Fox et al. 1985).

20.2/20.4: Aud-metronome, saccade to prev target pt with clicks (metronome; rhythmic saccades to previous target; see Fox et al. 1985).

20.3: Aud-metronome, "flex hands w/clicks" (metronome; oculomotor saccades, rhythmic hand flexion; see Fox et al. 1985).

30.1: Imagine sad situation (imagine a sad situation; see Pardo et al. 1993).

34.2: Aud-wds, 5-word recall, "recall wds aloud" (none; 5 word list, recall aloud; see Grasby et al. 1993).

34.3: Aud-wds, 15-word recall, "recall wds aloud" (none; 15 word list, recall aloud; see Grasby et al. 1993).

38.5: "oscillate arm" (none; oscillate extended arm; see Jenkins et al. 1993).

38.6: "extend arm" (maintain extension of arm; see Jenkins et al. 1993).

41.1: T-vibrate Rhand (vibration to right hand; none; see Tempel 1993).

41.2: T-vibrate Lhand (vibration to left hand; none; see Tempel 1993).

42.1: "repeat fing touch seq" (none; complex thumb-finger touch sequence; see Seitz & Roland 1992a).

43.1: T-rect solids, "explore objs w/Rhand, thumbs-up if longer" (solids; explore with right hand, thumbs-up if second object is oblong; see Seitz et al. 1991).

58.3: Vis-wds: "read par aloud" (visual words; read paragraph aloud; see Fox et al. 1996).

58.4: Vis-Wds+Aud-Wds, "read par in unison" (visual words; read paragraph in unison; see Fox et al. 1996).

108.13: Vis-Geo forms, "saccade away from stim" (geometric forms; saccade away from stimulus; see Paus et al. 1993).

108.14: T-finger: "lift nontouched finger" (light touch to finger; lift finger not touched; see Paus et al. 1993).

108.15: Aud-words:saywrongword (one of three verbs; say pronoun not previously practiced with the verb; see Paus et al. 1993).

108.16: Vis-Geo forms, "saccade to stim" (geometric forms; saccade toward stimulus; see Paus et al. 1993).

108.17: T-finger: "lift touched finger" (light touch to finger; lift finger touched; see Paus et al. 1993).

108.18: Aud-Wds, 1 of 3 verbs, "say practiced pronoun for verb" (one of three verbs; say pronoun previously practiced with the verb; see Paus et al. 1993).

159.1: T-itch, Rarm (intracutaneous injection of histamine in right upper arm; none; see Hsieh 1994).

179.1: T-Lfing (light tactile stimulus to left finger; none; see Bottini et al. 1995).

185.1: Aud-tone:liftfings (300 ms tones; lift finger after each test interval; see Jueptner 1998).

191.1: MoveFingers (none; sequential finger-thumb opposition; see Wessel et al. 1995).

219.1: "Describe a past experience aloud" (none; describe a specific experience from your past aloud; see Andreasen 1998).

219.2: "Say C Wds" (none; say words that begin with the letter C; see Andreasen 1998).

221.1: Aud-nouns, "silently generate verbs" (concrete nouns; silently generate verbs; see Weiller et al. 1995).

221.2: Aud-Wds-pseudowords; "silently repeat pseudoWds" (pronounceable pseudo-words; silently repeat pseudo-words; see Weiller et al. 1995).

Chapter 15. The websites subject to global replacement are real as of this writing, and can be very useful in researching consciousness. There are many other sites that could be on the list, and my short list should not be seen as a top-ten guide to consciousness on the Web. I hope the authors represented at these websites will not regard Porfiry's plan to sow confusion among them as satirizing their *current* efforts. Certainly no such insult was intended. The genuine Web addresses in the novel, in total, include this list, my own site, and the Brainmap and fMRIDC archives. The others given in Miranda's tale are fictions. I tried to coin domain names that do not already exist as websites, but the Web is a fluid medium. I apologize in advance if any of the fictional urls someday link to genuine websites. Of course, any discussion of these fictional sites in the book should not be taken to describe any actual website.

Chapter 16. The description of symptoms of a Prozac overdose are fictional. The antidote, "tryptosinate," is also a fiction.

Chapter 18. Max Grue's most jumbled ravings are derived from his less jumbled speeches using text-morphing software found in the McPoet Dadaist software package, written by the multitalented Chris Westbury. Westbury has developed a successor to McPoet, "Janusnode," available at Janusnode.com. The text-morphing process takes each word in an actual text and calculates which words from that text are most likely to follow. Morphing then generates a new text preserving the same word-to-word probabilities, but random otherwise. Such texts are enjoyable nonsense, but seem strangely haunted by the style and logic of the original.

Part Two: The Real Firefly

1. Often the detectors discovered in cognitive neuroscience are imagined to be located in specific regions of the brain. This idea has been called "localism." The idea that cognitive functions are localized areas is an old one, dating at least to Paul Broca in the nineteenth century, and to even older ideas about "faculties" in the mind. Localism also appears in proposals for the study of consciousness. In Chalmers 2000 and Varela 1999, for example, there is an expectation that particular states or types of consciousness will be the product of particular regions or "neural assemblies" in the brain. In addition to the discussion in the text, general critiques of localism include Uttal 2001. I use fMRI for an empirical approach to the issue in Lloyd 2002b.

2. In the ten short but explosive years since the development of fMRI, many methods for image interpretation have emerged, and the field is far from settling. So it's an oversimplification to suggest that simple subtraction is the universal method in functional neuroimaging. However, most of the methods share the logic of subtraction. They are attempts to understand a particular brain function by identifying specific regions of increased or decreased levels of activity correlated with the function. An excellent collection of papers on methods is available at <www.fil.ion.ucl.ac.uk/spm/>. This is the central Web repository for SPM (Statistical Parametric Mapping), a software package widely used in the fMRI community for image analysis. Also see the discussions of alternative image interpretation methods in Friston et al. 1995, 1996; and Price and Friston 1996.

For comprehensive introductions to functional neuroimaging, see Frackowiak et al. 1997, and the anthology edited by Toga and Mazziotta (1996). Lange 1996 is a comprehensive tutorial in the statistics underlying fMRI interpretation.

3. I've used Alumit Ishai's 2000 study to illustrate the standard methods in image interpretation; however, it should be noted that in fact, Ishai is critical of the localizing trend in functional neuroimagining. Her results and discussion support the idea that functional regions overlap, or in other words that parts of the brain are multifunctional. Later in this appendix, I will present new methods for image interpretation, but I share with Ishai the interest in exploring distributed processing in the brain. See also Ishai et al. 1999.

4. The anxieties of skepticism may be a Western preoccupation. "If you realize there is no connection between your senses and the external world," writes the Zen master Baizhang, "you will be liberated on the spot." (Thomas Cleary, ed. and trans., *Classics of Buddhism and Zen, vol. 1, Zen Essence* [Boston: Shambhala, 2001], p. 216.)

5. Superposition also implies a critical view of some contemporary discussions of consciousness by philosophers. Many philosophers single out a special form of conscious state, the awareness of "qualia," "pure sensations," or "raw feels." Examples include the color red, the taste of coffee, the feeling of pain, etc. Qualia then appear to pose a special difficulty for theories of consciousness, and failing to account for them allegedly dooms many hypotheses about the nature of consciousness. But phenomenology strongly suggests that the "qualia problem" is misguided. There simply are no experiences that can be exhaustively described as "seeing red." Every sighting of red, along with every taste and pang, is situated in a complex context, and awareness of aspects of that context are superposed on the sensory awareness itself. So the redness of a red thing is one aspect of the thing among many, an undetachable part of a state of consciousness rather than a special example of some kind of "pure awareness." When we do refer to redness as the quality in common to all red things, we have performed an act of abstraction, and the object of that awareness is a concept of redness rather than an object of sensation. In sum, phenomenology suggests that the issue of qualia does not arise as a *special* problem for a theory of consciousness. It is part of the problem of perceptual consciousness overall, but that is a problem of complex states of superposed interpretation. In the sections following, we will see how this orientation toward the problem of consciousness opens a way forward to some new solutions. See also the books by Austen Clark for careful philosophical treatments of the qualia problem and applications of ideas from multivariate statistics that inspired the interpretive methods used in this book.

6. There are borderline cases that seem to question the identification of transcendence and reality. Where one imagines a thing vividly, it sometimes occurs that one can discover something in the image that was not supplied by its author. Imagine two line triangles superimposed in the familiar Star of David pattern. How many triangles can you "see"? Are the eight triangles somehow *there* in the mental image prior to our mental exploration of it? Does this fact about the figure transcend our original awareness, prior to our imagined act of counting? These questions are similar to questions about the unmentioned properties of fictional characters. Do these properties belong to the character independently of our reflection? Negative answers to these questions deny that the examples display transcendence. But positive answers also reveal the same commitment to the equation of transcendence and reality, because ascribing factual properties to the geometric figure or to Miranda Sharpe ipso facto builds a case for the Reality of those entities. We find ourselves talking about the geometric properties of a physical image in the brain, or perhaps, with Plato, we become tempted to posit Real abstract or fictional entities residing in some alternate realm that is more-or-less independent of our awareness.

7. This conception of temporality has remained an enduring foundation of phenomenology. Husserl's followers have enlarged this basic picture through further

analyses of the structure and import of the components of temporality. Sartre, for example, stresses the absolute freedom experienced in the present, in contrast to the fixity of the retained past. Heidegger emphasizes the future, and the many ways its possibilities (and the ultimate fact of death) structure our values, desires, and acts. These and many other philosophers of time deserve careful study. But the basic structure described here has remained the starting point.

8. Husserl makes these points in characteristically high-density prose, as follows:

> The "source-point" with which the "production" of the enduring object begins is a primal impression. This consciousness is in a state of constant change: the tone-now present "in person" continuously changes into something that has been; an always new tone-now continuously relieves the one that has passed over into modification. But when the consciousness of the tone-now, the primal impression, passes over into retention, this retention itself is a now in turn, something actually existing. While it is actually present itself (but not an actually present tone), it is retention *of* the tone that has been. . . . Accordingly, a fixed continuum of retention arises in such a way that each later point is a retention for every earlier point. And each retention is already a continuum. . . . Thus a continuity of retentional modifications attaches itself to each of these retentions, and this continuity itself is again an actually present point that is retentionally adumbrated. (Section 11, *On the Phenomenology of the Consciousness of Internal Time* [trans. Brough]), p. 31

Husserl's "continuum" is his expression for the metaphorical "depth" of time discussed in the text.

9. Some cognitive scientists and philosophers have recently been promoting "enactive cognition" or "radical embodiment" as a theoretical framework for understanding consciousness and cognition (Clark 1999; Thompson and Varela 2001; Clark and Chalmers 1998). The "embodiment" framework is the mix of several claims, with some overlap with ideas in *Radiant Cool,* so it may be useful to draw some distinctions. *RC* shares with radical embodiment a rejection of some traditional ideas in cognitive science. We all reject the idea that the mind operates like a computer, and we agree that the kind of datastructures computers use are nothing like the kind of representations in play in the brain. In place of traditional computationalism we agree that the mind should be understood as a dynamical system. The artificial neural networks that play such a large role in this book exemplify such systems. We also agree that the way conscious thought is implemented in the brain is important. In this we reject a core tenet of classical functionalism, namely, that the mind can be decomposed into one or more functionally defined black boxes whose internal structure or processing can be implemented many different ways.

In addition to these claims, radical embodiment also claims that conscious states are not exclusively internal to the brain. For them, the proper science of consciousness is a study of brain+body+world, and states of consciousness should be understood to include elements of all three and their interaction. Embodiment captures this idea, along with "situated cognition" and "enactive cognition." In one sense, these claims are also compatible with *RC.* It would be impossible to understand consciousness (or cognition) without considering the special sensory and motor context of the brain. It is only through the interplay and harmony of multiple sensory channels that we achieve our awareness of an objective world. These various channels are embodied and their content decoded only through a complicated dance between our awareness of bodily position and other proprioceptive feedback and the particular inputs of other sense organs. Husserl's *Thing and Space,* for example, dissects this interplay at great length.

Husserl's phenomenology of reality is slowly spreading into cognitive science, a welcome development. (For example, see the anthology edited by Petitot et al., *Naturalizing Phenomenology.*) In other quarters, Husserl's insights are being reinvented in contemporary language, especially by the proponets of embodiment. For example, Alva Noë and Kevin O'Regan have advanced the idea of "sensorimotor contingencies" (O'Regan and Noë 2001; Noë 2002). As Noë explains:

> When you move toward an object, it looms in your visual field. When you move around it, it changes profile. In these and many other ways, sensory stimulation is affected by movement. These patterns of interdependence between sensory stimulation and movement are patterns of sensorimotor contingencies. (Noë 2003)

The body and its situation are essential; without them, human intentionality would not be possible. But do states of awareness *literally* include muscles and bones, along with actual parts of the physical environment? My view is that the body and its situation are necessary causal preconditions for consciousness and that change in one's body is a likely consequence of conscious action, but that these bodily events are not a literal part of the consciousness that is so intimately linked to them. The actual constituents of the awareness itself are brainy. They are made of neurons or elements that interact with the dynamics of a recurrent neural network. (These elements need not be carbon-based.) In defense of this "internalism," consider again the brain in a vat. The thought experiment seems to tolerate the wholesale substitution of simulations for bodies and their environments. But these substitutions leave one's states of consciousness intact. That interpretation of the results of vatting allows for bodies to vary greatly, but independently from awareness.

But the replace-and-simulate strategy has very different results when it is practiced on parts internal to the brain. Imagine, for example, a prosthetic frontal lobe, a black box plugged in to all the inputs to a normal lobe, and producing all the appropriate outputs. As with vatting, assume that a computer does the simulating, running "frontal.exe." Are you still conscious in this lamentable state? Is your prosthetic lobe conscious or semiconscious? My intuition is that this intervention greatly impairs consciousness, or at least makes it impossible to assess what survives after the implant. Internal structure and functional architecture matter inside the brain. But simulated embodiment, as experienced by a brain in a vat, doesn't impair consciousness, so long as the simulation preserves appropriate inputs to the unsimulated brain.

Thought experiments are a poor guide, however. It would be better to regard radical embodiment as an empirical claim. Then the decision between internalism and embodiment would be resolved as one outstrips the other in its yield of testable hypotheses. *RC* weighs in on this with a number of empirical predictions based on its internalistic approach. The empirical support for embodiment appears to support its welcome embrace of dynamical systems, a theme in agreement with this book. So far there has been little experimental support for the more radical claim about the inner+outer "spread out" elements of mind. But the science of consciousness is young, and the more radical claims of radical embodiment may also illuminate a future theory of mind.

10. Elman uses a method known as hierarchical cluster analysis, another means for extracting structure from the distance relationships in a high-dimensional space. The idea is simple. When a teacher says to her class, "Turn to your nearest neighbor," the class finds its own clusters. More formally, cluster analysis begins by finding the two points most near to each other in the high-dimensional space. They will be the first cluster. Treat the exact center of that cluster as a new "superpoint" and cluster again, entering this new point with all the remaining points, to find the next pair of nearests. (The superpoint may be part of the next pair, or get absorbed into a bigger cluster later.) With each pass, a new cluster emerges until all the points and all the lower-level clusters are absorbed into a single ultimate cluster. With clustering comes a helpful way of looking at the results, the dendrogram. A dendrogram links the partners in each cluster with a line to make a forking tree diagram out of the analysis. Toward the leaves lie the smaller clusters of nearby points. Toward the main trunk lie the big divisions of points. For an introduction to cluster analysis, see Kaufman and Rousseeuw 1990.

11. In linking the contents of consciousness to states of distributed activity in a neural network I'm endorsing what is generally called a "dynamical systems perspective." At the most general level, a dynamical system is a system of interacting components, where the interaction is complex and the resulting behavior of the system also complex. Planets orbiting a star constitute one such system, and as the discussion so far indicates, so do interconnected networks of neural processors, either simulated or (even more so) biological. As far back as the late 1950s, dynamical systems of the neural network variety were recognized to have capacities well suited to perception and cognition (Rosenblatt 1958, 1962). After a hiatus, dynamical systems were rediscovered in the 1980s (McClelland and Rumelhart 1986), inspiring a huge literature of theory, models, and methods devoted to understanding ourselves as dynamical systems.

The observation that dynamical systems could offer an attractive approach to consciousness appeared early in the renaissance of connectionism (e.g., Rumelhart et al. 1986), and is prefigured in William James and even Freud's *Project for a Scientific Psychology* (which was unpublished in his lifetime). Recent discussions include Dennett 1991, Port and van Gelder 1995, and my own papers listed in the bibliography.

The temporal dimension of the objects in experience is a further specification of the richness of consciousness, and I've argued here that it is the foundation of any plausible theory of consciousness, and endorsed most of Husserl's analysis of the temporal (see also Lloyd 2000a and 2002a). Francisco Varela (1999) and Tim van Gelder (1999) have also approached temporality from a dynamical systems perspective; all three of us have apparently arrived at our parallel conclusions independently of one another.

For Varela and van Gelder, as for me, an important facet of temporality is retention: Somehow information about the immediate past must inflect the present, so that the present carries some distinctive historical content. Both authors accordingly point out that the current state of any dynamical system is very sensitive to its own past conditions. So, even though at different times the system has "settled toward" or approached the same general condition, in the details of its configuration one could, in principle, extract information about the conditions prior to the moment.

This is a promising start, but too general. Examine the details and every system will bear traces of its past. Varela seems sensitive to this in his comments on van Gelder, where he proposes a more specific version of the dynamical systems hypothesis, linking temporal consciousness to transient oscillations of ensembles of neurons, "cell assemblies." In response to specific stimuli, collections of neurons that normally fire out of synchrony fall in with each other in a brief common rhythm. These oscillating assemblies, according to Varela, are states of consciousness. Varela regards this as a preferable hypothesis because the assemblies hold together for at most a few seconds, corresponding to the "specious present" of William James, that brief window of the Now wherein our temporal judgments are very accurate.

Both authors offer rich and interesting discussions of their perspectives, which I will not review. However, it may be helpful to distinguish the viewpoint of *Radiant Cool*. First, in this book and in prior papers, I've stressed the importance of recurrence or feedback as an element in the functional architecture of a conscious network. So, at the most general level of description, a network sufficient to sustain retentional information will have some form of the blueprint of a simple recurrent network, as invented by Jeff Elman. Both Varela and van Gelder introduce examples with recurrence or feedback too, but I think it is slightly more than a difference in emphasis. Husserl's challenge to us is not to show how a difference in the real past of a system can influence its present state—the actual past is excluded along with the rest of the objective world at the phenomenological get-go. Rather, Husserlian retention is the presence (now) of an apparent past experience, the prior Now in all of its richness. So, if a distributed pattern of activity is the network Now, then retention is achieved only if that pattern is inflected by *its own* prior Now-state, and not just some aspect of the prior now, but all of it. That consideration leads to the endorsement of a more specific version of the dynamical systems hypothesis, in which the dynamical system is specified as recurrent.

But Husserl's reconstruction of temporality is more specific still, and this further raises the bar for dynamical systems. As I discuss in the text, retention (and protention) preserve the order of time and the unity of objects over time. Like spatial boundaries, objects have their beginnings and ends, and each passing stage is held in retention in its correct place in the order of all. *In principle*, dynamical systems are generally capable of encoding these structures, but to establish any dynamical system hypothesis one has to demonstrate their success in reality. This need is sharpened when the dynamical system hypothesis becomes more specific, as it is here. You are entitled to say, "Maybe a simple recurrent network can capture the structure of retention, but maybe not. Show me!" Showing is indeed the plan. In this section, I've shown that an SRN operating in a temporal environment can embody all of the features of temporality discussed. In the next section, I will present evidence that human brains do it too, through the reanalysis of several human brain imaging studies.

12. I report much of this research in Lloyd 2002a, a scientific paper. This is the best source for the most detailed discussion of methods and results. The paper is available at <www.trincoll.edu/~dlloyd>.

13. Are exposure times of two or more seconds too long to catch the fleeting expressions of consciousness? Antti Revonsuo (2001) proposes what amounts to temporal localization at the conclusion of a perceptive essay on methods for neurophenomenology. Based on cognitive and neuroscientific evidence, Revonsuo calculates a minimal duration for conscious experiences, and further proposes that the fluidity of consciousness entails that all specific states of consciousness will be nearly as fleet as the minimum. Thus any scientific method for detecting the neural correlates of conscious experience must be tuned to rapid change in the nervous system. Functional brain imaging has a temporal sensitivity window of about two seconds—all of the images used for this book are time exposures. For Revonsuo, then, functional brain imaging is just too blurry to be of use. (It is also spatially blurry.) One reply to this is implicit in the text, and explicit in my comments on all the prima facie challenges to the science of consciousness (the hard problem, for example): Just go ahead with the tools available and see if there are results. But in addition, there is reason to hope for a positive outcome. Although each exact or specific state of consciousness is unique and fleeting, over longer periods, approximately similar states of consciousness endure. Hamlet pondering the skull of Yorick flashes through a dense poetic reverie, but something skullish persists over those seconds and minutes. Prosaic brain imaging studies use multiple repeating trials for exactly the purpose of producing similar patterns of activity over time, detectable through brain imaging.

14. Two specific adjustments in the calculation of t are designed to evade other effects that could confound the temporal interpretation. First, as mentioned previously, fMRI measures hemodynamics, not neurodynamics. That is, it detects physiological changes in blood flowing through brain tissue rather than neural activity. This hemodynamic response to neural activity takes a few seconds to build up, and, more important, attenuates slowly, with virtually all of the detectable response dissipating within around eight seconds. FMRI researchers generally assume that the attenuating hemodynamic response is purely physiological and not a reflection of a parallel attenuation in neural activity. If the scanner captures a full brain image every three seconds (as in the Ishai study), each volume will reflect a mix of neural action occurring over the last eight seconds. This blood flow spillover will guarantee that volumes adjacent in time will be very similar in patterns of activation (as indeed they are). But, assuming that this is mainly or wholly due to the physiology of blood vessels, this particular temporal effect almost certainly does not reflect neural activity. Accordingly, it should be eliminated from any

calculations of phenomenal indices. I did that by basing *t* and all the other indices on relations between volumes more than nine seconds apart. Beyond the interval of the hemodynamic lag and attenuation, multivariate relations were presumed to rest more on similarities among neural patterns rather than on accidents of blood flow.

A second problem lies in the tendency of voxel time series, the jagged line in figure 4.1, to exhibit overall trends. These general upward or downward drifts may be due to a variety of sources. Although there is some debate about the significance of these slow rises and dips, most researchers discount their relevance to underlying brain function. The data I worked with, the Ishai study and others, had already been detrended before I acquired it. But to further insulate my results from this possible artifact, I detrended each voxel time series again, using the function SPM_detrend from the SPM toolbox for Matlab (Friston et al. 1995). Thus, linear trends were removed prior to any analysis. A few further comments are in order. First, bear in mind that the nearest neighbors in time were excluded from the analysis to reduce the confounding effects of attenuating blood flow, but that exclusion also excludes their contributions to *t*. Thus, the *t* estimate is conservative. Second, we should note that no "noise reduction" was included in this analysis (except for detrending, which would also reduce *t*).

15. Here are a few details of the metanet exploration: The central idea of the analysis is to detect and decode patterns in the total state of activation recorded by the brain scan. No part of the brain is ruled out from this analysis, meaning that up to 15,000 voxels are in play. Also, because the task we set the metanet is to extract a prior (or following) state of activity, its outputs will also number around 15,000. Neural networks enable possible connections between any input unit pattern and any output unit connections, so, in this case, a network with no hidden units would require up to 225,000,000 variable connections. Although not completely intractable, this is a very big matrix to manipulate. Therefore, in the interest of computational efficiency, I embraced one standard technique of preprocessing for the metanets, which was to extract and work with the "principal components" of the brain activity over time, rather than with the 15,000 individual voxel time series.

Principal component analysis (PCA) is another form of multivariate analysis, somewhat like multidimensional scaling. (See Jackson 1991, for an introduction.) Principal component analysis exploits the redundancies among the 15,000-voxel time series. If the voxel time series are regarded as dimensions, PCA will compute a new "super-dimension" that captures a fraction of the variability in many of the other dimenions. This new dimension is a principal component. Once the first of these new dimensions is calculated, the PCA algorithm looks at what is left over, not yet compressed into the first principal component. The greatest redundancies in these residuals are compacted into a second principal component. What's left over from that becomes fodder for the next component, and so on. The first component in a typical analysis from the Ishai study accounted for about 25 percent of the variability in the entire set of voxels. The fiftieth component mopped up just .09 percent. The set of the first 50 components together accounted for about 90 percent of the total variability in all the voxels. That missing 10 percent is information lost, but the loss was accepted in order to complete the analyses during the present decade. (The PCA functions for Matlab are from the PLS Toolbox, Eigenvector Research, 1991–1998.)

A second issue also affected the analysis. As mentioned in note 14, one clear temporal effect in fMRI is the attenuation of blow flow over several seconds following an assumed neural event. In calculating the gradients I excluded several immediately prior and following time points, so that any temporal effect would be more likely to have a neural correlate, as opposed to simply reflecting an accident of circulation. In the metanet analysis, I dealt with the same problem in a different way. In this case, I assessed the metanet analysis for significance by contrasting it with another network, a metanet based on the same patterns, but in a different order. Shuffling the patterns for the random metanet (I argued) destroys any temporal relationship across patterns, while preserving every other pattern property. So far so good, but the shuffled patterns also lack the more basic signal attenuation attributable to blood flow. Perhaps, then, the metanet succeeds in its pattern prediction just by exploiting the blood flow tail-off in each voxel time series. In that case, the best prediction might be simply to anticipate that the next pattern in the sequence will be pretty much the same as the current pattern. This similarity from pattern to pattern is also known as autocorrelation (that is, the correlation of a time series with itself, one time point later). The blood flow attenuation does indeed result in a succession of volumes with substantial autocorrelation (around .4). It would be disappointing if the metanet learning was simply the effect of autocorrelation. To control for this possibility, therefore, I manipulated the shuffled time series for the random metanet to analyze, in order that it would also be autocorrelated to the same extent as the original series. To do this, a fraction of each voxel value was added to the value of the following time point. Thus, the shuffled pattern set also mimicked the blood flow attenuation. Any contrast observed between the learning of the original metanet and its randomized counterpart is therefore not due to simple autocorrelation, because both share this property. I discuss a second method for constructing a control for autocorrelation in Lloyd 2002a.

16. In this book, simulated neural networks have mainly served a heuristic function, providing a playground for testing interpretive methods and at the same time helping reconceive our research approach to the conscious brain. Nonetheless I've assumed that the brain is a dynamical system, i.e., that it more resembles an artificial neural network than it does a digital computer. The evidence for that position uses phenomenology as its warrant. Experience expresses many of the characteristics that a dynamical system brain would have. On grounds of phenomenology alone, one could argue that the brain is a big connectionist network (with a recurrent functional architecture). The methods introduced in this chapter assume this perspective. And they work—confirming the large-scale dynamics predicted by phenomenology.

Within the dynamical systems perspective we encounter the idea of distributed processing and distributed representation. This too seems warranted by the phenomenology of superposition and the overall complexity of human consciousness in the moment and over time. The idea of distributed processing in the brain has attracted a great deal of interest; the general topic in cognitive neuroscience is a topic for another book. For an overview, see Bressler 1995. Distributed representation meets multivariate analysis in the work of Shimon Edelman, whose conclusions about cognition parallel the dimension thinking about consciousness followed here. Also see Friston et al. 1996.

17. A classical distinction in the philosophy of mind is between "type identity" theories and "functionalist" theories. The first was advanced in the 1950s as a way of expressing materialism about the mind, in the form of statements such as "A pain is identical to a particular state of the brain." (The notional brainstate back then was the "firing of C-fibers.") A few years later, functionalism challenged type identity theory with the alternative position that mental entities should be identified with "black boxes" defined not by what they are but what they do. Very briefly, functionalists defended their view with the intuition that being made of our sort of neurons should not be essential to having a mind. Silicon-based Martians who talk about pain and react to it as humans do should not be peremptorily excluded from the mental club. For functionalists, it didn't matter whether pains were made of brains or mayonnaise as long as pain-states had pain-appropriate "inputs" and "outputs"—functionalism derived much of its appeal from analogies with computers. So here we are, linking consciousness and neurons, an enterprise that seems to resemble type identity theory. The motivated philosophical reader may be inclined to ask, on which side of the classic divide should one find *Radiant Cool?*

It depends. The distinction turns out to be a false one, for the reason that everyone is, *at some level*, a functionalist. Functionalists often turn to automobiles for analogies, and so will I, with some refinements. Imagine a world in which all autos are 1958 Thunderbirds, and our job is to provide a science of cars. From the beginning: Cars move. How do they do that? Inside are motors, and progress in car science will refine the understanding of motors, regarding them as internal combustion engines, then piston engines, V-8s, 1958 model T-bird V-8s, components in a certain arrangement, made of certain materials, having a particular molecular, atomic, and subatomic structure. A car functionalist might say, "All cars that we know of have piston engines, but that is not the only kind of internal combustion engine. What makes something an internal combustion engine is not its particular architecture, but a more general property of burning fuel inside the engine. Anything that functions in that way will be an internal combustion engine." The automotive type identity theorist, on the other hand, might say that internal combustion engines are always piston engines. Her claim that internal combustion is always implemented in the same way contrasts with the functionalist's allowance of multiple implementations of the same thing. But a few levels down, the type identity advocate sounds like a functionalist, for example allowing that the type "piston engine" can be multiply instantiated as V-8s, V-6s, etc. Both will agree that engines can be made of very different materials, including exotics such as superheated mayonnaise. (Having just one type of car around has no bearing on their discussion.) So the disagreement is about setting the appropriate level to begin allowing multiple implementations.

The approach taken here regards certain phenomenal structures to be essential to consciousness. So any conscious entity, brains included, must implement these phenomenal structures. But entities built of very different materials could also implement them—I can see no reason why you must be carbon-based to have awareness. So far that sounds like functionalism, but the functionalism is tempered by a further restriction, which will push it down a level or two. Throughout cognitive science, the mind is usually understood as a manipulator of representations. In classical cognitive science, fully enthralled with digital computation, representations are interpreted functionally. That is, the content of a representation depends entirely on its relations to other representations and the world. I argue in the text that representational content is not identical to phenomenal content, and that phenomenal content is a property of the form of the representation, or of the "vehicle" of representation, rather than its content (see also O'Brien and Opie 1999). That pushes the explanation of consciousness down a level from the pure functionalism of classical computational cognitive science. At this lower level, I keep company with the neural network modelers, who are generally noncommittal about the implementation of consciousness. (Usually they are concerned to show that their models are sufficient to implement some particular cognitive capacity.) In addition to construing phenomenality as a property of one's internal configuration, independent of representational content, I go on to specify some of what that phenomenal content must be. This amounts to a set of constraints on the internal structure of any implementation of consciousness. At this point, I suppose I drop even a bit below the neural network folks. They might claim that some sort of neural net is sufficient to generate consciousness, without specifying what sort. I'm saying that the right kind of network must have certain structures (approximately, fully recurrent and recursive self-mirroring, as in a simple recurrent network). At this point I can't imagine a classical computational architecture that could actually implement all this, and so it seems to me that consciousness not only does arise in a special sort of neural network, but can only arise in such a device. And if that's so, then I am a type identity theorist to this point.

Below that I'm as functionalist as the next person. Martians are fine candidates for consciousness. But they don't qualify because they squirm and squeak when pinched, but rather because they show us that they live in a temporal subjective world. Language is a preeminent way to display one's grasp of temporality, but it can also be seen in the behavior of smarter animals, discriminating stimuli on the basis of duration (in the absence of other sensory cues).

18. Philosophers of mind bring special worries to their discussions of consciousness, and to some of them a science of consciousness is challenged by armchair philosophical considerations. Foremost among these philosophical challenges is the notorious "zombie problem." A philosophical zombie is a being that in every observable respect looks like an ordinary human, but in fact has no states of awareness at all. In spite of the zombie's many avowals of awareness and its apparently human nervous system, there is "nothing but darkness" inside the zombie mind. The point of the thought experiment is to pose a steep requirement for a theory of consciousness. If a theory could be implemented by a zombie, that mere possibility is alleged to sink the theory, owing to the logical allegation that the theory will not be sufficient to entail that a being implementing the theory *must* perforce be conscious.

There is much that is fishy in this reasoning, but it holds a grain of truth as well. The fishy parts include the assumption that mere mortals can mull over a theory of consciousness and know with certainty that none of its entailments exclude the possibility of the theory applying to a being that lacks consciousness altogether. After all, any theory—and especially any scientific theory—leads to an infinite number of entailments, because the theory can be supplemented by any other premise known to be true, including premises from any other branch of science. Figuring out the entailments of a theory is life work for a scientist, whose entire career may be devoted to securing the smallest logical extensions of a particular theory. For a philosopher to claim that his or her ability to conceive a zombie short-circuits any scientific claims about consciousness reflects a striking combination of hubris and tunnel vision. For example, I find it perfectly conceivable that water has a chemical composition other than H_2O. Does my armchair exercise in imagination invalidate the scientific identification of water with H_2O? Of course not; my "conceivability argument" is nothing but a public demonstration of my own ignorance.

The grain of truth in the zombie problem is more of a worry than an argument. I suspect that the worry is ultimately a concern about generalizations about implementing consciousness. Cognitive science got off the ground with the big idea that cognition is information processing, an insight that has been expressed with a wide range of meanings over the last 50 years. Along with the big idea, cognitive scientists (and philosophers) generally embraced some form of functionalism, the idea that the human sort of information processing could be implemented in a wide variety of physical systems. The analogy, of course, is between software and psychology on the one side, and hardware and brains (or other systems) on the other. When these ideas were adapted for the problem of consciousness, the worry emerged that the big ideas were too permissive. Even if we had the right theory of information processing for human cognition, there seemed to be no obvious reason why one part of cognition would be conscious and another not. Moreover, functionalism seemed to entail that consciousness could be implemented in many systems that just didn't seem like the right candidates for such ennoblement. Of course, the concrete form of these worries featured the standard digital computer and its ability to implement virtually any program that can be specified. Surely those familiar metal boxes were not about to become conscious just by running some fancy software.

The worriers are right, I think, insofar as the basic ideas of cognitive science are indeed too permissive. But it would be an error in the opposite direction to completely reject all forms of the big idea, or all forms of functionalism. This book heeds the worries in several ways. First, the misleading aspect of the big idea is its general embrace of the detectorhead view of the mind. That works fine for cognition, but not for consciousness. Chapter 1 of the appendix attempts to explain why. Second, phenomenology does constrain implementation to some depth below the strata of traditional functionalism. This is discussed further in note 17. A useful way to explore these constraints is to ask what sort of system could implement the phenomenology described in chapter 2 of the appendix. Chapter 3 offers part of an answer, but one could go much further. Conscious gray boxes would not be excluded (and it would be chauvinistic to dismiss them *a priori*), but in their computational and sensorimotor capacities mechanical consciousnesses would necessarily have much in common with us, and be quite unlike present digital computers.

19. To be a candidate for interpretation is often the mark of Art. See, for example, Danto 1981.

References

fMRI Data Center Data Sets Used in "The Real Firefly"

Hazeltine, E., Poldrack, R., and Gabrieli, J. D. Accession #: 2–2000–11173. "Neural Activation during Response Competition." *Journal of Cognitive Neuroscience* 12, no. 2 (2000): 118–29.

Ishai, A., Ungerleider, L. G., Martin, A., and Haxby, J. V. Accession #: 2–2000–1113D. "The Representation of Objects in the Human Occipital and Temporal Cortex." *Journal of Cognitive Neuroscience* 12, no. 2 (2000): 35–51.

Mechelli, A., Friston, K. J., and Price, C. J. Accession #: 2–2000–1189. "The Effects of Presentation Rate during Word and Pseudoword Reading: A Comparison of PET and fMRI." *Journal of Cognitive Neuroscience* 12, no. 2 (2000): 145–56.

Postle, B. R., Berger, J. S., Taich, A. M., and D'Esposito, M. Accession #: 2–2000–1112R. "Activity in Human Frontal Cortex Associated with Spatial Working Memory and Saccadic Behavior." *Journal of Cognitive Neuroscience* 12, no. 2 (2000): 2–14.

Bibliography

Andreasen, N. "Remembering the Past: Two Facets of Episodic Memory Explored with Positron Emission Tomography." *American Journal of Psychiatry* 152 (1998): 1576–85.

Borges, J. L. *Collected Fictions*, translated by A. Hurley. New York: Viking Penguin, 1998.

Bottini, G., Paulesu, E., Sterzi, R., Warburton, E., Wise, R., Vallar, G., Frackowiak, R., and Frith, C. "Modulation of Conscious Experience by Peripheral Sensory Stimuli." *Nature* 376 (1995): 778–81.

Bressler, S. "Large-Scale Cortical Networks and Cognition." *Brain Research Reviews* 20 (1995): 288–304.

Cabeza, R., and Nyberg, L. "Imaging Cognition II: An Empirical Review of 275 PET and fMRI Studies." *Journal of Cognitive Neuroscience* 12, no. 1 (2000): 1–47.

Chalmers, D. *The Conscious Mind*. New York: Oxford University Press, 1996.

———. "What Is a Neural Correlate of Consciousness?" In *Neural Correlates of Consciousness: Empirical and Conceptual Questions*, edited by T. Metzinger, 17–40. Cambridge, MA: MIT Press, 2000.

Cherniak, C. "Philosophy and Computational Neuroanatomy." *Philosophical Studies* 73 (1994): 89–107.

Churchland, P. M. *The Engine of Reason, the Seat of the Soul*. Cambridge, MA: MIT Press, 1995.

Clark, Andy. "An Embodied Cognitive Science?" *Trends in Cognitive Sciences* 3, no. 9 (1999): 345–51.

Clark, Andy, and Chalmers, D. "The Extended Mind." *Analysis* 58, no. 1 (1998): 7–19.

Clark, Austen. *Sensory Qualities*. Oxford: Clarendon Press, 1993.

———. *A Theory of Sentience*. New York: Oxford University Press, 2000.

Danto, A. *The Transfiguration of the Commonplace: A Philosophy of Art*. Cambridge, MA: Harvard University Press, 1981.

Dennett, D. *Consciousness Explained*. Boston: Little, Brown, 1991.

———. "In Darwin's Wake: Where Am I?" *Proceedings and Addresses of the American Philosophical Association* 75, no. 2 (2001): 13–30.

Dickinson, E. *The Poems of Emily Dickinson*, edited by T. H. Johnson. Cambridge, MA: Harvard University Press, 1951.

Edelman, S., Grill-Spector, K., Kushnir, T., and Malach, R. "Toward Direct Visualization of the Internal Shape Representation Space by fMRI." *Psychobiology* 26, no. 4 (1998): 309–21.

Elman, J. "Finding Structure in Time." *Cognitive Science* 14 (1990): 179–211.

Fox, P., Burton, H., and Raichle, M. "Mapping Human Somatosensory Cortex with Positron Emission Tomography." *Journal of Neurosurgery* 67 (1987): 34–43.

Fox, P., Fox, J., Raichle, M., and Burde, R. "The Role of Cerebral Cortex in the Generation of Voluntary Saccades: A Positron Emission Tomographic Study." *Journal of Neurophysiology* 54, no. 2 (1985): 348–69.

Fox, P., Ingham, R., Ingham, J., Hirsch, T., Downs, J., Martin, C., Jerabek, P., Glass, T., and Lancaster, J. "A PET Study of the Neural Systems of Stuttering." *Nature* 382 (1996): 158–62.

Fox, P., Miezin, F., Allman, J., Van Essen, D., and Raichle, M. "Retinotopic Organization of Human Visual Cortex Mapped with Positron Emission Tomography." *Journal of Neuroscience* 7 (1987): 913–22.

Fox, P., Raichle, M., and Thatch, W. "Functional Mapping of the Human Cerebellum with Positron Emission Tomography." *Proceedings of the National Academy of the Sciences* 82 (1985): 7462–66.

Freud, S. "Project for a Scientific Psychology." In *Standard Edition of the Collected Psychological Works of Sigmund Freud,* vol. 1, edited by J. Strachey. London: Hogarth Press, 1895 (1974).

Friedman, W. *About Time: Inventing the Fourth Dimension.* Cambridge, MA: MIT Press, 1990.

Friston, K., Frith, C., Fletcher, P., Liddle, P., and Frackowiak, R. "Functional Topography: Multidimensional Scaling and Functional Connectivity in the Brain." *Cerebral Cortex* 6 (1996): 156–64.

Friston, K., Frith, C., Frackowiak, R., and Turner, R. "Characterizing Dynamic Brain Responses with fMRI: A Multivariate Approach." *Neuroimage* 2 (1995): 166–72.

Friston, K., Price, C., Fletcher, P., Moore, R., Frackowiak, R., and Dolan, R. "The Trouble with Cognitive Subtraction." *Neuroimage* 4 (1996): 97–104.

Ginsberg, A. *Collected Poems, 1947–1980.* New York: Harper & Row, 1984.

Grasby, P., Frith, C., Friston, K., Bench, C., Frackowiak, R., and Dolan, R. "Functional Mapping of Brain Areas Implicated in Auditory-Verbal Memory Function." *Brain* 116 (1993): 1–20.

Haldane, E., and Ross, G., trans. *Philosophical Works of Descartes,* vol. 1. Cambridge, UK: Cambridge University Press, 1969.

Hazeltine, E., Poldrack, R., and Gabrieli, J. D. "Neural Activation during Response Competition." *Journal of Cognitive Neuroscience* 12, no. 2 (2000): 118–29.

Hsieh, J. "Urge to Scratch Represented in the Human Cerebral Cortex during Itch." *Journal of Neurophysiology* 72 (1994): 3004–8.

Husserl, E. *The phenomenology of Internal Time-Consciousness,* translated by J. S. Churchill. Bloomington: Indiana University Press, 1964.

———. *Zur Phänomenologie des Inneren Zeitbewusstseins (The phenomenology of Internal Time-Consciousness),* edited by R. Boehm. Vol. 10, *Husserliana.* The Hague: Martinus Nijhoff, 1966.

———. *Ding und Raum (Thing and Space), Lectures of 1907,* edited by U. Claesges. Vol. 16, *Husserliana.* The Hague: Martinus Nijhoff, 1974.

———. *On the Phenomenology of the Consciousness of Internal Time,* translated by John Brough. Vol. 4, *Edmund Husserl, Collected Works.* Dordrecht: Kluwer, 1992.

———. *Thing and Space,* translated by Richard Rojcewicz. Vol. 7, *Edmund Husserl, Collected Works.* Dordrecht: Kluwer, 1997.

Ishai, A., Ungerleider, L. G., Martin, A., and Haxby, J. V. "The Representation of Objects in the Human Occipital and Temporal Cortex." *Journal of Cognitive Neuroscience* 12, no. 2 (2000): 35–51.

Ishai, A., Ungerleider, L. G., Martin, A., Schouten, J., and Haxby, J. V. "Distributed Representation of Objects in the Human Ventral Visual Pathway." *Proceedings of the National Academy of Sciences USA* 96 (1999): 9379–84.

Jackson, J. E. *A User's Guide to Principal Components.* New York: John Wiley and Sons, 1991.

James, W. *Principles of Psychology.* 2 vols. New York: Henry Holt and Co., 1890.

Jenkins, I., Bain, P., Colebatch, J., Thompson, P., Findley, L., Frackowiak, R., Marsden, C., and Brooks, D. "A Positron Emission Tomography Study of Essential Tremor: Evidence for Overactivity of Cerebellar Connections." *Annals of Neurology* 34 (1993): 82–90.

Jueptner, M. "Localization of a Cerebellar Timing Process Using PET." *Neurology* 45 (1998): 1540–45.

Kaufman, L., and Rousseeuw, P. *Finding Groups in Data: An Introduction to Cluster Analysis.* New York: John Wiley and Sons, 1990.

Kruskal, J., and Wish, M. *Multidimensional Scaling.* Beverly Hills, CA: Sage Publications, 1978.

Kuhn, T. *The Structure of Scientific Revolutions.* Chicago: University of Chicago Press, 1962.

Lange, N. "Statistical Approaches to Human Brain Mapping by Functional Magnetic Resonance Imaging." *Statistics in Medicine* 15 (1996): 389–428.

Lettvin, J. Y., Maturana, H. R., McCulloch, W. S., and Pitts, W. H. "What the Frog's Eye Tells the Frog's Brain." *Proceedings of the IRE* 47, no. 11 (1959): 1940–51.

Lloyd, D. *Simple Minds.* Cambridge, MA: MIT Press, 1989.

———. "Leaping to Conclusions: Connectionism, Consciousness, and the Computational Mind." In *Connectionism and the Philosophy of Mind,* edited by J. Teinson. Norwell, MA: Kluwer Academic Publishers, 1991.

———. "Toward an Identity Theory of Consciousness." *Behavioral and Brain Sciences* 15, no. 2 (1992): 215–16.

———. "Consciousness: A Connectionist Manifesto." *Minds and Machines* 5 (1995): 161–85.

———. "Consciousness, Connectionism, and Cognitive Neuroscience: A Meeting of the Minds." *Philosophical Psychology* 9 (1996): 61–81.

———. "Consciousness and Its Discontents." *Communication and Cognition* 30 (1997): 273–85.

———. "Beyond 'the Fringe': A Cautionary Critique of William James," *Consciousness and Cognition* 9 (2000a): 629–37.

———. "Popping the Thought Balloon." In *The Philosophy of Daniel Dennett, a Comprehensive Assessment,* edited by D. Ross, A. Brook, and D. Thompson. Cambridge, MA: MIT Press, 2000b.

———. "Terra Cognita: From Functional Neuroimaging to the Map of the Mind." *Brain and Mind* 1 (2000c): 1–24.

———. "Virtual Lesions in the Not-So-Modular Brain." *Journal of the International Neuropsychological Society* 6 (2000d): 627–35.

———. "Functional MRI and the Study of Human Consciousness." *Journal of Cognitive Neuroscience* 14, no. 6 (2002a): 818–31.

———. "Studying the Mind from the Inside Out." *Brain and Mind* 3 (2002b): 243–59.

Luria, A. R. *The Man with a Shattered World,* translated by L. Solotaroff. New York: Basic Books, 1972.

Lycan, W. *Consciousness.* Cambridge, MA: MIT Press, 1987.

Marcoulides, G., and Hershberger, S. *Multivariate Statistical Methods: A First Course.* Mahwah, NJ: Lawrence Erlbaum Associates, 1997.

McClelland, J., and Rumelhart, D. *Parallel Distributed Processing: Explorations in Parallel Distributed Processing.* 2 vols. Cambridge, MA: MIT Press, 1986.

Mechelli, A., Friston, K., and Price, C. "The Effects of Presentation Rate during Word and Pseudoword Reading: A Comparison of PET and fMRI." *Journal of Cognitive Neuroscience* 12, no. 2 (2000): 145–56.

Merleau-Ponty, M. *Phenomenology of Perception.* London: Routledge and Paul, 1962.

Muller, K. J., Nicholls, J. G., and Stent, G. S. *Neurobiology of the Leech.* Cold Spring Harbor, NY: Cold Spring Harbor Publications, 1981.

Nagel, T. "What Is It Like to Be a Bat?" *Philosophical Review* 83 (1974): 435–50.

Noë, A. *Art and Cognition Interdisciplines, 2002–2003* [cited 4 April 2003]. Available from <www.interdisciplines.org/artcog/papers/8>.

———. "On What We See." *Pacific Philosophical Quarterly* 831 (2002): 57–80.

O'Brien, G., and Opie, J. "A Connectionist Theory of Phenomenal Experience." *Behavioral and Brain Sciences* 22 (1999): 127–48.

O'Regan, J. K., and Noë, A. "A Sensorimotor Account of Vision and Visual Consciousness." *Behavioral and Brain Sciences* 24, no. 5 (2001): 883–917.

O'Reilly, R., and Munakata, Y. *Computational Explorations in Cognitive Neuroscience.* Cambridge, MA: MIT Press, 2000.

Pardo, J., Pardo, P., and Raichle, M. "Neural Correlates of Self-Induced Dysphoria." *American Journal of Psychiatry* 150 (1993): 713–19.

Pardo, J., Raichle, M., and Fox, P. "Localization of a Human System for Sustained Attention by Positron Emission Tomography." *Nature* 349 (1991): 61–63.

Pauleso, E., and Frackowiak, R. "The Neural Correlates of the Verbal Component of Working Memory." *Nature* 362 (1993): 342–44.

Paus, T., Marett, S., Evans, A., and Worsley, K. "Extraretinal Modulation of Cerebral Blood Flow in the Human Visual Cortex: Implications for Saccadic Suppression." *Journal of Neurophysiology* 74 (1995): 2179–83.

Paus, T., Petrides, M., Evans, A., and Meyer, E. "Role of the Human Anterior Cingulate Cortex in the Control of Oculomotor, Manual and Speech Responses: A Positron Emission Tomography Study." *Journal of Neurophysiology* 70 (1993): 453–69.

Petitot, J., Varela, F., Pachoud, B., and Roy, J.-M., eds. *Naturalizing Phenomenology: Issues in Contemporary Phenomenology and Cognitive Science.* Stanford, CA: Stanford University Press, 1999.

Port, R., and van Gelder, T., eds. *Mind as Motion: Explorations in the Dynamics of Cognition.* Cambridge, MA: MIT Press, 1995.

Posner, M., and Raichle, M. *Images of Mind.* San Francisco: Scientific American Press, 1994.

Postle, B. R., Berger, J. S., Taich, A. M., and D'Esposito, M. "Activity in Human Frontal Cortex Associated with Spatial Working Memory and Saccadic Behavior." *Journal of Cognitive Neuroscience* 12, no. 2 (2000): 2–14.

Price, C., and Friston, K. "Cognitive Conjunction: A New Approach to Brain Activation Experiments." *Neuroimage* 5 (1996): 261–70.

Reiman (1989).

Reiman, E., Fusselman, M., Fox, P., and Raichle, M. "Neuroanatomical Correlates of Anticipatory Anxiety." *Science* 243 (1989): 1071–74.

Revonsuo, A. "Can Functional Brain Imaging Discover Consciousness in the Brain?" *Journal of Consciousness Studies* 8, no. 3 (2001): 3–23.

Rosenblatt, F. "The Perceptron: A Probabilistic Model for Information Storage and Organization in the Brain." *Psychological Review* 65, nos. 386–408 (1958).

———. *Principles of Neurodynamics.* New York: Spartan Books, 1962.

Rumelhart, D., Smolensky, P., McClelland, J., and Hinton, G. "Schemata and Sequential Thought Processes." In *Parallel Distributed Processing: Explorations in the Microstructure of Cognition,* edited by D. Rumelhart and J. McClelland. Cambridge, MA: MIT Press, 1986.

Sacks, O. *The Man Who Mistook His Wife for a Hat.* New York: Summit Books, 1985.

———. *An Anthropologist on Mars: Seven Paradoxical Tales.* New York: Alfred A. Knopf, 1995.

Sartre, J.-P. *Being and Nothingness,* translated by H. Barnes. London: Philosophical Library, 1958.

———. *L'Etre et le Néant.* Paris: Gallimard, 1943.

Searle, J. "Minds, Brains, and Programs." *Behavioral and Brain Sciences* 3 (1980): 417–24.

Seitz, R., and Roland, P. "Learning of Sequential Finger Movements in Man: A Combined Kinematic and Positron Emission Tomography (PET) Study." *European Journal of Neuroscience* 4 (1992a): 154–65.

———. "Vibratory Stimulation Increases and Decreases the Regional Cerebral Blood Flow and Oxidative Metabolism: A Positron Emission Tomography (PET) Study." *Acta Neurologica Scandinavica* 1 (1992b): 60–67.

Seitz, R., Roland, P., Bohm, C., Greitz, T., and Stone-Elander, S. "Somatosensory Discrimination of Shape: Tactile Exploration and Cerebral Activation." *European Journal of Neuroscience* 3 (1991): 481–92.

Shepard, R., Romney, K., and Nerlove, S., eds. *Multidimensional Scaling: Theory and Applications in the Behavioral Sciences.* New York: Seminar Press, 1972.

Smolensky, P. "On the Proper Treatment of Connectionism." *Behavioral and Brain Sciences* 11 (1988): 1–23.

Stevens, W. *Collected Poems of Wallace Stevens.* New York: Alfred A. Knopf, 1954.

Tempel, L. "Abnormal Cortical Responses in Patients with Writer's Cramp." *Neurology* 43 (1993): 2252–57.

Thompson, E., and Varela, F. "Radical Embodiment: Neural Dynamics and Consciousness." *Trends in Cognitive Sciences* 5 (2001): 418–25.

Toga, A., and Mazziotta, J., eds. *Brain Mapping: The Methods.* San Diego: Academic Press, 1996.

Uttal, W. *The New Phrenology: The Limits of Localizing Cognitive Processes in the Brain.* Cambridge, MA: MIT Press, 2001.

Van Gelder, T. "Wooden Iron? Husserlian Phenomenology Meets Cognitive Science." In *Naturalizing Phenomenology: Issues in Contemporary Phenomenology and Cognitive Science,* edited by J. Petitot, F. Varela, B. Pachoud, and J.-M Roy, 245–65. Stanford, CA: Stanford University Press, 1999.

Varela, F. "Neurophenomenology: A Methodological Remedy for the Hard Problem." *Journal of Consciousness Studies* 3 (1996): 330–50.

———. "The Specious Present: A Neurophenomenology of Time Consciousness." In *Naturalizing Phenomenology: Issues in Contemporary Phenomenology and Cognitive Science,* edited by J. Petitot, F. Varela, B. Pachoud, and J.-M. Roy, 266–315. Stanford, CA: Stanford University Press, 1999.

Weiller, C., Isensee, C., Rijntjes, M., Huber, W., Mueller, S., Bier, D., Dutschka, K., Woods, R., Noth, J., and Diener, H. "Recovery from Wernicke's Aphasia: A Positron Emission Tomographic Study." *Annals of Neurology* 37 (1995): 723–32.

Weiskrantz, L. *Blindsight: A Case Study and Implications.* New York, NY: Oxford University Press, 1986.

Weizenbaum, J. *Computer Power and Human Reason: From Judgment to Calculation.* San Francisco: W. H. Freeman, 1976.

Wessel, K., Zeffiro, T., Lou, J., Toro, C., and Hallett, M. "Regional Cerebral Blood Flow during a Self-Paced Sequential Finger Opposition Task in Patients with Cerebellar Degeneration." *Brain* 118 (1995): 379–93.

Wise, R., Chollet, F., Hadar, U., Friston, K., Hoffner, E., and Frackowiak, R. "Distribution of Cortical Neural Networks Involved in Word Comprehension and Word Retrieval." *Brain* 114 (1991): 1803–17.

Zahavi, D. *Self-Awareness and Alterity.* Evanston, IL: Northwestern University Press, 1999.